One's Aspect To The Sun

Sherry D. Ramsey

One's Aspect To The Sun

Sherry D. Ramsey

TYCHE BOOKS LTD.

One's Aspect To The Sun

Published by Tyche Books Ltd.
www.TycheBooks.com

Copyright © 2013 Sherry D. Ramsey
First Tyche Books Ltd Edition 2013

Print ISBN: 978-0-9918369-5-6
Ebook ISBN: 978-0-9918369-6-3

Cover Art by Ashley Walters
Cover Layout by Lucia Starkey
Interior Layout by Ryah Deines
Editorial by M. L. D. Curelas

Author photograph by John Ratchford

Library and Archives Canada Cataloguing in Publication

Ramsey, Sherry, 1963-, author
One's Aspect To The Sun / Sherry Ramsey.

Issued in print and electronic formats.
ISBN 978-0-9918369-5-6(pbk.).-- 978-0-9918369-6-3(pdf)

I. Title.
PS8635.A668O54 2013   C813'.6   C2013-903994-5
                                        C2013-903995-3

Dedication

For Terry, who never stopped believing I could do it.

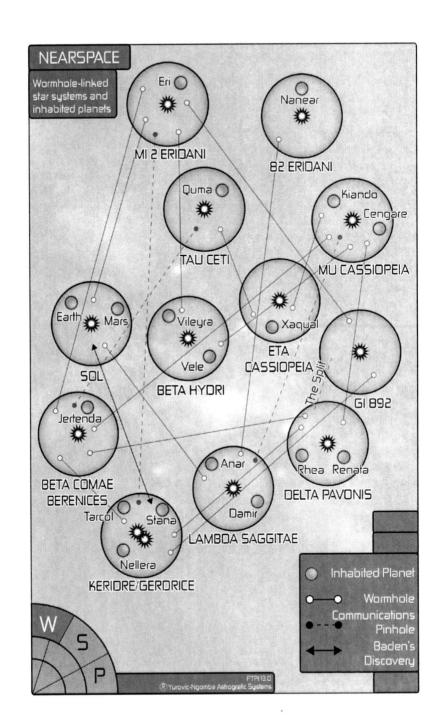

Contents

PART ONE

Earthside

Chapter One

Welcomes Warm and Cold

"Luta, we're about an hour from Earth. It looks good if the Captain's on the bridge when we dock." Rei's cheerful voice woke me over the *Tane Ikai*'s comm circuit. The dream faded slowly, fragments lingering in my mind like wisps of nebulae. It's always the same dream, when we near a planet.

I'm fourteen again, and I sprint through the crowded corridor of a space station, trying to keep my mother in sight, glimpses of her auburn hair taunting me. A press of people separates us. She doesn't slow, doesn't turn to look. I don't know if she knows I'm following her. Outside the station I catch glimpses of a ringed planet and the numinous dark shadow of a wormhole entrance.

Finally the crowd thins and I see her at a docking ring, waiting to board the ship. I call out, but no sound emerges. She turns and sees me, smiles sadly and shakes her head, lifting one slender hand in farewell. My chest tightens and I fight back tears. I don't want anyone to see me cry. She moves through the docking ring seconds before my leaden feet reach it. But there's no ship beyond. Only yawning, empty space, black vacuum starred with cold fairy lights. My mother is gone . . .

I fumbled a finger onto the ID biochip implant in my forearm to let Rei know I was awake and rolled onto my back. The ship's main drive throbbed like a giant heartbeat, pushing us closer to Earth, and my own pulse echoed the cadence. Outside the viewport above me, the pattern of stars was beginning to take on the familiarity of home. Earth always triggered the dream. Probably because it was the last place my childhood family had lived in peace.

Finally I swung my legs over the side of the berth and hauled myself up. After all these years I still don't sleep as well in space as I do planetside, but when you're the captain of a merchant far trader you learn to cope.

I slipped into jeans and a clean white t-shirt, splashed cool water on my face and dusted on makeup. I ran a brush through my hair, glanced at my reflection. I'd long ago perfected the skill of checking the presentability of hair, face and clothes without noticing all those little things I didn't want to see, the uncomfortable reminders that I didn't look a day over thirty.

Which would have been fine if I weren't due to turn eighty-five on my next birthday. Which still would have been fine if there were any logical, scientific explanation for my youthfulness. Hell, I'd even take an illogical, unscientific one, but there was no explanation. I was an anomaly, an aberration—a freak, for lack of a better word—but I tried not to dwell on it.

Datapad in hand, I left my cabin. Voices sounded from the galley off to the left, and the smell of freshly brewed caff wafted enticingly down the corridor, but I turned right instead, my footsteps echoing on the metal decking. Rei dam-Rowan, my pilot, turned in her skimchair to smile at me when I emerged into the bright lights of the bridge. Rei was the only one of my crew who knew my true age. There's something about Rei that invites confidences, and assures that they'll be kept. She's twenty-nine, looks twenty by way of good genes and better attitude, and we've been friends for the five years she's been part of my crew.

"Earth ETA twenty minutes, Captain," she said, then added with a grin, "How was your beauty sleep?"

I pulled a face at her. "Didn't need beauty sleep any more than you do. Everybody have something to do when we arrive?"

Rei nodded, her chestnut hair dark in the yellow-tinged light from the High Pressure Sodium overheads. "Viss says if we're going to be here more than a day he wants to clean out the plasma intakes, and he's planning to pick up a new thruster filter while we're Earthside. Yuskeya's downloading the star charts you requested and the datapoints for six new wormholes. Baden says after he sees the cargo unloaded safely he has a meeting with an old friend, if you don't need him for anything else." She rolled her golden eyes. "So it's either a woman or someone who owes him money."

"And what about you?" I settled myself in the command chair and punched up the incoming correspondence on my datapad. The servos kicked in and adjusted the chair for me.

"Easy," said Rei. She yawned delicately, the darkly beautiful tattoo-like markings around her eyes elongating like rivers of spilled ink across her clear, pale skin. All the women from Eri wore *pridattii*. I knew they weren't permanent, but I'd never seen Rei without hers. "I'm getting a facial and a manicure, and maybe—no, definitely—a massage."

I shook my head. "All work and no play, Rei. You should try to relax a little."

She stuck her tongue out at me and we both laughed, but my smile dissolved into a frown when a message from PrimeCorp displayed. They must have had it in the queue, triggered to send the instant my ship entered Earthspace, and with PrimeCorp, it was never good news.

Received: from [205152.59.68] PrimeCorp Main Division
STATIC ELECTRONIC MESSAGE: 25.7

Encryption: securetext/novis/noaud
Receipt notification: enabled
*From: "Chairman Alin Sedmamin" <chair.primecorp*web>*
To: "Luta Paixon" <ID 59836254471>
Date: Sat, 2 Nov 2284 17:57:29 -0500

Captain Paixon,

We would appreciate your finding some time during your stay on Earth to meet with one of our representatives for an exchange of information. Thank you for your time and consideration.

Chairman Alin Sedmamin
Per Beli Elaudoka

I sighed. Nothing new there. I'd only done the meeting-up thing once or twice, in the hope that they might actually offer some news of my mother. I'd given up in disgust after that. All they wanted was to pump me for information I didn't have, and get my permission to poke around inside my genes for anything that might belong to them, which I wouldn't give. Since the Genetic Materials Privacy Act came into being about a hundred years ago they couldn't force me, but I'd made my refusals politely—when I could. You never knew when they might have something I wanted. I wasn't sure I liked the notion that they were keeping a watch out for me, though.

Rei mistook my expression, or the reason for it, because she lowered her voice and asked, "Are you going to see Hirin right away?"

I nodded, carefully not looking up fr^m my screen when my heart lurched at his name. "It's been two months. He'll be getting anxious. And I picked up some herbal supplements on Vileyra that might help him some."

Rei was silent for a moment, then said, "Luta, don't you worry that sometime you'll come back and Hirin will be . . ."

"Dead?" I finished for her when her voice trailed off. "Of course I do. But we both agreed that this was the only way. I can't keep him in the best care unless I take the big-paying jobs, and those are all multi-skip runs. This is the practical solution."

"You miss him, though. It must be hard."

"I miss—I miss how we used to be. I don't know if I miss being around him all the time now. It's not easy."

She nodded and turned back to the pilot's screen, and I tried to bury myself in tenders for our next job.

Hirin is my husband. He's ninety-two. Unfortunately and unlike me, he's not an anomaly, an aberration, or a freak. He lives in an elderly care facility, and he looks and feels every day of those ninety-two years. With Vigor-Us treatments, even ninety-two isn't extremely old, but a virus Hirin picked up fifteen years ago left him damaged in ways that even the rejuv couldn't ameliorate much.

The rest of my crew had met Hirin, but they didn't know he was my husband. They thought he was some elderly relative for whom I had a soft spot. It was true enough. They'd also never met my children—didn't even know about them, in fact. Looking fifty years younger than my chronological age isn't something I flaunt. Too many uncomfortable questions for which I don't have the answers. Moreover, there's always the lurking presence of PrimeCorp, which would be a good reason to keep to the shadows all by itself.

More footsteps sounded in the corridor behind us and a soft

voice said, "*Bonan matenon*, Captain."

I glanced up with a smile as Yuskeya Blue slid into her seat at the navigation station and set a steaming cup down within easy reach. Yuskeya was the tallest woman I'd ever met, topping even Rei by a couple of inches, and she had the striking features and ebony hair of her American Indian ancestors. Her home planet was Quma, which a huge collection of Earth's aboriginal people had colonized for themselves about a century ago. Yuskeya was quiet, dignified, an excellent navigator and a competent medic, with a dry sense of humour and a taste for heavily spiced chai. She'd been part of my crew for over a year, but that was just about all I knew about her. I had a notion that on occasional nights she shared a cabin with Viss Feron, my engineer, but I wasn't certain and didn't know if I wanted to be. Everyone's entitled to their secrets.

"Good morning! I hear you're getting some new wormhole datapoints when we dock."

"That's right. Rumour says one of them might cut weeks off the trip between MI 2 Eridani and Beta Comae Berenices."

I raised my eyebrows. "Let me know what you get, then. It might influence what job we take next."

"Will do." Yuskeya nodded and began checking the nav computations for our arrival Earthside.

I opened a batch of new job postings and ran my eye down the list. None of them looked terribly promising, most looking for carriage to systems at least three wormhole skips away, but I stopped short of deleting any until I had the reports on Yuskeya's new wormholes. Any planet in any system could get a whole lot closer if an advantageous wormhole were discovered.

"Beta Comae?" a voice boomed suddenly right behind me. "We don't want to go to Beta Comae, do we?"

Baden Methyr was an outstanding communications officer, but his practical jokes were usually the juvenile kind. I was glad I hadn't jumped. He'd managed to sneak up behind me silently and look over my shoulder at the screen.

"We might," I said mildly. "Some reason you don't want to visit Jertenda, Baden? A woman with a grudge, perhaps?"

"A grudge and a plasma rifle, maybe?" Rei suggested sweetly. "Wouldn't be the only planet in Nearspace, would it?"

"Ladies, you wound me," he said, placing a hand theatrically over his heart and sliding into the comm station skimchair. He set down the mug he was carrying and docked the thumb-sized communications module into the implant on his left forearm. "Shall we let Earth know we're almost there?"

"Go ahead." I nodded. "And find out where they want to berth us."

"Do you want Central Mass for the cargo?" Baden asked. "Or somewhere else first?"

"Take Central Mass if we can get it. I'm going to visit Hirin, but I can take a flitter up to Nova Scotia. Judging by the number of job proposals on this list I'd say it's a busy time, so we'll have to go where they send us. If we can't get reasonably close to Boston, I'll hire out the delivery."

"See what I can do." He ran a hand through his cocoa-coloured hair and was all business suddenly, although I knew he would turn on the sweet talk if the situation warranted it. He'd just see who he got on the other end of the communications Wave Augmented Visual Emmission at Berthing Administration first.

"Where's Viss?" I asked. He should have been down in Engineering by now, but he hadn't reported in.

"Encrypted message came in for him," said Baden, putting a finger over the tiny mic on the comm module he was using to talk to Berthing. "He took it down in Engineering. I expect he'll be calling up any minute. And there's a live incoming for you via WaVE, Captain. Karro Paixon, Sagan Space Station."

"I'll take it in my quarters. That's my uncle," I lied easily.

Baden nodded, his fingers skimming the touchscreen as he transferred the feed. He turned his attention back to Berthing with a wide grin. "Well, hello again, *karulino.*"

I rolled my eyes. If he was flirting with her, it looked good for a berth wherever we wanted it. Baden has a certain touch.

I didn't run down the corridor to my quarters, but I hurried. "Karro?"

His face grinned at me from the screen. "All secure?"

I nodded.

"Great. Hi, Mom. Thought I'd tell you where I am, since you're passing through."

"Hello, *filo.* How'd you know I was here?" He looked good, happy. A little more grey at the temples, a few more wrinkles around the eyes. Whatever the secret of my longevity was, it hadn't found a way past the placental barrier and into my children.

He chuckled. "You're a hard woman to catch up with. I always leave a standing request at the station comm to notify me if the *Tane Ikai* passes heading Earthside. You look great."

"Thanks. How's everybody?"

"Aliande's here with me this time, just for a change of scenery. She's not going crazy yet, inside what she calls 'this metal cave,' but we're here for another month. Joash and Klaire are Earthside. We're all well."

Surely he'd have told me any bad news by now, but my chest felt tight as I asked, "And your father?"

Karro shrugged and shook his head, a frown threatening to overtake his features. "I don't know, Mom, he's up and down. Maja's trying to get him to try some new treatments but he seems . . . I don't know . . . too tired to be bothered."

I nodded. "I've got some medicine for him, from Vileyra. Maybe he'll try that."

"Are you going to see Maja?"

"Probably."

"Good luck," Karro said, his grin returning. He knew how well Maja and I usually got along. Or didn't.

"Oh, don't be mean. Your sister's just—"

"I know, I know. She's just Maja. I guess my time's about up. Will you be stopping at the station?"

"Don't know yet. It depends on what jobs come up. I'll be in touch, though."

"Okay. Give my love to Dad when you see him. Love you, Mom." He blew me a kiss, and I saw age spots on his hand that I hadn't noticed before.

"I love you, too, Karro. I'll try to see you soon. Love to Aliande." His face faded as the WaVE ended.

"*Kapitano?*" Viss Feron's gravelly voice emerged from the ship's comm.

"How's everything down there, Viss?" I asked.

"Clear sailing. Tell Rei the ship's ready to bring us in. Any idea how long we'll be in port this time?"

I knew he was itching to start tearing things apart, just so he could put them back together. "Not yet, Viss. I'll have a schedule soon. We won't leave 'til you get that new filter in place."

"I'd like to clean the plasma intakes, Captain. A day is all I'd need."

"Noted. I'll keep you up-to-date."

9

I switched the view on my screen to mirror the bridge view, and Earth floated before us, more beautiful, in my opinion, than any other planet in Nearspace. Humans have colonized enough planets to call many places home, but Earth is the one I love. I sat back in my desk chair and let the servos massage my back for a minute while I took in the vista of the slowly-spinning planet. We were home again, with a hold full of top-notch cargo and plenty of job offers on the board, the *Tane Ikai* was in fine shape, and my crew was still managing to get along. My family was well. Life was good.

The feeling lasted almost a full minute before a familiar knot of sick apprehension twisted in my stomach. How was Hirin, really? Would I have a fight with my daughter this time around, or would we just ignore each other? I was never sure which was worse. And would PrimeCorp back off or keep hounding me if I left their message unanswered?

Then there was the big question, the one that raised its head every time a planet, Earth or any other, shimmered to life on the viewscreen. Could my mother be here? Alive? She'd be getting close to a hundred and thirty years old, the average lifespan for humans these days, and she'd been on the run from PrimeCorp for decades. Every day I felt my chances of finding her dwindling.

I glanced down at my unlined hands resting on the datapad. Maybe I'd never understand why, but if I could find her, she might have some answers. That was the driving force that had kept me plying the vastness of Nearspace for over fifty years. As long as she was out there, I'd keep looking.

Chapter Two

Family Ties
and Knotty Situations

Harried-looking nurses nodded pleasantly to me as I made my way up the lavender-walled corridor to Hirin's room. A few new faces regarded me with interest. I wasn't an adherent of the latest fashions in biosuits and chameleon fabrics—take a good old-fashioned pair of organic denim jeans and a simple white t-shirt, throw a long black synth-leather coat over it and you can go just about anywhere, in my opinion. Rei had long ago despaired of getting me into any of the outrageous styles she favoured, though deep down I knew they'd garner me fewer stares than my usual clothes did.

I pushed the door of Hirin's room open gently, in case he was sleeping, but he sat hunched over an open datapad on his desk and turned when he heard the door. His grizzled face split into a grin when he saw me.

"Luta!" He tried to get up in a hurry, wavered and had to grasp at the edge of the cluttered desk for balance.

"Wait, Hirin, I'm coming." I crossed the room to steady him. He swept his arms around me as soon as I was in reach and pulled me close, and I leaned in, careful not to unbalance him again, and rested my head against his chest. His heartbeat was steady but somehow delicate, and tears pricked my eyes at the sound. He seemed to have . . . faded . . . since the last time I'd seen him, two months ago. Thinner now, more fragile.

He pulled back to hold me at arm's length. "You look beautiful, as usual," he said, and bent to place a chaste kiss on my lips.

I pulled the bag of herbs out of my knapsack and held them

out to him. "From Vileyra. Supposed to heal all sorts of muscle and nerve damage."

He took them with a smile and sniffed them, wrinkled his nose and put them on the desk atop a stack of papers. Gingerly he lowered himself back into his chair, swivelling to face me with a smile. "So how is everything? Easy run this time?"

I nodded, and sat on the end of the bed. "Good cargo, no passengers to babysit. What about you? How are you feeling?"

Hirin shrugged. "So-so. Karro's on Sagan Station again, did you know that?"

"He WaVed me when we went past. We had a nice chat. I hear Maja's giving you a hard time," I said with a grin.

"Not as hard as she gives you," he said, grinning back. Maja and I seemed to have more difficulties every time I saw her. I think it's because I look more like her younger sister than her mother now. Karro doesn't have a problem with it, but maybe men can deal with that kind of thing easier than women can.

Hirin's grin didn't last, though. "Maja's worried about me," he said with a sigh. "Keeps urging me to have this test or take that therapy. I know she means well, but . . ."

"You never liked a fuss."

He smiled at me. "No, I never did," he agreed. "Let's change the subject."

"*Okej,* what are you working on now?" I nodded at the overflowing desk.

He shrugged. "This and that. An idea for a new plasma intake system, some research. Nothing very exciting."

"That's what you always say, and it's always brilliant."

"You're my wife, you have to say that," he said, grinning. "Listen, want to hear some interesting gossip?"

"Sure."

Hirin leaned back in his chair and steepled his fingers in front of him, tapping them against his lips. It was a habit he'd had since we'd met and I almost teared up again. I focused on what he was saying.

"A doctor—a Vilisian doctor—came in here a few weeks ago," he began. "Said he was a geriatrics researcher or some such. Wanted data on all of us, how old we were, lifestyles, everything that was wrong with us now. Admin said it was okay with them, but they wouldn't just hand over our records. He had to talk to each of us himself and as far as Admin was concerned, we could tell him whatever we wanted.

"I had a pleasant visit with him—hell, it was someone to talk to—told him almost everything he wanted to know. He was a good listener. But he was an even better talker, if you got him started, and he let slip two things you'd want to know."

He coughed suddenly, the kind of cough that catches your breath hard and won't let go, and I poured him a drink of water from the carafe on his bedside table. I had to wait, with one hand on his back, while he fought to get control of his breathing again. His shoulder blades felt sharp and frail under my fingers as his body shuddered with the force of the coughing. A blonde nurse popped her head in, but smiled and left when she saw he wasn't alone. The smell of cafeteria food wafted in with her, not particularly appetizing.

"*Ho ve*, sorry," he managed finally, gasping in between sips of water. "Where was I?"

"The Vilisian doctor," I prompted. "Why is a Vilisian interested in human aging?"

Hirin shrugged. "Their lifespans are about the same as ours, a little shorter, if anything. He thinks maybe he can find something the two physiologies have in common. Anyway, he said he was looking for passage to Kiando in the next few weeks. Seems the Chairman of one of the colonies there has a serious interest in anti-aging research. Not just rejuv, something better than that."

I shook my head. "I hope it works better than the last time." Three decades ago a corporation—Nicadico, not PrimeCorp— had released an anti-aging treatment called "Longate" that was touted as the first tangible step toward human immortality. The research hadn't been sound, though; problematic data from medical trials was buried, a lot of money had changed hands surreptitiously, and a frightening number of people had consequently died. Turned out that the cumulative effect of several courses of treatment caused cascading organ failure on an irreversible scale.

The Longate disaster made anti-aging research a pariah field for a long time, although people gradually overcame their aversion as the beacon of immortality brightened again. No further real breakthroughs had happened, though—whether from over-caution or scientific obstacles, I didn't know.

Hirin nodded. "That little fiasco set the whole field back decades. This Chairman Buig, now, he seems serious. The kind of serious he's willing to back up with money. Big money, corporation money, but not for payoffs, for good solid research. Now, here's the thing. My Vilisian friend heard—by way of a long ravel of hearsay, mind you—that this Chairman has a lady researcher there with 'extensive experience' in the field. Supposedly has some revolutionary ideas." He stopped to let the words sink in.

"You think it could be Mother?" I didn't mean to whisper, but force of habit made me. I'd trained myself a long time ago to know that PrimeCorp could be listening anytime, anywhere.

Hirin shrugged. "No idea, but it made me wonder. Now, it's only rumour, and who knows how many times it's passed from one ear to the next. This doctor put enough stock in it to want to travel there to see if he could catch up with her. 'Course it's all supposed to be very secret—won't be for long if the doctor keeps blabbing about it—but there it is, for what it's worth."

I reached out to lay a hand on his age-worn one. His skin felt warm, but fragile as tissue. He'd been helping me look for her for decades now. "Thanks, Hirin. You never let me down."

A brief look of discomfort crossed his face and I added, "But Kiando! That's a long run, longer than I ever take. I'd be away for too long."

Hirin nodded. "Three months or more. I know you never like to be gone more than six weeks at the outside." He cocked his head disapprovingly at me. "I also know it's because of me, and I don't like that."

"I know. Because you never like a fuss," I said again. "I don't do it because I think I have to. I just—don't like being away that long."

"Well, that's what you always say, anyway. And if it's true, it makes this a little easier . . ." His smile faded and he sighed. "I have a favour to ask you, Luta. I was hoping I'd see you back soon for another reason, more than just passing along what I'd heard."

He looked so serious that fear gripped me. "What is it?"

Hirin pulled his hand from under mine and patted my arm. "Oh, it's pretty bad, no sense trying to hide the fact." He got up slowly and shuffled across the tiny room to the door, making sure it was shut tight before he turned to face me again, leaning back against it. He looked even paler against its cheery, robin's-egg paint. "I'm not going to live much longer."

I started to protest but he held up a hand. "No, it's true. The virus has resurfaced and it's attacking organs this time.

14

Everything they can think of to fight it will only do damage in other ways. Even the bioscavengers are overwhelmed. It's a no-win situation."

Tears stung my eyes but I fought them down, resolved that I wouldn't cry. If he could be logical about this then so could I. "Well, then, I'm certainly not going anywhere right now, let alone Kiando. I'll stay here for as long as you—"

"Last?" Hirin smiled. "You can say it, I don't mind, but that's not the favour I want, Luta. What I had in mind—I don't know. It might be even more difficult than staying."

I frowned. "What is it? You know I'll do it if I can."

He nodded. "I know, I know. All right." He left the door and limped back to sit beside me on the bed, taking my hand in both of his. "I think you should find the doctor, take the job, and skip him out to Mu Cassiopeia system. And," he took a deep breath, "I want you to take me with you."

As well as I knew my husband after almost sixty years together, I hadn't seen it coming. We'd agreed long ago that he wasn't up to space travel any longer. "But then you won't have access to any treatment at all! You'll probably die on the way there."

He just looked at me then, the blue-grey eyes I knew so very well steady on mine, and I realized suddenly that what I had said was exactly the point. My voice came out in a whisper again, although not from fear of eavesdroppers this time.

"That's what you want, isn't it?"

He leaned over and kissed me gently again, his lips papery and warm on mine. "I want to die in space. We spent so much time out among the stars—that's where I want to be at the end. Out there. With you."

That's when logic abandoned me and the tears would not be denied any longer. Hirin's arms were surprisingly strong around me while I sobbed against his sunken chest.

I didn't call Maja when I left Hirin, although that had been my original plan. Now I wanted to get back to the *Tane Ikai*, see if any of the requests for passage to Kiando might be from Hirin's researcher, and let the crew know that we'd be shipping out again soon.

I hardly remember walking back to the lot where I'd left the rented flitter, and I had to match up the numbers on the flight release chip and the hull to find the right one. My mind churned fretfully, trying to deal with too many things at once.

While the practical part of my brain was planning the next half-hour's worth of work and piloting the flitter through the light rain that spattered the windscreen, the emotional part thrummed chaotically. *Mother! Could she really be on Kiando, helping some Chairman extend his life?* It didn't sound like the altruistic woman I'd known until just after my fourteenth birthday, when she disappeared from our lives in order to protect us from PrimeCorp. Decades had passed since then, I reminded myself, and who knew what her financial—or ethical—situation might be now?

Then in mid-thought my mind would jump to *Hirin! Dying?* I'd known it would come, but I'd always hoped for a treatment, an anti-aging breakthrough—even a wild hope that if I found Mother, she might be able to help. She was a geneticist, after all. One thing about never aging oneself—it made aging in others much more difficult to accept. I didn't like to think about how many friends I'd lost over the years because things would just get too uncomfortable. After a while they'd start to look at me in a certain way, and I'd see them wondering. Then we'd slowly drift apart, and it was always painful.

Which led naturally to *Maja. She's not going to like this.* She meant well, but there were many things we just . . . clashed over. We'd been doing it since she was a child and hated living on board a far trader. She thought that I should "act my age," even if I didn't look it. That I should be staying on Earth, caring for Hirin. That I had an unreasonable distrust of PrimeCorp. She even thought my ongoing search for Mother was an obsessive waste of time that had played havoc in our own family. Sadly, we avoided each other most of the time. It was just easier that way.

I flew out of the rain somewhere over the White Mountains, but I wasn't in the mood for sightseeing. I kept my eyes on the controls as I turned things over in my mind.

Karro would be okay with Hirin's decision. He had a good relationship with both of us, loved us, but was too busy living his own life as a researcher to be overly concerned with ours. Maja would be a different story—Maja wouldn't want to say goodbye to her father, and she'd despise me even more for "taking him away." I could play out the conversation between us before I'd even spoken to her, and it wasn't going to be pleasant.

Right about then I realized someone was following me.

It had been a blip on my nav screen for the past while, but my mental distractions kept me from noticing the obvious—that it shouldn't have been keeping such a steady pace with me. I hadn't turned on the autopilot because I really didn't want to get back to the ship until I'd had time to sort things through. Consequently, my speed had been erratic. I'd slow down when I got too deep in thought, then speed up again when I realized what was happening. To stay consistently with me all this time, my follower must have been deliberately matching my speed.

The ship was just at the outer limit of my vision when I glanced out the rear view port, the sun glinting off a shiny hull of indeterminate colour. Too far away to tell what size or make it was. I checked my instrument panel, but the rental flitters were pretty basic, not equipped with magnification or scanning options. I slowed again, hoping it would catch up with me, but once again it matched my speed. That confirmed it. They were definitely following me.

I couldn't see much else to do but stay on course for the docking station. I kept my eyes on that glint behind me, doing nothing to make my follower think I'd spotted him. The rain started up again just outside Boston, and the glint became a small black dot against the darkening sky.

Back at the Central Mass docking station, I returned the flitter and found an excuse to chat with the rental agent for a few minutes, keeping a surreptitious watch on the other incoming flight traffic. Just about when I predicted, a top-of-the-line flitter landed at the outer edge of the ring, its bright titanium-coloured hull glistening with raindrops. No-one emerged, and the hull bore no logo or lettering. PrimeCorp, I suspected. It wouldn't be the first time they'd dogged me. Within a minute or two, it lifted off again and headed west, disappearing into the fog that had rolled in.

I finished my conversation and, without glancing back, followed the breezeway to the docking ring where the *Tane Ikai* lay berthed. I still felt an itch between my shoulder blades, as if someone were back there watching me, but I tried to shake it off. No-one had even gotten out of the flitter. What I couldn't figure out was why they'd followed me. I had made no secret of where we were docked, so if someone wanted to find me, they'd taken a round about route to do it.

PrimeCorp *bastardos*. I'd be damned if I'd let them rattle me. I resolutely put the whole incident out of my thoughts. I had enough to worry about.

I emerged onto a silent bridge, all the consoles dark and the skimchairs empty, the viewscreen black. It was like coming home to an empty house, depressing and lonely. I made my way down the short corridor to my own cabin to work. At least it wasn't unusual to be alone there.

The door of Baden's cabin slid open as I passed. "Captain! Back so soon? Thought you'd be visiting your family."

He'd changed out of the marine-blue biosuit he usually wore shipboard and was wearing street clothes, a chameleon-fabric shirt that clung to his upper body and cycled gradually and subtly through a range of cool colours, from aquamarine to emerald and all the gradations in between. His pants looked like denim, but they were more likely bio-weave from the planet Renata. One of two inhabited planets in the Delta Pavonis system, Renata did a big export business in the organic fabric that had an inherent temperature-modulating feature.

With his cocoa-brown hair still damp from the shower and the planes of his face freshly shaven, he looked, quite simply, gorgeous. He reminded me of Hirin when we were young, and it didn't improve my mood.

"Don't be too long if you're leaving the ship, Baden, we're probably shipping out again soon."

I must have spoken more sharply than I intended, because he raised his eyebrows. "What's—*okej*, Captain."

"Was all the cargo delivered?"

"Yes, the last client left about fifteen minutes ago. The hold's clear and the bots are sweeping up."

"*Bona.*"

"When you say, 'soon,' Captain, do you mean—?"

I relented. "Not before tomorrow night at the earliest, Baden. Probably not even that soon, really. Just check in tomorrow, all right?"

He looked like he'd say something more, but he only nodded and left, his footsteps echoing in the corridor. I turned and went into my cabin. Baden had tried his charms on me for a while when he first joined my crew, but eventually he'd accepted my rebuffs graciously. It would have been easy to say I was married, but that would raise more questions than it would answer, so I'd simply acted as if I wasn't interested. If it hadn't been for Hirin, I might have been, but we'd never had that kind of marriage and I wasn't about to start now, even in the strange circumstances that had entwined us. I thought that Baden and Rei sought solace with each other occasionally, especially on the longer runs. If it made them happy, it was fine with me.

It was something I never got used to, though, being the odd one out after all those years flying with Hirin.

I sighed and got down to work. The request for passage to Kiando was there on the job log, and the name matched Hirin's information. I sent an offer to the researcher, a Dr. Ndasa, knocking ten percent off the usual passenger fee just in case he had a tight fist. I did a quick scan for cargo offers going to Mars, the Cassiopeias or other systems en route, and sent out a few tenders. Might as well have the cargo pods full wherever we were going.

A knock sounded at the cabin door and Rei poked her head in. She looked fabulous, skin glowing, hair down and flowing around her shoulders like water. I wished suddenly that I'd gone for a facial, too. I could use some pampering.

"You're back!" she said, echoing Baden's words.

"I'm back," I agreed, "and on the trail of a new job. A few new jobs. We might not be here very long."

I'd tried to keep my voice matter-of-fact but Rei knew me too well. She came into the cabin and shut the door behind her. "What's wrong, Luta?"

"There have been some—unforeseen developments." I leaned back in my chair and tucked my feet up under me.

Rei flopped gracefully into my big reading chair, the one that I allow myself as a captain's luxury. She, too, was dressed in street clothes, if you could call them that. I know I wouldn't be seen on the street in them. Not even in my cabin. It was a two-piece golden biosuit, with flowing fabric bits intermixed with something that looked like medieval chain mail. Whatever you wanted to call it, Rei could carry it off.

"Hirin?" She said it softly.

"Well, yes, but probably not quite what you think." I thought maybe if I talked fast, I wouldn't start crying again. "He had a few bits of news. One was a possible lead on my mother. On Kiando." Rei was the only person in the crew who knew I was looking for her—but she didn't know everything about why.

Her eyebrows shot up. "That's a long run. Do you think it's worth investigating?"

I shrugged. "Might be. We might have a job that would take us that far. Hirin doesn't have much longer to live," I blurted suddenly.

"Oh, honey," she said, but that was all.

"But here's the interesting part." I swung my legs down and leaned forward, resting my elbows on the clear desktop. "He wants to ship out with us when we leave Earth this time. He wants to die in space."

There, I'd said it, and I still wasn't crying.

She thought about it. "Well, the guest quarters are empty," she said matter-of-factly. "I'd put him in there, it's closer to your room than the passenger cabins."

"So you think it's a good idea?"

Rei nodded. "If it's what he wants, I don't see any harm in it—except that it will be harder for you, right?"

I clamped my lips together tightly, because she'd hit upon the thing I'd been too cowardly to admit to myself.

"In the end it might be better for both of you this way. It's been a lot of years with a lot of distance between you."

I nodded. The incoming message alarm chimed and I shamelessly used the distraction to change the subject. As I'd hoped, it was from Dr. Ndasa, and I pressed the screen to take it realtime.

"*Saluton*," I said in Esper. "Good afternoon, Dr. Ndasa." He was an older Vilisian male, the amber-coloured flesh around his jowls wrinkled, the tips of his low-set, slightly upswept ears poking through ebony hair pulled back into the usual thick braid. A few pale amber streaks ran through his hair, the Vilisian equivalent of grey. He looked at me with eyes the shade of dark violet common to his race.

"Captain Paixon?" He seemed startled, looking at me with what, even on a Vilisian face, seemed an odd expression. "Th-thank you for your message," he stammered.

I couldn't imagine he had a problem with my speaking Esper; the Vilisians were generally good linguists and he could probably converse with me in several Earth languages, although they often clung to the older, more stiffly constructed Esperanto. When we'd first become allies with the Vilisians, during the Chron War, they'd had to use clunky computerized speakerboxes to converse with us, Vilisian voices being pitched too high for humans to hear. In the long years since then they'd fixed the problem with some kind of implant, and a distinct accent replaced the stilted mechanical voices. I gave him points for pronouncing my last name correctly, *pay-zon* and not *paxon*. Of course, he'd already encountered Hirin, so he had a head start.

"Were you interested in travelling on the *Tane Ikai*?" I asked. Perhaps he hadn't been expecting a female captain.

"Oh . . . oh yes, I am," he managed. He must have realized that he hadn't yet greeted me properly, and hurriedly made the usual Vilisian gesture, the touch of a palm to eyes, lips and heart. Then he blinked and seemed to make an effort to shake off whatever had made him uneasy. "I haven't had many other offers."

I wasn't surprised. Kiando was a long run—three wormhole skips with long insystem stretches between—and there wasn't much passenger traffic direct from Earth to the Cassiopeias. I mentioned Hirin, hoping to put the alien more at ease, and his face broke into a smile, the wrinkles in his skin thinning and flattening.

"My good friend Hirin Paixon! He is family?"

"He is family," I agreed. "He may be making the trip with us, so you can speak with him again if you like."

"But his health! Is it wise?" The doctor seemed truly concerned, which made me like him despite his initial weirdness. Maybe it was just an alien thing.

I shrugged. "It is—irrelevant," I said finally. "He wishes it."

The doctor nodded his head sagely, and we turned the conversation back to business. Rei waved silently to me and left the room.

When we had completed our conversation and terminated the connection, I sat back from the screen. Dr. Ndasa's words rang in my head. *Is it wise?* I smiled. No, it was not wise, but wisdom had not been a notably guiding principle of our lives together. It was too late to start taking much notice of it now.

Chapter Three

Shortcuts and Long Moments

I was busy following up cargo tenders an hour later when Yuskeya hailed me over the ship's comm.

"Captain?"

"Right here, Yuskeya."

"Do you have a minute? I have the wormhole data. I think you'll want to see it."

"I'm on my way." I went to the galley first and fixed myself a double caff. My eyes felt bleary after staring at cargo manifests for too long, trying to decide which were the most advantageous offers. If we made the skip to Kiando our first priority, which I wanted to do, it didn't leave much leeway for arranging other stops. The trip to Mu Cassiopeia involved skipping through three wormholes, taking us through the MI 2 Eridani and Beta Hydri systems. I could take on cargo for Mars, the planet Eri in MI 2 and either Vele or Vileyra in Beta Hydri, but that was as far as I wanted to stretch it for cargo hauling. Any more stops would add too much time, and the mysterious female scientist on Kiando could leave long before we got there. It had to be a balancing act.

I sighed and breathed the caff's enticing fragrance in deeply, the mug warm in my hands. Was she my mother? Was there really much chance, or was I still hanging on to a groundless hope that I'd been chasing for thirty years now?

Our life had been fairly normal, as far as I could remember, up until the time I was nine. Mother was a scientist and worked for PrimeCorp. I knew she worked on anti-aging research, but that was all I understood. She talked to me sometimes about how someday we'd live forever, would have probably found a way long before then if it hadn't been for the Chron War and then the Retrogression, but hell, I was nine, how closely did I listen? I went to school, I had friends. I was happy.

One day my mother came home from work and took Father into the study. They had a long, low-voiced conversation that lasted until my little brother Lanar finally pounded on the door and demanded some supper. They didn't say much when they came out, although they both looked grave. The next morning we woke to find our entire apartment packed up to move, and we left on a far trader before noon. There wasn't much in the way of explanation, only that this was "the way it had to be" and that it was for our safety. A succession of travels, moves, and midnight getaways continued until I turned fourteen.

That's when Mother said she couldn't keep putting all of us in danger and that she'd have to "go away" for a while. They fought about it, she and Father, but in the end there came a morning when she just wasn't there. For a while we received sporadic, untraceable messages, saying she loved us. Then— nothing. Father never believed that anything bad had happened to her, and after I'd stopped being angry and started noticing how neither Lanar nor I aged past about thirty, I didn't want to believe it, either. I wanted to find her. Lanar had used the opportunities presented by his Protectorate career to search for her for a long time, too.

"Captain? Are you coming?" Yuskeya's voice on the comm broke my reverie.

"Sorry, I'll be right there."

Yuskeya had been fidgeting while she waited for me; all the workstations were tidy, all the screens wiped clean. Yuskeya's one of those people who cleans when she needs to calm her mind. I've never understood people like that, but it's handy sometimes to have one on your crew.

Anyway, it was a good sign. It probably meant she had something interesting to tell me.

"*Okej*, what did you find?" I was hopeful there might be something to help on this new job, but I wasn't letting myself get too excited. Wormholes that actually made any of the trade routes shorter didn't turn up very often. In the first place, they were dangerous to explore and there weren't many hole-spelunkers. They're mostly either already rich or already dead. In the second place, wormholes didn't have to make sense.

24

They simply existed, had probably been around since the creation of the universe. They weren't all useful. If a wormhole led to a system with a habitable planet, eventually we colonized it, but most of them didn't. Occasionally a new one provided a shortcut to somewhere we wanted to go.

She looked up from her screen and grinned. "Two out of six useful, Captain. They're nice ones, too."

"Really?" I slid a skimchair over from communications to look at her screen. She pulled up a number of starmaps and overlaid them.

"Now watch." She typed in a command and twelve endpoints appeared in green, connected in pairs by broken yellow lines. Four of them started in Nearspace but ended in systems that didn't even have names yet, just Gliese Codes from the star catalogue. Two, however, looked promising.

"This one," said Yuskeya, tracing a broken line with a delicate finger, "starts near Eri and ends not far from Jertenda in Beta Comae Berenices, so that cuts a whole lot of time off that run."

She looked up at me and I nodded. "Impressive."

"And this one," she said, indicating the other wormhole, "goes between MI 2 and GI 892."

"Great." It was hard to keep the disappointment out of my voice. I know I had no right to expect it, but neither route was going to make the trip to Kiando any faster.

Yuskeya notices everything. "I thought you'd be pleased!"

"Well, I am. I was just hoping there'd be something that would work for the Cassiopeias. It was silly."

She pursed her lips and I realized she was suppressing a smile. "Want to take another look?"

I frowned and leaned in toward the screen, but I still couldn't see what she meant. "The Beta Comae Berenices route eliminates one skip, but the in-system travel times would still be longer." Since every wormhole seems to be similar in "length" no matter how distant the systems they connect, in-system travel times are the deciding factor in making routes longer or shorter.

Yuskeya grinned. "That's not it."

I grimaced. "I'm *stulta* today, I guess. You'll have to tell me."

"It's risky. You may not want to do it," she said. "Look at where this second hole terminates. It's only about two days from the Split."

I saw it then. The Split was a wormhole that connected the uninhabited system GI 892 and Delta Pavonis. Another wormhole out of Delta Pavonis terminated about a day's journey from Cengare, Kiando's sister planet. Yuskeya was right, that route could cut a good bit off the travel time.

The Split was rarely travelled, however, for very good reason.

I don't pretend to understand exactly how wormhole travel works—you'd have to talk to Viss for that and you'd probably come away feeling like you'd just stuck your head into a plasma drive. I do know that the skip drive generates a thin layer of what the physicists call "Krasnikov matter," enough to keep the wormhole from destabilizing while a ship is inside it. Then it uses alternating positive and negative energy pulses to launch the ship into the wormhole at one end. The effects of the Krasnikov matter and the pulses allow the ship to skip along the tunnel-like inside of the wormhole, much like a rock skipping on water. A Ford-Roman field holds the ship intact, countering the immense forces at work inside the wormhole and protecting it from the high-frequency radiation, which would prove disastrous for ship and crew.

However, *unlike* a rock skipping on water, the skips don't follow a straight line. As the Ford-Roman field repels from one side of the hole, the ship slides around to bounce the next time off the other side, to create a water-going-down-the-drain effect.

Inside the ship, one isn't aware of these sensations, or at least they're very faint. Some folks feel slightly nauseous, and occasionally someone takes a heart attack, but it's rare. The hardest thing for most people to deal with is that the pseudo-grav fields get intensified, so it's pretty difficult to move around during a skip. Possible, but not fun. Sit and stay until we're out the other side, is what I tell passengers. It's a whole lot easier that way.

The problem with the Split is this: once you get inside it, you realize quickly that it's only half a wormhole. From outside, the terminal point is just like any other. But inside, the usual tube-like passage is more like the half-pipe used in extreme gravity sports. While one half of the tube looks perfectly normal (for a wormhole), the other half of the tube—well, it either isn't there or isn't anything we can figure out. Instead of a brilliantly colour-shifting wall, that half is simply a plain grey haze, no sensors can penetrate it, and no probe that's gone through it has ever come back or been heard from again. So you can't skip through it the way you can a normal wormhole; you don't get that water-down-a-drain effect. Everything has to be tightly controlled—field, speed, pulses and other delicate factors—so the ship can go the whole distance like a skipping rock, in a relatively straight line down the normal half of the wormhole. Very few crews will take it on.

I'd done it once before. It was an emergency, it was unavoidable, and Hirin was piloting. I didn't know if I could do it with anyone else, even Rei. I'd have to think about it.

Yuskeya just sat there looking at me, her ebony eyes bright. She'd never say it, but she was daring me to say it was a bad idea.

"You might have a point, Yuskeya," I said with my best poker face. "Any far trader willing to go that route could offer some pretty nice discounts. I'll see what the others think."

"They'd do it if you wanted them to," she said.

"Maybe." What was she waiting for me to say? You'd think at my age I could read people better. "Good work, Yuskeya, and thanks for telling me about it. We'll discuss it with the others later."

I didn't bother telling her not to mention it until then. I was sure she wouldn't be able to resist anyway, and that way they'd be prepared by the time I brought it up. I could get a reaction they'd had time to think about, not an automatic one.

I heard the main bridge hatch cycle open as I went down the corridor to my cabin, still carrying my half-empty mug of caff.

Yuskeya said, "Viss! Come here for a minute. I want to show you something."

I smiled. Maybe I wasn't so *stulta* after all.

The next day I got a call from Hirin's nursing home. I was listed in their records as his next-of-kin, although to avoid questions about the age difference we hadn't specified the relationship.

"Ms. Paixon?" The woman on my screen looked very corporate, with grey-streaked hair pulled back rather severely from her pinched and taut face. Her dark grey suit was unrelieved by any hint of colour or pattern, and although she wore earrings, they were also grey. I didn't remember her from the time we'd admitted Hirin there.

"How can I help you?" I asked.

She folded her hands on her desk. "My name is Evlyn Travis, I'm an administrator at Holbencare. We've had a rather abrupt and worrisome notice from Hirin Paixon, that he intends to leave our care," she said. "I'm not sure that such a move should be permitted."

Permitted? Odd way to put it. "Yes, I've spoken with Hirin about this matter," I told her. "It may not be convenient, but it's his decision."

She leaned forward a little and softened her face. I had the impression it was a very deliberate gesture. "His health is really not good, Ms. Paixon," she said. "It is not in his best interests to leave here, but sometimes the older residents . . . well, they get these strange notions."

"I've spoken to him about his health, thank you, and I do understand the situation. But it is his decision to make—"

She interrupted me smoothly, as if I hadn't been speaking. "Now, you may not be aware that it's possible to apply to the courts for a declaration of incompetency—"

"Hirin is quite mentally competent, I assure you," I snapped. "I'm sure you'll have no trouble finding someone to occupy his room, if that's your concern."

She managed to look misunderstood and sorrowful. "Our only concern is for the welfare of our residents," she said. "Perhaps you haven't been fully informed concerning Mr. Paixon's health situation—"

"As I understand it, he's dying, and there's nothing to be done to save him," I said bluntly.

Evlyn Travis blinked. "It's—very serious, yes. So you can see why—"

"In which case," I continued, "I don't see that it makes a hell of a lot of difference if he's here, there, or orbiting Mars. His residence fees will be paid until the end of the month. If there's paperwork to be done, please have it completed as soon as possible. I'll sign anything necessary to relieve you of responsibility."

"It's neither the money nor the liability we're concerned about," she said stiffly. "We simply feel that the most beneficial health care option would be for Mr. Paixon to remain with us. His wish to leave does not seem . . . rational."

"Then thank you for your concern, Ms. Travis," I said coldly.

"It certainly seems rational to me. And I'll tell Mr. Paixon that everything is arranged."

I didn't wait for her to say anything else, and broke the connection. Yes, it was rude, but my heart was pounding and my chest felt swollen with repressed sorrow. And anger. To suggest that Hirin was not in his right mind! I pushed away from my desk and stood, pulling a deep breath and moving into the familiar rhythm of my tae-ga-chi workout to try and calm down. The fluid ease of the form, with its interlock of sweeping hand movements and choreographed steps, was my favourite way to regain focus and center my mind. *Block, bend, step, balance, reach* . . . muscles loosened and relaxed into a meditative, physical mantra, leading my emotions to follow suit. I could complete this particular form inside a three-foot square, making it perfect for small shipboard spaces. After only a few moments, my body settled into the well-known cadence and I started to feel better.

Another incoming call beeped and I moved to the screen, chest tightening again. This time it was Hirin himself. His grizzled face looked about as angry as I'd ever seen it, and he was breathing fast. "Luta? You won't believe the visit I got from the administration here this morning!"

I leaned toward him. "It's okay, Hirin, calm down. I think I can guess, as a matter of fact. They're trying to talk you out of leaving?"

He barked a short, humourless laugh. "As good as told me I wasn't *allowed* to leave, if you can believe that. I gave them a piece of my mind, I can tell you."

I smiled. I could just imagine how that had gone, and now I knew what had prompted my call from Evlyn Travis. "I hope you didn't give them too much. They already seem to think you're getting a little short in that department."

He stared at me, uncomprehending, then chuckled. "They called you."

"And I told them in no uncertain terms that you were sane, you were leaving, and that was the end of it. Don't worry. When the *Tane Ikai* lifts off, you'll be aboard. I promise."

Hirin drew a deep breath. "I haven't told Maja yet."

"Well, she's not going to like it, but she can't stop you."

"I think we should tell her together, if you don't mind."

I nodded. "I think you're right. Just let me know when, and I'll be there."

We ended the call, and I went back to my tae-ga-chi. It took a while before I felt better.

Three days passed in a frenzy of preparations. If PrimeCorp was following me around, they were being much more covert about it, because I didn't notice any more suspicious flitters or individuals as I made my way around the spaceport and the city. Dr. Ndasa had accepted my tender. I took cargo hauling jobs for Mars, Eri, Rhea, and Renata, but nothing beyond that, so that my ultimate destination wouldn't be on the records. I couldn't find any other passengers. I wasn't too disappointed about that. Most people would have backed out when they heard we were going through the Split, anyway.

Not surprisingly, no-one on the crew had a problem with that, and if they were willing, then I could accept the risks, too. Viss stated flatly that he was not going unless he had a chance to clean those plasma intakes and tinker with a few other things, but I gave him the go-ahead and then he was fine with it. Baden raised his eyebrows but said nothing. I already knew Yuskeya was willing, and Rei let out a whoop of joy.

"I get to pilot the Split!? No *blago*?" She turned to Viss. "Better get busy on those plasma intakes."

"*Tane Ikai* can do it, Rei dam-Rowan, she's done it once before. Have you?"

"No," Rei retorted, "but I know the drill. I've studied logs and field data from every known Split run that's ever been made."

Baden turned to her and drawled, "And why would you do that, Rei? It's not a common run."

Rei flushed suddenly, her clear skin a bright pink beneath her *pridattii*. It was something I'd only seen happen once—maybe twice—before.

"It was for another job," she said evasively. "We made a lot of runs in the vicinity. I wanted to be prepared, just in case."

Everyone had to know she was lying—the only ships that made regular runs through the Split were usually running *from* something—but no-one called her on it. We all had things in our pasts that we didn't care to talk about, and so we all naturally respected each other's right to those secrets. It was always interesting when a revelation happened by accident, however.

"*Okej*. If Dr. Ndasa's willing to take the chance, we'll do it. We'll have one other passenger, but I know he won't object."

Rei smiled and the others looked the question at me. "Hirin's coming with us," I said. "He'll be in the guest quarters."

"Hirin?" Viss frowned. "Isn't he rather—"

"Old?" I shrugged. "Sure. He's ninety-two, and he's quite ill. He wants to die in space, to be perfectly honest, and there's no telling when it might happen." I couldn't believe how steady my voice was. "I'm telling you this so that you won't be surprised if it does. Is everyone okay with that?"

Baden grinned. "The old space dog! I hope I'm thinking that clearly when it's my time to go."

Yuskeya snorted. "You! You'll be all safe and cozy in an old folks' home, whining and moaning and pinching pretty young nurses when they come to give you a sonic shower. No way you'll be wishing you were shipboard."

Viss still looked worried. "That's kind of you, Captain, but won't it be awfully difficult? I mean, he is a relative."

I nodded. "It won't be easy, you're right. But if I can do this for him, then I want to. I'll be fine." I stood up. "So that's everything. We start taking on cargo tomorrow and we ship out the day after that. Any other matters I should know about?"

No-one spoke up, so I told them to try and have a little fun in the short time we'd be Earthside and headed for my cabin. I wanted to change my clothes and mentally prepare for what lay ahead. Hirin and I were meeting with Maja, and while I know I shouldn't say such a thing about my daughter, I wasn't looking forward to it at all. With Karro on the space station, we'd have to tell him everything via WaVE, but he'd accept it. Maja would be another story.

I pulled a dove-grey biosuit out of my drawer and looked at it dubiously. It wasn't exactly me, but it was more refined and elegant than my usual jeans and t-shirt. Maja might consider it "acting my age." I drafted Rei to pin up my hair, something I can never seem to manage myself unless I'm going for the tousled, just-got-out-of-bed look, and kept the makeup to a minimum.

The last few years I've paid special attention to my appearance whenever I'm going to see Maja. She's over fifty, still looks a young forty, but her mother still looks thirty. Maja takes good care of herself. However, she can't possibly look younger than I do, and that's just not a healthy mother-daughter situation.

When I surveyed my efforts in the mirror, I still looked thirty. I sighed.

We met at the nursing home, where Hirin was waiting until it was time to ship out. They were still making some noises about bad ideas and paperwork, but I just kept telling them that Hirin was leaving with me and it was not up for discussion. I didn't get as many stares as I went down the lavender hallway this time. Maja's voice reached me before I opened Hirin's door, and already she wasn't happy.

"But Dad, I want to know—" she broke off and turned around when I pushed the door open. It was easy to see what had made her think something was up. Despite the paperwork issue, Hirin had already packed up all his belongings and the room was as stark as a hospital cubicle. Even his usually cluttered desk was clear. He was making a statement. He was going, no matter what administrative obstacles they tried to throw in his path.

The skin around her sapphire-blue eyes tightened when she saw me and she drew a deep breath. "Hello, Mother. I might have known you'd have something to do with this."

"Hello, Maja. It's nice to see you, too." *Damne.* I'd promised myself that I'd be polite and stay calm for Hirin's sake, and I was screwing up already. To mask the sarcasm in my words, I crossed to her and gave her a quick hug and a peck on the cheek.

I didn't say she looked good, although she did. She seemed to resent it when I remarked on her appearance at all, no matter how flatteringly. Her hair was still devoid of grey and hung in shining blonde layers to her shoulders, her makeup was impeccable, and she wore an emerald biosuit overlaid with a leaf-patterned swirl of translucent fabric. I sent up a silent prayer of thanks that we still might look like sisters, at least. The day she started to look like the mother would probably be the last day we'd see each other.

She briefly looked surprised, then narrowed her eyes. "All right, that was rude of me. Now that you're here, maybe you'll tell me what this is all about? Dad won't say a thing and his room looks like he's already moved out."

Hirin said calmly, "Would you both sit down? I've asked the nurse to bring us tea, and we'll have a nice visit, shall we?"

Ha, I thought, but I sat in one of the two worn brocade

armchairs and Maja perched on the end of the bed. Hirin sat at his desk chair, saying he preferred the straight back.

"Now," he said, "Maja, I'll tell you what's happening. I was just waiting until your mother got here. You must understand that this is all my doing. She's only helping me out because I've asked her to."

Maja opened her mouth as if she'd protest already, but closed it without saying anything.

The nurse arrived with the tea just then, so we had to wait while she settled it all on the desk and surveyed us with a sunny smile. *How nice, the man's daughters coming to have tea with him*, I knew she must be thinking. Finally she left us alone again.

"Honey," Hirin continued, and his voice was very soft, "Maja, I haven't got much longer. The virus is at it again and, well, there's just nothing they can do."

"But what about—"

He held up a hand, very gently. "There's nothing. Nothing I want, anyway. I do have one last request, and that's why I've asked for your mother's help. I don't want to die here, in this place. I want to go back to the stars, just one more time, and I want the end to come out there somewhere."

Maja's eyes widened. "You can't be serious! Dad, this is crazy! If you stay here they'll make you comfortable, at least, they'll look after you . . ."

"They won't make me comfortable up here," he said, tapping a wizened finger to his temple. "And that's what I want most now."

"But it's too dangerous! Think of the risks! You'll—" She saw his face and switched tactics. "Why don't you come home with me, instead? I can take care of you. And if you needed a doctor there'd be one close."

"That would be lovely, dear, and I'd come and stay with you for a while if I had more time. However, I don't, and this is my chance, when your mother heads out again. I want to take it."

"But does it have to be right away?"

I nodded. "I have jobs I'm committed to, and a passenger. And a lead on your grandmother," I added.

She rounded on me. "*Dio*, are you ever going to give it up? I can't believe you wouldn't stay here with him instead of hauling him off on some space bucket," she hissed. "But oh, no, you've got your precious *jobs*. How can you do this?"

I looked at her sadly. "I offered to stay here, Maja. I told him I wouldn't take another job as long as he needed me Earthside, but he doesn't want to stay here. This is his idea, it's his wish, and I have to help him as well as I can." I took a chance. "I love him too, you know."

She looked at me for a long moment, then her face crumpled and she buried her head in her hands. It was suddenly clear to me that for a long time now she'd viewed me, not as her mother, not as Hirin's wife, but as someone she had to compete with for his affection. Despite our shared past, to her I was more like the stereotypical younger stepmother than her real mother. That hurt.

I moved to sit beside her on the bed and put an arm around her. *Dankas Dio,* she didn't pull away. "Honey, I'm his wife. I've been his wife for almost sixty years. He loves us both. He always has."

Maja managed to turn a sob into a long, deep breath. "I know," she whispered. "I know. It's just so hard. I feel like I lost you so long ago. Now I'm losing him, too."

My heart clenched at that and I couldn't force any more words out.

Hirin got up and shuffled over to the bed, sat on the other side of Maja and silently put an arm over her shoulders.

"When do you go?" she asked finally in a muffled voice.

"Two days' time," Hirin said. "I love you, Maja."

We sat like that for a long time, grieving for what we'd had, what we'd lost, and what was about to change forever.

Chapter Four

Secrets Lost and Found

I arrived back at the *Tane Ikai* that night to find a notebug from PrimeCorp waiting for me, hovering outside the main bridge hatch. Viss Feron was there, too, lounging beside the closed hatchway with something cradled in the palm of his hand. His thick, greying hair was untidy, and he still had his shipsuit on—he rarely wore anything else. Took some ribbing about that whenever we were planetside, too, but his usual dry response was that women had always loved a man in uniform.

"Yes, but usually a clean one," Rei would point out. Viss would merely grin and shrug.

He nodded towards the notebug as I approached the hatch.

"It must be for you," he said. "It's already scanned all the rest of us. Wait a second," he said, holding up a hand to halt my approach before I got close enough for the bug to scan me. "I could take care of it if you want."

He opened his palm and I saw what he held—a bug scrambler, commonly known as a "zapper." They were illegal tech; they scrambled the bug's message and the ID implant tags of anyone it had scanned. They also eradicated the bug's memory cache so that it couldn't return home and was essentially "lost."

This wasn't the first time Viss had suggested something outside the strictly legal, and I knew it wouldn't be the last. In the five years I'd known him, I'd come to suspect that his former careers had included time in the military and on both sides of the law enforcement line. I also knew that in any situation, Viss would do what he considered "right," and on those kinds of decisions, we always saw eye-to-eye.

I considered it, I confess. But the appearance of a second message so soon was unusual. PrimeCorp had docilely accepted my ignoring them the past few years. I was curious to see what had changed.

"That's all right, Viss, I'll take this one." I didn't mention the zapper. "Who knows, it could be something interesting."

He snorted a laugh and I stepped up for the scan. The tiny 'bot settled delicately on my forearm over the spot where my implant lay, ran the initial ID scan and buzzed, "Luna Paxon?" Tiny antennae sprouted from the top, twitching as it waited for my response.

If it had been a real person I might have bothered to make the point that my name was Luta, not Luna, and that it had the last name wrong, too, but no-one ever bothers to fix bug software, and it had already identified me from the scan. The voice confirmation was just a redundancy. I rolled my eyes at Viss and said, "*Konfirmi*," and the notebug direct-transferred the message to my implant. I felt the usual small zap, like a shock of static electricity, to signal the end of the message, and then the thing flitted away. Trust PrimeCorp to go to ridiculous lengths to preserve its "privacy." They could have just sent me another e-note.

Viss watched the thing disappear past a battered insystem shuttle docked beside us, then opened the hatch and gestured me in ahead of him.

"Do you want the good news first, or the bad news?" he asked as we entered the bridge. Yuskeya and Baden were both there, and looked up as we arrived.

"I'll take the bad, I guess, unless you're going to tell me you couldn't get the plasma intakes cleaned. I don't want to hear that at all, now or later."

Viss grinned. "No, that's done and she's ready to take on the Split as far as I'm concerned. Actually, that was the good news. The bad news is that I don't think we should head into the Split with a full load of cargo on board. I don't know what plans you've already made, but I think the forward pod should be clear when we get to that point."

"Is there something wrong with the skip drive?"

"No, no, it's not that. The drive is fine. I just ran a new diagnostic I got from a friend who's had . . . experience with the Split. The runs seem safer when the field stresses are lowest, and that means reducing the weight load. Is it a problem?"

I shook my head. "No, we weren't going to carry a full cargo load anyway, and we'll be offloading some before we get to GI 182. I just wondered why. Baden can tell the steves to keep Pod One clear. Thanks for the input." Viss had some questionable friends, but sometimes they came in handy.

I headed for my cabin, wondering what the PrimeCorp message might say. When I outloaded it to my datapad, I saw that the tone had changed considerably from the previous missive.

Received: from [205152.59.68] PrimeCorp Main Division NOTEBUG-V.: 25.7

Encryption: securetext/novis/noaud
Receipt recording: internal/enabled
*From: "Chairman Alin Sedmamin" <chair.primecorp*web>*
To: "Luta Paixon" <ID 59836254471>
Date: Mon, 4 Nov 2284 10:29:32 -0500

Captain Paixon,

As I have not yet had a reply to my previous message, I have become concerned that you may be planning to depart Earth without contacting me. I would advise against this course of action. The synthetic virus organically embedded into this message should be treated at PrimeCorp Main as soon as possible. I will make myself available at your convenience.

Chairman Alin Sedmamin

Virus! I swore quietly. I hadn't downloaded any new virus definitions since I'd docked on Earth, and it seemed clear that Alin Sedmamin knew that. They must have a tap on my datalinks, which was unquestionably illegal, but hell, they were PrimeCorp, and who was going to do anything about it?

It followed that they'd be watching to see what I did next, so I didn't make a hasty connection and start looking for definitions. No sense in letting the *bastardos* know they'd rattled me. Instead, I went looking for Baden, and found him still on the bridge with Rei and Yuskeya.

"Baden, do you still have that virus scanner you ran for us

on Jertenda?"

He looked up, sea-green eyes concerned. "Sure. What's wrong, Captain, catch a bug?"

"Yeah, you could say that. Is it up to date?"

"Pretty much. It might not pinpoint some of the latest synthetics, but it could still return a general analysis. I could look for an update first."

"No, I don't want anyone accessing the datalinks now. Let's just go with what you have. I'm making a guess about something but I need some data to know if I'm right or not."

"Meet you in the galley in five minutes," he said, striding down toward his quarters.

Rei raised her eyebrows at me but I said, "Tell you later. Meantime, put an extra encryption filter on all incoming data and see if Viss has some 'special' gadget to look for a tap on the datalinks. I don't want anything outgoing until Viss checks it out. If anyone shows up with cargo, check the manifest down to the nanoprint and run an ID implant scan on whoever's loading it."

"Sure thing, Captain."

"Yuskeya, run a rootsource verification on that new wormhole data, would you?"

She started to protest but I shook my head. "I know, you got it from a friend, but it wouldn't be the first time someone used an innocent middleman for other purposes. Just verify it, *okej*?"

"No problem, Captain. You're right. Better safe . . ."

"If there is such a thing," I muttered as I left the bridge.

In the corridor near my cabin, a swift wave of nausea coursed through me. Hot sweat prickled on my forehead and I leaned against the door, closed my eyes and bent over, swallowing hard and hoping I wouldn't vomit. I couldn't remember what that would be like, but I knew it wasn't pleasant. There's a corollary to never getting older: I'm never sick, either. The most I ever feel is a general discomfort, usually gone within half an hour or so. Maybe a one-time churn of the stomach, or twinge of a headache. So while I stood panting and feeling wretched and cursing Alin Sedmamin, I was fairly certain that it wouldn't last.

I was right. In less than two minutes the nausea passed and I continued down to the galley. Baden was pulling an inky, pungent triple caff out of the machine when I entered.

"Want one?" he asked.

"Sure." It smelled damn good, and I wanted to be thinking clearly for the next little while. Nothing perks up the brain like a triple caff.

He brought the steaming mugs over to the table, where he'd set down his datapad.

"You planning to tell me what this is about?" he asked as he set up the scan.

"PrimeCorp."

"Really? Do they ever give up?"

"I guess not." The crew knew I'd had run-ins with PrimeCorp in the past, although they didn't know the details. As I said, we respected each other's secrets.

"You must have really pissed them off." He gestured with the datapad. "You ready?"

I held out my arm and he pressed the datapad over my ID implant, then wiggled it until it beeped to signal a good connection. He tapped the screen and a soft bioplas strap snaked out and wound around my arm, holding the datapad in place snugly but comfortably.

"Hey, mine doesn't do that!"

He half-smiled. "How old is yours?"

"*Okej, okej,* so I'm not a techdog like you."

The datapad chattered a sequence of beeps and Baden leaned in to read the screen. "You have a beacon implant there?" he asked.

"Oh, yes, does that matter?" *Damne.* I hadn't thought about that implant in ages. Hirin and I had bought them years ago, when our runs often took us to the more dangerous and then newly-explored reaches of Nearspace. I couldn't very well tell Baden that, though.

"No, the datapad just picked it up. It's pretty outdated, though."

I grinned. "I told you I wasn't a techdog." I thought fast. "Our parents bought them for us when we were kids. We travelled a lot, and they were always worried about us getting lost in some spacedock or something."

Baden nodded, leaned back in his chair and took a sip of caff.

"It's running the scan now. Shouldn't take too long. What exactly are we looking for?"

I considered. I didn't want to give too much away, but it's

always nice to get some credit if you turn out to be right. Helps crew morale if they think their Captain's at least mildly *inteligenta*. "If I tell you what I think, and I'm right, you'll just have to accept it. Deal?"

He pursed his lips. "Deal. I guess. Although it won't be nearly so interesting if I can't have an explanation."

"*Okej* then." I took a second to collect my thoughts. "I think it's going to find that I'm infected with a synthetic, organic virus, data-embeddable, probably not too nasty but annoying enough to warrant treatment. The virus won't be thriving, though. It'll already be partially dormant or dying."

Baden frowned. "That's pretty specific."

I shrugged and tasted my caff. It was heavenly—hot and creamy and sweeter than I would have made it, and good enough to make me consider the possibility that I'd been drinking it wrong all these years. "Let's just see if I'm right."

He took another sip from his mug, then said, "If I'm not allowed to ask you about that, can I ask you something else?"

"Go ahead." I smiled. "I can't guarantee that I'll answer that either, though."

Baden looked me in the eye. "Who's Hirin? I mean really. How are you two related?"

I opened my mouth to answer but he held up a warning finger. "It's only fair to warn you that if you tell me it's none of my business then I'm going to be pretty sure I know the real answer."

"Think so?"

"There's only one that I can think of that you might want to keep secret."

I picked up my caff very deliberately and took another drink. "It's none of your business."

He stared at me with narrowed eyes, then nodded. "*Okej*. It leaves more questions than it answers, but okay."

The datapad trilled, and he reached over and gently released it from my arm. "It'll take a minute to compile the analysis."

"No problem." I leaned back in the chair and tucked my feet up on the seat. Baden was busy tapping the screen and I watched him carefully.

I wondered if he'd actually guessed the truth about my relationship with Hirin. Probably. There was nothing slow about Baden. The question was, why did he care? I hoped it was pure curiosity. I didn't have time for complications.

"That's weird," he said suddenly. He was frowning down at the datapad screen.

"What?"

"Just a second." He watched the screen intently for another minute or so and then fiddled with the touchpad. He shook his head. "Do you mind if I hook you up again and take another sample?"

"It didn't work?"

He grimaced. "It's not that. I've got the virus nailed down, I think. I'm getting data on another entity as well—but it keeps disappearing before the analysis can run. One second it's there but before the program can collect enough data, it's gone."

Wordlessly I stuck out my arm, my heart thudding uncomfortably against the walls of my chest. *Another entity.* I shivered despite the warmth of the galley and the hot caff. It might be a clue—if Baden could get enough information about it to be useful.

The datapad locked itself on my arm and emitted its string of beeps. I looked up from it and met Baden's intent regard.

"You know what it is, don't you?"

"No," I said truthfully, "I don't. But I have a few ideas, and I'd sure love to know if any of them are right or even close."

Baden got up and took his mug over to refill it. "You?" he asked, but I shook my head. When he came back and sat down he said, "Everybody has things they don't talk about. I think this crew has more than the usual complement. But I'm beginning to think that you've got more than all of us put together."

"You may be right," I admitted. "I'd have to know all of everyone else's secrets to know for sure. You want to go first?"

He laughed. "Not at the moment. Maybe someday. But what if you have to give up one of yours because of this scan?"

"If I do, I do." I shrugged. "None of my secrets are life-threatening. Just uncomfortable." I sipped at my still half-full mug of caff. "Well, as far as I know, anyway."

The datapad trilled and Baden swiftly removed it from my arm, touching the commands to run the analysis as quickly as possible. I felt certain that if he didn't get the data this time there would be no sense in trying again. It was the nature of the "entity," as he'd called it, to be almost invisible. I'd learned that much long ago.

"*Damne,*" he whispered, and I knew it hadn't been quite fast enough.

He sat back in his chair and smiled humorlessly. "Want to know what we got?"

I nodded.

"The virus is or was a synthetic-organic virus, data-embeddable, probably one that would cause mild vomiting, fever, and other unpleasantness for a week or so. However, the virus is not thriving. All the fragments we caught were already disintegrating or dying." He set the datapad down on the table and tapped it lightly with his knuckles. "Exactly like you said."

"What can I say? I'm a good guesser."

"Mm-hmm." He turned the datapad so he could read it. "As for the other stuff, whatever it was, it seemed like it didn't want to be found. I think it was only partially organic. It was attaching itself to the virus and then detaching again quickly and either breaking down or—reorganizing itself. The program couldn't get a clear read on it."

"That's *okej*." What might these slim clues mean? *Partially organic. Attaching and detaching from the virus cells. Then breaking down or changing—on a molecular level? Which would explain why the analysis program couldn't maintain a fix on it to keep reading data?*

"What?" I jerked out of my thoughts as Baden touched my hand.

"I said, I want to connect the datapad one more time and update your virus protocols and a few of your modules, *okej*? Since it seems you're too busy to do it yourself." As the datapad trilled and chattered, his grin faded and he looked serious. "Captain, does any of this make sense to you? Part of what we found was what you guessed."

I nodded. "It makes some sense. It was what I was hoping for, the virus part, anyway. That was a little unsolicited gift from PrimeCorp, one that I won't forget about anytime soon. The rest—I don't know. It's something I'm still trying to figure out."

"And that's all you're going to say about it?"

"For now. Thanks, though, Baden. I'm sorry I can't say more."

He laughed. "Hey, like I said, we all have our secrets." He stood up and was suddenly serious. "Just be sure you tell someone if you need help, Captain. PrimeCorp—I've heard some things. They're not very . . . scrupulous."

"Yeah," I said, "I've figured that out."

I wasn't about to cancel my cargo jobs to leave early, so I couldn't just laugh in PrimeCorp's face as we were thrusting for the upper atmosphere. They'd know by now exactly when we were scheduled to leave Earth, and if they'd abandoned whatever slim scruples they used to have I wasn't about to walk into Alin Sedmamin's plush office at PrimeCorp Main. However, I couldn't leave the situation as it was, either.

I called him an hour or so later, when I was sure the nausea wasn't coming back. My "entity" appeared to have done a thorough job. The PrimeCorp secretary-avatar, synthetically beautiful in the way only corporate avatars seem to be, put me through right away.

Sedmamin's face, when it came onscreen, was paunchier and paler than I remembered from our last talk. It made his small dark eyes look even more pig-like, although I guessed he'd had a Vigor-Us treatment since then. He'd pressed me pretty hard that time to come into the research department for some tests, even making thinly-veiled threats, so I'd had to end the conversation by closing the connection abruptly and shipping out that night for Quma with the cargo pods only half-full.

Might as well get to the point. "*Saluton,* Chairman Sedmamin. This is Luta Paixon. I'm not planning to come in and see you this visit, so I'm placing this call instead."

"*Saluton,* Captain Paixon. Did you receive both my messages?"

"I did. Your notebugs are highly efficient. By the way, don't bother sending another one. It will not be accepted."

Sedmamin smiled thinly. "You seem irritable, Captain. Are you feeling unwell?"

"Actually, Chairman, I'm feeling fine. Perhaps the virus in your note has malfunctioned. Or come to other grief. It was a rather unusual way of extending your hospitality, I must say."

"You've ignored my previous invitations." He shrugged, not an elegant gesture for him. "I felt other measures were in order."

"Chairman Sedmamin, let's stop dancing, shall we? You want to know if I have any information on the whereabouts of my mother. I do not know where she is. You want me to come into your research facility and submit to tests to determine if I'm carrying around any bits of my mother's research that you consider to be the property of PrimeCorp. I am refusing to do so; I have a ship to run and business of my own to attend to, and I am fully within my rights. I know without asking that you have no information you're willing to share with me—"

"Ah, but that's where you're wrong, Captain Paixon, and I'm wounded by your mistrust." He didn't look wounded in the least; in fact, he seemed to be gloating. "I have solid information that your mother was alive and well as recently as one month ago."

"Really?" I kept my face impassive. For the second time that day my heart was going a couple of rounds with my rib cage. "And what would you call 'solid' information?"

"Would you consider a first-hand encounter with a PrimeCorp associate, who has identified her convincingly from hologrammatic representations, to be 'solid'?"

"I might. Was this associate hunting for her? He may be lying to try and impress you. What sort of evidence do you have?"

"It was a she," he corrected me, "and she wasn't 'hunting' your mother, as you so crudely put it. She merely thought the face was familiar. She had seen a hologram of your mother here, or she would not have noticed her on—when she saw her. She then confirmed the sighting with the hologram back here at home as the woman she'd spoken to."

"Impressive." I did my best to look bored. "And where did this exciting face-to-face encounter take place?" He'd almost let it slip.

"Oh, no, Captain." He waggled a chubby finger at me as if I were a naughty pet and sat back in his leather chair. "Information *exchange* is what I'm after, not a one-way transfer. Come in, let us take some samples, and I'll give you open access to the file on the most recent verified sighting of your mother."

I sighed. "Well, I'll think about it. We ship out tomorrow. I don't know if I can fit it in."

"Before you go," Sedmamin said, leaning forward slightly in his chair, "I'd like you to meet some one."

This was unusual. Generally it was just me and Sedmamin in not-so-cozy privacy. "Certainly," I said.

Sedmamin gestured to someone off-screen and a woman

moved in to my field of view to stand just behind him. It was difficult to tell, but she seemed tall, and looked fit in a sleek black pantsuit with the PrimeCorp logo embroidered tastefully on one lapel. Dark blonde hair was pulled back from her face, except for a few tendrils that curled around it, softening her angular features. She wasn't exactly smiling, but had arranged her face in a pleasantly neutral expression.

"Luta Paixon, this is one of my administrative assistants, Dores Amadoro," Sedmamin said. Dores nodded politely. It could have been just the video feed, but her eyes seemed cold and appraising as they surveyed me, like I was an interesting specimen of something.

"Nice to meet you, Ms. Amadoro," I said.

"Likewise, Captain Paixon," she said. I didn't get the impression she thought it was very nice at all.

"Ms. Amadoro will be your liaison with PrimeCorp for the next while," Sedmamin said, smiling as if we were all good business partners. "She's very ambitious. Any questions or concerns, you can bring to her, and she'll be speaking to you for me. Anything that comes from her, you can assume has my approval."

Not that I really cared, but I asked anyway. "Are you going somewhere, Chairman? Not unwell yourself, I hope."

He kept smiling. "No, nothing of the sort. I simply have other matters to attend to, so I'm, well, delegating. Something I'm sure I should do more of."

Ha, I thought. *Downloading me to some poor sucker because I'm a pain in your azeno.* I would have felt sorry for Dores Amadoro if she'd seemed like a person with any feelings. Then I wondered if she'd been the one to spot my mother somewhere, and this was her reward—a step up the administrative ladder. Any hint of warmth I might have felt for her dissipated immediately.

I plastered on a smile, however. "I'm sure we'll get along just fine, then. I don't expect to be in Sol System much for the next while, however, so I guess we won't have the chance to get to know each other very well."

"Captain," Sedmamin said, leaning forward and trying to look solicitous, "I don't mind telling you that there are some members of the Board who feel that we've been too . . . accommodating in our dealings with you. I've done my best to convince them that polite discourse will eventually lead to a satisfactory conclusion for all of us, but they're growing restless."

"Sending a virus in a notebug is your idea of 'polite discourse,' Chairman? It's not exactly the best way to earn my trust. And I'm within my rights under the Genetic Materials Privacy Act."

He shrugged again. "Laws are meant to be challenged, and as I said, there are some who think we've been polite enough. As for trust, you may want to give some thought to where you've already placed it, Captain."

"What do you mean by that?"

Dores Amadoro still stood half-behind Sedmamin's chair with that neutral look on her face. I wondered if she knew what he was talking about, or if she was just too well-trained to show any reaction.

"Call it free advice. You may not know as much as you should about that crew of yours." He smiled in a knowing way that infuriated me.

"My crew is no concern of yours."

"Of course it isn't. But one more thing, Captain Paixon," he said seriously. "I like you, although we've had our differences. So here's a warning. There are changes in the wind, changes that are going to play more in my favour than in yours. It would be . . . prudent . . . on your part to simply come in, give us our samples, and go on your way. That way, there will be no complications."

Sedmamin liked me? I doubted it, and I certainly couldn't return the compliment. "Complications? What kind of complications?"

"I can't elaborate. Let's just say it would be better to be a friend of PrimeCorp than an enemy."

I grinned at him. "Well, that's always been true, hasn't it, Chairman? Thanks for the warning. I'll think about what you've said, and get back to you, or to Ms. Amadoro. *Gis la revido.*" I broke the connection.

I leaned back in my own chair—not leather—and closed my eyes. I hated talking to anyone at PrimeCorp, and Sedmamin was just about at the bottom of the list. My first impression of Dores Amadoro didn't put her much higher. Sedmamin had definitely stepped over a line with that virus trick—I had no doubt the idea had been his, no matter what he said about restless board members—and we'd have to be careful until we shipped out tomorrow. Chairman Sedmamin had taken my rebuff a little too graciously. He could well have other plans to delay us or try to get to me, although I couldn't imagine what they might be.

On second thought, I could imagine a few. I didn't like them.

I called Hirin and set the encryption to maximum. It took a moment for the administrator to connect us, and then his dear, wizened face came up on the screen. "Hirin, do you think you could come aboard this afternoon instead of tomorrow?"

"Are you shipping out early?"

"No, I don't have all the cargo on board yet. I'm just a little worried about . . . security, that's all."

"Well, they're throwing me a going-away party here this afternoon, and Maja's coming over for it." He looked uncomfortable. "I didn't tell you about it because it might be . . . awkward."

"That's okay," I reassured him. "I'm busy getting everything set here, anyway."

"*Okej*, well, as soon as I've made my appearance there I could come on over. Everything's packed. I don't like to disappoint them; the only going-away parties here are usually wakes." He chuckled until he started coughing again.

I smiled. "That'll be fine. Can I send Viss over to get you?"

He nodded. "Sure. I thought it would be you, though."

"I think I'll stay on board until we leave. It might be wise in light of some recent developments, and you know how I love to be wise."

"Yeah, right. Our old friends giving you trouble?" Given my history with PrimeCorp, he knew exactly what I meant.

"They might be. I'm not taking any chances. Just call when you're ready and I'll send Viss over. Enjoy your party."

"I will. See you later."

Just to be on the safe side, I sent messages to Maja and Karro, letting them know that PrimeCorp seemed to be at it again. Karro had had his own encounters with Sedmamin in the past, and though they were never as dramatic as mine, he didn't like the company's intrusions any better than I did. As for Maja—well, she actually seemed to get along with PrimeCorp and thought I was paranoid about the company. She didn't know why I wouldn't just cooperate with them and be done with it. Even knowing the details of my family's history with PrimeCorp didn't seem to make a difference to her. No doubt she thought I'd made half of it up or exaggerated it. She'd probably delete my warning message in a huff. I sent it anyway.

I knew one thing. If Alin Sedmamin—or this new, unknown quantity Dores Amadoro—tried to get to me through Hirin or anyone else in my family, I'd have to leave the ship in order to kill them. I really hoped it wouldn't come to that.

The only other person PrimeCorp bothered as regularly as me was my brother Lanar, but when I tried to message him I got an automated reply that he was currently outsystem, so I left it at that. With the Nearspace Protectorate fleet at Lanar's back, PrimeCorp tended to tread gently around him, anyway. I wondered if he'd know what Sedmamin might have meant by "changes in the wind," but that could wait until the next time we spoke in real-time.

That was all I could do. Unfortunately, that left my mind free to consider the other things Sedmamin had said.

First, was the story about my mother true at all? He could have fabricated it as another ploy to get me onto PrimeCorp property, but I didn't think so. He wouldn't gloat over a lie. No, the PrimeCorp person had seen my mother—or someone they were certain was her.

A month ago. I idly punched up the star charts and wormhole routes on my own screen, including the new ones. If the story was true, and considering that the identifier was already back on Earth, she could have been in almost any inhabited system. In the time since then she could have gone anywhere in Nearspace.

The other question was, where had Sedmamin obtained a hologram recent enough to make any kind of identification likely? Whatever he'd have "on file" would be decades old.

He hadn't said anything else about her, only that she was "alive and well." For half a second I considered actually storming in to PrimeCorp and demanding to see what else was in that file, then shook my head. Chances were I wouldn't learn a damn thing more than I knew now, and I could be walking into something very bad. It was probably exactly what Sedmamin was hoping I'd do.

As for that crack about my crew—I wanted to brush it off as nothing but pure nastiness on Sedmamin's part, but it nagged me. I trusted my crew and considered them all my friends, but in truth, I hadn't known most of them very long. I did know they all had secrets. Could one of them be keeping quiet about something that could ultimately hurt us?

I closed down my screen and went to talk to Viss about picking up Hirin. One worry at a time.

Chapter Five

Dark as Space and Twice as Dangerous

Dr. Ndasa and Hirin both arrived on board just at suppertime, which made for a busy couple of hours. We got Hirin settled in the guest quarters, right across the hall from my cabin. It didn't take long. He didn't bring much with him.

He shrugged when I asked him about it. "I don't need much," he said. "And you'd only be stuck with it after . . ."

"After you croak and we jettison you off into the depths of space?" I finished for him.

He laughed. "Exactly. Oh, Luta, I'm so glad you can joke about this. I was worried that it would be too hard on you."

"It's the hardest thing I've ever had to do." I hugged him. "But if you can take it, I guess I can, too."

He stroked my hair briefly with a hand that trembled just enough to notice. "There never was much we couldn't take on together, was there?"

"Nope, there never was," I agreed. "Let's go see how Dr. Ndasa's doing. If you feel up to it."

"I feel better than I have in a long time, to tell you the truth. One thing, though," he said, squeezing my hand instead of letting it go. "The crew—they still don't know about you, do they? And me—us."

"Only Rei," I said. "She knows some of it."

"And we'll keep it that way? I don't mind, but I thought you might be wondering if I would."

Sudden tears stung my eyes. "It's not the way I've ever wanted things to be, Hirin. All this secrecy. Especially now."

"I know. But I've had lots of time to think about it, and it's

51

just the way things are. Frankly, I'm surprised you haven't left me for a younger man before this."

I looked up, stricken, but his eyes twinkled as he tried to suppress a grin. I put my hands on my hips.

"Keep that up and I just might, old man. Now are you coming with me?"

"I think I'll have a lie down and rest until supper time. I'll come to the galley to eat. I can't wait to have different people to talk with."

Since Dr. Ndasa was our only other passenger, I'd put him in one of the two larger cabins. He'd shown up with a lot more gear than I'd expected, but I let him put that in the smaller cabin that adjoined his, since it was empty anyway. He thanked me sheepishly. A mild scent of grapefruit hung around him, a sign of nervousness in Vilisians. I'd been studying up on the Vilisian scent-language in preparation for his time with us.

"I've never been away from my laboratory for this long before," he apologized. "It was difficult to leave things behind."

"If you do it often enough you learn to travel light, but it's no problem." I leaned against his stack of mismatched luggage. "I'm curious, Dr. Ndasa. Are you really travelling all this way on the off-chance that you'll catch up to this researcher? She could be long gone by the time we get to Kiando."

He nodded. "Yes, yes, I know. But Chairman Buig, her employer, is reputed to have connections to many of the best longevity researchers. He has a miniature research facility set up there, but the work coming out of it is not small. If this particular lady has moved on, it will still likely be a worthwhile journey for me." He flushed slightly, his amber skin darkening. "And besides, I have never taken an out-system journey before. I was born on Earth. I believe everyone should experience wormhole travel once in their lives."

I smiled. "I think so, too. I hope you'll be comfortable with us."

He looked around the cabin, the long smooth plait of his dark hair swinging across his back. "The room is quite perfect," he said. "And I love the name of your ship, *Tane Ikai*. Do you have an interest in longevity as well, Captain Paixon? I assume you know for whom your ship is named?"

"A passing one," I said easily. "I know it's named for the Japanese woman who lived to one hundred and fifteen back in the twentieth century."

Dr. Ndasa nodded eagerly. The grapefruit scent was fading. "Most people live that long now, but back then it was notable. I believe, however, that it is possible to extend the human and Vilisian lifespans almost indefinitely."

"We've thought that for a long time, but we never seem to make a breakthrough."

"The Longate tragedy certainly set the research back," he said. "But I think people might be ready to trust again. The knowledge is out there. I think we are very close. There have been rumours in the scientific community—but of course, they are only rumours." He was staring at me intently, his dark eyes unreadable. Could he suspect . . . no. Surely just an alien thing.

"What's the name of this researcher you hope to find on Kiando?"

"Demmar Holsey," he replied. "Although Chairman Buig is building quite a stable of researchers there. She is only one of perhaps a dozen, but I have heard especially good things about her work."

The name meant nothing to me, but I had hardly expected it would. My mother had been living under aliases for so long she might not even remember her real name.

Dr. Ndasa rubbed his long-fingered hands together and looked around the room again. His skin smelled mildly floral now, with excitement. "I hope to learn much on this voyage. It should be an excellent spot for quiet study."

I laughed. "I don't know about that, but we'll see. I've never thought of this crew as 'quiet.'"

I left then to see what was happening for supper, found that Baden and Yuskeya had things well in hand with some spicy Vileyran dish underway, and went back to the bridge to look over the cargo manifests. Everything was on board except one shipment of ore bound for Renata, so we'd leave as soon as that arrived, early in the morning.

Supper was a jovial affair and I was optimistic that this would be a restful run. Sometimes passengers complicate things and everyone ends up ill at ease, but I didn't need to worry about Hirin, and Dr. Ndasa seemed to get along well with everyone. He had an endless supply of interesting stories from his interview subjects. I wondered what he'd think if he knew my true age. No doubt he'd want to interview me every day for as long as the journey lasted.

That night I found it difficult to fall asleep. It wasn't that my circadian rhythms were out of sync with Earth's—we always made the necessary adjustments in the approach to a planet to make sure we didn't suffer from space lag. I sleep better planetside than out in space, but not planetside on a silent ship. That's the worst. No pulse of engines for comfort, no sprawling, majestic vastness of starry space outside the viewport. Not even the normal sounds of the world beyond the spaceport. Just utter silence in a big metal can.

That wasn't the problem tonight. I knew very well what it was—Hirin was only a few scant meters away from me, just across the hall, and I longed to go over and curl up in the bed beside him.

Not for sex—we'd not looked for that very often since he'd become sick. Just for the warmth and companionship and because there wouldn't be many more nights when I could listen to his breathing beside me and feel the soft rise and fall of his body next to mine. There were nights when I missed him no matter how many light years and wormhole skips separated us, but it was easier to dismiss when time and distance were insurmountable obstacles. When I could cross the hall to him in less than ten seconds, it was harder to ignore.

I looked at the clock: one a.m. already, and I hadn't closed my eyes yet. I weighed the consequences. What if someone saw me? I had no idea if the rest of the crew were sleeping or pursuing their own nighttime activities. How could I explain creeping into the bedroom of my elderly "relative" in the middle of the night? It would raise more than eyebrows in this bunch. They wouldn't rest until they knew everything.

Yet here I was, Captain of the ship, and afraid to venture outside my cabin door? It was ludicrous. I could always plead a trip to the head or a midnight snack if someone saw me emerge, after all.

After another hour of debating, I decided to risk it. I pulled on my robe and threw together some clothes for the morning. I felt silly, and excited, like a teenager sneaking around on her parents.

When I stealthily opened my door, the corridor was dark, broken only by a pale yellow glow from the guidelight in the galley. No-one else seemed to be stirring. I picked up my bundle of clothes and stepped out into the hall. A noise halted me.

It didn't come from the direction of the crew quarters, but

from the stern. I knew that peculiar tinny echo, the click of a step on a metal ladder. Someone was climbing up the hatchway from the lower decks. Trying to be quiet about it.

I took a silent step backward to the doorway of my cabin and let the clothes I was carrying slide to the floor. I shrugged out of my long robe and let it slip down as well—I didn't want any encumbrances. Whoever it was would find out that I favoured biosilk sleepsuits in bright colours, but at that moment I didn't care.

What really worried me was that I couldn't get to the weapons locker. To do so I'd have to run towards the intruder climbing up from the engineering deck, and that just wasn't practical or smart. I should have stepped back into my room and hit the general alarm button on the comm pad, but to be honest I just didn't think of it.

I took one more careful step inside the doorway of my room, just to be out of the glow from the galley guidelight. Whoever was coming would have to step through that glow, however, and I wanted to be able to see them without being seen.

Another light step sounded on the corridor decking. A shadowy figure rounded the corner of the weapons locker, close enough to notice me if the lights had been on.

The figure gestured with something I couldn't discern, and the guidelight went out.

I hadn't seen a face, only a dark silhouette, but it obviously wasn't anyone who belonged here. It took me a nanosecond to make up my mind. I launched out of my doorway at a dead run.

My shoulder hit the intruder in the chest with as much force as I could gather. I swung for a neck pressure point, and yelled, "*Intruder!*" Strong arms thrust around me in a vise-like grip and started to squeeze. Good thing I'd gotten one good yell out first.

My right knee came up reflexively and I knew the assailant was a man, since he arched deftly away from the blow. As soon as both feet were on the ground again I squatted low, then sprang up like a coil, twisting away at the same time. He couldn't keep the pressure steady and his grip loosened, enough for me to drop to the floor and swing my leg at his feet, knocking him off balance. He thudded against the airlock door, and the vibration triggered an automatic overhead emergency light. One step brought him close enough to kick me sharply in the solar plexus, though, and my breath *whooshed* out in a painful gasp.

I twisted around to try and get a look at the intruder, but a black biosuit concealed him from head to toe. He bent over me swiftly and something cold and sharp pierced the flesh of my upper arm, right through my sleepsuit. I swore, jerking and rolling away from the pain, still gasping for breath. The intruder moved away, back toward the hatchway, although all of this happened in a fraction of the time it takes to tell it.

I think it was about then that I heard other doors opening and the soft pounding of bare feet in the corridor. Someone was answering my summons.

I heard a step on the ladder, no attempt to be quiet this time, just as two sets of legs flashed past me. There was a bit of yelling and thumping then, as Viss and Yuskeya attempted to catch hold of the escaping intruder and haul him back up from the ladder.

Dr. Ndasa emerged from his cabin, inquiring sleepily about the disturbance. A faint metallic scent—confusion and apprehension—wafted from him. I was trying to mumble something reassuring when there was a yell and an ominous thud from far below.

Viss swore under his breath, turned to me and barked, "Are you all right?"

"He just—jumped," Yuskeya said in a low voice. Her eyes were wide and her voice shaky. "Viss had his arm and then— *idioto!* Did he think he could fly?"

Still breathless, I crawled over to the open hatchway and looked down the nine meters to the decking of the cargo level below. A dark shadow lay sprawled and still on the unforgiving metal, and I really, really didn't want to be the one to go down there.

Viss saved me the trouble. "Yuskeya, see why the Captain has blood on her pretty sleepsuit, would you? Doctor her up if she needs it. I'm going down to see what's cluttering up our nice clean cargo pod."

I found my voice. "Viss, wait, don't go alone. Here's Baden, he'll go with you." Baden came down the hall at a run then, shirtless, eyes wild.

"What the hell—?"

"Baden, go down to the cargo deck with Viss. There was an intruder aboard, he fell down the hatchway, and we need to know what shape he's in."

One thing about Baden, he never asks needless questions. He started down the ladder after Viss without another word.

Suddenly all the lights went up, and Rei called from up the hall, "All clear, Captain?"

"Clear, as far as I know," I answered back, looking up the corridor. Rei emerged from the alcove that led to the head, cradling a plasma rifle and taking in the scene warily.

It was probably nerves, but I couldn't help it. I giggled and said, "What the hell are you doing?"

She looked momentarily hurt. "When I heard the racket I didn't think it was a good idea for all of us to run headlong into trouble. I grabbed this," she said, hefting the rifle, "slipped out of my cabin, went up through the bridge and around through Sensors and the First Aid station. Thought I might need to catch someone by surprise."

"They would have been surprised, all right." Rei doesn't sleep in the nude, but the diaphanous rose-coloured thing she was wearing came pretty darn close. Alien genetics notwithstanding, Dr. Ndasa was trying not to gape and failing miserably.

"Wait," I said, "you keep a plasma rifle in your quarters?"

"It's one of my souvenirs," she said with a wicked grin.

"Come on, Captain," Yuskeya said, tugging gently at my uninjured arm. Her hand was trembly. "Let's get up to First Aid so I can take a look at your arm."

"All right, all right." I winced at the pain in my chest as I stood. "Dr. Ndasa, I think you can safely go back to bed now. I'm terribly sorry for the disturbance; things like this don't happen often on the *Tane Ikai*. When we know what it was all about I'll let you know."

He turned away reluctantly as another voice sounded from the corridor. "Rei dam-Rowan, you'd best cover yourself. My eyes are enjoying the view, but it's sure a strain on my old heart."

"You're a dirty old man, Hirin Paixon," Rei said, and stuck out her tongue at him. She headed down the hall towards her cabin, but I knew she'd be back to find out what she'd missed.

Hirin stood in the open doorway of his cabin as Yuskeya and I passed by on the way to First Aid. He smiled sheepishly.

"Figured I'd better stay put," he said. "Old men tend to get in the way without meaning to. Are you all right, Captain?" He managed to ask it very casually, although I knew how difficult it must have been for him to hang back.

"I think so, thanks. Just a flesh wound. And some bruises, I expect. Yuskeya's a good medic—she's handled much worse than this. I'll fill you in on everything later." I knew he'd expect me to report in before the night was over. If that was awkward for me, well, too bad. Hirin was an eminently reasonable man, but he was still a husband.

Yuskeya pulled me along relentlessly, so I threw Hirin a helpless look in passing and he winked and nodded. Rei came back down the corridor, still toting the plasma rifle, but now covered up with a floor-length crimson kimono. The kimono was another one of what she called her "souvenirs"—things that reminded her of one adventure or another. She had quite a collection in her quarters, everything from clothing and jewelry to weapons. Most of them were from exploits I'd rather not know about, but occasionally she'd tell me a story to go with an item. She grinned at me and continued down the corridor, curious, I knew, to see what Viss and Baden had discovered.

In the First Aid station, Yuskeya deftly checked me for broken ribs, then rolled up my sleeve and tsk-tsked. "I can't imagine that this was caused by a weapon," she said, cleaning away the congealing blood. "It looks more like he was trying to—I don't know—give you a needle or take a sample or something, and the instrument raked along through the skin. It's not just a clean piercing."

"You're right." I frowned, remembering. "He wasn't attacking me when this happened—not in the usual sense, anyway. He had some kind of techrig."

She smeared a clear gel on the wound—it felt very cool and soothing—and pressed a healstrip over it. "Well, it looks clean, and unless the instrument was contaminated—"

"Or poisoned?"

Her face froze. "I didn't think of that! Do you think it's possible?"

I shrugged, then grimaced at the stab of pain in my chest. He'd kicked me hard, the *bastardo.* "I doubt it, but he wasn't here to ask me for a date."

"I'll run a blood scan," she said, pulling a datamed from the shelf above where I sat. "What else is wrong? I saw you wince."

"Bah, he kicked me, too. It'll leave a bruise, I guess, but it's not that bad. The blood scan's probably not necessary, either." I was sorry I'd brought it up. Chances were, even if he had been trying to poison me, it wasn't going to work. I'd withstood a lot of nasty things in the last six decades, and none of them had made a dent. I really wanted to get back and see what the others had found.

However, Yuskeya didn't know about my seemingly limitless immunities, or that, left alone, the wound would have been gone in twenty-four hours anyway. She shook her head firmly. "It will only take a minute. I won't be able to rest until I've checked, now." She touched the datamed to my implant for a few seconds, then to the inside of my wrist and the side of my neck. She pressed a command into the screen and watched it as the analysis ran.

"*Okej,*" she said after a moment. "No toxins. I think you're clear."

"Sorry I mentioned it."

"No, you were right. I should have thought of it myself." She scanned my chest and abdomen and narrowed her eyes at the results. "No fractures, either. Ice and painkillers for that," she said with a smile. She put the datamed back on the shelf and cleaned up the small mess we'd made, after watching me down a couple of little tablets she produced. "What do you think he wanted, Captain?"

"I don't know," I said, sliding carefully off the gurney, "but I'm going to see if we can find any clues to that. Coming?"

She hesitated, as if about to say something else, but then she nodded. "You bet," she said, and we left the First Aid station together.

"We're in here," Rei called from the galley as we made our way back down the corridor.

We entered to see a strange tableau. Hirin sat in one of the big armchairs, looking extremely pleased to be included. Viss, Baden and Rei stood around the big central table, and on it lay the dark-suited figure who had assaulted me. He wasn't moving, and the unnatural stillness of his chest told me that he wasn't going to.

"*Morta?*" I asked.

"As a careless wormhole explorer," Viss answered. "He had this," he said, passing over a shiny multipurpose techrig, "and not much else. No ID, and look at this." He held up the man's left arm and pulled back the sleeve of his biosuit. A fresh healstrip covered the spot where an implant should have been nestled in his skin.

"No implant? That's illegal!"

Baden shrugged. "So's using that thing to bypass the airlock protocols and the alarm system, tamper with any internal systems it wants—"

"Like the guidelight," Rei said.

"—and try to take blood and tissue samples from you without your permission," Baden finished. "Anyone who's up for all that isn't going to balk at having his ID biochip removed for a while."

I shook my head. "Not having an ID biochip is serious—it's a Primary Statute crime. He was taking a big risk, and so was whoever sent him." Planetary statutes were instituted and enforced by planetary governments, whether corporate, Protectorate, or autonomous. Primary statutes, though, were put in place by the Nearspace Worlds Administrative Council itself, and applied to every citizen in Nearspace. They were the most serious, by far, and not having an ID biochip was considered to be very serious indeed. All the governments of Nearspace depended on them for keeping track of their citizens—and their criminals. If caught, the intruder could still be identified, through the information on record in the Nearspace Inhabitant Database—retina scan, fingerprints, DNA and hologram—since everyone was sampled and entered at birth and updated at intervals. But only top-clearance government officials had access to the database.

They'd pulled the mask from his face. I studied the features. High cheekbones, a nose that had been broken once or twice, a pale, thin scar tracing his jaw on one side. He didn't look familiar. "Well, I don't know who he is."

"Neither do we. But we have a guess at who sent him," Viss said.

"PrimeCorp?" I suggested.

"PrimeCorp," Rei said flatly. "They're beginning to get annoying. Baden told us about that notebug virus."

Well, I hadn't sworn him to secrecy. I'd only said he couldn't ask me any details about it. I sighed. Was there any sense in trying to keep secrets anymore?

"I wonder if this has anything to do with the flitter that followed me back from Nova Scotia the day we got here?"

Hirin frowned. "Someone followed you? You didn't mention that."

"I know." I shrugged. "It didn't seem that important—they

kept their distance, just followed me as far as the docking ring and then left again. It's not like we were making any secret of where we were docked."

"They get a look at you?" Baden asked.

"Sure, they could have. I wasn't hiding, and I hung around the rental kiosk to get a look at *them* if I could. But no-one got out of the flitter, and it didn't have any markings."

He looked down at the dead operative thoughtfully. "So, say if someone wanted to confirm who you were, so they'd know you at a later date—"

Goosebumps prickled my skin as I followed his glance. The cut on my arm stung again. "You think I was being pointed out to someone? Maybe this guy?"

"It would make sense. If he was coming after you, he'd want to be able to identify you without a doubt."

I shuddered. "Ick."

"You might want to mention it the next time someone follows you," Rei suggested with just a hint of sarcasm, and I nodded.

"If you don't mind, Captain," said Viss, obviously changing the subject, "I'll take that techrig back. I'd like to have a closer look at it. Might be a handy thing to have around sometime."

I passed it back to him, knowing he couldn't wait to strip it down and see how it worked and what it could do. "It's contraband tech, Viss. Keep it to yourself."

He grinned. "Captain, that hurts my feelings."

"Where's PrimeCorp getting something like that to outfit its ops?" Baden asked. "They're medical and research. You can't just go out and order a batch of illegal tech."

Each of the big corporations had its own area of specialization, and they usually stayed within their own boundaries. Stepping outside would lead to conflict with some other corp, and they'd at least learned that it was more productive for everyone if they simply stayed out of each others' way.

"Well, technically, you could—no pun intended—if you weren't too worried about getting caught," said Yuskeya. "But they took over GintenoTech a while back, didn't they?"

"GT's always been non-weapons tech, though," Baden argued. "I can't see them making something like this. It's way outside the boundaries."

Viss shook his head. "Who knows what direction PrimeCorp

might have steered them in, if they had an agenda. And if they're sending out stripped ops now, they've crossed all kinds of lines."

"Captain," Yuskeya said suddenly, and I knew she was thinking about my suggestion that the intrusion could have been an attack on my life, "is there anything else you ought to tell us?"

I didn't answer right away, staring down at the man who'd come to steal the most personal of items from me and died rather than be caught alive. He must have known he had little chance of surviving that fall.

"Probably," I said finally, "but not right now."

They had to be content with that.

"So what do we do with him?" asked Viss. "You going to call the police?"

I crossed my arms over my chest and stared at the intruder unsympathetically. Yes, he was dead, but he'd broken onto my ship and attacked me, and the problems didn't end there. If I called the police, it would throw our departure schedule completely out the window—questions, statements, a full-blown investigation. I was loath to trigger that because it could cause me to miss Mother, if it really was her on Kiando. I couldn't very well tell the crew that. But there were other reasons, too.

"If he's a PrimeCorp operative, it seems kind of pointless, doesn't it?"

Rei chuckled humourlessly. "Gee, trying to get a police force on a PrimeCorp planet to do something PrimeCorp doesn't like? Why would that be a problem?"

Viss nodded. "Absolutely right. If he was working for PrimeCorp, you're never going to prove that on Earth."

"So how about this?" I said. "We put him in the secret locker until we get a little further up the gravity well. Then we put him in a cargo crate and park him on a lonely little asteroid, where he won't be causing anyone to ask awkward questions we don't want to answer. But if we were ever in a position to need him, we'd know where to find him."

Every good far trader has a secret locker—because in space, you just never know—and while I'd never used one to hide a dead body before, it seemed like a handy place. I didn't really like the plan, because it did seem disrespectful—but I could live with it. No-one else had a problem with it either. Viss snapped a picture of the dead face. "Just in case," he said. "I've got a few friends I could show this to. Someone might know who he is." I suspected that Viss's "friends" could range from a Protectorate secret agent to an underworld crime lord, so I left that up to him. We settled the intruder in a cargo pod. The locker was on the bridge deck, so we put him in a refrigerated pod to lessen the . . . unpleasantness.

After all that, I managed to fall asleep pretty quickly in my own bed, and as soon as the last of the cargo arrived the next morning we lifted off. The weight that lifted from my spirit when we reached the limits of the atmosphere was no less than the pull of gravity itself.

I shouldn't have been so quick to relax.

Chapter Six

Brother in Arms

When Baden contacted Mars Central Berthing a day and a half later to offload the cargo destined for the red planet, we were comm-flagged by the Mars Planetary Police and told to assume a geosynchronous orbit. It was routine, they assured us—they had the same questions for all ships that had departed Earthspace around the same time we had.

Every corporate-controlled and autonomous world has its own planetary police force, and the Protectorate polices the worlds it administers, as well as the spaceways. Mars was governed by Schulyer Corp, but most of the planets had reciprocal agreements for dealing with legal matters. I know we all had the same thought when the police message came through. But surely this couldn't have anything to do with the lonely body reposing in the locker?

Baden acknowledged the request and Rei put us in a parking orbit and then they both looked at me.

I shrugged. "No sense worrying until we know what they want."

"Of course not," said Baden, "but I think I'll just go and check that all our cargo is secure, while we're stopped here anyway."

"Probably just coincidence," Rei said. "They could be looking for data runners, smugglers, pirates . . ."

". . . local criminals, world-jumpers, illegal tech . . ." Yuskeya added.

I wondered what Viss had done with the dead man's techrig. I knew we were all thinking the same thing, so I said it aloud. "Or they could be looking for missing PrimeCorp operatives.

Let's just wait and see, shall we?"

Baden came back after a few minutes and said that everything was secure, and not long after that, the MPP hailed us again.

I told Baden to put the main screen on. "Captain Luta Paixon here. How can I help you?"

The MPP officer on the screen was an older man, not recently shaven and with the look of someone who'd already done this too many times. He sighed and nodded once. "Flight Officer Halderan. Thank you for waiting, Captain. Would you mind sending your cargo manifest, crew and passenger lists down the datalink?"

"Not at all." I nodded to Baden. "I'd be sending that to Central Berthing in a moment anyway. What's the problem, Flight Officer?"

"I'll just ask you to wait another few moments, Captain," he said, ignoring my question and blanking the comm signal. The words "Please Wait" flashed on the screen in Esper, New Asian, Vilisian, Lobor, and a couple of other Earth languages.

I signalled to Baden to cut our outgoing signal as well and looked around at the others. "What do you think? Does he suspect something or is he just rude?"

Baden shrugged. "There's nothing in any of that information that anyone should look twice at. It's the same stuff we download to every docking authority—well, except for the specifics of the cargo."

"And our two passengers," Rei reminded him.

"I doubt anyone's looking for them," I said, shaking my head.

"Ship's coming up from the planet," Yuskeya said. "Signature reads as an MPP Ironwing."

"So someone's coming to visit us." I took a deep breath, wishing the intruder's body was already floating somewhere between here and Mars. I'd wanted to get further away from Earthspace before we jettisoned it, but now it seemed that might have been a bad idea. "Okay, folks, we're just going to cooperate, here. If they find anything they shouldn't, I'll tell them what happened and take full responsibility. PrimeCorp's not quite as popular on Mars as it is on Earth, so that might run in our favour."

Viss' drawling voice came over the comm from Engineering. "Just as a point of interest, Captain, the *Tane Ikai* could fly circles around an MPP Ironwing and be gone outsystem before they finished getting a signature reading."

I smiled. "Noted. But I'd rather not put us on the Nearspace fugitives list if I don't have to. And we do have cargo to deliver."

"Just a thought, Captain."

"Hail the Ironwing, Baden. I may have to put up with this, but I don't have to pretend that I like it." When he gave me the nod, I said, "Mars Planetary Police vessel approaching the far trader *Tane Ikai*. Please respond to this comm and state your purpose."

The face on the viewscreen was not that of the weary Flight Officer who'd hailed us first, but a woman, much younger but with a stern set to her jaw.

"MPP Red Wing Arla Jansen here, Captain Paixon, and my Flight Officer, Tamri Ongolonan is with me. We'd like a word with you on board your vessel, if that's convenient."

"May I ask why? We seem to be having a perfectly clear conversation over this comm."

She wasn't easily rebuffed, though she kept glancing at her controls, not holding my gaze. "My orders are to speak with you in person, Captain. We're investigating several criminal matters at this time and we're hoping you may be able to assist us."

I was about to give in when another voice broke in on the comm.

"Thank you, MPP Ironwing. The Nearspace Protectorate is assuming authority in questioning this vessel. Your revised orders should appear on your console any second now."

I almost grinned, but kept my face impassive. The voice was one I knew well.

Red Wing Jansen's lips tightened a little as she looked at her console. She didn't resume eye contact with me. "Certainly, Admiralo," she said with cold politeness. "*Bonan tagon*, Captain." The comm screen went blank, only to spring to life again a moment later. The face filling it now was grinning.

"*Saluton*, little sister! *Kiel vi fartas?*"

"I'm fine, thank you, but it's *big* sister, remember? Just because you're an *Admiralo* doesn't put you first in everything."

He laughed aloud, showing even, white teeth. His dark hair showed no signs of grey and his face was as unlined as mine. He didn't look eighty any more than I looked eighty-four. "All right, you're still the boss. Now tell me, what have you been doing to annoy the Mars Police?"

I looked as innocent as possible. "Absolutely nothing. I'm just passing by on my way outsystem, about to dropdown some cargo, when—"

"They want to question you about something with no provocation whatsoever, I know, I know. You sure seem to attract bad luck, Luta." He shook his head in mock sympathy.

Baden snickered quietly. Out of the corner of my eye I saw Rei punch him in the arm. The crew knew, of course, that Lanar was my brother, and seemed to take an inordinate amount of pleasure in the teasing he gave me. "Okay, I might have a couple things I'm not really eager to tell them about," I admitted. "But nothing they need to know."

"No data runners on board?" he asked. "I hear PrimeCorp's keen to track down a cagey one who's managing to avoid all their traps between Earthspace and the Cassiopeias. Seems he—or she—is playing fast and loose with PrimeCorp data, and they don't like that at all."

I shook my head. "No data runners that I'm aware of."

"Hmph. Like you'd tell me." His grey eyes sparkled with amusement. He leaned back in his chair, and I saw that he was in his shipboard office. The wall plaque behind him, with the insignia and motto of the Protectorate, framed his face. "Okay, know anything about any mysterious disappearances before you left Earthspace?"

My heart thudded but I said coolly, "No, but if it were Alin Sedmamin who disappeared I confess I wouldn't shed any tears."

Lanar snorted. "*Azeno!* Is he bothering you again?"

"Nothing I can't handle. Although one thing he said made me wonder. Something about 'changes in the wind' that would favour PrimeCorp. Any idea what he might have meant?"

Lanar pursed his lips. "He said this over a real-time link?"

I nodded. "He was trying to convince me to come in and see him, as usual."

"I'm surprised he'd say that. It almost sounds like an admission of something, doesn't it?" His face wasn't giving anything away.

"It might, if I had any idea what you were talking about."

He seemed to consider, then said, "Not just yet, Luta. But yes, we think PrimeCorp is up to something."

"Gee, what a surprise."

He grinned. "Want to do me a favour? Where are you headed next?"

"I have cargo for Eri," I said cautiously. I didn't want to volunteer the information that we would be heading for the Split after that. Lanar would try to talk me out of it, and I wasn't in the mood to fight with him.

"Perfect! Will you courier a datachip to the Protectorate headquarters there? It will save me a stop."

"No top secret information that's going to make me a target, is there? I have enough trouble on my hands already."

"Cross my heart," he said solemnly. "I was about to pick it up from the Superintendent on Mars, but I'll message him and tell him to deliver it to—who will you send to collect it? Viss?"

"Sure, he'll probably have some part or something to pick up anyway. But you'll owe me one," I warned. "I'm not the one who signed on to be an errand runner for the Protectorate."

Lanar laughed. "I haven't actually run that many errands since I made Admiral, but I don't mind being in your debt."

Curiosity got the better of me. "You won't really be, anyway. Not that I'm complaining, Lanar, but why did you step in with that Ironwing? You didn't think I was actually in trouble, did you?"

He chuckled again. "No, I just wanted to talk to you and I didn't have an hour to wait for MPP to finish jabbering. I know what they're looking for and it wouldn't apply to you anyway. They're boarding every ship that's left Earthspace in the last three days."

I felt a little pang at his trust, thinking about what was concealed in the secret locker, but I brushed it off. "So what's up?"

He went suddenly serious. "We were docked at Sagan and I spoke with Karro. He told me about Hirin. I'm—it will be a big loss—for the family. Is he there?"

"It sure will." I brushed away a tear that had sprung up too fast for me to try and blink it back. "He's doing fine so far, though, and he's happy—really happy. He's in his cabin. Do you want to talk to him?"

"I'm glad you can do this for him, then. Yes, put me through. I've got a run to Lambda Saggitae on the board but I have a minute. Oh, and little sister," he added, the grin sneaking back across his face, "try to stay out of trouble, would you? I'll tell them to let you sidestep the red tape this time, but I'm not always going to be there to get the MPP or anyone else off your tail."

I stuck out my tongue at him. "I don't need a babysitter anyway, but thanks. It saved me a chunk of time, if nothing else."

"No problem at all. See you 'round Nearspace," he said, and I signalled Baden to transfer the feed to Hirin's quarters.

After we'd contacted Mars Berthing again and arranged for the cargo dropdown, I realized that Lanar hadn't mentioned Mother. He usually asked—in an oblique way—if I'd had any luck with the search, even though I think he'd lost his own hope of finding her long ago.

I tried to brush it off. We hadn't had a long conversation, he was in a hurry. But it emphasized the hollow ache in my chest, that dark suspicion that no matter how much I wanted it, I was never going to find her.

Chapter Seven

Dead Assailants and Other Mortalities

I was finishing my morning session of tae-ga-chi when Rei signalled me on the ship's comm. We were seven days out from Earth, still two away from the vicinity of Jupiter and the wormhole to MI 2 Eridani.

"Good place to get rid of our unwanted cargo," she advised. "The only thing on the scanners is a big asteroid. If I calibrate it right I can set him down right on that."

I wondered if anyone else on board shared my pangs of guilt about getting rid of this inconvenient body. Sure, he'd broken onto my ship, assaulted me and tried to steal my genetic secrets—but did he really deserve to be jettisoned unceremoniously onto some nameless asteroid in the empty vastness of Nearspace? It gave me a twinge. I also still felt bad for lying to Lanar about it, and worried at how quickly word of the intruder's disappearance had spread to the outer planets Earthside.

However, options were limited. He currently reposed in the frozen confines of Cargo Pod Two, but he'd already been there for a week and he couldn't stay there forever.

"Okay, Rei, give me twenty minutes and I'll be on the bridge."

She hummed a few melancholy bars of what I imagined must be an Erian funeral dirge, then chuckled and broke the connection. I shouldn't have been surprised. Rei can find the humour in almost any situation, and if there isn't any she'll find a way to inject it. Forcibly.

I slipped out of my bodyglove and pulled clothes out of the

dresser. Tae-ga-chi is not a sweaty kind of workout, but it does tend to focus mind and body into such a mellow state that you move in slow motion for a while afterwards. I was only half-dressed when a knock sounded at the door of my cabin.

Hirin's voice called, "It's me, Captain."

"Come in, Hirin."

He entered the cabin and quickly shut the door behind him. When he saw the state of my attire, or rather lack of it, his eyebrows shot up. "I swear, if I were twenty years younger—"

"You'd still be wrinkled," I laughed, but I stepped over to plant a kiss on his cheek. His arms came around me in a surprisingly strong embrace and he moved his head so that our lips met instead. He kissed me with unexpected ardor.

When he released me, my pulse rate was higher than it had been during my workout. I stepped back in surprise and looked at him suspiciously.

"Hirin Paixon, are you getting better?"

He laughed, but then he said, "Honestly, Luta—I don't know. I feel so much stronger than I did back on Earth, you can't even imagine. Dr. Ndasa commented on it yesterday."

I studied him, cataloguing the slow changes that had been taking place in the week since we'd left the confines of Earth. Not only did he stand straighter, but his walk had lost much of its shuffling quality, and his face had filled out. His breathing was smoother and no longer wheezy. It was as if the faded version of him had been recoloured. Granted, the ship's artificial gravity was only 80% of Earth-normal, and the air a little richer in oxygen, but those things alone wouldn't account for the differences—would they? It seemed an unbelievable change for only seven days.

"Does he have any ideas about it?"

"I don't know—he did ask me if he could run some tests. I think he's going to start them today."

"What about the virus?"

Hirin shrugged. "I'm going to ask him if he can find out what it's doing now. When I decided to come out here, I wasn't going to worry about it, just let things happen, until I came to the end. But now . . . now I'd like to know what's changed."

"Me, too." I finished dressing quickly. I'd managed to sneak into Hirin's room a couple of nights since we left Earth and we'd slept curled against each other in the pure bliss of being together again. If Hirin kept getting stronger . . . well, one of those nighttime visits might turn into something more.

When we left my cabin, Hirin headed down to the galley to join Dr. Ndasa for tea, and I went to the bridge. The rest of the crew was there, an impromptu send-off party for our uninvited visitor.

"He's in a cargo crate in the jettison tube, all set for departure," Baden said with a grin when I entered.

"Why does everyone think this is so funny?" I snapped. "The man is dead, not going on vacation."

They went quiet. "Rei, get the calibrations right and just do it. I want this over with."

"Right you are, Captain," she said. "It's all set. Do you want me to activate the homing beacon on the crate?"

I considered. It didn't actually seem very likely that we'd ever want to find this particular asteroid again—in fact, I felt like if I never saw it again, I'd be just as happy. But the homing beacon was fairly weak, and you really had to know the calibration codes in order to find it. Cargo crates could go missing from time to time, so the beacon was useful to the vessel that owned them—but it wasn't like any passing vessel was likely to notice it and go to investigate. "Sure, turn it on, Rei. Launch when you're ready."

It took less than a minute for the image of the nondescript cargo crate to glide onto the viewscreen as it cleared the side of the ship. The asteroid Rei had targeted as a landing spot hung in the distance, a pockmarked, slowly rolling shape with a cluster of smaller followers.

We watched for a few moments as the crate slid silently through the vacuum, on course for its asteroid gravesite. I was about to turn my attention from it when—it vanished.

Someone gasped. I blinked.

Viss said, "What the hell?"

"Rei, scan for that crate," I ordered.

Her fingers flew over the console for a few seconds, then she said, "I can't get it. It isn't there anymore."

"It has to be there," Yuskeya said. "Did you calibrate for the beacon?" She sat down at one of the sensor screens and ran several scans in quick succession. Then she sat back and dropped her hands to her lap, dark eyes puzzled. "*Okej*, it's not there."

"Wormhole?" Viss suggested, but Yuskeya shook her head.

"We'd know if there was one that close. Hell, we'd be almost inside it. And without a skip field generator the crate would have been spit back out by now."

Baden snapped his fingers. "But maybe not if it's a pinhole." He sat down and rapidly fed commands into the communications console.

"I didn't think there were any pinholes out here," Rei said.

"Neither did I. Neither did anyone else, as far as I know," Baden answered. He was grinning. "If I've found a new one, I'll get to name it."

"If it goes anywhere useful," Yuskeya reminded him. "Communication pinholes aren't much good if they carry your message out to some unexplored system like Zeta Tucanae."

"Hey, don't ruin this for me, huh? At least wait until we know for sure."

"Excuse me." I cleared my throat. "Captain here! Does anyone want to tell me how a cargo crate three meters long could disappear into a pinhole? Because that's what it sounds like you're saying might have happened, and I've never even heard of that possibility before. I thought they were only good for transmitting messages."

"Mostly they are," Baden said, not taking his eyes off his screen, "but some of them are large enough that small items or craft can slip inside. You're right, it doesn't happen very often. And they don't work like the big wormholes—they're a different kind of phenomena. They seem to have an internal force that draws from both ends and streams continuously down the length of the tunnel, and they don't need Krasnikov matter to keep them stable. That's why messages can travel so fast and reliably through them, although not as fast as a ship going through a wormhole."

"Thank you, Baden. Now, can you tell me where the hell this one goes—and where it's taken our unwanted and unlamented visitor?"

He looked up at me with a grin. "Not yet. I've sent out a tracer scan, but it will have to exit the pinhole, pick up data, and bounce off the crate and back into the hole to be picked up again at this end before I'll know anything else."

"And how long will that take?" It all sounded doubtful to me.

"Anywhere from ten seconds to a week," Baden said.

"A week? We can't stay here a week!"

Baden shook his head. "No, seriously, I doubt it will take

that long. It takes a week to get a return message through the pinhole between MI 2 Eridani and the Keridre/Gerdrice system, but that's because of the insystem distances. I expect we'll hear back from this one much faster than that."

How badly did I want to know where the crate had come out? It all came down to that. I sighed.

"A day," I decided. "We can't wait more than a day to find out about this. Rei, hold this position for twenty-four hours. The crate had no identification markings, so it would be almost impossible to trace it back to us anyway. I'll wait a day to see if Baden gets to name a pinhole, but that's it."

I turned and left the bridge before there was any further comment or complaint. Suddenly I just wanted to get away and think for a bit.

One of the biggest problems with Nearspace travel on a far trader is how small the ship seems after the first few days. My cabin was four and a half meters by almost three, the largest of all the crew or passenger cabins, but it still felt mighty confining at times. The galley was bigger, but it never seemed to be empty. I passed by it, hearing Hirin and Dr. Ndasa laughing over their tea, and climbed down the hatchway to the engineering deck.

While that had some more wide-open spaces, it was likely that Viss would be back before too long, so I kept climbing down. This brought me eventually to a metal catwalk vaulted high above the floor of Cargo Pod Four. I came here when I needed to think. The biggest volume of empty space on the ship could surround you here, over six hundred square meters of it, and it was heavenly.

Jettisoning the body of my mysterious assailant had started my mind down the path I'd been avoiding in the days since we'd set out from Earth. What did PrimeCorp really want from me? Well, sure, they wanted to know if my body contained anything they could legally claim. But what could that something be? I thought I might have an answer—at least I had a theory, which recent events had helped me solidify. Here, in the relative vastness and quiet of the cargo pod, I wanted to consider that theory.

What were the facts? First, not aging. I'd had my personal doctor check me over in every imaginable way when I'd turned fifty, and he'd been completely baffled. "You're in wonderful shape for fifty, Luta," was what he'd said, but we'd both known it for the massive understatement that it was. If it had just been me, I might not have made the connection to my mother, but since Lanar showed the same persistent youthfulness, well, it made sense. That was when I started looking for her in earnest.

Additionally, I didn't get sick. The notebug virus was only the latest example. Hirin and I had suffered exactly the same exposure to the virus that had debilitated him on Vileyra—I'd come through unscathed. No colds, no influenzas, no infections, nothing.

I also seemed, if not impervious to injury, at least somewhat protected. Toxic fumes didn't damage my airways; poisons were flushed from my system with no effect; cuts and bruises healed in twenty-four to forty-eight hours. I'd never tested anything truly severe, like a plasma burn or getting smashed up in a collision, but there had been times I'd been tempted to try something serious, just to see. Luckily, my curiosity had never driven me that far.

So it was undeniable that something was protecting me—internally—something that did not occur naturally in the human body. I had two theories about it. Initially, that it had something to do with childbirth, since I'd seemed to stop aging after Maja was born. But Lanar's similar condition seemed to disprove that one. The second was that my mother had done something—the details of which were beyond my imagination—to effect this protection for both of us. Even so, no blood scans or DNA tests had ever detected anything out of the ordinary, not even the first ones I'd allowed PrimeCorp to conduct.

Now Baden had discovered this strange "entity" when he'd scanned for the virus. An entity that was difficult to detect, that rendered itself somehow invisible immediately after it had been observed, that apparently changed its molecular appearance at will—to avoid detection? Whatever I was carrying around was over sixty years old, but perhaps the tech was finally catching up with a leap my mother had made long ago. Baden's "entity" made me wonder if that leap might have involved those helpful little constructs we called bioscavengers.

They'd been around as early as the middle of the twenty-first century, protein constructs that could counteract the effects of certain toxins, like nerve gases, in the body. The research had grown in leaps and bounds for a while, producing cancer and other disease-specific bioscavengers, then trauma-repair nanobioscavengers. We got that far, and then the Chron war put a stop to everything. Even after it ended, tech made a slow comeback through the thirty-odd years of the Retrogression. First, we were too busy trying to save the species from destruction to worry about how long we could live if the war ever ended, and then we were too busy being thankful and reflective about our salvation. Technology seemed like something that had only gotten us into trouble by catching the attention of the Chron in the first place and was best avoided for a while.

But finally we went back to wondering how we could keep the body going, keep it healthy, fix it up and make it last. That's where my mother came in, and I had to assume that she'd made a breakthrough. A breakthrough that, for some reason, caused her to break with PrimeCorp. A breakthrough that had set our family on the run. A breakthrough that Nicadico Corp and their Longate treatment had attempted to duplicate, with disastrous results.

The intruder who'd made his way aboard the *Tane Ikai* had wanted samples from me: blood and tissue, judging by his techrig. What if he'd been hoping to find, not those things specifically, but something *in addition* to those things, something that might be present *in* them? Like a sixty-year-old nanobioscavenger that could do all the things its many predecessors could do, and more, all at once? Such a construct would be a gold mine to someone who could break it down, perhaps reverse-engineer it, and learn its secrets.

It would answer a lot of questions. It made a lot of sense. It was also pure speculation.

It was more imperative than ever that I find my mother. Because whatever it was, she must have put it in me. And only she could tell me exactly what it could do, and how long it would last.

If I were scheduled to live *forever*, I wanted to start making some plans. If not, I'd like to have some idea just when my expiration date might come up. Neither medicine nor the mirror was telling me anything useful.

Baden's voice over the ship's comm interrupted my musings.

"Captain, you might want to come back to the bridge now. I've got some news about the pinhole."

I sighed. No matter how much time I spent thinking about

things, the answers I needed were simply not in my brain.

"I'll be right there."

I started the long climb back up to the bridge deck and realized halfway up that I was humming—it echoed eerily down the hatchway. I puzzled for a moment over where I'd heard the tune, and then it came to me. It was the little funeral dirge Rei had treated me to earlier in the day.

I climbed the rest of the way in silence.

Chapter Eight

Pinholes, Wormholes, and Holes of the Heart

"It's back!" Baden said as I strode onto the bridge. His face was alight with excitement.

"Your tracer scan?"

He nodded. "And you'll never guess where the other end of the pinhole is."

"That's right, I won't. So just tell me."

"It's in the Keridre/Gerdrice System. There's only one other reliable comm pinhole to that system and it's always overloaded, plus it comes out light years away from any of the inhabited planets, which is why messages take so long. If this one turns out to be reliable, I'll be famous! I even got readings from Nellera, so the terminal point is not very far out in the system."

I tried not to frown. "Doesn't this mean that the crate came out in the same vicinity?"

"Well, yes, but I wouldn't worry about it. No-one's going to notice the homing beacon, and even with that, there aren't any traceable identifiers on either the crate or the body. Unless someone finds it and runs a government Nearspace database search, and what are the chances of that?"

"Not very good," I agreed, although I had some misgivings. I smiled. "So what are you going to name it?"

"I don't know yet. I have to think about it." He grinned evilly. "I was thinking of naming it after Rei, since it *is* a communications pinhole and no-one talks more than—"

He ducked away from the punch she swung at him.

"Well, you won't have to worry about me talking to *you*," she

79

said loftily. "Captain, would you ask the communications officer if he's done here now, or do we have to hold this position indefinitely while he brags about his discovery?"

"No, I won't," I said. "Members of this crew are not permitted to stop talking to each other while on duty. Captain's orders. Rei, get us back on track as soon as Baden's finished with any other readings or scans he needs. I'm going to the galley to have some tea and talk to some grown-ups for a change."

The only grown-up still there when I arrived was Dr. Ndasa, who was engrossed in something on the datapad propped up on the table before him. He didn't look up until I'd fetched a cup of hot chai for myself and sat down opposite him at the table.

"Oh, hello, Captain," he said vaguely, glancing up from his screen. "I'm just looking over some of Hirin's data from my interview with him Earthside. I haven't done any physical testing on him, but his condition is markedly improved since that time, judging by my own observations."

I nodded. "I've noticed that, too. Do you have any ideas about why?"

"Some thoughts, but nothing concrete," he said. "The lighter gravity, and the slightly richer atmosphere inside the ship, probably have something to do with it. It's likely he's eating better—both the nature of the food itself and the effects of having more engaging companionship to share it with. But to pin down exactly what's at play is impossible. After all this time we're still not sure about all the effects deep space travel has on the body, human or Vilisian. Most of the research is looking to see how we can address the negative effects—now I'm beginning to think there may be positive things we've overlooked."

"That would be wonderful." I remembered how Hirin had been when he was younger—how *we* had been.

"He's told me about the virus. We talked about it Earthside and again since we embarked on this journey. I'm curious to know if space travel has had an effect on its progress in his body. That would be quite a valuable bit of information." The excitement on his face was an alien mirror of Baden's a few minutes ago.

I sipped my tea carefully. It was almost too hot to be drinkable, and redolent with spices. The heat of both tingled down my throat. "He mentioned that you plan to run some tests."

"Yes. You don't mind if I use the facilities in your First Aid station? I notice you have more than the usual single-function datameds and healstrips in there."

"Please feel free. I think one of the previous owners of the *Tane Ikai* suffered health problems, and he had her outfitted to provide more than just patch-up medical needs." It had been Hirin, but I didn't say that.

"Thank you, Captain." He smiled sheepishly, the amber skin around his eyes puckering. "I'm finding space travel a bit more—tedious than I'd expected, to be perfectly honest."

I laughed. "It can't be all hurtling through wormholes and marvelling at nebulae, Doctor. There'll be plenty of excitement soon. Our first skip is tomorrow and we're only a week away from our trip through the Split after that."

He sipped at his teacup and shuddered. It had obviously gone cold long before I'd arrived. "Well, there are many different sorts of excitement, aren't there, Captain? I'm not looking forward to that part of the journey now, as intriguing as it sounded back on Earth."

"Me, neither." I finished my tea and pushed my chair back. "Look forward to seeing the other end of the Split, Doc. That's what I'll be doing."

We arrived at the wormhole out of Sol system just after noon the next day, shiptime. Although there's no actual "night and day" in space, we cycled through the same hours we would have on Earth or any other planet with a similar-length day, just to keep our own rhythms as normal as possible. Humans seemed remarkably unable to adapt to six- or forty-hour days—our circadian programming was too deeply encoded in our genes to be undone in less than two brief centuries of space travel.

Rei brought the ship to a halt well away from the almost-invisible dark spot that marked the end of the wormhole. Like any wormhole, it wasn't easy to see; hell, you'd never spot it without sensors to tell you where to look. Think of a black cat on a moonless night, or a shadow on the pupil of an eye. The communications relay, parked a few hundred meters away from it, was a dead giveaway, though.

Normal wormhole runs are an unremarkable way to travel

these days, although it's always interesting to watch passengers make their first one. They're welcome on the bridge, so long as they stay out of the way; it's the only place on the ship with a decent viewscreen, and even if you're a seasoned Nearspace traveller, the inside of a wormhole is something to see.

It's quite a pretty place. All the radiation pouring into the wormhole gets blueshifted to high frequencies and reacts with the thin layer of Krasnikov matter the skip drive generates to hold the wormhole open. The result is a breathtaking swirl of constantly moving colour, like a hundred rainbows spinning down a drain. As the skip starts and the ship bounces from one side of the wormhole to the next, the effect is dizzying, and not a few meals have been lost in wormhole transit. Of course, the X-rays and gamma rays would fry you in an instant if the shields failed, but we don't talk about that with the passengers.

Hirin and Dr. Ndasa had both come up to the bridge to watch. Hirin was grinning like a kid and Dr. Ndasa looked nervous, the scent of grapefruit wafting from his skin again. I was glad Hirin was there. If he were going to have any negative reactions to the skip, I wanted him close. He came and stood behind my skimchair while the others were busy making preparations.

"I never thought I'd see another wormhole," he whispered. "Thank you, Luta."

I swivelled my head around to smile up at him and realized that there were tears in his eyes. "You're welcome," I whispered back. "Now go and sit with Dr. Ndasa before you make me blow our cover!" I turned back to the viewscreen.

He squeezed my shoulder and strode over to sit by the Vilisian.

"Tracer scan reports no other ships in the wormhole or near the other terminal point," Rei said. "Initiating skip drive sequence." She looked over for my approval and, when I nodded, launched us into the wormhole.

No matter how many skips you've done, the wild beauty inside a wormhole always takes you by surprise. I glanced over at Dr. Ndasa just after the wormhole mouth closed around us and the swirling tunnel of colour curved out ahead. He stared at the viewscreen transfixed, his mouth open slightly, nodding at something Hirin was telling him. His long-fingered hands tightened on the skimchair arms when the first skip sent us spinning to the other side of the wormhole, but that was all.

Hirin looked over and winked at me, so I stopped worrying about him, and a minute later we were in the MI 2 Eridani system, heading for its lone inhabited planet, Rei's homeworld Eri. We'd be on Eri just a day, with one cargo shipment to unload there and fuel to take on, and then we could head for GI 892.

We were just about to leave Eri when Maja caught up with us.

I know I stared stupidly at Baden when he said, "Live incoming for you, Captain. Maja Tacan."

"What? Where is she?" It couldn't be a live message if Maja was back in Sol system. My heart thudded heavily in my chest. If Maja were here, or close enough to send a live message, something must be wrong.

"Maja Tacan, message originates from the *P. Keinen*, Dock 34." Baden half-turned in his skimchair, sea green eyes quizzical. "Is something wrong, Captain?"

I shook my head. "No, Baden, it's all right. It's—it's Hirin's daughter. He's asleep. I'll take it in my quarters. Secure messaging."

My knees felt watery as I scurried down the corridor to my cabin. "Maja? What's wrong?" I asked as soon as her face appeared on my screen.

"Hello, Captain," she said. Her face was set in a serious look that I knew well. She wasn't interested in sparring with me today. Whatever had brought her here was more important, but she didn't seem upset.

"We're secure, Maja, and I'm alone in my quarters. Where are you?"

"I'm here on Eri, Mother. Nothing's wrong. How's Dad?"

I knew she hadn't come all this way, hating space travel as she did, just to ask about her father. "He's doing fine, Maja. He's actually improved since we left Earth. Please, why are you here?"

She took a deep breath, audible over the comm line. "I decided—I wanted to be with Dad. At the end. I want to come with you, if you have room."

Her voice was harsh; it was difficult for her to ask favours of me.

"Maja, you hate space travel!"

"I know. It doesn't matter."

"What does Taso think about this?"

Maja shook her head, pressing her lips into a thin line before she spoke. "Taso and I have been separated for six months, Mother. The divorce will be final soon. He has nothing to do with this."

I stared at her. I didn't say, "Why didn't you tell me?" because I knew why she hadn't. Instead I asked, "Does your father know?"

"I didn't want to worry him. He seemed so frail . . ." Her voice trailed off, but she kept her eyes steady on mine. There was a core of steel in my daughter that I could admire when she wasn't wielding it against me. Perhaps I hadn't done her any favours by accepting and mirroring her aloofness.

"What about work?"

"Leave of absence," she said. "It's not a problem."

I smiled at her, flooded with relief that the news hadn't been worse. "Well, you seem to have thought of everything. Come aboard, Maja, and we'll talk some more. There's room if you want to stay. Your father will be happy to see you, and I think you'll be pleasantly surprised when you see him." I pretended not to notice the suspicion in her eyes as I broke the connection.

Since our scheduled departure time was getting close, I stuck my head in on the bridge before I went to see Hirin and said, "Slight delay on everything, folks. Looks like we're taking on another passenger. Yuskeya, since Dr. Ndasa has both cabins on the dock side, would you run down and check out the starwise cabins and make sure they're presentable?"

"No problem, Captain. Should I go now?"

"Please."

Rei looked at me and raised her eyebrows. She'd have to wait for an explanation, though. "Rei, would you double-check stores, make sure we have enough laid in to handle another mouth? We shouldn't be held up too long, she's already here at the port, so everyone just stay ready, *okej*?"

Then I went down the corridor to Hirin's room before anyone could ask me anything else. I eased the door open gently, expecting to see him still asleep, but he was standing in the middle of his small cabin, his arms and body twisting slowly in the fluid motions of tae-ga-chi.

He stopped when he saw my face, and grinned.

"I still remember how to do it," he said proudly. "And now I can do it again."

"Hirin, that's wonderful. But we've got company."

His eyes narrowed, and he looked like a fierce, grizzled bulldog. "PrimeCorp?"

I shook my head. "Maja."

"What the—Maja's *here*?"

"Here on Eri, yes, and on her way to the *Tane Ikai*. I just spoke to her. She followed us because she didn't want to be away from you when—at the end."

Hirin closed his eyes and shook his head slightly. "Maja hates space travel."

I crossed the few steps between us and hugged him. "But she loves you."

Hirin sighed. "She loves you, too, Luta."

"Maybe." I pulled away. "Anyway, she'll be here soon. You want me to bring her here?"

He thought a moment, then said, "I don't think so. She isn't finding the same man she said goodbye to on Earth. I'm not an invalid, and I think I'll meet her in the galley. She may not even want to come along once she sees me."

"Or it may make her more determined. If she wants to come, I'm not going to stop her."

"No, I won't, either," he said. "But it's not going to make things any easier."

"Nothing ever does." I kissed his cheek and went to meet my daughter.

She was there ten minutes later.

"*Saluton,* Mother," she said when the rear airlock hatch cycled open and she could see that I was alone.

"Hi, Maja." I smiled carefully. "I still can't believe you came all this way."

She shrugged. "It just didn't seem right not to. And I didn't have any reason to stay behind."

"I'm sorry about Taso."

Maja nodded. "I knew you would be. You always liked him."

That wasn't what I meant, but I let it go, knowing even as I did it that someday I was going to have to stop just letting things pass with her. I wanted to ask her more about it, offer to listen if she wanted to talk, but we hadn't had that kind of relationship in a long time. We'd been together ten seconds now without a fight and I wanted it to stay that way as long as possible.

"Well, your Dad's waiting for you in the galley." I pointed down the corridor. "It's this way."

"I know, Mother, I used to live here too, remember?"

I bit back a retort and followed her silently down the hall. *Fifteen seconds and counting.*

Hirin sat at the big table with two mugs of double caff in front of him. He didn't stand when we came to the doorway. I guessed he didn't want Maja to be too shocked all at once. His appearance itself should be a surprise.

"Hi, honey," he said in a voice that had regained so much strength and timbre that she stopped halfway across the room. "What's all this about, now?"

I slid quietly along the wall so I could see both their faces. She was looking at him quizzically. "Dad? You—you sound great."

He nodded. "I'm feeling so much better, Maja, you wouldn't believe it."

She crossed the rest of the way to where he sat and took the chair beside him, leaning in to give him a quick hug. Then she put a hand on his cheek and said, "And you look great, too."

"And watch." He pushed his chair back easily and stood, straight as a man half his age, walked confidently over to one of the big armchairs and sat. He crossed his legs and held his arms wide, obviously pleased with himself. "What do you think of that?"

Maja shook her head in obvious amazement at this performance and turned to me. "What did you do?" she asked, her sapphire eyes dark with suspicion.

"Not me." I shrugged. "Dr. Ndasa thinks it might be the lower gravity and richer air. Better food. Or something else. We don't really know."

"But you should have taken him back home so his doctors could—" she stopped when she saw the look on Hirin's face. Maja sat back in the chair and crossed her arms. "So I suppose you think this will make me change my mind and go on home."

Hirin got up and went back to the table. "You're welcome to come along if you like, Maja," he said. "But if you're here for a funeral, you might be disappointed. Really, honey, if you'd rather go back home I think you can go with an easy mind. I'm not so sure anymore that this is going to be my last run."

Maja looked at me and I shrugged.

"Your decision, Maja. There's an open cabin waiting if you want it, but I agree with your father. It's probably not going to be the trip you thought you were taking. I know you don't like this kind of travel."

I knew the look on her face before she said a word. "I don't understand this," she said slowly, "and I don't trust it. You could get worse again, Dad. I still want to go along. I can pay my way, at whatever you usually charge."

"Honey, cost isn't an issue. Family always travels for free on the *Tane Ikai.*" Surprisingly, she didn't seem to take offence.

"*Okej,*" she said, nodding.

"Right this way, then. We were just getting ready to leave when I got your message." I led her through the door at the back of the galley, leading to the starwise passenger cabins. These had been Maja and Karro's rooms when they were children. I wished the ones on the other side were open, so that Maja couldn't accuse me of trying to make her feel like a child, but I forced the thought away. These were available, and Maja was here unannounced. I'd let her choose, though.

"These are the only two open, but you can take your pick," I said.

To my relief, she didn't make any remarks, and chose her own old room. She opened the door, and I followed her inside. Yuskeya had been efficient, as usual, and the room looked as clean and inviting as it was possible for a far trader cabin to look.

"I'll get Baden to bring in your things."

"Home sweet home. I assume I should just call you 'Captain,'" she said, looking around the cabin and not at me. "You and Dad are still carrying on with your little charade?"

"Everyone knows you're Hirin's daughter, but only Rei knows where I fit into the family portrait," I said evenly. "So your father and I would appreciate it if you went along."

She met my eyes then, and hers were as cold as the vacuum that would soon surround us. "Seems like this family is always trying to keep secrets. I guess 'family always travels for free' comes with conditions."

"I'd rather say that family comes with some expectations." I chose my words carefully. "Your father and I have agreed that this is the best way for us. I'm asking you to respect that."

"The way you've always respected what I think?"

"I respect what you think, I just don't always agree." I took a deep breath. "Look, Maja, I don't want to fight with you. I know we clash sometimes, but it's not that I think you're wrong about everything." I blew out a long sigh and leaned back against the door. "Do we really have to do this now?"

Maja sighed and sat down on the bed. It looked like she was blinking back tears, but I couldn't be sure. "No, I suppose we don't. I just don't like any of this," she said. "I thought I was prepared for Dad to die. I came out here to face it, even though it was hard. Now things have changed again, but who knows if they'll stay this way?"

"I certainly don't. Right now, I'm taking one day at a time. For your father's sake, I'd like us to try and get along."

She didn't exactly smile, but her face softened and she nodded. "We can try," she said, although she didn't sound too certain.

"You unpack, and we'll talk again later," I said, and left with at least a tentative peace in place.

Rei threw me a sympathetic glance when I popped my head in at the bridge to ask Baden about Maja's gear, so I knew she'd found out who our new passenger was. I smiled and shrugged. For now, I was just trying to roll with the punches.

To give Maja credit, she made every effort to fit in unobtrusively with the rest of us. She graciously accepted Baden's offer of a tour of the ship (since she couldn't very well explain that it had been her childhood home), showed up on time for every meal, and stayed away from the bridge. Hirin told me that she tried to coddle him for the first couple of days but finally seemed convinced that he could look after himself again. She played *quozit* with Yuskeya in the galley, talked politics with Viss, and laughed at Baden's jokes.

She didn't say much to me, but that was just her way of trying to get along, and she did nothing that would hint at our relationship.

Hirin was worried about her, though. "She seems distracted to me, Luta," he said to me when we were a couple of days out of Eri, and alone in the galley fixing lunch. "She's worried about something."

"She's worried about you," I reminded him. I added some

re-hydrated tomatoes to our salads and handed him one. "That's why she's here."

"No, I think it's something else. She's still trying to 'look after' me a little, but overall I think she's accepted that I'm feeling better. Did she say anything to you about Taso?"

I sat at the table and he pulled out the chair beside me. I shook my head. "Only the bare fact of the breakup. We aren't prone to mother-daughter confidences, in case you haven't noticed."

"She didn't give me any details, either. Do you think I should talk to her?"

I smiled at him and sighed. "No, I think *I* should try to talk to her. I'm her mother. I guess I've been putting it off. I don't know if she'll talk to me about Taso or not. More likely just get angry."

Hirin put a hand over mine. "Maybe not. Maybe she needs to tell someone about it. She might appreciate your asking."

I pulled my hand out and patted his instead. "I thought you weren't going senile anymore."

"Very funny. People change, you know."

"Well, it's worth a try. And if it doesn't go well, I promise not to say 'I told you so.'"

I let another day pass before I went looking for her. She was in her cabin, reading.

"Mind if I come in for a few minutes?" I asked when she opened the door.

She shrugged and turned away, going back to sit on the bed. "I guess not. Is Dad all right?"

"He's fine." I closed the door behind me and sat in the desk chair. "Maja, I wanted to talk to you about Taso. Are you okay?"

"I'm doing fine. I suppose you think it was my fault."

"No, and I'm not trying to pry. These things happen, but they're never easy. I just wanted to know how you're dealing with it." I smiled. "It's a mother thing."

She hesitated, looking down at her datapad. "We just grew apart, I think. And then he found someone else."

I didn't know how she'd take it if I tried to hug her, so I stayed where I was and just said, "Honey, I'm really sorry."

"She's quite a bit younger," Maja said. "Old story, I guess." She clamped her lips together and I wondered what else she had been about to say.

I nodded. "Is everything settled, then? What about the house?"

"He didn't want it, so we split things so that I could keep it," she said. "The money wasn't a problem. I took a leave from the school for this term, because I didn't want anything personal to affect how I taught the kids."

I smiled. "You seem to have everything under control, as usual."

She sighed. "Except for the things I'd like to control. Is that all? I'm fine, really, but . . . thanks for asking."

"Well, that's what mothers do, worry about their kids." I didn't know if she meant it or was just saying it to get rid of me, but either way I wasn't going to argue. It was the first non-confrontational conversation we'd had in a long time and I wasn't about to push it. "I'm glad you're doing okay. If you do want to talk, well, you know where to find me. See you at supper."

Outside her door, I took a deep breath. That hadn't gone too badly at all, and she appeared to be dealing with the breakup in her usual businesslike way. Maybe this trip together would turn out to be a positive thing for us. If Maja and I could have a few more conversations like this, we might actually start to get along.

I wasn't going to get my hopes up just yet, though, and it didn't explain what was worrying her—if anything was. Hirin might have just been picking up on her ongoing concern for him. I'd tell him about our conversation, I decided, and let him take what he wanted from it. If he still thought she had something else on her mind, he'd have to try his own luck at finding out what it was. I didn't feel like pushing mine any further.

PART TWO

NEARSPACE

Chapter Nine

Bodies, Minds, and
Other Well-Kept Secrets

Maja stayed in her cabin when we made the wormhole jump from MI 2 Eridani to the uninhabited GI 892 system, sulking, I think, because she and Hirin had fought about his being on the bridge for the skip. She thought it was too dangerous, and he'd laughed and told her he felt well enough to pilot the ship himself. Aside from that, by the time another three days had passed we'd all settled into a comfortable routine. Mid-afternoon of that day we arrived at the Split.

Viss and Rei spent some time running every conceivable check on the ship's systems; stabilizers, hull integrity, skip drive, plasma drive, field generators, steering thrusters and half a dozen more. Meanwhile, Yuskeya ran reams of data calculations on everything that was known about the Split and fed all the analyses into the nav computer.

Hirin was on the bridge with them. He'd earned a place there as the only one aboard who'd piloted the Split before, even if it had been over thirty years ago. Skip drives and Ford-Roman field generators apparently hadn't changed much in that time, because he was discussing technical fine points with Rei and Viss and seemed completely at ease. From my chair at the command station, I admired him covertly. The changes in his health were still all positive, and he looked about as close to dying as anyone else aboard.

Maja was in her cabin, feigning disinterest, but I expected she and Dr. Ndasa would appear on the bridge by the time the skip drive kicked in.

I tried not to fidget, and I knew Baden was feeling the same way by the sympathetic look he shot me. The two of us really had nothing to do while we waited, and the suspense was killing us. I wasn't surprised when Dr. Ndasa appeared in the archway that led to the bridge.

"May I come up there with the rest of you?" he asked sheepishly, twisting the end of his long braid around one finger. "It's slightly—unnerving, waiting back there and not knowing what's happening."

"Completely understandable." I turned in my seat to smile a welcome. "I was planning to call you before we went in to ask if you'd like to come to the bridge. We're still running checks, but you can have a seat at one of the empty stations and make yourself comfortable."

As I said, I'd been through the Split once before. However, since I was busy at the time trying to subdue an alien—a Lobor pirate who was attempting to strangle me—and listening to Hirin swear because he couldn't leave the controls to help me with the alien in question, I can't tell you what it looks like inside. All I know is what I've heard, that it's not like a normal wormhole. Apparently that's all Hirin noticed about it at the time, since *he* was dividing his attention between piloting the ship and watching his wife fight off an alien pirate. I was looking forward to this time, when I hoped I could let others do all the work and just watch the show.

Rei sat back in her chair and fetched a deep breath. "I think we're ready," she said. She turned and grinned at me. "This is going to be interesting."

I raised an eyebrow. "Not too interesting, I hope. Just get us safely out the other side and that will be plenty interesting for me, thanks."

"No problem, Captain," she said, and snapped off a completely irreverent salute.

"Viss?" I asked.

He nodded. "She's as ready as she's going to be—the ship, I mean. She's in good shape as far as I can tell. I'm going to monitor everything from the engineering console here." He grinned. "I don't want to be stuck down on the other deck and miss any of the fun."

"Yuskeya?"

"All ready. All the data we have has been compiled and

downloaded into the nav computers and the skip drive compensators."

Hirin snorted. "The time I piloted the Split," he said in true cranky-old-man mode, "we arrived in this sector at top speed and fired up the skip field generators on the fly. We had no wormhole data to speak of, mostly rumours, and I had to do everything myself as the rest of the crew was engaged with—another emergency. Rei's a *perfekta* pilot and the ship is in good shape. Let's get going, already!"

"Not much I can say after that." I smiled. "I hope you're still as lucky as you were back then, old man. Go ahead, Rei. Take us in."

Rei and Viss busied themselves at their stations and the ship hummed to life. The buzzing whir of the skip drive matter generator soon drowned out the usual comforting throb of the main drive. Once it got going it faded into white noise, but for the first few minutes after it started up it sounded like a hive full of angry giant bees had invaded the ship. You definitely knew that something out-of-the-ordinary was going to happen. It was at this point that passengers usually arrived on the bridge.

Right on cue, Maja appeared and, when Hirin crooked a finger at her, took a skimchair from an empty console and wordlessly slid it over beside him.

We began to move toward the wormhole, the black spot where no stars shone growing even darker as we approached. To outward appearance it looked like any other wormhole.

The difference was obvious as soon as we entered the mouth, however. The tunnel that stretched and curved ahead of us swirled with the usual spangle of colours down one side, but the opposite side was a barely discernible gauzy grey, opaque yet seemingly insubstantial. My head spun with a vertigo that was completely unlike the sometimes-dizzying beauty of other wormholes. This was more like standing on the edge of a steep, crumbling precipice.

"Holding steady on one-hundred-eighty degree skip course," Rei said, and her voice was the tiniest bit shaky. "Advancing Krasnikov matter generator to full power."

It was like going over the crest of a snowy hill on a sled, the slightest hesitation and then a quick drop as the ground fell away. We skidded along the wormhole like a skipping rock, one that ricocheted off the sides of a watery half-circle in a smooth defiance of gravity.

"Drives at one hundred percent," Viss reported. "No problems."

The colours were beautiful, but I couldn't keep my eyes away from that half-circle of grey that demarcated near-certain death. It looked almost soft, inviting. I wrenched my eyes away from it. My suicidal curiosity was kicking in again, but I had more lives to consider here than just my own.

We hurtled along the wormhole at nearly full speed now, the colours blurring almost painfully. I heard Dr. Ndasa gasp but didn't turn to him.

"Rei? How are you doing?" Her hands skittered over the touchscreen like frenzied spiders, making the numberless tiny adjustments that would keep us away from the deadly grey zone.

"*Okej.*" It sounded like her teeth were clenched. "The ship wants to make the full circle skips. Hard to hold to one-eighty."

"Should we reduce speed?"

She shook her head. "No, I think it would only make it worse. I don't know how the hole gravity would affect us."

A tremor shook the *Tane Ikai*, only a small one, but anyone who knew the ship felt it. Viss punched in adjustments. I glanced over and saw that Maja was holding Hirin's hand, her face ghostly in the bright bridge lights. My own fingers dug painfully into the armrests of my chair, and I deliberately disengaged them. We seemed to be swinging closer to the dangerous edges of the coloured walls with every skip, but it might have been my imagination and I didn't want to put any more pressure on Rei.

"Time?" Rei asked. I looked over and saw that her skin, beneath her *pridattii*, had gone very pale.

"Probably halfway through," Baden said. The muscles were working in the side of his jaw. Inaction at a crucial time was a difficult thing for a man like Baden. He was a lot like Hirin in that respect, I thought with a pang.

"Luta," Hirin gasped suddenly, and I turned to look at him. His face was ashen, the same grey as the half-wall of the wormhole, and he clutched his chest with one hand and Maja's hand with the other. Maja stared at him, her mouth open. *Heart attacks happen occasionally during skips.* The words appeared with horrible clarity in my mind.

"Hirin!" I dove out of my chair toward him. Dr. Ndasa and Yuskeya moved only seconds behind me.

"Luta?" That was Rei, her voice tight.

"Never mind us!" I yelled. "Keep the ship on course."

We eased Hirin out of his chair and onto the bridge's cool metal decking, and Dr. Ndasa loosened Hirin's shirt. Maja hadn't said anything, but she still gripped her father's hand. Yuskeya leapt up and staggered against the inexorable forces that pulled at her, heading for the First Aid station.

"His pulse is jagged," Dr. Ndasa said. The metallic scent of his worry belied the calmness of his voice.

"Feel like . . . can't breathe," Hirin managed to gasp. "Too tight . . ."

"Dad . . ." Maja croaked.

"It's all right, Hirin." I took his other hand. It was ice cold. "We're going to help." I looked at Dr. Ndasa hopefully, but his dark alien eyes were unreadable.

Yuskeya hurtled back onto the bridge and dropped to her knees beside us. I hardly knew what she was doing as she and the doctor worked over Hirin. A datamed. A scanner. A pulse injector for meds. Other implements I couldn't name.

Maja met my eyes for a second, hers dark with fear and something else I didn't want to name. I couldn't let go of Hirin's hand, although the weakness of his grip was frightening. *I must have been crazy to think I could handle this.* Then I looked back down at Hirin, and in his eyes was a look of finality, and love, and regret. *He had been getting better! It isn't fair!*

"Luta!" Something was wrong. Rei was shouting.

Then I felt it—the ship was shaking as if we were entering an atmosphere far too fast and at the wrong incline.

"What's wrong?"

"The swing force is too much. I can't hold us to one-eighty!"

"You've got to!"

"Twenty seconds, Rei," Baden shouted. "Just twenty seconds more!"

"I can't do it! We'll be off the safe side in two more skips at this rate!"

"Viss? Can you do anything?"

He didn't answer me right away. "Viss!"

His hands never stopped moving over the engineering console, but he shook his head. "I'm trying. Nothing's working."

Hirin whispered something. Yuskeya bent over him. "What?"

"The main drive," he rasped, a little louder. "Shut it down."

"We can't shut down the main drive," Viss said calmly. "The drag would disrupt the skip. I don't know what it would do to the ship."

"Rei?"

"I don't know." Her voice was as panicked as I'd ever heard it. "We'd probably break apart."

"No." Hirin's voice was stronger, but not much. "The plasma drive's started . . . a resonance flux with the skip drive. That's what's wrong. You have to . . . shut it down. Now." He tried to smile, but it came out as a grimace. "Trust me."

I released Hirin's hand and stood up, swaying against the warring energies that clawed at the ship. "Viss, do what Hirin says."

"But Captain—"

"Shut it down, dammit. Now!"

He didn't argue again, and his hand didn't hesitate as he punched the command to shut down the drive. The shaking stilled immediately and the ship shot forward even faster than it had been travelling.

"Hey!" Rei's hands still flew over the board, but I could tell from that one word that she was back in control—both of the ship and of her fear. The arc of the skips lessened perceptibly, and ten seconds later, we shot out of the terminal point of the wormhole into the starry, empty space of the Delta Pavonis System.

"Help me get him to First Aid," Yuskeya said, wrapping Hirin's arms across his chest so we could carry him.

I was shaking so badly I knew I couldn't support his weight, and I let Baden push me gently aside so he could help. Maja held fast to Hirin's hand, and she hadn't looked at me again. Before I followed them, I laid a hand on Rei's shoulder. She was trembling, too.

"Good work."

She shook her head. "I almost lost it."

"Not your fault. You got us through. We're here in one piece."

"What about Hirin?"

"I don't know. He's still alive, and we're out of the wormhole." She shuddered. "If anything—"

"I know. But he wanted to come. Yuskeya and Dr. Ndasa will look after him. He wanted to come."

"Oh, Luta," she said, and tears welled up in her golden eyes and flowed over the beautiful dark swirls on her cheeks.

"I know, Rei," I said, and my own tears came then, too. "I know."

A week later Hirin was still alive, but barely. He was extremely weak and short of breath, always feeling shaky and tired. Dr. Ndasa ordered complete bed rest, but it was unnecessary—Hirin couldn't have walked the length of himself. Maja nursed him almost ceaselessly, while Yuskeya and Dr. Ndasa took turns caring for his immediate medical needs and trying to figure out what had happened to him. It had been a heart attack of sorts, the result of some strange surge the virus had taken when we entered the Split. But there was no real explanation. Even Dr. Ndasa was, on the whole, mystified.

I kept waiting for Maja's anger at me to explode, but this time it didn't. She wasn't saying much, her eyes burned when she looked at me sometimes, but we weren't fighting. It was eerie. Finally, I mentioned it to Hirin when I took some lunch into his room.

"What's up with Maja?"

"What do you mean?" he asked, struggling to sit up.

"I mean she hasn't tried to bite my head off for taking you through the Split." I sat on the side of the bed and handed him the bowl. He took it shakily.

"This time," he told me with a characteristic grin, even though his voice was quavery, "I confess. I interfered."

The effort of talking exhausted him, though, and he motioned for me to take the bowl again. I filled a spoon with spicy, saffron-coloured broth and held it to his lips.

"You told her not to get mad at me?"

He slurped and nodded.

"Even you haven't been able to manage that little miracle before," I observed, spooning up some more. "How'd you talk her around this time?"

Hirin swallowed carefully before he answered. "I told her that if I found out you two were fighting," he said, and paused to draw a deep breath, "it would probably kill me."

I stared at him, mildly shocked. I'd never known Hirin to resort to any kind of emotional blackmail before.

He shrugged. "I figured that if I only have a short time left, I might as well use it to get you two to be civil," he said. He took a few breaths, gathering strength. "You can go back to sparring after I've gone."

I pressed my lips tight together, willing the tears away. "Well, I'm not saying I'm buying into the whole 'I'm a goner' thing, but thank you. At this point I don't care why she's doing it. I'm just too tired to worry about anything else."

Hirin took my hand, although his grip was very weak. "Luta, I do wish you two could learn to get along. You'll both be alone now once—"

"I know, I know," I interrupted him. "I don't have to hear it again." I leaned over to kiss his wrinkled forehead. "As long as you feel up to it, keep saying nice things about me. Maja might actually listen to you one of these times."

"I'll do my best," he whispered, and closed his eyes to nap again.

I went in search of the doctor to ask for what seemed like the hundredth time if he'd discovered anything new. He and Yuskeya were drinking triple caff in the galley.

He made the strange Vilisian waggle that was the equivalent of shaking his head. "I still don't understand it. The tests I ran just before our arrival at the Split showed that the virus had gone dormant, probably since Hirin left Earth. I was going to start running some theoretical data extrapolations to see if I could come up with an explanation."

"You really think that just being in space was causing the virus to back down?" I asked, my heart heavy. If that were the case I would have kept Hirin on the *Tane Ikai* years ago instead of letting him go into the nursing facility on Earth. But at that time he'd seemed to be getting steadily worse.

He shrugged. "I was hoping to verify that theory. It could have been conditions in space, or it could have been conditions he left behind on Earth. Two sides of the same coin, but knowing the causal relationship could provide information that might be applied to other diseases, or to others suffering from this virus or ones like it. Since it's a synthetic virus—"

"A synthetic virus?" I asked. I'd never heard of the doctors mention that before. "What does that mean?"

"The virus that infected Hirin is a bio-engineered entity, not a naturally occurring organism," he explained patiently. "Actually, it looks like a recombinant version of two originally separate viruses, with a synthetic element. This is the first chance

I've actually had to look at it, treating Hirin since his . . . relapse," he said. "I thought you would have known that."

Yuskeya said carefully, "I thought bio-engineering viruses was illegal."

"Well, it is," Dr. Ndasa said. "Unless it's done as part of a project that doesn't have the creation of viruses as its ultimate goal, and everything is destroyed once you're finished with it. It's a fairly common practice, really, and sometimes—well, sometimes the protocols fail, and a virus does get out and flourish 'in the wild.'"

"So, doesn't that mean it should be easier to treat?" I asked. "I mean, knowing what it's made of?"

Dr. Ndasa smiled slightly. "If only it worked that way," he said. "In truth, that's why bio-engineering viruses is illegal, except under highly controlled conditions for research purposes. Often synthetic ones are more resistant and difficult to treat."

"Was there much damage to his heart?" I'd been putting off asking that question.

Yuskeya frowned. "That's the weird part. There doesn't seem to be much damage to the heart muscle itself, and yet he's not getting any better. It's like the virus is running rampant now, and everything in his body is affected."

"Even though we're back to the same conditions as when the virus was dormant," I added. "It doesn't make sense."

"Ah, but we don't *know* if they're exactly the same conditions or not," said Dr. Ndasa, "because we don't know what those conditions were. We're in a different part of the universe, don't forget, and although it all may look the same from the viewscreen of a starship, every system could have subtle differences we can't even detect. Particles, rays, who knows what? Maybe things we wouldn't see even if we ran extensive scans and readings in the system."

It sounded grim. "Can you think of anything that might help him?" I asked, hating the pleading sound in my voice. "We're almost at Rhea, and we've got a cargo dropdown for there. I could go planetside, find whatever you need . . ."

Dr. Ndasa nodded slowly, the folds of skin around his eyes puckering as he thought. "There might be a few things," he said, "if you could find them. I'll make a list tonight."

Tears pricked at my eyes. "Thank you."

He reached over and patted my hand. "I can't make any

promises," he said seriously. "There might not be any improvement at all."

"I know," I said, blinking. "But it's worth a try."

Maja insisted on going planetside with me on Rhea, to try and fill Dr. Ndasa's wish list. I was surprised.

"I thought you'd want to stay here with your father."

Strangely, she flushed. "I do, but I want to feel like I'm doing something, too," she said. "Do you mind if I come?"

There was no trace of the old belligerence in her voice. She was just asking a favour.

"No, I don't mind at all," I said. "I'd be glad of the company."

Once we'd berthed at the spacedock outside Undola Mines and the steves had started to unload the cargo, we took the slideway into the city proper. We could have rented a flitter but Maja suggested that since the day was fine we might as well get all the fresh air we could. After being cooped up in the ship for so long, I had to agree with her. As we walked, I felt some of the stresses of the last few days dissipating in the cool air.

The city was an old one, the first one to spring up after humanity had discovered the wormhole to Delta Pavonis and explored the two planetary jewels of Renata and Rhea. Rhea's crust was riddled with rich deposits of uranium, and most of the settlements had grown up around mining colonies. Undola Mines, though, had transformed itself over the decades from a simple mining station to a large, cosmopolitan city, and I wouldn't have known where to start looking for Dr. Ndasa's supplies if it hadn't been for the handy data kiosks peppered around the streets. I touched my datapad to the screen and the whole of the city lay in my hand, mapped and ready for us to explore.

Maja wasn't quite as impressed with it as I was, but she was busy taking in the sights. There was a considerable Lobor population on both Rhea and Renata, and Maja was watching the wolf-like aliens with covert interest. There were Lobors on Earth, but they were uncommon.

"Stop staring," I whispered.

She turned to me impatiently, then saw my grin and chuckled. "I guess I was, a little. I didn't realize what I was missing, staying on Earth this long."

I consulted the datapad and we set out down a wide street lined with shops. Electric cars hummed past in both directions, and the walkways were crowded.

"That's one thing your father and I always enjoyed," I said, "just being in a place completely unlike anything you'd ever seen before."

It was the wrong thing to say. At the mention of Hirin, the air seemed to pick up a chill that permeated both of us.

"This way." We turned down a side street that was less busy, but still humming with activity. We found the shop we sought easily. The Lobor behind the counter was brisk and professional, consulting our list without questions or comments. I caught Maja staring at the pale umber skin on his hands and the line of dense russet fur that showed when the hem of his sleeve pulled back from his wrist, and nudged her foot. He had all but two of Dr. Ndasa's items in stock.

Back on the street, I consulted the datapad again. We might find what we needed at another of the smaller shops listed. It was on the other side of the city and too far to walk, but slideway routes arched over the busy streets, and we climbed a set of steps up to the nearest one. They moved much slower than the traffic, but twice as fast as we could have walked.

Maja seemed relaxed again, so it seemed an opportune time to have another talk with her. "You seem to be adjusting well to space travel after all. Is it not as bad as you'd remembered?"

"It's fine." She stared over the rail at the traffic below us.

I tried again. "You do seem a little distracted though, and worried. Anything you want to talk about?"

This time she turned. "I'm worried about Dad, of course," she snapped.

My mercurial daughter. "I know that," I said gently. "But he thought you had something on your mind earlier, before we went through the Split and he got worse. I wondered if Taso—"

She shook her head, blonde hair wafting around her face in the breeze. "No, I told you, I'm fine with that. After the first little while it was—actually sort of a relief. We were together, but not in any way that really mattered." She looked as if she might say something more, but stayed silent.

"*Okej.*" I turned away lightly. "I was just asking."

We rode the rest of the way in silence. Our stop was in a much quieter part of the city, away from the main routes. The streets here seemed a little darker, more shadowy, although the sky was still clear above.

The buildings were dingier and not as well marked here, the streets narrow and crooked. We walked slowly, peering through dust-coated windows and trying to decipher signs in Vilisian and Lobor as well as Esper. There were almost no other pedestrians, but I didn't turn to look when I heard footsteps behind us. I was studying the datapad, trying to locate the store, when a black-clad pair of arms went around me roughly from behind. I jerked in surprise, dropped the datapad, and heard Maja scream.

Reflexively I kicked out backwards, but missed my attacker's legs and stumbled forward. He was ready, however, and didn't loosen his grip. I tried the opposite end, throwing my head back in an attempt to smash it into his face, but he ducked that, too. I heard a nasty chuckle.

I twisted my head to try to see Maja. She was in the same state I was, held tight in the grip of a man in a dark biosuit. I caught a glimpse of his face but I didn't recognize him. A bruise was darkening beneath his left eye, so Maja must have had better luck than I'd had in landing a blow. I felt a flash of surprise at that, but I didn't have time to think about it then. I had a brief impression of two or three other dark-suited figures. Something small and cold pressed against the back of my neck, I heard the snick of a pulse injector, and my vision dimmed. A wave of nausea rolled over me.

I heard Maja gasp, "What are you doing? Not now!" just before I lost consciousness, and wondered foggily what she meant.

Chapter Ten

Various Items Stolen and Recovered

Whatever they'd injected fortunately wasn't meant to kill me or incapacitate me for very long—or perhaps my mysterious internal defence systems had come to the fore again. I fought back to consciousness with the realization that I was being trundled along on a cargo sled, arms bound in front of me. For a wild moment I thought the cargo sled meant we were back at the spacedock, but I didn't recognize the rhythmic thumping noise that echoed around us, and when I gingerly opened one eye a crack I saw what looked like the inside of a warehouse or factory. The air was thick with an oily smell I couldn't place.

I didn't want to move around enough to attract attention, but I could hear the treads of another sled behind us, presumably carrying Maja. The footfalls of our captors were soft, and they didn't speak. It sounded like all five or six of them must still be with us.

At last we stopped and someone punched a code into a keypad on the wall. The cargo sled moved through a doorway into a darkened room. The second sled nudged up beside mine, and something hit the floor nearby with a *clunk*. I caught the glint of Maja's fair hair before they shut the door, closing us into the dark. The oily smell was less noticeable in here, and the thumping quieter.

I tried to sit up and realized that something bound my ankles as well. A wave of dizziness swept over me when I raised my head and I almost fell sideways again, but I bowed my head and fought it off. The only other sound in the room was Maja's even breathing. She didn't seem to have moved yet.

I felt around my ankles for what held them, and was disappointed to feel the smooth, hard lines of ultraplas cuffs, not good old-fashioned ropes and a knot. My wrists were doubtless held by the same kind of cuffs, since there was no give to the binding at all. I took a deep breath and slid off the edge of the cargo sled to stand, swaying a little until I gained my balance. It felt good to have accomplished even that much.

Shuffling as quietly as I could over to the other cargo sled, I leaned down close to Maja and whispered her name. She didn't stir. She lay on her side, facing away from me, curled up almost into a fetal ball. Blindly, I ran my hands over her wrists and ankles—they were bound just as mine were. I shook her, gently at first, then more urgently, but she still didn't show any sign of returning to consciousness. Panic threatened to overtake me, but I told myself that she was okay; her breathing sounded steady and strong. They must have injected her after they put me out, or given her a stronger dose. Or my "entity" had allowed me to wake early.

Belatedly I thought of the beacon implant in my ID biochip— if I could activate it, the *Tane Ikai* would know that I was in trouble, and the crew could follow the signal to me. I hadn't even thought about the implant until the day Baden had asked me about it, but it was worth a try. If it still worked—he hadn't been kidding when he'd said it was outdated. And if the factory we were in wasn't wire-blocked. And if anyone back on the ship was on the bridge and listening.

With the ultraplas cuffs firmly locking my wrists together, though, I couldn't reach my forearm to activate it. One good press was all it took, but it was impossible with the cuffs on. I swore under my breath. I looked around for something to extend my reach, realized it was too dark to see anything, and knew that I had to get Maja awake to help me.

Hard as I shook her, though, she didn't wake. I whispered into her ear as loudly as I dared, but with no response. Finally I shuffled around to the other side of the cargo sled and leaned over her, trying to maneuver one of her limp fingers into position on my implant. If I pressed against her finger hard enough, I thought, it might activate the beacon. I was just thinking that I might have done it when the door to the room opened, spilling blue-tinged light around us. It was too late to feign being still unconscious, so I stood up as if I had merely been trying to rouse

Maja and faced my captors with more confidence than I felt.

"Kidnapping is a Primary Statute crime, you know," I said conversationally to the figure outlined against the light in the doorway.

The figure said nothing, just reached toward the wall. Overhead lights sprang to life and I blinked in the sudden glare. When my eyes had adjusted, I saw three of them in the room with us. All were dressed in black biosuits, two men and a woman. I didn't recognize any of them. One of them shut the door.

The shortest of the three, a blocky man with thin grey hair sparsely peppered across the top of his head and a jagged white scar across his upper lip, pulled a chair out from a computer console and pushed it in my direction. "Have a seat, Captain Paixon," he said. "You and your daughter can be on your way in a few minutes."

Like I believed that. I hesitated, hating to give in to his orders, but there wasn't much I could do to resist. With my hands and feet bound by the ultraplas cuffs, any one of them could have me on the floor in a second without breaking a sweat.

"Why hasn't my daughter woken up yet?" I asked as I sat.

"She hasn't been out as long," the same man said, unclipping a techrig from his belt. It looked familiar to me, but at first I didn't realize why. "She should be coming around any time now." As if she had heard him, Maja twitched her head and groaned.

"Do I get to know what this is all about?" I asked, to hide my relief.

"Come on, Captain, I think you already know." He was busy with the touchpad on his techrig, and I glanced over at the other two. They stood just inside the door, their faces impassive. One was the man with the blossoming bruise under his eye, the skin around it taut and swollen now. Maja must have landed a hard one on him. The short man looked up from his screen at me and grinned, not a friendly grin. "And if you don't, your daughter can explain it all to you when she wakes up."

He nodded to one of the guards and she moved behind me, clamping her hands on my shoulders. The short man pressed the end of the techrig to my upper arm, and when I glanced down at it, I realized where I'd seen one before. The intruder on the *Tane Ikai* had carried the same kind of modified datapad. I'd only had a glimpse of it before Viss tucked it away for further study, but I was sure this one was the same. The prick of a needle stung suddenly where the techrig pressed against my arm. I twitched away, but the woman's hands held me like a vise and the needle didn't dislodge.

"Almost done," the man said, and pulled the techrig away from my arm. He moved it over my ID implant, about to link into it. I remembered Baden's datapad beeping when it recognized the beacon implant. *If he linked to me, he'd know I'd set the beacon.* I had to try and delay that, to give someone on the ship more time to get to us.

The guard behind me had relaxed when the other man had taken the techrig away, and I twisted to the side, swinging my wrists in the ultraplas cuffs up toward the techrig. They connected with a solid *thunk* and the rig flew out of his hands and skittered across the floor, into the alcove where he'd gotten my chair. Unfortunately, it didn't smash.

He cuffed me across the face, hard enough to bring tears to my eyes, and I heard Maja gasp.

"Mother!" she said, struggling to sit up. "Just—just let them do this. Then they'll let us go."

I turned to look at her. Her face was set, but her eyes were frightened. *Your daughter can explain it all to you when she wakes up*, the short man had said.

"How would you know that?" I asked her.

The short man had retrieved his techrig and was fussing over it, while the woman's hands gripped my shoulders again, even harder this time. Maja pressed her lips together, then said in a rush, "They only want the samples, and then you can go. I—it wasn't supposed to be this way." She glared at the short man, who was paying no attention to her. "They were supposed to wait . . ."

"Wait for what?" I was amazed at how calm my voice sounded. She had managed to wind up sedated and bound herself, but Maja had obviously known something about this in advance. My mind was having trouble processing that information.

I was going to have to wait for an explanation, though. The short man was advancing toward me, techrig in hand, his face hard. The woman clutched my shoulders in a death-grip. I wouldn't be able to take them by surprise again.

In the next breath the room went dark. The short man swore. "See what's going on!" he barked at the man still standing guard.

I heard the click of the latch, but no light spilled in when he opened the door. The muffled thumping noise had also stopped, I realized, and the entire building was eerily silent.

I wished it meant that someone had come to rescue us, but there was no way the crew could have gotten to us that fast, even if I had managed to trigger the beacon. I realized I was holding my breath, and let it out in a long, silent sigh.

"Get out there and tell me what's happening," the short man hissed, and as my eyes adjusted to the feeble amount of light coming from the huge room outside, I saw the guard move out.

I barely heard a soft thud outside the door, and then two beams of blinding light pierced the room, playing around quickly and coming to rest on our two remaining captors.

Baden's voice said casually, "Now, these lights are the targeting beams on a couple of pin-beam plasma rifles. Let the ladies go and you won't have to find out just how painful a pin-beam plasma burn can actually be."

I couldn't understand how it was possible, but my body went limp with relief.

The man and woman were obviously not as willing to die for their cause as the intruder aboard the *Tane Ikai* had been. They didn't move from where they stood, although the woman released my shoulders.

Someone else slipped into the room, careful to avoid walking through the targeting beams, and I felt Yuskeya's hand on my arm a second later. She touched the cuffs and said, "Viss, maybe we could have the lights back in this room. I'll need to see to key in the disengage code that one of our friends here is going to provide."

"Sure thing," Viss said, and the lights came on overhead. The targeting beams dimmed under the overheads, but were still visible, playing with ominous brightness on the chests of our captors. I noticed that Viss held a techrig very like the one the short man had used on me—it had to be the one he'd taken from the intruder's dead body. I grinned in spite of myself. He'd said it might be useful sometime, and he'd been right, as usual.

Yuskeya looked pointedly at the short man and he snarled the code to disengage the cuffs. "You all right, Captain?" she asked as I rubbed my wrists where the hard ultraplas had bound them.

"We're not hurt." I glanced over at Maja as Yuskeya used the code on her cuffs as well. She wouldn't meet my eyes. I was far from all right, knowing my daughter was involved in this somehow, but I was willing to let it wait until we were alone.

I stood and took the techrig from the short man's unresisting hand.

"What shall we do with them?" Baden asked me.

"Well, it seems a shame to let these perfectly good cuffs go to waste." I passed them to Yuskeya. "And at least one of them has a pulse injector that might have a few doses left in it. There were more than just these three, though."

Viss nodded. "Already taken care of, Captain."

"Do you think that fancy techrig could extract names and personal data from their biochips, Viss?" I asked.

He grinned. "I'm pretty certain it could, Captain."

While Yuskeya trussed them up, and Viss got their data. "Sylvana Kirsch, Ben D'Epiro, and Anshum Chieng, Captain," he said when he'd finished.

None of the names were familiar to me. I found the bag that they'd tossed into the room with us. My datapad was inside, as well as the things we'd bought from Dr. Ndasa's list. I tossed the second techrig inside and crossed to the short man, now sitting in the chair I'd occupied only a few moments before. Yuskeya had cuffed his hands and feet and held the pulse injector close to his neck.

"One second," I told her. I stuck my face close to his. "Tell your bosses at PrimeCorp that next time, we won't be leaving live bodies for them to find. You just got lucky today, Mr. D'Epiro. Stay away from me and my family."

He didn't say anything, and I nodded to Yuskeya and left the room. My stomach churned with an anger so intense I could almost taste bile in my throat. The rest of the factory lay in darkness, but when the others followed me a moment later Viss used the techrig to pull the lights back up. Nobody said anything else until we were outside again, and Viss and Baden quickly loaded their weapons into a flitter that waited near the door with an anxious-looking Rei in the pilot's seat.

I climbed inside. "I don't understand how you found us so fast. I wasn't even sure I'd activated the beacon, and you were there only a couple of minutes later."

Baden turned from the front seat and grinned at me, a little sheepishly. "Remember when I updated your virus protocols, after PrimeCorp sent you that bug?"

I nodded. Rei started the flitter and we rose above the street level and up past the elevated slideways.

"Well, I thought if PrimeCorp was ready to start playing dirty, it might be a good idea to update that beacon implant, too, and I keyed the signal into all the crew datapads. We got a signal from it as soon as you went unconscious. By the time you tried to activate it, we were probably almost there."

I took a deep breath. I wanted to hug him, but I had to be the Captain first. "But you didn't see any need to let me know about those little modifications?"

"You would have told me not to bother," he said with a shrug.

I smiled. I was a long way from laughing just yet. "Your're probably right. Well, thank you, Baden. It's nice to know that you've all got my back." Maja was sitting beside me, but I still hadn't looked at her. There was one person in the flitter who most definitely hadn't had my back, and once we got back to the *Tane Ikai* I was going to find out why.

I had to let Yuskeya and Dr. Ndasa fuss over us for a few minutes, and I gave the doctor what we'd been able to find from his list.

"I'll come and check on Hirin in a little while," I told him, "but I have a few things to take care of first."

He nodded, and his eyefolds were puckered with what I had come to recognize as Vilisian worry. The coppery scent of his emotion suffused the First Aid station. "You should have a rest, Captain. You've had a traumatic experience today."

I patted his arm. "I know, and I will. I'm going to talk to Maja now and see how she's doing." He made as if to protest, and I added, "And then I'll have a lie down, *okej*?"

Maja had managed to slip away to her cabin, but she wasn't getting out of this that easily. I had to know what part she'd played in the day's events. I was confused, because although she'd obviously known something about what was happening, they had knocked her out and cuffed her, too. I stopped in the galley on the way through to her cabin and pulled myself a triple caff. As I held the steaming mug I realized that my hands were ice-cold and not as steady as usual. I pressed them tightly around the mug to keep them still.

She didn't answer when I buzzed her door, but when I reached out to press the button again it slid open. She sat on the side of the bed with her head in her hands, and she didn't look up. I crossed the room and sat down in the desk chair, setting the caff down on the desk beside me.

"I'm sorry," she said in a muffled voice after a minute. "I am so, so sorry."

I was still angry, and though I kept my voice calm, it sounded hard and cold even to my ears. "That's wonderful and I'm glad to hear it, Maja, but I'm still not exactly sure what it is you're sorry for. How were you involved in what happened today?"

She sat up and swallowed hard. Her eyes were puffy and rimmed with red. "I wasn't. Not involved. But I knew right away what it must be about, although that wasn't how it was supposed to go."

She stopped and took a deep breath.

"I'm listening."

She didn't look at me. "A woman named Dores Amadoro contacted me after you left Earth," she said. "She works for PrimeCorp, for Alin Sedmamin."

"I'm familiar with her," I said dryly.

"She told me that you were still refusing to cooperate with PrimeCorp even though they had a legal right to ask you for what they wanted—samples for their research."

"And you believed her, of course."

"Yes, I did. I . . . thought it sounded like something you would do." She looked up at me defiantly. "You've always hated PrimeCorp, irrationally, I thought. And you don't always play by the rules, Mother. Even Dad admits that."

"Neither does your father, but I'll grant you that." I took a careful sip of caff. "What did Amadoro want you to do? Come with us and set me up somehow? Is that why you're really here?"

"No! I'd already booked passage on the *Keinen* to try and catch up with you. Amadoro knew that when she contacted me. She knew Dad was dying. She was very sympathetic."

"I'm sure." I bit my lip. I was trying to let her tell it her way, but my anger kept slipping out.

"All she asked me to do was plant a beacon on the ship after Dad had . . . passed. I wasn't planning to stay aboard after that. She said she just wanted to be able to keep track of you this time, so that they could pursue proper legal channels to get the samples. She said you never stayed in one place long enough for them to track you down and serve notices."

"So you agreed."

She met my eyes. "Yes. It didn't seem like such a big deal. And. . . I thought you were in the wrong."

I wanted to tell her that I'd consider betraying one's own mother to be a very big deal indeed, but I didn't. "But then your father got better, not worse—"

"And I didn't know what to do," she finished.

I looked at her, trying to imagine just how much she must dislike me. "When Amadoro told you that she just wanted to keep track of me, did you believe her?"

She looked away. Her hands twisted in her lap restlessly. "Yes. At least I told myself that I did. But then today, when they attacked us . . . I realized that I'd been fooling myself."

"Did you ever plant the beacon?"

She shook her head. "No. She told me the cargo hold would be the best place, but I never did it." She crossed to the desk and opened a drawer, pulling out a shiny foldcase with her name on the front. From it, she extracted a fingernail-sized button and held it out to me. "You can get Baden or Viss to check it. It hasn't been activated."

I let her drop it into my hand. "Seems like PrimeCorp wasn't planning to wait around for you to use this, anyway. Gee, could it be that they weren't playing straight with you?"

"Look, you don't have to tell me I was an idiot," she said. "But I didn't plant the beacon and I didn't have anything to do with what happened today. I tried to stop them, after they put you out."

"And that's why they took you, too."

Neither of us said anything for a moment. Then Maja said, "I wonder how they found us today?"

I shrugged. "There's not much PrimeCorp can't find out about if they want to, not on Earth, anyway. Dores Amadoro could easily have looked up the planets I took cargo for, and had PrimeCorp ops watching the spacedocks for a chance to get at me. When they saw one, they took it."

"Then why would they need the beacon?"

I stood up. "Because I only filed a flightplan to a certain point. Once I made the last cargo dropdown from Earth, there'd be no record of where I was going next."

Maja licked her lips. "I guess I was wrong about that Amadoro woman. I am sorry, Mother."

I'd let a lot of things slide with Maja over the years, even since she'd come aboard, just trying to keep peace in the family. I wasn't ready yet to forgive her for this one. "So am I, Maja." I left the cabin, and she didn't try to stop me.

We didn't waste any time in leaving Rhea. PrimeCorp's actions lately were outside the scope of what I'd encountered from them before, so it was impossible to predict how they might react to anything. We had cargo to dropdown on Renata as well, but I intended to do it as quickly as possible and not let anyone off the ship. Then we'd make the skip to Mu Cassiopeia, and we'd find out if my mother was still on Kiando.

The night before we reached Renata, I dreamed again.

As usual, I'm running through the crowded corridor of the space station. The silvery walls curve with the compass of the station, never allowing a long line of sight ahead. I know my mother is there, in the crowd, but I can't even glimpse her this time. I push past humans, Lobors, Vilisians, but I never seem to get any closer.

At last I reach the docking ring, but she isn't outside it this time. I've missed her. I run up to the ring anyway, punch in an access code with numb fingers. The docking ring doors roll open but there's no ship beyond, no sign of Mother. This time it's the swirling rainbow colours of a wormhole outside the ship, and a wild surge of force threatens to push me out of the station. I hang on to the door, pull myself back inside and key the doors to close. Exhausted, I lean against a viewport I hadn't noticed before, and I'm shocked when a body floats by outside with no EVA suit. It rolls gently, free-floating as if in water, and I see the dead face.

Hirin.

I don't think I screamed aloud, but I jerked awake, my face wet with tears. I sat up in the bed, panting, heart racing, the burn of adrenaline tingling up my arms and legs. I couldn't bring myself to look up at the viewport overhead. My head throbbed painfully. A single thought pulsed in my mind, one I'd been trying the past few days to ignore.

I couldn't take Hirin through another wormhole. Not in his current condition. Not after what had happened to him in the

Split.

Unless . . . unless I put a certain plan into action. I got out of bed and paced the tiny room. An idea had sprung into my head after what happened on Rhea, but it seemed so crazy I didn't know what to do with it. I'd kept it to myself, rolling it over repeatedly in my mind while I waited to see if Hirin improved with Dr. Ndasa's care. But he hadn't, and I couldn't wait much longer. I paced the inadequate length and breadth of the cabin, wishing I could go out in the corridor, but I didn't want to wake anyone or have to answer any questions. I finally went back to bed and forced myself to stare out the viewport at the star-flecked darkness beyond, but I didn't venture into sleep again that night.

In the morning after breakfast, I went to see Hirin. He was dozing when I entered his cabin. There wasn't much sense in keeping him in the First Aid station, with its utilitarian cot, so we'd hauled all the equipment we thought we might need in a hurry and set it up in the guest quarters. The tiny room was crammed. For once, Maja wasn't there with him. He must have sensed my presence, even though I tried to move quietly, because he opened his eyes as I crossed to the bed.

"Come to cheer me up?" he asked. "I'm all right, really, Luta. This shouldn't be a surprise to either one of us."

"I know that." I sat on the side of the bed and took his lined hand in mine. His skin felt cool and fragile again. "It doesn't help."

He shook his head ruefully. "No, it doesn't, does it?"

"Where's Maja?"

"She went for a nap when I said I was going to sleep for a while." Hirin sighed. "I'm supposed to call her on the ship's comm as soon as I'm awake."

No time to waste, then. "Hirin, I have an idea."

"Mm-hmm? Should I be worried?"

I smiled. "Probably. It's a little crazy, but you might think it's worth a try. I'll let you make the decision, though."

"I never was one to refuse to consider a crazy idea, especially when it came from you."

"Let Yuskeya give you a blood transfusion—from me. We have compatible types, so that's not a concern."

He was frowning slightly. "No, it's not, but why?"

The words tumbled out. "Think about it, Hirin. I never age. I never get sick. I didn't get this virus when we were both exposed.

The chemical fire on Eri that time, or the snakebite when we were mountain climbing in Brazil. *Nothing affects me.* Why? What if it's something in my blood?"

"But you've been tested," he said, shaking his head. "No-one's ever found anything."

"I know that, but what if the tech simply couldn't find it before? Baden ran a virus scan on me before we left Earth and he found something—something the datamed couldn't get a reading on. Maybe that's why PrimeCorp is bothering me again, because some new tech might find it and analyze it. Now I'm wondering, what if it's something that I could transfer—to you? We've never known the explanation, but what if it's not something natural, or even enhanced? Something completely— I don't know—autonomous. It might help. That's all I'm saying. It might help." I ran out of breath and blinked at sudden tears.

He reached up to stroke my cheek, his gnarled hand gentle on my soft, unlined skin.

"And if you're wrong, I don't have much to lose, do I?"

I laughed. "You said it, old man, not me." I took his hand in mine. "But it's all just conjecture, things I've tried to figure out on my own with not much to go on. Even if I'm partly right, and it is something blood-borne, it could be specific to me. It could even kill someone else, their body could reject it, or—"

"Shh. I know. I saw all that while you were talking, because I'm not quite senile yet." Hirin rolled sideways with obvious effort and propped himself up on one elbow. "Luta, the last couple of weeks, before the Split—they've been better than the last few years put together. Being out here, with you, feeling better for the first time in a long time . . ." He shook his head. "I think I'd take any risk rather than go back to staying an invalid again."

My heart thudded painfully in my chest. "So you want to try it?" I realized I'd been just as afraid that he'd say yes as that he'd say no.

"Maja won't like it."

I felt my jaw tense, but I hadn't told Hirin about Maja's betrayal, and I wasn't going to put that on him now. "Maja," I said, "will go *freneza*. But it isn't her decision to make."

He nodded. "I'll tell her. How will you explain it to Yuskeya?"

"That, I don't know." I ran a hand through my hair. "Frankly, I'm so tired of trying to hide the truth that I'd just as soon tell her—tell all the crew—at least part of what's really going on. They're all good at keeping secrets. I think they'd understand."

"What about Dr. Ndasa?"

I hesitated. "I'm not so sure. I mean, I like him, don't get me wrong, and it's nothing to do with his being Vilisian. I simply don't know him that well. I think we'd all have to keep up the charade for him at least. But some of the pressure would be gone."

Hirin laid back on the bed again. "Think he'll go planetside at all when we're on Renata? When we're unloading cargo?"

"I think so. He mentioned a colleague on Renata he thought he'd look up if we were staying long enough. I wasn't sure if I'd even let anyone off the ship, but if I tell him he has time I think he'll go."

"So we could explain everything to the crew and do the transfusion while he was off ship. That would make it easier."

"That's what I was thinking. Hirin, are you sure you want to risk this?"

He reached up a shaky hand and drew my head down to his, placing his lips gently on my cheek. "No risk is too great," he said in a low voice, "when the prize is worthy enough. Tell Rei to get this space crate to Renata as fast as she can. And you'd better go tell Maja I want to talk to her."

Maja stormed into my cabin a short while later without even knocking. I was ready for her.

"How could you?" she demanded, before the door had even closed behind her. Her eyes were wild and she didn't come all the way over to where I sat at my desk.

It was strange, but I was still so angry with her myself that her emotion didn't touch me the way it usually did. I set my datapad carefully down on the desk. "Maja, I think it's his only chance."

"And he'll do whatever you think, even if it kills him," she said bitterly. "He always does."

I shook my head. "That's not fair and you know it. Your father's always made his own decisions."

"Fair? You want to talk about fair?" She stalked the rest of the way to my desk and leaned over it, glaring at me. "Is it fair that he still listens to you when I'm the only one who's stood by him all this time? The only one not roaming all over Nearspace while he sat in that place? I went every day—*every day*. Is it fair that I'm always the odd one out in this family? Is it fair that you look like that," she spat, pointing at me, "and I look like this?"

She'd never actually come out and said it before, and my stomach lurched. But, good. It was finally out. I stood up. "So that's why it's all right to betray me, is it? Because life isn't fair? Grow up, Maja."

For a second she looked like I'd slapped her. "I didn't plant the beacon!"

"Only because you didn't have a chance."

"Stop trying to change the subject. I'm here about Dad."

"Fine." I crossed my arms over my chest and took a deep breath. "I think this is the best chance he has, now. We've been through this before, a hundred times. I can't help the way I am, Maja. I don't understand it, I certainly didn't ask for it, and I've told you all I know about it. Don't you think if I knew how to share it I would have done that long ago?"

"I don't know," she said nastily. "You seem to think you know how to share it now."

"Maja, I have a theory, that's all. I don't know if this will work for your father. It's something I've just figured out recently, because of things that have happened."

"Right."

"Look at the incident on Rhea. PrimeCorp seems to think there's something in me worth going to a lot of trouble to get."

She ignored that. "So this plan of yours is something you just 'figured out.' How convenient."

I threw up my hands. "*Dio!* Do you really think I'd *want* to outlive your father and you and Karro and the children? To stand by and watch you all grow old, die, and not do anything about it? Am I a monster?"

"What if it kills him? Has that occurred to you?"

"Of course it has. But as far as he's concerned, he's as good as dead already. He was ready to die when we left Earth. How much better is it for him to sit around suffering? Can't you go along with it because it's what he wants?"

Her blue eyes pierced mine. "Oh, I won't try to stop him. I don't seem to have any choice in the matter. I'll tell you one thing, though. If he dies because of this," she said between clenched teeth, "I'll never speak to you again."

"He's dying anyway, Maja." My voice was harsher than I'd

intended. She didn't say anything. I wanted to shake her, to ask her why he mattered so much more to her than I did. "And what if it makes him better? Will all be forgiven then?"

She didn't answer, just turned on her heel and walked out. I didn't try to stop her.

Chapter Eleven

Revelations and Risk

We touched down on Renata in the middle of a wintry morning. The first thing that met me was a static message from Dores Amadoro, which didn't improve my mood. I read it in my quarters while the crew finished docking procedures.

Received: from [205152.59.68] PrimeCorp Main Division
STATIC ELECTRONIC MESSAGE: 25.7

Encryption: securetext/novis/noaud
Receipt notification: enabled
From: "AdminAssistant Dores Amadoro"
*<admin.amadoro.primecorp*web>*
To: "Luta Paixon" <ID 59836254471>
Date: Mon, 25 Nov 2284 1:42:13 -0500

Attention Luta Paixon

Further to our last conversation, and under instruction from Chairman Alin Sedmamin, please be advised that I have instructed our legal department to begin proceedings for an exemption under the Nearspace Genetic Materials Privacy Act, in order to obtain samples of your blood and tissues. The same proceedings will be undertaken against your brother, Lanar Mahane, and your mother, Emmage Mahane.

Please advise the nearest PrimeCorp Division of your travel plans within Nearspace for the coming six months, so that we may serve the necessary documents as they become available. This will facilitate matters for all concerned.

Any information you may have concerning the whereabouts of your mother, the aforementioned Emmage Mahane, should be transmitted to any PrimeCorp Division to avoid later charges of obstruction or complicity.

Dores Amadoro, Administrative Assistant
for Chairman Alin Sedmamin

I glared at the screen. So Sedmamin, the *bastardo,* had decided to send his little flunky after me via the conventional legal route now, since his illegal plans hadn't worked? That didn't seem like him, but it could be true. Or it could be the influence of this new thorn in my side, the oh-so-chilly Dores Amadoro. I erased the letter from the datapad with a contemptuous flick. Like hell I was going to tell PrimeCorp where they could find me. Let them chase me all over Nearspace.

The nerve of them, asking for—no, demanding—information about my mother's whereabouts! If Sedmamin had been present, I probably would have punched in that puffy face of his, and slapped Dores Amadoro into the bargain. I stood up, sending my desk chair skimming across the room. It clattered against the bed. My quarters seemed suddenly too small, so I went out into the corridor, paced evenly down to the bridge entry, then turned and went back, as far as the galley, and turned again. The steady thud of my feet on the metal decking had a calming effect on my nerves, and the crew wouldn't ask questions. When I paced, they left me alone.

This Amadoro woman must feel very confident if she was dragging my brother Lanar into it. Lanar had the pull of the Nearspace Protectorate behind him, and the Protectorate had very clearly told PrimeCorp years ago to stop bothering him. Maybe Sedmamin hadn't warned her about that. Or maybe this sudden turnaround had something to do with the "changes" Sedmamin had hinted at in his conversation with me. I'd send Lanar a message as soon as I finished pacing, to see if he'd heard from anyone at PrimeCorp, and ask if we could meet up to discuss things. Between my unpredictable travels and his patrol duties it wouldn't be easy, but maybe we could manage it.

After traversing the length of the hall a few more times, I'd decided that was all I would do. I wasn't going to contact the PrimeCorp Division on Renata and tell them anything whatsoever. If this were another bluff, I'd call it, and if it were something else, I'd deal with it when the time came. I'd send Lanar's message, and then I had a meeting with my crew, and Hirin to worry about. Everything else would have to wait.

The capital city of South Colony, Serous, had a spaceport widely known for its hospitality. I got some curious looks when I told the crew we were having a meeting before any of them left the *Tane Ikai* for shopping, drinking, or any other planetside pleasures.

"This had better be important," I heard Baden grumble as they filed into the galley.

I'd confided in Rei some of what I was going to say to them all, and she shot him a look that he must have read pretty well, because his eyebrows raised and he looked suddenly more alert. Dr. Ndasa had left for a meeting with his friend from one of the Universities, with my blessings to stay away until suppertime. I had already helped Hirin down to the galley and settled him in one of the two big armchairs that flanked one end of the room. Maja perched on the arm beside him, not meeting my eyes. The others took the chairs around the big table.

"We have about an hour before the first cargo is due to be unloaded," I said without preamble, "and I have a few things to explain that are going to take a little while. So I'm just going to jump right in and you'll figure it out as we go along."

They were a pretty solemn bunch right then, and I wondered what they thought I was going to dump on them. If the situation had been less serious, I would have laughed.

I started with a brief synopsis about my mother, how she'd worked for PrimeCorp when I was a child and that her focus had been in longevity research. I could tell they were wondering what that had to do with anything, so I dropped the first bombshell.

"I suspect, but have nothing but my own observations as evidence, that her work is responsible for a curious fact about me. I'm going to tell you my actual age. Most women don't hide it anymore, I know, but I have good reasons to do so. I'll be eighty-five on my next birthday."

Baden snorted a laugh, then fell silent. Looks and mutters of disbelief made their way around the table and I kept quiet to let it sink in. Three pairs of eyes stared at me like they never had before, and I knew they were taking in every detail of my appearance in a very different context.

"*Okej*," Viss drawled. "The last fifty years or so have been mighty good to you, Captain. And you think your mother's anti-aging research when you were a child had something to do with it."

I nodded. "My brother Lanar is the same way. It would make sense."

"How old is your brother, Captain?" Yuskeya asked sharply.

"He's eighty. But you wouldn't know it to look at him."

"And that's why PrimeCorp is always dogging you? Because your mother stiffed them over half a century ago?" Baden asked incredulously. "*Hola*, do they have long memories."

"Well, it's more than just that, Baden. Don't forget the disaster with Nicadico Corp and Longate. They have Vigor-Us, but PrimeCorp would love to be the company that comes out with a treatment like Longate—a version that doesn't kill everyone who uses it."

"Yeah, that would be a definite improvement," Viss said.

"PrimeCorp seems to think that some of my mother's research into that sort of treatment is still floating around in Nearspace. To be precise, in me."

"Do you think they're right?" Yuskeya asked.

I shrugged. "Quite possibly. It's the only thing I can come up with that would explain why I seem to be virtually immune to disease, toxins, aging, everything negative that affects the body."

"The thing my virus program couldn't quite identify?" Baden asked.

I nodded. "I think so."

"So why are you telling us now?" Yuskeya asked. "I can understand your keeping it a secret for so long, but what's changed?"

"That would be me," said Hirin, his voice still raspy and soft since the heart attack.

"Bombshell number two." I crossed to Hirin's chair and settled on the other armrest. "Hirin and I have been married for sixty years, and Maja is our daughter."

"Unfortunately, I don't share my wife's immunities, as is too painfully obvious," Hirin added. Maja said nothing.

"I knew it!" Baden gave one bark of laughter. "I thought it was one of those May-December things, but I knew it. Hirin, I confess to you now that I did my best to seduce your wife when I first came on board the *Tane Ikai*, but she resisted with ego-smashing ease."

Maja remained stony-faced, but Hirin smiled. "I can't blame anyone for trying to seduce her," he said. "She's easily the best-looking octogenarian I've ever seen."

Baden laughed again.

"I still don't—"

"I know, Yuskeya. Here's the part where it all comes together." I got up again, walked over to the counter and drew off a double caff. "On the chance that whatever's in my system would help Hirin recover from the virus, even slightly, we want you to give him a transfusion, from me. We have to make the last skip to Kiando in a week and a half, through a brand-new wormhole, and it may not have been just the Split that made the virus and Hirin's heart go berserk."

She frowned. "But a transfusion! When you don't know anything about what might or might not be in your blood? That seems so risky. What if—"

"Sorry to keep interrupting you, but we've been through all the 'what ifs,'" I said. "Hirin's willing to take the chance and so am I, but it's too difficult to keep it secret any longer, at least from all of you. If things happen as a result, we can't keep trying to hide the facts. I'm tired of it, and we need your help to do this."

"What about Dr. Ndasa?" Viss asked.

I shook my head. "I'm not willing to share with anyone outside this room yet, and I might never be. I have to trust you all to help me keep the truth hidden from everyone else. It would just be easier if we were in this together."

"Count on me," Viss said easily. "The whole thing's so damned interesting that I'd be willing to keep my mouth shut just to know what's going to happen next."

"Me, too," said Baden. "If you don't tell anyone I came on to a little old lady. My reputation would be shot."

Rei punched him in the shoulder. Not gently, either. He winced.

"I'll attempt the transfusion," Yuskeya said. "But how are we going to keep it secret from Dr. Ndasa? That won't be easy."

"We'll do it now, while he's off the ship." I took Hirin's hand. His skin felt cool and wrinkled as a withered leaf. "If Hirin gets better, he'll put off any more of Dr. Ndasa's tests on the grounds that he's just happy to be recovered, and doesn't feel like any more medical stuff right now. If he doesn't—"

"He knows how sick I am," Hirin finished for me. "It wouldn't be that surprising if I were to die. Just don't let him do an autopsy," he said with a chuckle. It caught in his throat and he coughed, clutching my hand harder with each spasm. *Just like back on Earth*, I thought. *Oh, this has to work.*

"One more thing," I said.

"*Dio!* There's more?" Baden widened his eyes in mock surprise.

"Yep. The researcher Dr. Ndasa is going to Kiando to meet? One of the reasons I wanted to take him there is that I'm hoping she might turn out to be my mother."

Maja shook her head impatiently, but no-one else seemed to notice.

"Your mother? Wait a second, Luta, she'd have to be—"

"I know, I know. Don't bother doing the math. If she's alive today, she's almost one hundred and thirty. But—I suspect she doesn't look it."

Viss nodded. "You think she experimented on herself, too?"

I shrugged. "I haven't seen her since I was fourteen, but I do remember her and what she was like, and I can tell you one thing: she'd never have used anything on us that she didn't use first on herself."

"Well, the clock is ticking, folks," Yuskeya said, getting up from the table. "I'll go get some things ready. Fifteen minutes?"

I caught Hirin's eye and he nodded unwaveringly. "Fifteen minutes," I told Yuskeya, "will be *perfekta*."

I gave Viss, Rei and Baden all the information they might need to see to the unloading of the cargo and told them they were free to take a break in Serous as soon as that was complete. Hirin and I made our way slowly down the length of the ship to the First Aid station, pausing to peek out the front viewscreen at the spaceport. It bustled with humans and Vilisians, some of the humans from the various worlds exhibiting such cultural diversity that they might have been other aliens. We shared a glance, remembering how exciting it used to be to visit a new spaceport for the first time, years ago on those early trade skips.

In the First Aid station, Yuskeya was fidgeting around, creating a pile of datameds and other instruments on the cot.

"What are you doing?" I asked when we entered, Hirin leaning heavily on my arm. "I thought Hirin would have to lie down there."

She shook her head. "We should just do it in Hirin's cabin," she explained. "I'm sorry I didn't think to tell you that. There's no room here for both of you to get comfortable—wait a second." She stopped what she was doing and stood with her hands on her hips. "There isn't really room in his cabin, either. We'll have to do it in yours, Captain, unless you want to use the galley."

"No, if Dr. Ndasa comes back early I'd rather not be out in plain view. My quarters are fine. We'll start back."

Hirin and I headed back down the corridor. "I'm getting my exercise for the day, anyway," he joked. His feet shuffled hollowly on the metal decking.

"You take the bed," I directed once we were in my quarters, "and I'll sit in the armchair. I'll just push it over as close as it needs to be. Is it cold in here?" My hands felt icy.

Hirin shook his head. "I don't think so. I think it's just nerves."

"Maybe so. I hope this works."

"Me, too. Now that they all know we're married, I could be spending every night in your room."

I laughed in spite of myself. "Men. They never change."

Maja came in then and wordlessly sat on the floor with her back against the wall. She radiated anger, but maybe it was conflicting with the guilt she felt about conspiring with Amadoro against me. Hirin smiled at her and got a half-hearted response.

Yuskeya bustled in with an armload of supplies. "Get comfy, folks."

"What is all this stuff? I pictured a couple of needles and some kind of tube to connect us. Isn't that how they used to do it?"

Yuskeya gave me a look. "Let's just say I'm not taking any chances. I've never done this before, remember. Person to person transfusions were never common, and since the development of artificial blood, we don't even have to collect it and store it very much anymore. I've had to improvise."

She held up what looked like a datamed with bioplastic tubing protruding from each side. "This is what will connect you. I'll set you both up with transcutaneous diverters and then attach the bioplas tubes. I'll use the gadget in the middle first to make sure your blood is compatible—"

"We have the same blood type," I interjected.

"Yes, well, I still have to do a crossmatch, if you don't mind," she said mildly. "I'm the medic here. Regardless of—and because of—those extra-special additives that might be floating around in you, I want to make sure that your blood isn't going to cause any adverse reaction in Hirin. I'm sure you don't want to kill him instead of saving him."

I gulped. "No, of course not. How long will it take?"

"Only a couple of minutes, with this." She held out the gadget she'd indicated and I pressed my finger on a soft, clear pad. I felt the slightest prick as it took a sample. She did the same thing with Hirin.

"We're lucky. This part used to take about an hour before we'd have a result," she said as she studied the screen, reading the output. Then she looked up with a smile. "Everything looks good."

I let out the breath I'd been holding. I hadn't realized my entire plan could have failed before we'd even begun.

Yuskeya set the datamed down on the night table. "Now this will regulate the blood flow so that we have a nice smooth transition." She held up another one. "Hirin, I'll connect you up to this one, too. It'll monitor your blood pressure to make sure we're not adding too much too fast. How much do you want to transfer?"

I hadn't thought about it. "Maybe half a litre or so? Does that sound right?"

Maja opened her mouth, then clamped it shut without speaking.

Yuskeya shrugged. "What's 'right'? Nobody's ever done this before, or at least not for the same reasons. You're the one who said this was all theory."

"It is. Well, let's try half a litre and see what happens. I guess what I meant by 'right' was, can I lose that much and Hirin gain that much without any other physiological problems?"

"Probably. That's why I'm monitoring his blood pressure and other vitals. Just to be sure."

"Okay. Let's do it."

After all the talking and Yuskeya's fussing and puttering

around were finished, the actual transfer took about forty-five minutes. "In the old days it would have been a little faster," Yuskeya said, keeping an eye on Hirin's readings in the datamed, "but I would have had to actually pierce your vein with a needle. Transcutaneous is slower, but less painful and intrusive. And I didn't want to put too much of a strain on Hirin's pressure."

Truthfully, I hardly felt a thing, just the pressure on my arm where Yuskeya had taped the transcutaneous extractor, and the pangs of worry that it wouldn't work. Next to those, a little physical discomfort was nothing.

Yuskeya checked our vital signs periodically during the procedure and again when the process was through, fetched us glasses of chilled fruit juice from the galley, and suggested that we simply rest for a little while before trying to go anywhere else on board. She and Maja looked after cleaning everything up despite my protestations that I would help.

Maja said, "I'll check on you later," as she went out the door. I couldn't tell if she was speaking to just Hirin or both of us, but she shot me an appraising glance that I couldn't really interpret.

As Yuskeya was leaving, she paused. "Feel better," she said with a smile from the doorway. "Both of you."

Hirin looked over at me. "I wonder what will happen now?"

I took a deep breath. "I don't know. We'll just have to wait and see."

He nodded. "Thank you, Luta," he said quietly. "I know it hasn't been easy—"

"Shhh." I stood hesitantly and walked, just a little wobbly, the couple of steps to the bed and lay down beside him. He wriggled over to make room. "It hasn't been easy for either of us. But we've always done our best. It's worked so far. Well, except with Maja, I guess."

He put an arm around me and closed his eyes. "That it has. And Maja will be all right. We'll just have to trust that things will work out, one more time."

We both slept then, not knowing what forces worked inside us, but content in the knowledge that it was one more thing we shared.

The next few days left me wondering if we'd made a terrible mistake. Hirin ran a fever that soared well over a hundred and stayed there for two days, despite the meds Yuskeya gave him every few hours. He was delirious some of that time, his mind wandering the pathways of the near and distant past. He talked to Karro and Maja as if they were present and young children again, assured me that we'd keep looking for my mother for as long as it took, and recited data on skip runs we'd made long ago. We had to invent excuses to keep Dr. Ndasa away, for fear of both what Hirin might say and the medical tests the doctor might want to perform.

I spent as much time in Hirin's room as I dared risk without arousing Dr. Ndasa's curiosity. Maja was there almost constantly and seemed to be getting a head start on her vow never to speak to me again. We spoke about as much as strangers on a gravlift. Yuskeya helped run interference with Dr. Ndasa by explaining that Hirin was feeling down about his condition and had requested some time to spend alone with his daughter and me, his only family on the ship.

She told me later that Dr. Ndasa had asked, "What is the relationship between Hirin and the Captain? I've never asked."

"I told him you were a niece or something," she told me. "Was that all right?"

"Sure. Just as long as I can remember to tell the same story if he asks me, too."

Four days after the transfusion Hirin's fever was suddenly gone, and he was awake and demanding some "real" food. Three more days and he was out of bed and back to normal. I was so relieved I felt almost ready to forgive Maja for her pact with Dores Amadoro, and that she might be ready to relent a little toward me, too. In fact, she didn't seem so angry, just quiet and aloof.

"I can't believe how he's improved," Dr. Ndasa said one morning as we sat having breakfast in the galley. Hirin had just come in and was digging in the cooler for something interesting.

I sighed. "It's a great relief, I'll say that. Thank you for all you've done, Doctor."

Dr. Ndasa shook his head. "I don't know that I made much of a difference. He seems to have just fought back on his own. He's a strong man."

Hirin winked at me over Dr. Ndasa's head. "Clean living and good eating, and all bad things in moderation, that's what I always say."

"Well, it certainly seems to have worked for you. Tell me, Hirin, will you let me run those tests to study your virus soon? Are you feeling up to it? I would love to know what it is doing now."

Hirin sat down across from the doctor. "I would, too, Doc, but to tell you the truth, I've had enough of datameds and scans for a while. I'd like to just enjoy this good feeling while it lasts."

The doctor looked disappointed and the scent of fresh bread wafted gently from his skin, but he nodded. "I suppose I can understand that. But you will tell me when you think we can get back to the tests, will you?"

"Oh, sure, Doc. I'll definitely let you know." He tackled his breakfast with great gusto.

He was a better liar now than he'd ever been in his younger days, but I was glad to see him having fun with it. I left him and Dr. Ndasa to their chatter and went to the bridge to check on our status. I had more than enough on my mind as we drew closer to Kiando and whatever—and whoever—we would find there.

Before we made it out of the Delta Pavonis system, though, I had a very different worry.

Chapter Twelve

Piracy and Other Questionable Pastimes

We were a week out from Renata when an urgent call over the ship's comm woke me from a deep sleep.

"Captain, Yuskeya here."

"Go ahead." I struggled to get my bearings. Beside me, Hirin sat up, too.

"I'm alone on bridge watch and there's a vessel on fast approach. I've commed it but no reply. I don't like the look of it." Her voice was clipped and businesslike.

"I'm on my way. Wake Baden, Viss, and Rei and get them to the bridge."

"Aye, Captain."

I swung my legs past Hirin and reached for the jeans I'd left on the desk chair. He was right behind me.

"You stay here," I told him, pulling my t-shirt over my head. "You should rest. I'm sure it's nothing. We're all just a little jumpy."

He was already fastening his shipsuit. "Like hell," he said mildly. "I feel fine, and I still have a vested interest in this ship, remember."

I didn't wait to argue any more, since it was obviously a waste of my breath anyway. The ship lurched hard to the left just as I got the door open, and I stumbled inelegantly into the corridor.

"*Damne,*" I swore aloud, and ran for the bridge.

Yuskeya was still alone there. She didn't look up from the piloting console when she heard me come in.

"It's an unmarked Stinger-class," she said, "and the ship's sig is scrambled. I don't know what he's trying to do. He's not hailing us on the comm; he's not shooting at us. He just keeps trying to get up under us. I'm taking evasive maneuvers."

I wondered where Yuskeya, a navigator, had learned to take evasive maneuvers, but she seemed to know what she was doing and I didn't have time to ask. Rei and Viss both arrived on the bridge at that second, and Rei slid into the secondary pilot console while Yuskeya gave her a clipped rundown of what she'd just told me. Viss went to the engineering console and punched up the screen.

"Viss, try and get a reading on it. What the devil is he doing?"

Baden ran onto the bridge then and slid into the comm console. "What's up?"

Before I could answer him, Viss barked, "Goddamn—Cargo Pod One airlock override just engaged!"

"Anything you can tell me, Baden—"

The ship shuddered again and Viss yelled, "Cargo Pod One dockside door open."

"What the—close it!"

Viss punched commands into the computer but he shook his head. "Can't. Something's overridden the controls. I'm going down there."

He turned and sprinted from the bridge before I could tell him not to. Yuskeya was about two steps behind him.

"*Damne!* Baden, come with me! Hirin, you have the bridge," I shouted over my shoulder as Baden and I followed Viss and Yuskeya. They'd left the weapons locker open and I pulled two of the remaining plasma rifles out of it and handed one to Baden. It sounded like Viss was mostly sliding down the metal ladder to the engineering deck below. Baden put a hand out to make me let him go first, and we went down the hatchway.

"What the hell?" Baden asked me as we climbed down. "Is there even anything in Cargo Pod One?"

"No, Viss thought we should leave it empty if we were going through the Split. They must have just picked that one as a way to board the ship." *Board the ship.* My own words sent a chill down my spine. Piracy wasn't unknown in Nearspace, but the Protectorate kept it reasonably well under control. Those who practised it anyway were ruthless, hardened, and no-one I wanted to run into.

We reached the engineering deck and jumped off the hatchway ladder. The ship pitched hard again to dockside and I stumbled, almost falling into the open hatch. I caught a rung of the ladder and pushed myself back. The hatch continued down to Cargo Pod Four below us, and I had no wish to take the same leap the masked intruder had taken a few weeks ago.

"You *okej?*"Baden gasped, and I nodded. We sprinted through Engineering toward the hatchway to Cargo Pod One at the front of the ship. The pods didn't interconnect on the lower level; each had its own airlock and cargo doors. Viss's footsteps echoed on the metal decking as he ran ahead of us down the long corridor between the fuel storage cells. I had no idea where Yuskeya had gone, but she wasn't ahead of us. The hatchway to the cargo pod was at the very end. Viss was kneeling beside it when we caught up.

"Viss!" I yelled, and he stopped and looked up at me, one hand on the hatch lever. "Red light!" The warning light beside the hatch glowed bright crimson, indicating that the pod below was not pressurized. The hatch shouldn't have opened without a keycode anyway, but I wasn't sure how clearly any of us were thinking.

Viss let go of the lever, stood, and kicked the wall beside the hatchway viciously. None of us had stopped to put on an EVA suit, so the hatch had to stay shut. He turned and started to run back past me headed back to Engineering and the EVA suits stored there.

He almost ran into Yuskeya. Her arms were loaded with EVA suits, and Maja was with her, carrying more.

I blinked. Maja's blonde hair was still tousled from sleep and she'd thrown only a short jacket over her sleepsuit, but she looked totally in control of herself. She'd obviously stopped at the weapons locker for a handgun since she was toting a pin-beam Viper in one hand. I know I stared. She let Viss pass her and ran down the hall toward us.

"Are you *okej*? What's happening?" she demanded.

"I wish I knew. Pirates, apparently. What are you doing down here?"

"What was I going to do, cower in my cabin while the ship was being attacked?" she asked.

Viss was on his way back down the corridor. He'd closed and sealed the bulkhead at the engineering end of the corridor behind him and took a suit that Yuskeya offered him. "Get these on quick," he ordered. "If they blow this hatch from the other side—"

Damne, I hadn't thought of that. The *Tane Ikai* had bulkhead hatches between each deck, but we almost never kept them closed. I touched my biochip implant to comm the bridge and told Hirin, "You and Rei get into EVA suits, just in case. Wake Dr. Ndasa. With the pod bay doors open—"

"Already done," Hirin said. "What's happening down there?"

"I'll keep you posted." I struggled into an EVA suit as quickly as I could. My fingers trembled as I wondered if the intruders would blow the hatch from the depressurized pod before we had our suits on. The others were quick, too. Baden helped Maja with the unfamiliar fastenings.

"What are they doing down there?" I wondered aloud. "There's nothing in that pod to start with, and they're not coming up."

Viss gave me an unreadable look and said, "I'm going to open the hatch." He'd been the first into his suit and had stood fidgeting, waiting for the rest of us.

"They'll probably be watching it," Baden warned. "Don't do anything rash."

Viss just grinned at him and pulled the hatch lever. There was an almost immediate burst of plasma fire from the cargo pod. Viss glanced up at me and then dropped through the open hatch. Yuskeya and Baden followed him and there was more fire.

"Stay here," I ordered Maja, and went down the hatch myself.

When you drop through a cargo pod hatchway you have two options. You can keep climbing the metal ladder down the nearly five meters to the floor of the pod, or you can head to the side on one of the raised catwalks. Going in blind, I hit the catwalk, dropped, and crawled right. There hadn't been any lights on in the pod, although Viss must have hit the switch when he left the bridge. They were still very faint, warming up, so the pod was cast in general gloom.

I could make out a few things. The doors were still open, though mostly blocked by the stinger, which had attached itself to the *Tane Ikai*'s hull just outside the doors. Its own cargo door was open, and some crates rested just inside. A couple of figures in EVA suits crouched behind the crates, and one more was trying to hide behind a crate on our pod floor. The tableau didn't make sense to me. They'd boarded the ship to put cargo *into* our pod?

A few short bursts of plasma fire shot out from the stinger, but they were out of range and didn't reach us on the catwalk. The final pirate left on the *Tane Ikai* made a run for the stinger under the covering fire, and Viss let loose a couple of shots. One went wide, but one took the pirate in the leg and he stumbled and fell, skittering across the floor of the cargo pod toward the open door. He dropped both his weapon and a techrig, clutching at the burned patch of fabric and flesh on his calf with one hand and trying to catch the door ledge with the other. He stopped sliding, hauled himself upright, and managed to launch himself across the space separating the two ships just as the stinger's cargo door slid down, blocking our view. Viss gave a yell of rage, muffled by his helmet, and slid down the ladder. Yuskeya fired at the stinger but the distance was too great and the plasma dispersed harmlessly.

At the same moment, Maja jumped down onto the catwalk beside me and immediately rolled to one side, coming up with the Viper steady in her hand as she looked around. I was speechless.

She grinned at me. "Warrior Chi self-defence classes. I had to do something to vent after Taso left."

Well, that explained the bruise she'd left on the PrimeCorp operative back on Rhea, anyway.

The second the stinger's door closed the ship released itself from us and moved off, slowly at first but then with mounting speed. I wished the *Tane Ikai's* torpedo bays were full and I could order the little *bastardo* taken right out of the sky, but it was an empty desire. I hadn't carried torps since Hirin and I had downgraded from really exciting cargo to more mundane loads, and with the Protectorate on patrol, the notion of pirates had dimmed to a memory of a long-ago threat.

Viss crossed to the control panel beside the open doors and punched in some commands. The pod bay doors began to close, and once they did, the pod could be re-pressurized. For now we'd have to talk over the comm channel. I left the plasma rifle on the catwalk and climbed down the ladder, Baden and Maja right behind me. Yuskeya had already made it to the floor and was collecting the pirate's weapon and techrig.

Hirin's voice came over the comm. "Luta? What's happening? Should we pursue this guy?"

I thought fast. "No, never mind. We'd never catch a stinger; they're just too fast. Is everyone *okej* up there?"

"We're fine. You?"

"No problems. You can probably shuck the EVA suits, too."

By this time I had reached the floor, and I realized that there were still a dozen crates sitting in the tie-downs. Slowly my confusion cleared—somewhat. The pirates hadn't been loading anything into the pod; they'd been taking it out. This pod, however, was supposed to be empty.

"What *is* all this stuff?" I asked.

No-one answered, and the question hung in the air, caught in a sudden tension. Then Viss said, "I suppose I could say, 'ask your brother,' but that probably wouldn't cut it, would it?"

I turned to look at him and put my hands on my hips. "No. No, it wouldn't. What does Lanar have to do with any of this?"

Viss sighed. "You want to go up to the galley and get a triple caff? This could take a while."

I scowled at Viss, but it's hard to feel you're really conveying your anger from behind an EVA helmet.

"I think we'll take it on the bridge."

It wasn't often that I saw Viss looking sheepish, but that's the face he presented me once we assembled back on the bridge. The viewscreen showed a magnificent nebula swirling in the distance, but none of us paid much attention. Viss and I faced each other near my command chair, but I didn't sit. The others went to stations, turning in their chairs to face us. Tension hummed in the air as if the skip drive were warming up.

"Are you sure you don't want to do this in private?" Viss asked me.

I glared at him. "You've put every member of this crew in jeopardy. I think they have a right to hear what you have to say."

"There might be . . . higher powers . . . who might not appreciate that," he said.

"The higher powers can kiss my *azeno*. You have one chance to tell it, and this is it. So get on with it." Generally I got on exceedingly well with Viss, not because I was under any illusions about his shady past—or present, for that matter—but because I thought we shared the same bearings on our moral compass. The possibility of this kind of betrayal had never crossed my mind. First Maja, now Viss. The thought left a bitter taste in my throat.

"Guess I'm not a very good smuggler," he said with a half-grin.

I didn't return it. "Oh, I don't know, you had me fooled, and it's my ship. What's in those crates in the cargo pod?"

"Illegal tech," he said.

I closed my eyes. Carrying illegal technology was a Primary Statute crime that could land us in jail for what would be, even for me, a very long time.

"And why is it on my ship?"

Viss swallowed. "Because your brother asked me to deliver it to Kiando, or as close as I could get it, for him."

"Her brother?" Yuskeya broke in. "You mean the *Admiralo*?"

"That's the only one she has, as far as I know," Viss drawled.

"I don't believe it." Yuskeya sat back in her skimchair and folded her arms, looking as angry as I felt. "He wouldn't put the Captain in that kind of danger."

I rubbed a hand across my eyes. "You'd better just tell me the whole thing."

"Mind if I sit?" he asked, and pulled a skimchair away from the secondary pilot's console without waiting for my answer. He turned it to face me and sat, leaning forward with his elbows on his knees. "Here's what I know. The *Admiralo* contacted me when we arrived Earthside, and then again shortly before we shipped out again. I've done some . . . favours . . . for the Protectorate in the past, so that wasn't unusual. He told me that they've been keeping an eye on PrimeCorp for some highly irregular activity at their new tech subcorp for a while now, and they've managed to . . . acquire . . . some of PrimeCorp's illegal tech." He paused.

"I've got my own issues with PrimeCorp, but I don't see how this ties in."

He shrugged. "Well, it doesn't. See, the Protectorate wants a chance to have a look at this stuff, so they need to get it to a planet controlled by one of the other Corps. They have to tread carefully around PrimeCorp and they don't want any hint to get out that they're involved. It's too chancy for a Protectorate ship to transport the stuff. But we were going to Kiando anyway, it wasn't a big load, and I knew we weren't carrying a full cargo shipment . . . if I just told you to keep one pod clear . . ."

"And what happens if we get caught with it on board?" I asked.

"The *Admiralo* said he'd make sure that didn't happen, and if the worst happened and it did, he'd make it right. Remember how he jumped in when that Mars Planetary Police ship was heading for us? I figure that's why."

"It was on board then?"

Viss nodded, but had the grace to blush. "Once I got you to leave Cargo Pod One empty, I had room for it, and that pod wouldn't have to be opened again, so the secret would be safe. The *Admiralo's* message came for me as soon as we were close to Earth."

I threw my hands in the air. "And who's out here looking after my back now? I didn't see any Protectorate ships coming to the rescue when we were breached and boarded a little while ago!"

Viss frowned. "I don't think they were expecting that. The *Admiralo* didn't mention that anything like that might happen."

"Who the hell were those guys?"

"I don't know." Viss stroked his grey-peppered beard. "I'm kind of worried about that, to tell you the truth, since they knew exactly where to find us and where on the ship to look for the stuff."

"Unless it was a coincidence," Yuskeya suggested, but she didn't sound like she believed it. She stared at Viss coldly.

"Viss, did you tell Lanar we were going to Kiando?" I asked. "Maybe the message was intercepted?"

He shook his head solemnly. "No, Captain, because I didn't tell him that. I said I'd see how close I could get it, and let him know where the Protectorate could pick it up. We have some . . . mutual contacts . . . and I was sure I'd be able to arrange something. But I knew you wanted to keep the Kiando thing quiet."

"I think it had to be PrimeCorp," Baden said suddenly.

"Why?"

"If they've got an eye somewhere inside the Protectorate, found out where the stuff was headed and how, it'd make sense to come out and try to take it back."

"PrimeCorp has an informant in the Protectorate? No way," Yuskeya said, shaking her head.

Hirin spoke up. "If they were going to go to all that trouble," he said, "Why didn't they just blow the hatch and come right through the ship after Luta, too? We know they're still after her. They could have taken care of two birds with one stone." Everyone fell silent, picturing that scenario, I suppose. I know I was, and I didn't like it. Then Rei snorted delicately.

"Different departments," she said. "These guys probably don't even know anything about Luta. PrimeCorp's huge—big enough to make the Protectorate nervous. Not everyone's going to know what everyone else is doing."

"Great, now we have two groups of PrimeCorp operatives after us? Makes me want to skip into the nearest unexplored wormhole and take my chances." I turned back to Viss. "Did Lanar tell you why the Protectorate is tiptoeing around PrimeCorp? That doesn't sound right to me."

Viss shook his head. "He didn't really say. But he said that PrimeCorp's planning something—he didn't say what—that the Protectorate is working to stop. But he said it's a 'delicate operation.'"

"If the Protectorate's worried, then I'm worried," Baden said. Yuskeya looked like she was about to say something, but she scowled and stayed silent.

I sighed. "Okay, let's get back on track. Viss, get down and check the integrity of the cargo pod. I want to know how they got the doors open and if they damaged the ship at all. Yuskeya, set up a maximum range in-system scan and keep it running. I want lots of warning if anyone else comes looking for us."

Viss nodded and stood.

"Viss, you know I'm going to have to check your story with Lanar."

He grinned. "I wouldn't respect you if you didn't, Captain," he said. "I'm half-surprised you're not locking me in my quarters."

"Don't think I didn't consider it. Now get going."

Viss flashed me a grin and headed down to the cargo deck.

"Baden, check all the crates that are in that pod, would you? Just make sure they're all secure again."

"Aye, Captain," he said.

I saw the gleam in his eye. "And don't *open* the crates. I know you'd love to get your hands on some of that stuff, but it's strictly off-limits, understood? Whatever's left, I want to deliver to Lanar intact."

"Oh, Captain! Just a peek? I swear I won't take anything!"

I shook my head. "No opening the crates." I grinned. "I know you wouldn't be able to resist the temptation. Think of it as me saving you from yourself."

"You're a hard woman," he said, shaking his head as he left the bridge. Maja followed him.

I stood up from my chair, although my body felt that it barely had the energy.

"Rei?" I stretched, feeling the kinks pull out. "As soon as you get the okay from Viss and Baden, get us back on track for the wormhole to Mu Cassiopeia, please. Once we're underway, I want to double up on bridge shifts. No-one's on duty alone. I am going back to bed, and if anyone wakes me before morning, I'm converting one of the cargo pods into a brig."

In my cabin, I lay down on top of the bed without bothering to change my clothes. I wanted to shoot a message off to Lanar right away, lambasting him for first, using the *Tane Ikai* as a mule ship, and second, not coming to me with his problem instead of Viss. I know Lanar likes to think that I've always been squeaky-clean in my operations, but it hurt that he hadn't simply asked me to help.

It wasn't safe to send that kind of message, though; PrimeCorp owned the subcorp that had a monopoly on almost all the communications systems in Nearspace, and it was far too likely that any message might be scanned or intercepted. I considered asking Viss if he counted any data runners among his questionable friends and contacts, but decided against it. The ship was hot enough with all that contraband tech in the hold. I didn't need to add any other illegal activities to the list.

Anyway, I was still too mad at Viss to ask him for any favours. I sighed, rolled over, and resolved to put all worries out of my head and get some sleep. It must have worked, because I didn't even notice when Hirin climbed back into bed with me.

Chapter Thirteen

Face to Face
With Certain Unreality

Hirin improved every day after that. We both felt certain that whatever secret helpers functioned in my body were now hard at work in his. He had already regained the improvements we'd noticed on the beginning leg of the trip, and seemed poised to make even further gains. Still, the thought of the next wormhole filled me with trepidation.

Our encounter with the pirates had one positive result. Maja and I arrived in the galley at the same moment the next morning, and I realized that sometime around the moment she'd arrived at the cargo hatch with a pin-beam Viper in her hand, I'd stopped being quite so angry with her.

"Thanks for your help last night." I pulled double caffs out of the machine for both of us.

She half-smiled and shrugged. "I didn't actually do much."

"But you were there."

"Sometimes families have to stick together regardless," she said, handing me a plate of *pano* with an uncharacteristic grin. "Pirate attacks fall into that category."

Rei came in then and we didn't say anything more, but I felt as if maybe there was hope for us yet.

We were still a day out from the skip to Mu Cassiopeia when Baden hailed me on the ship's comm. Hirin and I were playing *quozit* in my quarters.

"Captain, incoming WaVE for you, although the signal's weak. *Admiralo* Lanar Mahane, on board the Protectorate Patrol Ship

S. Cheswick."

"Thanks, Baden." I switched to the incoming. Hirin mimed going to the galley for a snack and I nodded. My brother Lanar's face appeared on the screen, grinning through the grainy reception.

"*Saluton*, little sister! We meet again!"

This time I let the "little sister" thing pass. I was too angry to play games with him just then, but I knew the comm could be monitored, too, so I had to choose my words carefully. "*Hola*, Lanar. Calling to talk to Viss?"

"No, why would I—" he broke off and his grin disappeared. He swallowed. "Oh, how's Viss doing, then?"

"He got quite a surprise when we were breached and boarded by some space pirates. They were interested in some cargo I'm hauling."

"*Dio*! Is everyone all right?" He looked stricken, and I felt perversely satisfied.

"Yes, and they didn't get away with much. What I can't figure is how they knew we had that particular cargo aboard. They must have had some kind of inside information. I think the shipper must have been careless."

"You'll want to speak to him first chance you get, I guess," he said carefully.

"Yes, I'm pretty much livid about the whole thing. He'll get an earful when I catch up with him next."

"I imagine he'll feel pretty badly."

"He'd better," I said grimly. "So, what's this about? I didn't think I'd see you again this soon."

He looked relieved that I'd changed the subject. "I wish this reception were better—we're just outside the wormhole to Beta Comae Berenices, ready to make the skip. Thought I might catch you before you left the system."

"You did, just barely." Apparently we weren't going to have much time. "Hirin's doing better. He's better than he's been in years."

"Really? That's wonderful news, Luta. What happened?"

I grinned. "You might say I worked a little magic on him."

He narrowed his grey eyes at me. "I wonder exactly what that means? I think we need to get together, face to face, sometime soon."

"You're right about that. Did you get the message from

PrimeCorp? About legal proceedings?" I hardly cared if they intercepted my feelings about that charade.

Lanar snorted. "I did! I think they're bluffing."

"I don't know. From what I've seen of them lately it seems like they're a lot more intense than they used to be."

"You're right about that." He leaned closer to the screen, his eyes serious. "You've had more than one . . . encounter with them?"

"Yes, but I think the details will have to wait until we have that realspace chat. Listen. Does this have anything to do with those changes Sedmamin mentioned? They've always steered clear of you in the past."

Lanar's lips flattened into a thin line. "I'd say it has a lot to do with that. I would have expected Sedmamin to be playing his cards a little closer to his chest, but he tends to forget that people can figure things out on their own."

I sighed. "I love chatting with you, Lanar, but the riddles get tiring after a while."

He laughed suddenly. "You're probably right, but that's all I can say now. You're doing okay, then?"

I nodded. "I'm fine. I have one passenger headed outsystem and I'm going to have a look around when I drop him off."

"Hmmm . . . something interesting where you're headed?"

"Maybe." I shrugged. "Maybe not. I'll keep you posted."

"Do that." He paused. "You don't think anyone is following you now, do you?"

I shook my head. "I don't think so, but I don't know for sure. I have Yuskeya running a constant in-system scan so we'll have lots of notice if anyone turns up. There shouldn't be any public record of where I'm headed next. I could be taking any one of the skips out of Delta Pav."

"Well, if they're following you, remember that not every world is under PrimeCorp control. There are other corps out there, like Schulyer and Duntmindi, that don't like them any better than we do. You'll have better protection there."

"I don't think it's going to be a problem."

"Are you going to get in touch with PrimeCorp about the legal proceedings?"

"Are you kidding? The only thing I'll be telling them is to kiss my thrusters."

He laughed again. "Good girl! I'd like to see Sedmamin's face

145

if you sent that message. But listen, Luta," he said seriously, "don't worry too much, okay? Whatever you think, I've got your back. And watch out for those quilberries."

The reception began to fade. "What do you—Lanar!"

He grinned and mouthed *gis la revido*. I shook my head and waved to him as the carrier wave dispersed. "Yeah, see you soon, little brother."

"What did Lanar have to say?" Hirin asked, coming back with some honey *kuko* for us.

I blew out a long breath. "He had the grace to look guilty when he realized I knew about his arrangement with Viss. And somehow he knows we're going to Kiando."

"What? I thought you didn't log that."

"I didn't. And Viss said he didn't tell Lanar where we were heading." I frowned. "But he told me to watch out for quilberries. I got sick on them once when we were kids, visiting Kiando. That had to be what he meant."

"Weird." Hirin shook his head. "Must be a Protectorate thing. Maybe he knows about Dr. Ndasa?"

I shrugged. "I don't know. He told me not to worry too much, because he has my back. So he's keeping tabs on me—somehow. I don't know what he can do, though, considering that within ten minutes or so he's not even going to be in the same system. And if Lanar knows where we're going . . . well, what if PrimeCorp does have an informant in the Protectorate?"

Hirin chuckled. "Don't they have a saying in the Protectorate—'Worry never won a battle'?"

"Something like that." All I knew was, I wished I had some of Lanar's confidence.

We arrived at the wormhole into Mu Cassiopeia around midnight by the *Tane Ikai's* clock, eleven days after the transfusion. I hadn't bothered going to bed, since I knew we were this close, but apart from Viss, taking his nighttime shift on the bridge, the ship was silent; I thought everyone else had retired. I'd spent the evening alone in my cabin, curled up in the big armchair, reading. It wasn't easy to keep my mind on the book, but I knew nothing else had any chance at all of distracting me. The swiftly approaching wormhole presented a host of potential problems that I'd already been thinking about for a week and a half.

While I was encouraged by Hirin's progress, I was still worried. If this wormhole skip caused another heart attack he might not survive it, and if he did, there was no way I was going to undertake a further skip with him on board. That meant that the *Tane Ikai* and I would have to remain in the Mu Cassiopeia system indefinitely. There were two inhabited planets in the system, Kiando and Cengare, and while either one of them made a nice place to visit, I wasn't sure I wanted to be stuck on them. I also didn't think any of my crew would want that, which would mean letting them go, and that would be heart-wrenching. After a lot of trial and error, I'd put together a crew that really worked well together, and losing them would hurt.

Furthermore, while I could probably find a few jobs running goods between the two planets, a far trader would be expensive to use for in-system runs, and a waste of resources to boot. Even with just me and Hirin to run her, though we had done it before, I might have to trade her in for something smaller, and I would truly hate to do that.

If my mother wasn't on Kiando, I wouldn't be able to follow her trail any further, even if she'd left one. PrimeCorp would eventually track me down and I'd have nowhere to run.

I had managed to forget all of that temporarily in the pages of my book, and I looked up, startled, when Viss's voice came to me over the ship's comm.

"Captain, we're here," he said in a quiet voice. I think everyone on board was worried about the skip, and it touched me how much they cared about Hirin for his own sake and for mine.

"Do you want to tackle it now, or wait till morning?" he continued. "It won't cost us much time to wait."

It was tempting to put it off a little longer, but as I was considering it, a knock sounded on my door. Hirin's knock, I thought, and sure enough he poked his head in without waiting for my answer.

"Are we there yet?" he said with a grin.

"We're there. Do you want to wait till morning before we run the skip?"

He shrugged. "I doubt anyone's actually asleep, although I think Rei could pilot a skip even in that state if she had to. Why don't we just get it over with?"

He looked so confident, so like the old Hirin, that I felt

marginally better. "*Okej*, Viss, we'll go now. I'm on my way. I guess you should let the others know."

Viss chuckled over the ship's comm. "Actually, Captain, they're all here already. Except Dr. Ndasa. I'll tell him."

"*Dio!* Am I that predictable?" I smiled despite the worry.

The bridge hummed with quiet efficiency when Hirin and I got there. Maja sat in a skimchair close to Baden's at the comm station. Their heads, his dark and hers fair, almost touched as he explained something to her and I was struck by the sudden realization that I'd seen them together frequently in the past few days. I'd just been too preoccupied to wonder about it. Now I did. My motherly instincts jumped into the red zone when I considered Baden's womanizing ways, but I fought them down. Maja was certainly old enough to look out for herself. I'd keep an eye on the situation, though. Those instincts don't die easy.

I tugged my attention firmly away from my daughter and to the viewscreen, searching for the telltale dark blotch of the wormhole. From this vantage point, it hung in an area of space with fewer faraway stars in the background, so the spot where no stars shone was not as pronounced, and it took me a moment to find it. We all took our assigned spots—almost the same ones we'd occupied when we entered the Split, but Maja didn't leave her seat beside Baden although she turned to watch her father. Hirin gave me a thumbs-up signal and I told Rei to take us in.

This hole was a "normal" one, not like the truncated Split, and the swirl of colours was as spectacular as in any other wormhole I'd ever traversed. This time, though, they brought back the memory of my painful dream and I kept one anxious eye on Hirin. He seemed perfectly fine, and everyone relaxed visibly the further we travelled through the tunnel. Perhaps fifteen skips later we sped out the other end and into the star-spangled darkness again. Rei laughed with relief and the men cheered. Maja gave Baden a quick hug and my intuition nudged me again. Even Dr. Ndasa heaved a sigh as if a great weight had lifted from him.

Only Yuskeya kept her eyes on her screen. She frowned as her fingers danced over the holo controls.

"Anything wrong, Yuskeya?" I asked.

She shook her head. "I don't know—I don't think so." She turned around to look at me and shot a significant glance at Dr. Ndasa. "Just a reading that looked off, but it seems fine now."

Hirin was grinning widely. "I'm not sure if you're happy I made it through in one piece or if you're just looking forward to the pleasures of Kiandon *jarlees* wine. Either way, what do you say I treat you all to a drink when we get planetside, and you can use it to toast my health?"

There was hearty agreement all around as the others headed for their cabins, but I hung back to talk to Yuskeya. When only she, Viss, and I remained, she said, "The sensors caught a ship signature somewhere behind us when we entered the wormhole, but then it just—stopped. The wormhole might have cut it off, but it also could have been deliberately damped."

"Could you get anything on it?" Viss asked.

She pursed her lips. "It *might* have been a PrimeCorp sig, but I can't say. I thought I should mention it, though."

"They're a long way behind if the signature was just coming into range," Viss mused. "But I'll keep the in-system scanners on maximum, just in case."

"Thanks, you two. I appreciate everyone staying on the alert."

I left them then, my mind already leaping past PrimeCorp and Maja and *jarlees* wine to the answers I hoped I might find on the next planet. Now I just had to come up with an innocent way to get Dr. Ndasa to take me with him when he went to find the researcher he'd travelled so far to meet. And to decide what I'd say to her if it turned out to be the woman I'd been chasing for fifty years.

Getting an invite to the Chairman's palace proved an easy task. I offered to help Dr. Ndasa get his massive pile of luggage and equipment unloaded and safely transported to its new home, and he accepted gladly.

"I didn't like to trouble the Chairman for assistance, when I had just arrived," he confided in me. "He's already invited me to attend an informal gathering he's holding tonight, and pressed me to bring any acquaintances I liked. I think he's rather keen to have a wide variety of visitors at these salons whenever he can. They're a regular event, or so I've heard. Do you think the others would like to go?"

I told him I could virtually guarantee it, but I could tell there was something else on his mind.

"It's only, well . . . he calls them informal, but I believe the

Chairman likes his guests to—er—dress for the occasion, if you know what I mean." He blushed, the pink undertones of his amber skin deepening into a human-like flush.

I smiled. "Doctor, you needn't worry. Just because we favour plain biosuits, or in my case, jeans and t-shirts, while we're working, doesn't mean the crew of the *Tane Ikai* can't rise to the occasion. I know that Rei, for one, will be absolutely thrilled at the prospect of dressing up for a change. Don't worry. We won't embarrass you."

"Oh, now, I didn't mean—"

"Not another word about it. What time shall we be ready? We'll pile all your goods into the groundcar from Cargo Pod Two and arrive in style."

I went the rounds of the crew and told them about our invitation. When I stopped off in Engineering, I asked Viss, "How soon will Cargo Pod One be cleared out? I don't want those crates in there a minute longer than they have to be."

He grinned. "Already scheduled, Captain. They'll be gone within an hour. Do you want to know the details?"

I stopped him with a wave of my hand. "No, thanks. Just let me know when it's gone and I'll be happy."

"Aye, aye," he said with a mock salute, and I continued my mission.

Everyone else was delighted by the idea of a party, but I hit a snag when I told Maja about the evening's plans.

She shook her head. "I don't think I'll go."

"Why not? It might do us all some good to actually have some fun for an evening."

She turned to look out the viewport above the dresser. "I don't have anything to wear."

I knew that wasn't it. "I'm sure you could borrow something from Rei or Yuskeya." I tried to joke with her. "I'd loan you something myself, but my closet's not exactly overflowing with dresses."

She smiled briefly and shrugged. "Maybe I just don't feel like a party."

My gut reaction was to let the issue drop, as usual, but this time I didn't. I'd seen a glimpse of a Maja I didn't know when she'd jumped down onto the catwalk beside me, and I wanted to see more of that person. I was never going to do that by walking away from her.

I leaned my back against the door for support and said, "You don't have to come, Maja, but I'd like it if you did."

"Is that an order, Captain?" she asked, but there wasn't any bite in the words. I felt like they were an automatic response, the way mine had almost been.

"No, it's just a request. Honestly, I don't know what or who we're going to find there. If it's your grandmother, I'd like you there with me. And if it's anything else—like a PrimeCorp trap— I'd be happy to have another Warrior Chi graduate watching my back." I chanced another smile.

She looked at me thoughtfully. "You're not quite the way I remember you, Mother," she said. "Sometimes I don't know . . ." her voice trailed off and she shrugged. "I don't know what to expect."

I nodded. "I'm finding the same thing. You're surprising me." I grinned. "I like it."

"I guess I have a couple of things that might be suitable for tonight," she said finally.

I smiled. I felt like I was dealing with a skittish animal, this new Maja, and I didn't want to scare her off. Happiness welled up in my chest, but I kept my tone light. "Great." I opened the door. "Thanks, Maja."

She smiled. "No problem."

With a lighter heart than I'd expected, I went off to face the daunting depths of my own closet.

The crew was as good as my word. When we gathered in the cargo pod I had to blink at how absolutely stunning we all looked. Rei was resplendent in a dress of artfully arranged amber and gold scarves that seemed dangerously close to falling down around her ankles whenever she moved, and a gold chain that looked like something from ancient Egypt.

When I asked her about it and she said, "Oh, it's a souvenir from one time on Xaqual . . . there was this exec from IndioCorp—"

I held up a hand. "Never mind. You can tell me sometime over a bottle of *jarlees* wine."

"It's a good story," she said, grinning evilly. "It might even take two bottles."

Baden wore a pale grey biosuit interwoven with nano-optic

fibres that subtly illuminated the planes of his body. Yuskeya looked quite regal in a swirling, multicoloured robe that molded itself to her curves and swept upward to meet the dark fall of her hair, and even Viss had traded his blue shipsuit for a dark synthsilk sherwani jacket and pants. I hadn't even known he owned such a thing.

Maja was radiant in a layered cornflower-blue and silver tunic and nodded to me with the hint of a twinkle in her eyes. I wondered whether her good mood had more to do with our tentative peace or the effusive compliments Baden paid her. She seemed anxious below the surface, however, shooting covert looks at me when she thought I wasn't looking. Was it something to do with Baden? Or Hirin? Our conversation? Or the prospect of meeting her grandmother? There was no opportunity to ask her, though.

I had been worried about what Hirin would wear—I knew he hadn't brought much on board with him and nothing, I was sure, that could be considered formal. He'd told me not to concern myself over it, however, and appeared now in a jacket that took my breath away. I knew it—from the crimson silk embroidered with two rampant ebony dragons, to the elegant wide, white cuffs, to the small yin/yang symbol placed just above his heart— he'd worn it when we were married. My eyes filled with tears and I turned so that Dr. Ndasa wouldn't see.

Viss had offered to drive, and I went to the furthest back seat in the groundcar. As I'd hoped, Hirin clambered back to sit with me, and Dr. Ndasa sat up with Viss. Hirin leaned over and whispered to me.

"I brought it to wear when you jettisoned me," he said wryly. "I didn't know I'd be going to any parties."

"It looks wonderful," I whispered back. "I couldn't believe it."

"And *you* look absolutely *bela*," he said. "Where did you get that?"

"That" was a dress I'd bought on Quma a couple of years ago, and I have to admit that I loved it. It was an intermixed fabric of bio-synthetic fibre and velvet in deep purple, the skirt studded with tiny optics that twinkled like stars. It clung close and rose in a high neckline, while the sleeves shifted to an open braidwork of velvet and silver. Whatever the Chairman thought of us all, I was certain he couldn't find fault with our dress.

The spaceport lay on the outskirts of Ando City, Kiando's

capital, and while the streets were not in bad shape, the neighbourhoods we passed through held a general air of shabbiness, as though there wasn't quite enough money to keep everything up to standard so it all just slipped a little. The city was busy, even at this hour when the sidewalks began to shimmer with a nighttime guideglow and some of the shops and businesses had closed.

The atmosphere changed perceptibly as we drew closer to the Chairman's palace, however. Duntmindi Corporation, the mining conglomerate that owned the heavy metal mines riddling much of this part of Kiando, ran the planet with the Nearspace Authority's blessing. Chairman Buig had been at the top of the corporation for thirty years, and rumour had it that he wanted to retain that top spot indefinitely. Hence his interest in anti-aging technology, I supposed. He reportedly ran the corporation like a well-maintained skip drive, engendered loyalty among his workers, and kept the shareholders happy. His only enemy, it seemed, was time, and he was doing his best to eliminate the effects of that.

It was apparent that money clustered around the palace of the Chairman like moons clung to their planet. As we approached, the homes grew larger, the streets broader, and the people obviously wealthier. Some stared at us with open curiosity. I'm certain a groundcar from a far trader was something of an oddity on these streets.

The palace itself, when we reached it, was what I would call a mansion, although if it pleased the Chairman to call it his palace then who was I to argue? Whatever one called it, it was magnificent, an architecture stolen straight from late twenty-first century Earth, with its juxtapositions of styles in chrome and brick, greenspaces and ultraplas. I noted with interest that security was minimal and we passed through into the parking area after Dr. Ndasa gave his name to the single guard who appeared to be on duty.

I say "appeared," because the Chairman was obviously a perceptive man and doubtless liked to give the impression of open gates while maintaining a reality that was rather more secure.

Luxury groundcars and flitters sat around the parking area in small groups, as if holding their own salon. Viss settled ours near a group of flitters, and I wondered fancifully if it would have some interesting tales to add to the conversation.

Inside the palace, a notebug recorded our names and likenesses, and a multi-armed 'bot arrived to relieve us of outerwear and offer a variety of refreshments. When we had made our selections, another guidebot led us down the green-marble-floored hallway to an ornate set of gilded double doors, muffling but not quite muting the sounds of conversation within. The doors slid open silently when the guidebot reached their sensor range, and we had a sudden panoramic view of the gathering beyond.

The room was enormous. Vaulted ceilings arched gracefully overhead, painted a dark midnight blue and dotted with "stars"— tiny lights that sparked and twinkled, but did little to illuminate the room below. In contrast, the floor glowed with squares of pale, multicoloured light, and wall sconces arrayed around the room completed the lighting. Small groupings of chairs and tables invited people to sit, talk, and eat from several bountiful sideboards, which numerous attendees were doing. An open area in the middle of the room might have been for dancing, had the music been right for it, but it was mostly occupied by small knots of people holding drinks and chatting. A few heads turned when the doors opened, but most of the crowd seemed too engrossed in their discussions to pay attention to newcomers. Some of those who had turned to look stared at us with surprising rudeness, especially for Kiandon society. The five colonies on Kiando had a reputation for their strict social rituals and concern with etiquette.

One man did more than turn and look when we entered. He was tall, with greying hair and a confident bearing, and he turned and crossed toward us immediately. His two-piece biosilk suit was almost unrelieved black, but for a white Duntmindi Corporation logo over the left breast and a neat row of four white circles below it. The asymmetrical hemline of his jacket fell to his knee on one side, and to his ankle on the other. This, then, must be Chairman Buig himself, and Dr. Ndasa stepped forward to greet him.

"You must be Dr. Ndasa! Come in, come in! And your guests as well." His smile took us all in, although I had the strange impression that it faltered when his gaze fell on me. He stopped far enough away from the doors so that we could enter easily and allow them to close behind us. He clasped his hands over his heart and bent forward twice from the waist, in the classic Kiandon greeting. "Welcome, guests."

"I am Dr. Ndasa, and I'm very pleased to meet you, Chairman." Dr. Ndasa returned the ritual bow smoothly, and added the Vilisian gesture of greeting, the touch of a palm to eyes, lips and heart. Then he turned to the rest of us. "Allow me to present my friends from the far trader *Tane Ikai*," he said, "starting with the incomparable Captain Luta Paixon."

I made the Kiandon greeting for an uninvited guest, the same but with only one bow. Buig's eyebrows had lifted slightly at the name of my ship, and I knew he'd made the connection. He obviously took his anti-aging research very seriously indeed to catch such an obscure reference. I wondered what he'd think if I told him my age.

"Thank you so much for your generous invitation, Chairman," I said. "Your home is quite magnificent."

When I lifted my head from the bow I caught a glimpse of an unabashed stare from his pale, ice-blue eyes, before he rearranged his face into a gracious smile. He looked gratified and perhaps relieved that I'd known the custom and responded properly. "Please promise that you'll tell me more about your ship later, Captain Paixon," he said, and Dr. Ndasa continued with the introductions. Buig shot me another glance when Dr. Ndasa introduced Hirin, too polite to ask about the relationship. His gaze lingered long and appreciatively on Rei, Yuskeya, and Maja, and I wondered if womanizing was one of the Chairman's techniques for a longer life. It didn't seem to be the same kind of stare he'd treated me to, though. I wondered if I should be insulted.

The Chairman gestured for us to mingle and afford ourselves the pleasures of the various refreshment tables, and with a final sidelong glance at me, moved off to chat with Dr. Ndasa first, as was only proper.

Hirin leaned over to whisper in my ear. "I'm getting something to eat. We've had to leave enough parties early and I haven't forgotten my old rule of getting fed first."

I suppressed a giggle and watched him stroll over to the nearest buffet table and help himself to a plate. He piled it high with a reddish salad, slabs of spiced meat, and a selection of intriguing-looking appetizers. If his appetite were any indication, his recovery was going well. Maja followed him and asked him something I couldn't hear, then glanced over her shoulder at me.

Viss, Rei, Yuskeya and Baden were still huddled in a little knot, sipping their drinks and sending covert looks around the room. I strolled over to them.

"Relax, you people," I hissed. "It looks like you're casing the place to come back later and loot it."

"Did you notice this floor?" Rei asked. "This much lumistone probably cost as much as the *Tane Ikai*!"

I had to admit it was beautiful, perfectly cut and matched blocks of multicoloured stone that emitted its own soft light when stepped on. The floor seemed like a living thing, breathing colour as it interacted with the other creatures in the room. The light was never harsh, just a glow that limned the lower half of the room in a wash of blue, pink and mauve.

"Well, don't just stand here gaping," I ordered. "Walk, talk, and find out who everybody is. I've never known any of you to be exactly shy or retiring!"

They laughed and moved off, breaking into pairs to go in search of conversation. Standing alone for the moment, I had the eerie feeling that half the people in the room were looking at me out of the corners of their eyes. While the purple dress was not intended to deflect attention, it certainly wasn't the most noteworthy in the room and had never caused this much of a stir before.

I felt a touch at my elbow. Chairman Buig had circled back to me.

"Thank you so much for bringing Dr. Ndasa all the way here from Earth," he said. "It's a long run, I know."

His pale blue gaze was earnest and intense. I felt myself withdraw a little from it. "We were pleased to have the opportunity, and a new wormhole has cut a considerable amount of time off the journey."

"I'd heard about that. It could be we'll have more visitors in the near future." I couldn't tell if he thought that was a good thing or not.

"But tell me about your excellent ship," he continued. "I recognize her name. One of the longest-lived Japanese women on Earth in the twentieth century."

I nodded. "That's right. Of course the ship herself is not nearly that old."

He laughed politely. "Did you name her? Or did she come to

you with her personality already set?"

"No, I named her myself. I've always had an interest in longevity research." He would take all night to get around to actually asking me, I could tell. Not a man to speak before thinking.

"Personally, I do not understand why more people are not fascinated by it," he said, nodding approvingly. "Aging, death, they are the only things that bind us all, are they not?"

Well, most of us. "Dr. Ndasa mentioned that he'd be joining other colleagues in the anti-aging field here. I'm impressed that you're throwing so much support behind the work. No scientific research comes cheap."

"No," he said seriously, "it is an expensive endeavour. I have sixteen top researchers here now, and Dr. Ndasa makes seventeen. It is one of the largest groups working on the problem in tandem anywhere in Nearspace. Although some people continue to think it's just a silly hobby on my part, they are wrong. Only Earth's PrimeCorp and the Schulyer Group on Mars are larger."

"Really? Are the researchers here tonight? I would love to meet some of them, if I might."

He nodded, looking around almost agitatedly. "Yes, there's someone I'm particularly interested in having you meet. Some of them are here already . . . I see Dr. Admelison over there, speaking with *Sinjoro* Paixon. You and he are related? It is an unusual name."

"Distant relatives," I lied easily. "He's no stranger to aging himself, but had a yearning to return to space one more time. I was glad to be able to offer him a berth on the *Tane Ikai*."

"Most commendable," he said. "Now, where are the others? I had thought they would all be present tonight. Perhaps, if you will excuse me, I'll round them all up, especially . . . well. Enjoy yourself in my absence."

He moved off, but I saw him pull out a small datapad and input something. Was he calling someone? Or making notes about me like a good corporate executive, so he could "remember" me later?

I strolled over to Baden and Rei, who each held a plate piled high with brightly-coloured exotic fruits covered with a sweet-smelling sauce. "Does anything seem kind of strange here, to you?"

Rei grinned as she delicately licked her fingers. "Here's the big one, there are more people staring at you than there are at me. That's definitely a first, although you know I think you're beautiful, Luta."

"I know, there's nothing catty about you, Rei." The room hummed with an undercurrent of conversations kept deliberately muted as guests cast covert glances my way. "That's what I've noticed, too. It feels *bizara*."

"I take it you haven't seen her," Baden whispered.

"No, even taking into account how she might have changed, I don't see anyone who could be her. But Chairman Buig said he thought all the researchers would be here tonight, and he's gone to hunt them up. I should know soon if she's here or not."

Hirin came up to us then and unobtrusively gave my hand a little squeeze. "Nothing yet?"

I shook my head. "No. Soon, though, I think."

He hesitated a moment. "That man I was talking to—Dr. Admelison—he said none of the researchers was over seventy."

"She might not look seventy."

"I know," he said. "I just hate to see you have another disappointment."

Maja stepped up behind me and said in a low voice, "Mother, I was thinking about what you said earlier—that this could be a trap. If you don't see her, maybe we should leave. I have a bad feeling—"

A hush fell over the hall, as suddenly as if someone had damped the volume with the flick of a switch. Another doorway stood open, one that led from somewhere inside the palace, and a woman stepped through it. Even Chairman Buig stopped speaking to someone at the other side of the room and turned to look. It was as if the entire room had been waiting for her to arrive, and now held its breath.

She was exquisitely dressed, in a sweeping emerald dress of organic velvet trimmed with spun gold brocade. A tall collar studded with tiny sparkling sunrubies and moonpearls framed her face and reached high above the mass of auburn curls looped and twisted artfully on top of her head. She was stunningly beautiful. She entered the room confidently, gracefully, a little smile on her lips, then halted her steps to look around at the sudden and unexpected quiet.

My heart pounded once, then felt as if it paused in mid-beat as the moment stretched into eternity.

She was me.

I heard Hirin's sharp intake of breath as if it came from very far away, felt Maja's hand touch my arm. With agonizing slowness, the woman's quizzical gaze swept the room, landing on each face in turn, until it came to us.

To me.

All the speed that had been drawn from the moment came back in a rush. The woman's hand flew to her throat and she took a step forward, mouthing a name.

Luta.

Then she crumpled silently into a heap on the gently pulsing lumistone floor, and the room erupted into chaos around her.

Chapter Fourteen

Schrödinger's Cat Is Alive and Well and Living Under an Assumed Name

I don't know if Chairman Buig ever had a stir like that at one of his salons before, but I doubt it. As my mother collapsed, the noise level in the room swelled from a moment of stunned silence to at least double what it had been. Buig himself actually *ran* the length of the room to get to her, but Yuskeya, bless her, was there first, and had Mother's head resting comfortably on a pillow she'd swiped from somewhere before Buig ordered her out of the way.

For myself, I was rooted to the spot, feeling like I'd swung off the safe side of the Split into a soft grey nothingness. There was no exultation at the conclusion of my fifty-year quest, no feeling of relief or disbelief or even satisfaction. It was as if the world had dropped out from under my feet and left me hanging in space without an EVA suit. I simply didn't know what to feel. The only things that seemed real were the presences of Hirin and Maja beside me.

There was no shortage of doctors in the room, and Dr. Ndasa was there as well. His presence gave the scene an even more surreal feeling—he'd travelled all this way to find her, and here he was, having to minister to her only moments after her appearance. In short order Mother was conscious again, although so pale it seemed you could see through her skin. As soon as she was back on her feet Buig took her arm, gestured for us to follow with a peremptory jerk of his head, and led her from the room through another door. The stares of the other salon attendees were no longer guarded or covert, but open and unabashed. I held my head high and walked beside Hirin, with Maja still gripping my other arm tightly. My breath came in short gasps. I couldn't seem to fill my lungs. I heard Hirin tell Dr. Ndasa to come with us, but his voice seemed to come from a long way off.

The room beyond the door was a small sitting-room, and as soon as the door closed behind us my mother let go of Buig's arm, turned to me, and held out her arms. Her hands trembled like leaves in a windstorm, but when I stepped into her embrace the shaking stopped and she held me as if she meant never to let me go.

I don't know what effect tears have on organic velvet, but mine flowed freely onto her collar.

"Remarkable," Chairman Buig said in a low voice. "They must be twins. I could hardly believe my eyes when she walked into the ballroom. Demmar, you never told me!"

No-one answered him because, stupidly, we hadn't rehearsed any story to tell if we actually found her. I guess after so long, I hadn't really expected it. I hoped, but I had long ago given up on expectations.

She recovered more quickly than I did, holding me off at arm's length and studying me, but speaking absently to the Chairman. "I'm sorry to have caused such a scene, Gusain. It's a long time— a very long time—since Luta and I have seen each other."

There was still a little part of me taking notes, and it spoke volumes that they used each others' first names so easily. I wondered if all his researchers were that informal.

"You must have known I was here?" The question was casual, but the intensity of her eyes locked on mine revealed its importance.

"I'd heard a rumour." I was surprised at how normal my voice sounded. I smiled. "And I had a job in the vicinity anyway."

She laughed then, a sound I remembered with a sharp pang of joy and pain intermingled. She hugged me again. "Well, as long as you didn't go out of your way!"

Chairman Buig cleared his throat. "Well, Demmar, if everything is all right?"

"I'm fine now. Go on back to your guests. Do you mind if we take a little time . . .?"

"No, no, that's fine. Stay here as long as you wish." He chuckled. "I'll go and see if I can stop the rumour mills from grinding."

"Good luck with that," Hirin murmured as the Chairman left. Through the open door, we glimpsed huddled knots of people in the throes of wild conjecture.

When the door closed behind him Mother's composure slipped again. "Luta, can it really be you?" Her voice was harsh with tears that I suspected she'd been holding back too long to cry even now.

I squeezed her hand. "It's really me. These are my friends—my crew—and my family. They. . . know a lot."

She glanced around at the others. "If you trust them, I trust them," she said finally.

"This," I added, pulling Hirin forward, "this is my husband, Hirin Paixon."

He swept as low a bow as he could manage. "I am as honoured as I could be to finally meet you," he said.

Her eyes filled with tears then. "Oh, Luta, I'm so sorry! No, I mean. . . Hirin, I'm so pleased to meet you. . . I knew, of course. . . how it must be. . . it's just—I've made things hard for you both, impossible, I know that—"

He shook his head and slipped an arm around me. "Please. It's been my profound pleasure and honour to be married to Luta," he said elegantly. "I would not trade one moment of our life together. I want you to believe that."

She smiled through her tears. "Oh, I do. I can see it in your eyes. Thank you, Hirin."

"And this is our daughter, Maja." She was still a quiet presence just behind me. "Your granddaughter."

Maja smiled and nodded reservedly to Mother. It was hard to reconcile the relationship between them, looking at the two together. Now that I had seen her at closer range, Mother did look older than I did—a gathering of fine wrinkles hemmed her eyes, and her hands showed the rigours of time more than mine—but she'd been older when she'd done . . . whatever she'd done. She and Maja could have been of an age. Maja might even have been the older of the two, and speaking the words made it absurdly obvious.

"Maja, I can't believe I'm meeting you at last. My beautiful granddaughter! I knew about you and Karro, naturally," Mother said, eyes still glistening. "I'm sorry I had to watch from the shadows, but please believe that it wasn't because I wasn't interested in my family."

Maja seemed to be searching for a way to respond, so I came to her rescue.

"Here's someone else who has travelled a long way just to meet you," I said, turning to find Dr. Ndasa. He'd retreated to the back of the room, behind everyone else. He seemed pale—or the Vilisian equivalent of pale, a sickly greyish cast replacing the usual pink undertones of his skin. I stepped toward him, hand outstretched. His scent, when I caught it, was a jumble that I couldn't sort out, but he said nothing.

"As you might have guessed, Dr. Ndasa, Demmar and I are related."

He looked at me intently, the amber skin around his eyes crinkling. "So, Captain, all this time, while we were travelling— you knew who she was . . .?"

I smiled and shook my head. "No. I hoped, and I suspected. But I didn't know. In fact, I have you to thank."

"You, too, were searching for her." He shook his head slightly, as if trying to clear it, and swallowed with an audible gulp. I caught a breath of the anxious grapefruit-like scent that had clung to him on the bridge just before his first wormhole skip. "This is—not what I expected."

Mother made the Vilisian greeting gesture in a fluid motion and said, "I'm very pleased to meet you, Doctor."

"It is a very great pleasure to meet you, *Sinjorino* Holsey," he said valiantly as he returned the gesture. "I—I . . . oh, dear, this is awkward." Unexpectedly he slumped down into a chair that was fortuitously behind him and dropped his head into his hands.

There was a brief silence. I felt the crew go into alert mode. Don't ask me how I knew, but I knew. I dropped to my knees beside the Vilisian. "What is it? What's wrong?"

I glanced up at Mother. Alarm had spread visibly across her face. Dr. Ndasa didn't move. I put a hand on his arm and shook him a little.

"Dr. Ndasa, what's wrong? You have to tell me." I used my captain's voice. "That's an order."

He sat up then, and heaved a sigh. "I have a message for Doctor Holsey," he said quietly. "But under another name, which I'm . . . not sure I should mention here." He glanced around the room and gulped again. The grapefruit smell was almost overpowering now.

"A message? From whom?" Mother's voice was harsh.

"PrimeCorp?" I could barely say the word.

"From the Schulyer Group," Dr. Ndasa said, barely above a whisper. The Vilisian didn't look up at me. He smelled damp and cold, like wet earth. Viss quietly moved to stand behind the Vilisian's chair.

"Dr. Ndasa." I waited, but he didn't look up. "Does the Schulyer Group know where we are right now?"

"Yes," he mumbled, keeping his gaze fixed on the tabletop. "But they're not coming here. No-one from Schulyer is following us," he added quickly.

"You're sure about that?"

He nodded.

"What about PrimeCorp?"

"I have nothing to do with them."

I could tell Viss was resisting the urge to shake him. "You said you had a message for Doctor Holsey?"

The Vilisian heaved a great sigh and finally lifted his head. He spoke when he found Mother, perched uneasily on the edge of one of the brocaded armchairs. "I have a message," he said, "for Doctor Emmage Mahane. I was shown a holo," he glanced back to me, "although as it turned out that wasn't really necessary."

So that explained why he'd looked so startled at seeing me, the odd stares I'd occasionally catch. Not an alien thing at all. A curiosity thing.

"I did not realize that you were unaware of her presence here," he said, his curious violet eyes sorrowful. "I now feel that I have betrayed your hospitality."

"Deliver your message," Mother said coldly. She sat back in the chair and folded her arms across her chest. "This is all I needed, another corp tailing me everywhere I go."

Dr. Ndasa shook his head vehemently, his dark braid swinging. "No, no, please, it isn't like that. I'm here to ask for your help, nothing more."

Mother narrowed her eyes at him. "Go ahead."

"The Schulyer Group has been developing a new anti-aging technology for twenty years," he said. The words came in a rush now, as if he were tired of holding them in. "It's similar to Longate, but yes, they've solved the problems Longate caused. They bought out all of Nicadico's research years ago so they could see where Longate went wrong. They're certain their basic data is sound," he added emphatically, perhaps because Mother had already begun to shake her head. "But there have been . . . incidents."

"Incidents? So perhaps the data is not as sound as you think."

The Vilisian tilted his head to one side. "No, that is not what I mean. They believe someone—I'm certain you can guess who they suspect—has been sabotaging their efforts. Subtly altering data. Interfering with samples. Trying to access classified data, although we do not think they have been successful. They would like to have their work—especially the groundwork—verified by a trustworthy outside source, by someone who has been working in this field longer than anyone else. By you, Dr. Mahane."

"How did they find me?" Mother wanted to know.

Dr. Ndasa waggled his shoulders in the Vilisian equivalent of a shrug. "They did not tell me that, only who you were and why it was important to find you."

"And why did they send you, in particular?" She regarded him with narrowed eyes.

He flushed, his skin darkening from amber to ochre. "Perhaps because they knew that once I knew about you, I would have to meet you. I share your obsession, Dr. Mahane, and I've made no secret of that. And perhaps because I am so very . . . non-threatening." He twisted a tentative half-smile at her, then grew serious again. "Please, Doctor, I don't have to tell you how important this could be. I know you already understand."

"Only too well." Mother sighed and turned to me. "Luta, I assume you were not privy to Schulyer Group's machinations?"

I couldn't read her voice. An outraged protest rose to my lips but I didn't speak the words. How could she know anything about me, really, after all this time? Could I blame her for being suspicious?

"No. He told Hirin he'd heard there was a female anti-aging researcher doing work for the Chairman on Kiando, and he'd wrangled an invitation to join his colleagues there. Hirin passed it on to me. It was only a guess hitching a ride on the back of a rumour, but it seemed worth a try."

"That's all?" She raised her eyebrows. "It's a pretty thin rumour."

"I started following thinner rumours than that a long time ago." I regretted the words when I saw the look of pain that flashed across her face, and shook my head. "Don't apologize again. I'm pretty sure I understand some of the reasons—"

A staccato knock sounded on the door and it opened to reveal Chairman Buig. He stepped inside and closed the door behind him quickly. He didn't look happy. The skin around his pale eyes was taut and worry lines creased his forehead.

"Pardon the intrusion," he said, and his eyes quickly found my mother. "Demmar, we need to speak. It's urgent."

Her face stayed calm, but I saw her fist clench ever so slightly. "Gusain, what is it?"

He flicked a glance over the rest of us. "Perhaps it would be better to speak privately—"

Mother shook her head. "It's all right. Whatever it is, you can say it here."

He pulled a deep sigh, looking even more unhappy, if that was possible. "I've had a very unsettling communication from a vessel that's on its way here," he said. "I really think this should be private, but . . ." He must have recognized the stubborn look in my mother's eye, because he seemed to make up his mind. "The vessel is from Earth, a PrimeCorp far cruiser named *Trident*— apparently belongs to their police branch. They just came through the wormhole from Delta Pavonis. They say they have a warrant for your arrest—although they used a different name— for corporate data theft and other Planetary Statute crimes. And a second warrant to obtain genetic samples. They had a holo for identification, it's—it's definitely you, Demmar. Their assertion is that I am constrained by interplanetary Nearspace law to hold you until they arrive, and deliver you to them."

Mother didn't say anything, and Buig turned to me. "They have a similar warrant for you, although it's only for the genetic samples. I believe if you allow them to take those, they have no interest in detaining you."

I caught Maja's eye. She shook her head almost imperceptibly. *I had nothing to do with this.*

Damne. My stomach roiled and I felt sick, a weird echo of Alin Sedmamin's trick with the virus. This feeling, though, came from my own emotions. *They must have followed me, somehow, despite my precautions. I've led PrimeCorp straight to my mother.*

"Chairman Buig, did they say how long it would be before they arrive?" I asked.

"Several hours. It's a far cruiser, and they're still in the outer system."

My mother spoke then. Her voice was flat, emotionless, as if she'd gone completely cold. "And what did you tell them you would do?"

He didn't flinch under her gaze. "I told them I wasn't certain of your whereabouts, either of you, but that I would see what I could do to locate you." He flashed a quick grin. "It's called, *stalling for time.*"

Mother let out her breath in a quiet chuckle and I felt my stomach unclench. It looked like Chairman Buig, at least, was our ally.

"Why would they give you so much notice? Why not just show up and make their demands?" Baden asked.

"That's PrimeCorp for you," Mother said with a humourless smile. "Supremely confident in their own power. It wouldn't occur to them that Gusain would question their authority or not comply. He works for a *smaller* corporation."

"Well, they don't know us very well either, then," Rei said. "So what's the plan? Make a run for it?"

"If they're still that far out, we can outrun them easily," Viss added. "Far cruisers aren't built for speed."

Mother turned to me with a half-smile. "You're docked nearby?"

I took hold of Mother's hand. "My far trader's at the Havering dock. And when we say 'we,' you're included in that. I'm not letting you go so soon. Not for a long time yet." I smiled. "Just so you know."

She squeezed my hand in return. "You couldn't if you tried. Can you give me a few minutes to grab some of my things? I'll be quick."

Gusain Buig opened his mouth as if he might protest, but I said "I'll be right here," and without hesitation she opened the door that led to the salon. The Chairman followed on her heels and they merged into the crowd. I saw him catch up to her and cup a hand under her elbow as he leaned in close to speak.

"But we have to be fast," Yuskeya said. "It's silly for everyone to wait here. Why don't I go with them, and I'll bring her back to the groundcar? If we meet back there we'll get underway faster."

"And if I ask the Chairman to give me access to his communications crew, I might get some better details on the ship and how soon it might be here," Baden suggested.

I nodded. "Good ideas. Go catch up to them, and we'll meet back at the car." The two of them hurried after Mother and the Chairman.

I looked at Dr. Ndasa. "Doctor, I'm afraid I'll have to insist that you come with us until we have this sorted out," I said. "We're in enough trouble now. I can't take any more chances."

He looked startled, then nodded.

"Bring him," I told Viss. He took Dr. Ndasa's arm with smooth efficiency, and the Vilisian doctor didn't try to pull away.

Maja slid into the crowd and found one of the waiters, and we asked him to show us the quickest way out, avoiding the salon. He seemed unfazed by the strange request—perhaps guests often wanted to leave unseen—and led the way through a twisting maze of hallways. All were sumptuously carpeted and gently illuminated by elaborately blown glass sconces. Finally we rounded a corner, and the waiter let us out a back door to the parking area. All the time I followed him, I tried to calm the pounding of my heart, sick with the fear that I'd led my mother's enemies to her safe haven.

Kiando's moons were on the rise and shone brightly, painting pale puddles on the ground and deep shadows under the parked vehicles as we waited at the groundcar. None of the others were back yet, but I couldn't make myself get inside the groundcar to wait. Hirin and Dr. Ndasa climbed in, and Maja sat on the running board, but I paced nervously across the silver-limned space next to the car. I felt as if I'd just opened the box and found Schrödinger's cat alive and well, but that there was no guarantee of maintaining that state.

Rei leaned back against the groundcar and crossed her arms, watching me. "Congratulations, Captain," she said suddenly. "Slow down a minute, would you, and take a breath? You did it! I mean, you really did it, you found her. After all this time." She grinned. "PrimeCorp notwithstanding, that's a good thing."

I stopped and took a deep breath, closing my eyes. "Thanks, Rei. You're right. Although I think I'm still in shock, mostly."

Out of the corner of my eye I saw Viss glance at his datapad. "I hate to say this, but what if she doesn't come back?" he said slowly. "She said she'd be quick, and that PrimeCorp ship is getting closer by the minute."

"She'll come back." I'd seen the look in her eyes. She wasn't going to run away again—not just yet, anyway.

Baden came around the corner at a run and practically skidded to a stop, leaning on the groundcar and panting. "I thought you might leave without me," he said between breaths.

"Oh, we would have, if Yuskeya and Luta's mother had raced you back," Rei drawled. "However, since you're here, did you find out anything useful?"

He paused to stick his tongue out at her, then said, "Judging by the timestamps on the comm signals between the ship and the Chairman, we should make it off the planet before they're in sensor range. Even if they've sped up considerably since then, we should have a decent window of opportunity." He glanced toward the Chairman's palace. "As long as we don't waste too much time."

I started pacing again. What could be taking them so long? I assumed that my mother, in her years of running and hiding from PrimeCorp, could be packed and out of anywhere in short order. Unless Gusain Buig was trying to talk her out of it. Or wasn't really on our side, after all. But Yuskeya was with them, and she was more than competent to make sure my mother was able to come with us. I sent her a quick message from my datapad. *Where are you?*

Coming!

But after five minutes they still weren't back. I messaged her again. *Everything okay?* This time she didn't respond. Well, maybe she wasn't paying attention to it and had the sound off. Maybe she was busy trying to hurry mother along, or talking to the Chairman. After another five minutes of silent pacing, and two more unanswered messages, checking my datapad every thirty seconds or so as the moons climbed higher into the sky, I said, "I can't take any more of this. I'll have to go and find—"

My words were cut short by the appearance of one of Chairman Buig's uniformed security personnel, who appeared in the doorway we'd come through into the parking lot. He held the door open and beckoned a finger in my direction. I took off at a run, although I heard Viss say, "Captain, wait! It could be a—" Then his footsteps followed mine. I knew the others would be watching from the groundcar, so nothing too bad was going to happen.

When I got close enough, though, my heart tightened in a painful spasm in my chest. On the richly carpeted floor of the hallway next to the guard lay a figure whose long, tousled dark hair I recognized immediately. Her multicoloured robe lay wreathed around her like a shattered rainbow.

Yuskeya.

Chapter Fifteen

Lost and Found and Lost Again

I must have stopped in shock, because somehow Viss was there before me, kneeling beside her and feeling for a pulse at her neck. I felt a hand on my arm—Maja had come, too. The guard said to me, "She's unconscious, but otherwise she seems fine. The Chairman found her in a hallway, and said to bring her—"

"Where's the Chairman now?" I interrupted him. "And there was a scientist with her, a woman—red hair, looks a lot like me—"

He shook his head and gestured toward Yuskeya, whom Viss had now lifted up from the floor. He held her cradled against his chest as if she weighed no more than a child. I noticed distractedly that he looked unusually pale. A dark bruise stained one side of Yuskeya's forehead, and the blow that had done it had raised a nasty-looking lump, as well.

"She's the only one I saw," the guard said. "The Chairman said to contact him on this channel." He fished a torn scrap of paper out of his pocket and handed it to me.

"I have to see him—" I started, but Viss cut me off.

"Time, Captain. We don't have much. Let's get Yuskeya into the groundcar and you can call him. No point running around here looking for him."

"Just call him, Mother," Maja urged. "It'll be quicker."

Damne. I wanted to grab the guard, shake him, and demand that he take me to Gusain Buig, but Viss and Maja were right. We were on a deadline. And now I didn't know whom I could trust. Swearing under my breath, I punched the code from the scrap of paper into my datapad. The Chairman appeared on my screen almost immediately.

"What's happening, Chairman?" I asked. I was surprised at how calm my voice sounded.

His face was pale, and he puffed out a sigh of relief upon seeing me. "Captain, you're all right. Is Demmar with you?"

My fingers tightened reflexively around the datapad. "No," I said evenly. "The last I saw her, she was with you, and so was my navigator, who *is* with me, but currently unconscious."

His image jumped unsteadily on the screen, and I realized he was walking quickly as he talked to me. The glass wall sconces flickered behind his image as he passed them. "I don't understand," he said. "Your crewmen caught up with us. She— your navigator, I assume—went with Demmar. I took your communications officer, Mr. Methyr, to a console and connected him with my comm station, and told them to give him any information he needed."

We had reached the groundcar by now, and Baden heard the end of what the Chairman said. He nodded his confirmation. Buig was telling the truth—at least to that point.

"Then what?" I stood beside the car while Rei and Viss manoeuvred Yuskeya inside. She still hadn't stirred. They settled her in one of the seats, her head still leaning on Viss's shoulder, his arm around her. Baden clambered behind the wheel.

Buig ran a hand across his forehead. Tiny beads of sweat glistened on his skin and his hand shook slightly. "Then I went to find Demmar. I wanted—I wanted to say goodbye, properly. To find out where she was going to go, and when I might hear from her. But she wasn't in her room, so I thought I'd missed them. I was on my way to see if I could catch up to you in the parking area when I found your navigator, unconscious, and called a guard." He was in a darker hallway now, the light from the datapad throwing his features into caricature-like relief.

"Where are you now?" I could feel the eyes of everyone on me: Hirin, Rei, Baden, Viss, Dr. Ndasa. Waiting for me to tell them what we would do next.

"I'm trying to find her, goddammit!" Buig snapped. "But it's like she's vanished. I hoped she'd already found her way to you."

I swung around, searching the parking lot. The dual moons painted it in a clear, bright glow that reflected off the many vehicles still dotting the area. But nothing moved, the air was silent, and the lot seemed empty of anyone but us. "I don't see her. She hasn't come outside."

"Do you think she'd go straight to your ship?" Buig looked up from his screen, searchingly, as brilliant light flared in front of him. It darkened again, and he looked back down. "She's not in the labs."

"I didn't tell her the name . . . but who knows, she might know it." I tried to think clearly, logically, but my mind raced from awful possibility to awful possibility. Which was worse: that she'd been somehow kidnapped practically right in front of me, or that she'd run away from me again, despite what she'd said?

I felt a firm hand take mine and looked up to see Hirin's blue-grey eyes. They were dark and serious. "Let's go and check the ship. She might be there. We can't be much help here . . . we don't even know our way around."

I swallowed hard. He was right, as usual. "I'll call you again from my ship, Chairman," I said. "Keep looking." *And if you're lying to me . . .* I climbed into the groundcar beside Hirin and we wheeled out into the Kiandon night.

The drive back through the nearly-deserted streets to the spacedock seemed to take forever, and the silence was making me crazy. There would be a rowdy area of the city, where the clubs and bars and shopping venues were open late, since it was predominantly a mining colony and there were always miners whose shift had just ended. Our path wove through more residential and business areas, where lights had been extinguished for the night and streets lay in soft darkness. None of us spoke much. I felt torn between by the certainty that I should not be driving in the opposite direction from where I'd last seen my mother, and the crushing fact that perhaps this was exactly what she wanted. *Could she have lied to me that thoroughly? Could I have read her so wrong?* I don't know what consumed everyone ease's thoughts, but I guess we were all either too worried, too angry, or both, to talk. Hirin and I kept an eye on the road behind us, but no-one followed.

When we arrived back at the Havering spacedock Baden jumped out to disable the alarms and open the cargo pod doors. I wanted to call Chairman Buig again, but I wasn't going to do it until we'd reached one of the wire-blocked decks above the cargo level. The engineering and bridge decks had wire blockers on a constant sweep and scramble so that onboard communications were private, but the cargo deck didn't—the required electronics would limit the types of cargo we could haul. I was glad that we'd spent some of the travel time to Kiando making security modifications, but I was suddenly sorry that I'd stopped carrying torpedoes a while back, if PrimeCorp was sending far cruisers after me now. At least the personal ordnance locker remained well-stocked for emergencies.

Hirin's hand on my arm brought me out of my musings and I realized the groundcar was inside. Baden and Maja were already securing it. Viss lifted Yuskeya gently out of the car, and Rei had a hand on Dr. Ndasa's arm. It was lucky they knew instinctively what to do, because my head seemed too jumbled to think of everything. I gathered up the heavy folds of my purple dress and climbed out of the car.

"Go ahead, Captain," Baden said. "I'll help Viss bring Yuskeya up."

"Put her in First Aid," I said with a nod, and headed for the metal stairway that had been locked in place next to the ship when we docked. It led all the way up to the airlock door on the bridge deck. The rhythmic mindlessness of the climb up the stairway felt somehow soothing, and I didn't stop until I'd reached the top. Hirin was right behind me all the way. It didn't occur to me that it was a long climb for him or that I should slow down, but he kept pace without complaining. I took five minutes to change out of my dress and into jeans and a black t-shirt, then strode straight to the bridge. I called Buig as soon as I was sitting. Hirin took a skimchair and slid it over near mine. Maja came in and sat at the communications console, since Baden wasn't there yet.

"Anything?" I asked without preamble when the Chairman appeared on the screen.

He shook his head. He looked a little calmer now, although no less worried. "I can only assume that she knew this might happen someday, and had a plan ready," he said. "She's very resourceful."

"Or she might have been kidnapped!" I said, trying to keep my voice calm. It didn't work very well. "*Someone* knocked out my navigator, and I doubt it was my—Demmar."

"Is your navigator all right?"

"She's still unconscious. You don't think this looks like Demmar was taken by force?"

Through my anger and anxiety I was trying to read the man. I had only his word that he'd found Yuskeya unconscious—what if he'd knocked her out himself? But if he had, why had he allowed

176

me to retrieve her?

"It's possible Demmar was kidnapped," the Chairman said, "but I don't think it's likely. Why would PrimeCorp do that—a criminal act, something so risky—when they think they're going to walk away from here with her anyway?"

"Then who attacked my navigator?"

He shook his head, his brow furrowed. "I'm sorry, I just don't know. Maybe they were accosted by someone, and there was a struggle, but Demmar got away. Perhaps your crew member will be able to tell us something when she regains consciousness."

I wanted to drop my head into my hands and cry, but there was no time for that. "You'll keep searching on your end?"

He regarded me seriously, his eyes dark with worry. If he was a liar, he was damn good at it. "I will. What are you going to do?"

"Consult with my crew. I'll get back to you shortly," I said, and broke the connection.

Rei came onto the bridge. She'd also taken time to change out of her golden finery and into a plain blue shipsuit, and had tied her chestnut hair back in a ponytail. "Dr. Ndasa is back in his room."

"Think he'll stay put?"

She nodded. "Seems pretty glum about the whole thing. Also, I locked the door from the outside," she added with a grin.

Viss and Baden came in through the archway to Sensors. "Yuskeya's settled in First Aid," Baden said. "All her vitals are good, she's just sleeping now."

Viss passed me a cocoa-coloured leather satchel, a little worn around the edges as if it had seen a lot of use. "This was slung over Yuskeya's shoulder," he said. "Don't know if you noticed it. I've never seen it before, and I don't think she had it with her when we went to the Chairman's place."

I took it, puzzled. "I'll ask her about it when she wakes up," I said. "Thanks."

Rei was in the pilot's chair. "I assume we're getting out of here?" she asked, flicking switches to start the engines and thrusters warming up. The bridge screens sprang to life.

"I—" I stopped. I didn't want to leave the planet without knowing what had happened with my mother.

Hirin put a hand on mine. "No matter what else has happened, you still don't want to give PrimeCorp those samples, right?"

I pulled a deep sigh and shook my head. "No."

"The Chairman might be able to protect your mother if she's still down there, but he can't do a thing for you if we're sitting right here in plain sight. I know it's hard to leave." He squeezed my hand. "But we can come back."

Tears sprang to my eyes and I blinked them back. I swallowed hard. "Right. You're right. Rei, get us off Kiando, fast. Baden, try to get a reading on that PrimeCorp ship. Wherever it is, take us in the opposite direction. Once we're well outside their sensor range, we'll figure out what to do next."

Maja said, "I'll go and sit with Yuskeya in case she wakes up and wonders what's happening." She left the comm station to Baden and hurried off to First Aid. Baden commed the docking authority and told them we'd be leaving. After a brief discussion about docking fees they agreed to release the clamps.

Viss settled in at the auxiliary Engineering console. "Once we're off the planet, I'll go down to make modifications to the main drive. I might be able to alter the drive signature slightly, to make us more difficult to detect in case PrimeCorp is scanning for us. It'll only be temporary, but it might work."

"Great. Are we ready to lift off?"

Rei nodded. "Firing thrusters now." A low, steady hum had been building in the ship for the last thirty seconds or so and it increased sharply when Rei took us up. Other than that, it was a smooth lift. Probably not even enough to wake Yuskeya. Even under pressure, Rei had a steady hand at the helm. Maybe especially then. I got ready to contact Chairman Buig again.

"Luta, look at this," Rei said, although she didn't look away from her screen. A map of the Mu Cassiopeia system popped up on my screen. "The PrimeCorp far cruiser came through the wormhole from Delta Pavonis not long ago. No matter what wormhole we decide to go through, we're going to have to wait until the cruiser is docked here in order to get close to any of them. Instead of hightailing it out to the other side of the system to stay out of their scan range, why don't we just try to hang out in the planet's sensor shadow until they land at Ando City? Then once the planet's turned so that the spaceport is facing away from the wormhole we want, we'll slip out of the shadow and run like hell for the terminal point."

I hesitated. "How much time will it save us in getting through the wormhole?"

"Depends on how fast the PrimeCorp cruiser is moving, and where we decide to go. But it'll be here in a few hours. If we spend that time putting distance between us and them but then have to backtrack . . ."

She was right. "Go ahead, then, Rei, but be careful. Block all outgoing transmissions except from the bridge. I'll speak to Chairman Buig if I have to while we're there, but otherwise we don't want anything going out that PrimeCorp could pick up on."

I sent a ping to Chairman Buig and he came up onscreen. I quickly outlined our plan. "Will you send me an encrypted message when they dock at Ando City?"

"*Certe,*" he said.

"What are you going to tell PrimeCorp?" I asked.

A glimmer of a smile touched his lips. "Why, that *Sinjorino* Holsey went off to visit someone at the spaceport, and I haven't seen her since. Naturally, I'll keep my men searching for her."

"And you'll leave out our little conversations?"

He grinned. He looked quite nice when he did that. "I don't know what conversations you mean, Captain. I've also instructed my docking authority to 'lose' the documentation on when you left."

There wasn't much to do then except sit and watch as Rei piloted us up and around the planet. On the viewscreen, Kiando spun slowly below us, the ochre swirls of its many arid deserts interspersed with verdant dots of scattered oases and small blue seas. *Was my mother still down there somewhere?* Any number of small vessels and mining ships had lifted off since the message had come from the PrimeCorp ship; the spaceport at a busy mining colony rarely went quiet, and a silvery starliner hung in orbit, with a busy stream of shuttles flitting between it and the surface. But if she'd wanted to get off the planet, why hadn't she simply come with me?

"We're just about in a perfect position," Rei said.

"Oh, thank goodness," said a voice from the archway. I looked up to see Yuskeya, very pale and with a somewhat messily wrapped bandage encircling her head, leaning against Maja. Her robe was a wrinkled mess but she seemed supremely unaware of it.

"She insisted," Maja said, shaking her head.

Yuskeya stared at the bag in my lap. "Where's your mother?"

I jumped up and went to her. "I wish I knew. But I know where you should be. Lying down," I told her.

She shook her head, then half-closed her eyes, grimaced, and pointed to the empty skimchair at her nav station. Maja and I helped her into it and I knelt beside her. "What in the world happened?"

Yuskeya closed her eyes. "I was hoping you could tell me. We had your mother's things—she gave me that bag to carry for her—and we were on the way to meet you." She touched the tips of her fingers gingerly to the lump on her head. "Whoever or whatever hit me, I never saw it coming. The next thing I knew, I woke up in First Aid."

"Who was with you?" I wanted to check out Gusain Buig's story.

"Just me and your mother," she said. "The Chairman went with Baden to hook him up with the comm centre. Did you send me a message?" She squinted as if she were trying to remember something.

I nodded. "Several. You only answered the first one." I kicked myself mentally. My message had probably been the distraction that let someone sneak up on Yuskeya. "I'm sorry," I told her.

She shook her head, then winced again. "No, I'm the one who's sorry. This never should have happened."

I patted her hand and went back to my chair, where I'd left the leather bag. It felt a little voyeuristic to go through it, but I justified snooping by telling myself there could be a clue inside to tell me where Mother was now. To be honest, I think I just wanted to feel a little closer to her. I sat down and opened the top.

It looked like a pretty ordinary travel bag. I pawed through carefully. A denim-blue t-shirt and rolled-up pair of jeans. A set of tiny earphones. A chipcase. A personal bag with toothpaste, toothbrush, soap and other toiletries. Socks. Mints. A tiny light and an actual paper book, *Ring of Tears* by Juris Lell. A hand-drawn wormhole map of Nearspace, a red pen, and a sheaf of papers filled with scientific diagrams and notations that made less than no sense to me.

I sighed. It was all pretty standard, and what I would have expected. Could have belonged to almost anyone, really, except for the scientific stuff. And the wormhole map, I supposed.

But . . . there was the chipcase. I drew it out and opened it. There were slots for six chips, but only three of them held anything. Two were labelled *NB2897* and *PC35411*, respectively. The third was labelled, *L/L*.

Luta/Lanar? Or was I being silly and sentimental?

"Yuskeya," I said slowly, "my mother didn't say anything about this bag, did she? Or anything in it?"

"No. She just asked me to carry it. She had a few bags."

"Rei, we're okay here for a bit, yet, right?" I asked her.

She nodded, leaning back from the piloting console and folding her arms. "Until we hear from Chairman Buig that the PrimeCorp ship is down, we just have to stay in geosynchronous orbit."

"Then I'm going to my quarters for a bit. Hirin, Maja, would you come with me?"

I saw the quizzical glance that passed between them, but they both got up to follow me. "Yuskeya," I added, "Go lie down, okay? There's nothing for you to do here, and you could use the rest."

She smiled and nodded. "I've felt better, I have to admit. Thank you, Captain."

I knew it wasn't necessary, but I added, "Keep an eye on her, Viss."

"Aye, Captain."

I took the whole bag with me to my cabin. Hirin and Maja trailed after me, and we stopped in at the galley for hot drinks.

"What's up?" Hirin asked, drawing off a chai tea for himself. Yuskeya seemed to have won him over to her favourite drink.

"Maybe nothing," I said. "But maybe a message from my mother. I'd like a little family support if that's what it turns out to be."

Hirin squeezed my arm and Maja simply nodded, spooning sugar into her own tea. "That's what we're for," Hirin said.

We settled in my room, Hirin in the big armchair and Maja on the edge of the bed, while I sat at the desk. I twisted the screen around so that we could all see it. When I inserted the chip marked *L/L*, a message popped up. *Please enter the password to view this data.*

I slumped back in my chair. "Well, this might be a short meeting. Having not seen the woman in seventy years, I doubt I can guess this password."

"There's nothing else in the chipcase, or the bag?" Maja asked.

I passed the bag to her and opened up the chipcase, showing it to her and Hirin. "Two other chips, that's all. Everything in the bag looks pretty normal."

While Maja went through the contents of the bag, I tried the other two chips, but they were both password-protected as well. I put the first one back in and tried the labels of both the other chips as the password for this one. I thought that was pretty clever, but neither of them worked.

Hirin leaned back and steepled his fingers in his characteristic "thinking" pose. "Okay, let's think about this. Assuming she meant this for you or Lanar, she must have made the password something you could figure out."

"Assuming that, I suppose. I don't even know for sure that's what *L/L* means, but we're working under that assumption."

"So it's likely something that relates to your life together," he went on, "before she had to leave."

"Well, I was only nine when she left PrimeCorp, and fourteen when she went off on her own," I said. "I doubt that I remember very much from that time. What if there was something that she thought was important, but I didn't?"

"All we can do is try."

For ten minutes or so we tried street names, pet names, teachers, schools, my father's and grandparents's names— anything we could think of that tied to my early life. We moved on to places we'd lived, friends, children; still no luck. I ran my fingers through my hair in frustration.

"What about things you and your mother have in common?" Maja suggested.

I typed in *red hair*, but that wasn't it.

"Very funny," she said. "No, really. So you've been separated all this time—that doesn't mean you have nothing in common."

I typed in *PrimeCorp*, but that wasn't it, either. *PrimeCorpSucks?* No.

"Something you have in common, something important to you both," Hirin mused. "But maybe with a more positive connotation?"

I sat back and closed my eyes, thinking about the all-too-brief conversation we'd managed to have. Had she said anything that might be a clue?

. . . it wasn't because I wasn't interested in my family.

Family. We did have that in common. I typed in *KernenEmmageLutaLanarKarroMaja.*

And we were in.

Chapter Sixteen

Sounds in the Vacuum

There were several files on the *L/L* chip, but they were all labelled *Luta & Lanar vid*, followed by a number. I paused only long enough to take a deep breath and pat myself mentally on the back for guessing correctly about the contents of the chip. Then I tapped the screen to play the file that ended with *-01*.

Mother's face filled the screen. She sat at a scarred, metal-topped desk, and the background looked like any one of thousands of small passenger rooms on any one of hundreds of starliners that operated around Nearspace, carrying folks between planets and systems. She looked pretty much exactly the same as she had when I'd spoken to her earlier, although she wore an azure mandarin-collared shirt and her auburn hair was piled in a messy updo—that kind I can never achieve myself.

She took a deep breath and began to speak.

I'm not sure who'll be watching this, Luta, or Lanar, or maybe both of you together. So hello to you both, and before I say anything else, I love you. I'm sorry I haven't been able to say it more often.

She blinked away tears that had threatened to spill over, and smiled. *I have a lot to tell you. I doubt that it will all happen at once. I'll number the files consecutively so that you can watch them in order, and they'll make sense. If you're watching these videos, it's because I'm dead—which I sincerely hope is not the case—or for some other reason, they've come into your hands without me. I hope we'll be able to talk this over together, but if*

183

not, it's important for me to tell you everything. She smiled. *Or at least a few things.*

"She sounds like you, too," Maja said quietly.

"She does," Hirin agreed. I had no opinion, not really knowing what my own voice sounded like. But my mind was busy elsewhere. I felt guilty to be watching this without Lanar. He deserved to be here as much as I did. I couldn't send him any kind of message without possibly alerting the PrimeCorp ship to our presence, though, and I needed to know if there was going to be anything in these files that might help me decide on my next move. Mother began to speak again.

PrimeCorp has been dogging me—sometimes subtly, sometimes blatantly—for as long as I've been away from you. She breathed a deep sigh, letting it out slowly, as if she were releasing more than just breath. *That's a long time.*

They have always maintained that they have a proprietary interest in all the research I carried out during the years I worked for them. Sometimes their attempts to find me have seemed almost cursory, but then they will ramp things up again. They stopped almost completely for a time, when they brought Vigor-Us to market, but the reprieve did not last long. In the past two years, they've appeared to be growing more desperate. They want my data and knowledge, and they want it now.

Mother paused and took a sip from a mug. She positioned her hand to cover the ship's logo imprinted on the side of the mug. Always careful.

"They probably know or suspect that Schulyer is getting close with their own research," Hirin commented.

Let me be clear, Mother continued. *Legally, they do own all my data up to the point when I left. It's plain as plain in the contract we all signed when we went to work there. I can't argue with that, legally or ethically. But I don't want them to have it.*

It's a complicated story, but I'll try to be concise. I worked for PrimeCorp for fifteen years doing research on what was then the next generation of bioscavengers.

Even though she couldn't see me, I nodded once, my heart thumping. *I'd been right.*

We were looking for a way to incorporate all the functions of the previous generations—cancer and disease fighting, trauma repair, toxin purification—into one super-protein, and supply an extra function as well: age-related change suppression. Once we could create nanobioscavengers to deal with the main causes of aging—telomere shortening and damage, DNA glycation, and oxidative stress—in addition to everything else they could do, it would be easy. PrimeCorp fed us a lot of encouragement about the philanthropic value of what we were doing, how this would change humanity forever, how their business model would make it universally accessible. We believed them.

She smiled. *It was probably the most exciting time in my life. We all thought that we were on the verge of offering virtual immortality to the human race.*

And then—we discovered PrimeCorp's actual agenda. We'd just had a breakthrough. We had a prototype designer protein for bioscavengers that could self-replicate, and delay aging by about seventy years before an individual would need an infusion of new proteins. Then we discovered a way to make that protein indefinitely self-replicating. It would mean something close to human immortality.

I heard someone, Hirin or Maja, take a deep breath. I couldn't take my eyes off Mother.

She brushed a few stray hairs back from her face and went on. *PrimeCorp stood to make enormous profits, because effective as the bioscavs would be, they couldn't be inherited. Each new generation would have to have an initial infusion.*

That's when we found that PrimeCorp had no intention of using the research to the full benefit of humanity. They planned to halt the research where it was, and manufacture only the non-replicating bioscavengers. They'd offer them for distribution only to colonial and planetary governments—at exorbitant prices. A huge advertising campaign would practically force governments to pay whatever PrimeCorp asked. If people knew the technology existed, they'd demand it from their governments, and if the governments didn't come through, the people were sure to revolt.

Mother folded her hands, set them on the desk in front of her. *When we found out, some of my colleagues wanted to argue with PrimeCorp about it, try to fight them. Someone mentioned starting legal action on the basis that we'd been encouraged to work under false pretenses. That didn't make much sense to me;*

I could see where that would go. We'd all had to sign non-competition contracts when they hired us so that we couldn't take our data or even our experience and go start working for some other genetics firm. We couldn't just move to a less greedy company. It would be tied up in the courts for years, and meanwhile PrimeCorp would let the news slip out, and the demand would be so great that they'd win in the end.

So I took matters into my own hands. I was the project head, after all, and most of the original ideas had been mine. Before PrimeCorp began to suspect that we weren't happy, I stole all the data and we ran with it. She leaned back in the chair and looked suddenly very tired. *I've been running ever since.*

The image froze and I realized that was probably the end of the first video file. I was about to tap the next one when Maja said, "If they were after her for that long, how do you think they finally caught up with her now?"

I started guiltily and turned to face her. "I'm afraid I must have done something to lead them here," I said. "Although I don't know what. I tried to be careful."

Maja tapped her fingers against her lips in an echo of her father's gesture. "Somehow, they keep finding us. Could they have put something on the ship?"

I shrugged. "All the decks except cargo are wire-blocked, so it wouldn't matter if they managed to smuggle something on with one of us. And a tracking device on a piece of cargo doesn't really make sense—it could be offloaded anywhere."

"What about the intruder?" Hirin said suddenly. "Didn't you say he came up from the cargo deck?"

"What intruder?" asked Maja.

"It was before we left Earth," I said. "Someone, I'm assuming Sedmamin, sent a stripped operative to break into the *Tane Ikai* and get a biological sample from me without my permission. He didn't get it," I added when I saw the worried look on Maja's face.

"What happened?"

"He tried to fly from the bridge deck to the cargo deck, without stopping at Engineering in between," Hirin said wryly. "But PrimeCorp hadn't thought to give him wings first. He left a mess on the deck, and we left what was left of him in the outer Sol system."

"And then in the Keridre/Gerdrice system," I added. "He slipped through a communications pinhole when we jettisoned the body in a cargo crate. We planned to tuck it away on an asteroid until we'd decided what to do."

"Were you hurt?" Maja asked.

I shrugged. "A bit of a scratch, that was all. Yuskeya fixed me up."

"I didn't know about that," Maja said, frowning.

"That was before you caught up with us," Hirin explained, patting her hand. She still looked troubled and pale. "Could he have—I don't know—injected you with something to make you trackable somehow?"

I hadn't thought of that possibility before, but then I remembered my "entity." "I don't think that would be very useful. I'm almost always on one of the wire-blocked decks."

"So where was he on the ship?" Maja asked.

I waved a hand. "Pfft. Everywhere, I guess. Well, no, that's not true. I came out into the corridor as he got to this deck. We had to assume he got in through the airlock on the engineering deck. He could have been in any of the cargo pods, and anywhere on Engineering. I don't think he got anywhere on this level before he ran into me. Or I ran into him." I grimaced, remembering.

Hirin stood up. "He could easily have planted something on the cargo deck. Did we run any scans after that?"

I shook my head. "I don't think so."

"Then let's go check."

I popped the chip out of the reader and put it back in the chipcase, pocketing the whole thing. I wasn't letting it out of my possession until I'd watched everything that was meant for me.

Rei and Baden were on the bridge, and Yuskeya was still there, too. Someone had been to the galley, since they all had empty mugs and a plate specked with crumbs sat on the console next to Baden.

"Didn't I tell you to go and lie down?" I demanded of Yuskeya.

She held up her hands in surrender. "I'm resting. I haven't moved from this chair since you left. Rei and I were just chatting, and we sent Baden to the galley for us."

"Oh, all right. Next time I'll make it an order." I turned my attention away from her. "Baden, nothing from Chairman Buig yet?"

"Not a word."

"Is Viss in Engineering?"

"As far as I know, yes."

I opened up the comm to the Engineering deck. "All right, then listen up, everyone. We have reason to suspect that the intruder who boarded the ship before we left Earth might have left a tracking device on the cargo deck."

"He came in through cargo pod Four, Captain," Viss said. "I got that much from that techrig he had."

"All right, we'll start there. What do we have for scanners? It'll probably be minuscule."

Baden held up his updated datapad. "This will pick up any transmission that would be strong enough to use for tracking. I'd just have to scan for the right frequencies."

"So that could have been a *putra* PrimeCorp ship behind us when we jumped for Kiando," Yuskeya said, already halfway out the door before I could tell her to sit back down. "I'll get the datameds from the First Aid station. The implant bioware could scan for transmissions if I tweak the sensors a little."

"My datapad's got the same capabilities as Baden's," Hirin said, following Yuskeya. "He got me a new one when we were on Renata. I'll be right back."

Diable. I didn't know Hirin had a new datapad. I think I gaped after him a little. The changes in that man just didn't stop.

"I have a new datapad, too," Maja offered quietly. "I bought it to come on this run. I don't know everything it does yet, but if Baden will show me how, I'll help."

"And if I shut down the wireblocker on the engineering deck I can scan the cargo deck from the diagnostics station," said Viss.

"All right. At this rate, I can't imagine not finding it, if it exists. Let's go."

There didn't seem to be anything for me to do but go along and . . . watch.

I stood to one side, watching the others move around the half-empty cargo pod in their search. I wasn't sure if I hoped they'd find something, or not.

Yuskeya tired more quickly than she'd expected and came to stand next to me, having handed her scanner over to Maja. "You know, Captain, just going through the Split might have been enough to throw anyone off our trail."

"Thanks, Yuskeya, but they found Mother somehow," I said grimly. "If this was how they managed it, I guess I'd rather know."

I got my wish.

"Got it!" It was Baden, over in a far corner of the cargo pod. He knelt beside a cargo lockdown slot.

Everyone rushed over. "I can't see the damn thing yet," he said, "but this reading shouldn't be here. There's nothing else it could be."

"Let me see." Rei knelt near the lockdown slot, tucked a tendril of chestnut hair back from her face, and pressed something just behind her right ear. A bright, slender beam of light emerged from somewhere near her temple and shone wherever she looked.

"Huh," Baden grunted.

"I knew this implant would be useful someday," Rei said, not looking up from the search. "Ah-ha! There it is." She ran a fingernail over a spot just under the lip of the lockdown slot and came up with a tiny black and silver circle on her fingertip. It was no bigger than the stud Baden wore in his ear. "Nice."

I hailed Viss over the comm. "We've got it. I'm bringing it up to you."

"Excellent, Captain," he said, "I'll reset the wire blocker, and once it's up here it'll be mute. If I can reprogram it, it might be a handy little thing to have around, don't you think?"

"Good idea," I agreed. A thought struck me and sent a chill down my back. "Has this thing been transmitting to the PrimeCorp ship ever since we left the planet? Do they already know we're here, hiding behind it?"

Viss didn't answer right away, but Baden said, "I doubt it. This type of signal would get lost really easily once we were inside a planet's atmosphere, to say nothing of all the extra chatter coming from the planet and the ships coming and going—and the *Trident* is still pretty far out. I don't think they'd have any chance of picking it up."

"*Okej.*" I didn't feel entirely safe, but Baden knew his stuff. Anyway, there wasn't much we could do about it now except stop the transmission and hope for the best. We left the cargo pod and climbed back up to Engineering.

I handed the minuscule bug to Viss and Maja said suddenly, "But if PrimeCorp knew their operative had left a beacon on the ship, why did Dores Amadoro try to get me to plant one, too?"

"What?" Hirin exclaimed, frowning. He put his hands on his

189

hips. "Seems like I haven't heard all of this story."

The others, who didn't know about the way Amadoro had conned Maja either, stared at her uncomprehendingly.

I held up my hands. "Sorry, Hirin, you were out of the loop on that one. We'll fill you in as soon as we're done here."

He didn't look entirely happy about that, but he nodded. I thought about Maja's question

"Because Amadoro wouldn't have known if this beacon was in place or not. All she—or she and Sedmamin—knew then was that the virus trick had failed, and the op hadn't come back from the mission. If they couldn't stop me from leaving, they at least wanted to be able to track me."

In a display of unusual tact, none of the others asked for details. Rei looked a query at me, but I shook my head a little and she seemed to accept that.

Viss said, "The tracker probably wasn't set to start signalling until we made the first skip out of Earthspace, to minimize the chances of it being found."

"So when Amadoro learned that you were coming after us—"

"She thought she could set up some 'insurance,'" Maja finished bitterly.

I squeezed her arm. "Stop worrying about it. We've put that behind us, right?"

She nodded. "What do you mean, 'virus trick'?"

"That was before we left Earth, too. Chairman Sedmamin sent me a notebug infected with a virus in an attempt to get me in to PrimeCorp for some 'discussion.' It didn't affect me in the way he'd hoped, so I guess that's when he sent the operative to break in."

"How did you know he came from PrimeCorp?" Maja asked.

"Well—we don't, not for sure," I said. "He didn't have any identification, not even an ID chip. But he did try to get blood or something from me. Makes sense that he was from PrimeCorp."

"Too bad you can't prove it," she said. "If you had actual proof of some of the things they've done to you, maybe you could make them stop."

I stared at her. "But it's . . . PrimeCorp," I said. "We wouldn't stand a chance against them. Anything we said—they'd find a way to bury it, or make it go away. Buy people off." I shook my head. "They're just too big."

Maja cocked her head at me, considering. "It's PrimeCorp,

yes. But maybe they're bigger in your mind because you've spent so much time feeling attacked by them. They can't be free to act completely outside the law. Surely they can't be so big that in all of Nearspace, we couldn't find enough allies to move against them."

"She's right," Baden said, leaning back against one of the Engineering consoles and crossing his arms. Viss cleared his throat and Baden stood up straight again. "I mean, you seem to have found one in Chairman Buig. PrimeCorp might think he'll accommodate them, but he's under no real obligation to. Duntmindi Corp has its own sovereignty rights on its own planets."

"And its own legal rights and justice system," Hirin added slowly. "The things that happened on Earth and on Rhea—they're both PrimeCorp-controlled planets. I wouldn't think you'd have much luck there. But if you could manage to bring charges here . . ."

Yuskeya snapped her fingers. "The pirate attack! That happened in open Nearspace, not on any planet, which means you can bring the charges on any planet with an ambassador in the Administrative Council."

My mind was whirling. "But we don't have much evidence from that. A techrig and a weapon. Maybe a bit of DNA or a fingerprint, if we could recover it from the weapon. And we'd have to be able to link that stuff to PrimeCorp."

"Yes, but if you start the proceedings here, you can bring in the other incidents as well," Yuskeya said. She'd sat down at one of the auxiliary engineering consoles, but she leaned forward in the skimchair, eyes bright. Viss didn't seem to mind her sitting there. "You'd have to prove that they were all related, but you could build the body of evidence for everything at once."

"And maybe you don't even have to win," Rei said thoughtfully. "If it even looks like you have a chance of winning, you may be able to get PrimeCorp to negotiate, or at least leave you and your mother alone."

An ally in Chairman Buig, I thought suddenly. An ally who had access to the Nearspace Database, and might be willing to access it on our behalf.

"I need to think," I said. Which meant I needed to pace. I opened the bulkhead leading from the Engineering station to the long corridor between the fuel storage cells, where so recently we had raced in response to the pirate attack on Cargo Pod One. Before I stepped inside, I said, "Maja, take your father up to the galley and fix him a double caff while you explain about Dores Amadoro, would you? He's a patient man, but he has his limits."

Maja didn't look like she relished the idea of telling that story again, but she nodded and took Hirin's arm. I wasn't too worried about how he'd react. If I'd forgiven Maja, I knew he would, too. But I had to let them handle this one themselves. I had too many other things to think about. I stepped through the bulkhead and pulled the door shut behind me, signalling my need for a few minutes alone, and stalked down the corridor. I used the easy rhythm of my feet on the decking to shuffle my thoughts into order.

What evidence did we have against PrimeCorp, if I stacked it all up together? We had a photo of the dead intruder, which might be enough to provisionally identify him. It wouldn't be enough on its own to do much damage to PrimeCorp, but if he were identified, then we'd know if he could be linked to PrimeCorp. His techrig might not be much use, since Viss had taken it apart, put it back together, and used it since then. *Body of evidence*, Yuskeya had said. I wished again, mightily, that we still had the body, but put that thought aside for now.

I had Alin Sedmamin's notebug message about the virus. I had the names of the thugs who had kidnapped me on Rhea, and I had the techrig, weapon, and if I was lucky, some DNA or a fingerprint from one of the pirates.

I reached the end of the corridor and turned, then slumped back against the wall as another thought hit me. There was also the illegal tech cargo that the pirates hadn't managed to get, which we—or Viss, anyway—had delivered to the Protectorate agents on Kiando. That meant they now had hard evidence of PrimeCorp's manufacture of illegal tech. If they'd help us. If they could do so without jeopardizing their own case against PrimeCorp, and the things Lanar had hinted at so obliquely. I couldn't say anything to the others about that yet. I needed to talk to Lanar—securely—and find out what the Protectorate could do to help.

I leaned my head back against the cool metal wall of the corridor, letting its solid bulk comfort me. The ship always had a way of doing that. Maybe the evidence wasn't much, even taken all together. It didn't tell me where Mother was now or why she'd disappeared as suddenly as I'd found her. But at least it gave me something to do.

Chapter Seventeen

Souvenirs and Circles

I hurried back towards Engineering. It said a lot about how well the rest of them understood me that none of them had followed me into the corridor or moved from the spot. Only Hirin and Maja had gone.

"Baden," I said, as soon as I was within earshot. "Do you think I could talk with the Chairman for a few minutes, and send him some data packets, without jeopardizing our situation with that PrimeCorp ship?

Baden pursed his lips. "I think so. I'll make it as narrowband as I can; the quality might suffer a bit, but the ship should still be far enough out that they wouldn't pick it up. There's lots of that other chatter I mentioned down here to mask it, and they shouldn't even be looking for us out here. If they pick us up at all, they'd likely think we were still on the planet."

"*Okej.*" I outlined what I'd been thinking. "If he'll help us, I'll send him the photo of the intruder, the names of the kidnappers, and anything we might get off that pirate's belongings. If Buig can identify any of them and link them to PrimeCorp, we'll have something to start with."

"We can do even a little better than that," Rei said suddenly. "Wait right here."

Without another word she swarmed up the ladder to the upper deck. Everyone looked at me, but I shrugged.

She was back inside a minute, swinging something small and soft and black from her hand, and she tossed it to me, carefully, as she passed. "I'll bet you can get a better identification of the intruder with some of his skin cells, and maybe a hair or two . . ."

She dropped into one of the skimchairs and let it spin her around, looking extremely pleased with herself.

I picked it up. It was the intruder's mask.

"How?"

Rei tilted her head to one side and grinned. "Souvenir," she said. "I thought it would be a good one. I had it in the secret locker in my room so it wouldn't be out in plain sight if anyone came asking about the man. I kept it after we took it off him that night. Didn't think he'd miss the warmth. No-one else has had it on, so anything in there belongs to him."

I hugged her. "Remind me never to call your souvenir habit crazy again."

She pulled back. "You think my souvenirs are crazy?" But there was a smile in her eyes.

"Okay, folks," I said. "Here's what we're going to do. Yuskeya, if you're feeling up to it, would you try to extract some information from this mask and the pirate's belongings, and package the results to send to Chairman Buig? Ask Dr. Ndasa to help you. I'll go and retrieve that message from Sedmamin about the virus. Viss, you took the photo of the intruder, would you send a copy to Baden? And Baden, you can cobble all of this together, make it as small as you can, and get it ready for me to narrowband down to the Chairman after I've spoken to him."

A chorus of *ayes* met my requests, and I led the way up the hatchway ladder. Yuskeya said she'd need about half an hour, and I headed to my quarters to call up Sedmamin's nasty message from the notebug. I settled at my desk and tried to load it, the one where he'd admitted that there had been a virus in my notebug message. I should have realized he wouldn't be that sloppy, though. The message was a corrupted mess of gibberish, obviously set to self-destruct after it had been read. I made several attempts to rebuild or decrypt it with some filters I'd gotten from Lanar, but it was no use. I wondered briefly if Baden could make anything of it with his superior techrig. Somehow I doubted it. Sedmamin was a master when it came to covering his tracks. Maybe we wouldn't need it anyway.

A knock at my door took my attention from the screen, and I crossed the room to answer it. It was Maja, and she looked pensive.

"May I come in?"

I nodded and pushed the door open, stepping inside and

holding it for her to follow me. "Of course. How did it go with your father?"

"Oh, fine," she said absently. "He's more angry at Amadoro than he is at me."

She crossed the room, looking around as if she'd never seen it before, and sat down in my big armchair. She stared across at the wall, saying nothing, as if she were searching for a way to begin. Her fingers drummed a nervous staccato rhythm on the arm of the chair.

I sat on the bed and waited. She obviously hadn't come here because of Hirin.

"I didn't know you'd been attacked," she said finally. "Besides what happened to us on Rhea."

I shrugged. "Well, like your father said, it was before we left Earth. It wasn't a big deal."

She stared at the wall above my bed, not meeting my eyes. "But . . .twice? I think it was. Is. A big deal." She met my eyes, her blue ones thoughtful. "And the things Emmage said in that vid . . .it all makes me realize that I never really listened when you tried to explain why things were the way they were."

I raised my eyebrows and half-smiled at her. "I noticed."

Maja stood, walked around the chair slowly, running her manicured fingers gently over the soft woven fabric. "All I could see was that it wasn't fair. I always seemed to be on the outside. You and Dad and Karro, even Uncle Lanar—you all loved space so much. I hated it. Never staying in one place, living on a far trader. You all thought it was so exciting. For me, it was just . . . unsettled."

"It isn't the life for everyone. I suppose I didn't pay enough attention to what you wanted. But there was always PrimeCorp to think about—"

"I understand that now." She sighed. "I just thought it was a stupid excuse then. I stayed angry about that for a long time. PrimeCorp never seemed like such a threat to me. Then it started to be obvious that you hadn't passed on whatever was keeping you young. I hated you for that, too—and you wouldn't cooperate with PrimeCorp to find out about it. And later," she went on, as if she were determined to make a full confession, "when Dad got sick. That was your fault, too, as far as I was concerned. And then I couldn't forgive you for putting him in that facility and leaving."

"Maja, I—"

"No, no, you don't have to say anything. I understand. Now I do, at least. Then when Taso and I . . . he went off with someone else." She smiled wryly. "She was much younger. And even though it didn't make any sense, I blamed you."

"Honey, I'm sorry." I didn't know what else to say.

She shook her head. "It doesn't matter now. Really. It was just one thing after another, all our lives, and now I see that I always got it wrong."

"I wouldn't say you always got it wrong." I looked up at the viewport, at the incomprehensibly vast expanse of stars beyond it. I'd thought of the whole thing as my home, never understanding that Maja needed something else. Never paying enough attention, I realized. "I spent a lot of time when I was younger being angry with my mother, too. It took time, and learning to understand the situation, before I could see her reasons for acting the way she did."

She stared at the fabric of the chair, lightly tracing the design. "I think I should have been able to find that clarity sooner."

"I didn't make it any easier for you to do that. It wasn't exactly a normal life."

"No, it wasn't," she agreed, almost smiling. "But that's no excuse." She'd circled the chair and sat down again, leaning her arms on her knees. She looked forlorn, her blonde hair tumbling over her eyes like it had when she was a little girl. "These last few weeks, being here on the ship, I started seeing things differently, even though I didn't realize what was happening. Then when I saw you finding out things even *you* hadn't known, from Emmage—I'm afraid I can't call her 'Grandmother' yet—it came into focus. And knowing that there was real danger from PrimeCorp . . . I can't blame her, either . . ." She sighed. "I'm not quite sure what I'm trying to say."

I knelt down and put my arms around her. "That you don't hate me?"

She laughed a little at that, or maybe it was a sob, but at any rate, she hugged me back. "That's it, Mother. I don't hate you."

"That's good to know, Maja." I smiled. "I don't hate you, either."

I told Maja that Rei would fill her and Hirin in on what we were planning and she left then. I looked at the time; Yuskeya wouldn't have things ready yet. I was intensely aware of the chipcase in my pocket, and the unwatched messages from my mother waiting for me to view them. I hesitated only a moment before I pulled out the *L/L* chip, slotted it into the reader, and touched the second vid file to start it.

The background had changed from the last vid; Mother was obviously in a different place, although it was impossible to tell how much time had passed between the last message and this one. Her hair was swept into one long auburn plait and hung over one shoulder. She wore a baggy, loosely-knit sweater in shades of green and blue. A bank of bookshelves covered the wall behind her, but I couldn't make out any of the titles.

Mother smiled, a bit tentatively, it seemed. *I've been wondering what you both may be thinking about my decisions and actions from an ethical standpoint,* she began. *We—most of us, anyway—felt that we had a moral right to decide how our research would be used, if not a legal one. In the end, I alone took the action, and the responsibility, of removing the data. But that was seventy-five years ago. You probably wonder why I've worked so hard to keep it secret for so long.*

She took a deep breath. *You may be thinking that even if they made untold billions from the product, at least PrimeCorp would have made it available. That there are thousands upon thousands of people who've died in that time, who would still be alive today if they'd had the bioscavengers.*

I can't even count the number of nights I've lain awake and thought about that. Mother's voice was weary, those little lines around her eyes more pronounced. *I hunted for ways I could safely get in touch with you, Luta, when Maja and Karro were young, so that I could offer you the choice for them. But I knew they would be monitoring you, watching. I had to consider both the benefits and the risks. If PrimeCorp had this data, it would effectively rule the entirety of Nearspace. I think I did the right thing; look how they've exploited their monopoly on the rejuv market with Vigor-Us. If PrimeCorp could offer virtual immortality, every government in Nearspace would be under its thumb. I simply couldn't take the chance. I was afraid of the kind of society I might be creating if I let it happen. No single corporation should have that much power.*

Even the alien governments, the Vilisians on Damir, and the Lobors, would have come under PrimeCorp's sway. We had samples of Vilisian and Lobor DNA even then, and some researchers were working on modifying first- and second-generation bioscavengers to work for the alien races, too. We share a certain amount of basic biology. It would only have been a matter of time before they had a prototype that would work against alien aging, too.

Mother took a drink from a delicate china teacup that sat on the table or desk next to her. Graceful tree branches wound around the sides of the cup and the curving handle echoed their shape. *I did wonder if some other company would come up with the same data at some point,* she continued, *or with a similar product. I always felt that in the event another company developed a self-replicating bioscavenger, I'd send everything back to PrimeCorp and let them go to it, or maybe leak the data on the public nets, because at least then there'd be competition. No one would have sole control of human aging. However, I felt that the possibility of that happening was unlikely, for two reasons.*

*One was the breakthrough I mentioned. Like the discovery of penicillin at the beginning of the twentieth century, or the Krasnikov matter we depend on for wormhole travel, our breakthrough was something of an accident. We wanted nanobioscavengers that would not only deal with disease, trauma, and aging, but that would be self-replicating as well. The self-replication was the roadblock. And then—I suppose you could call it a twist of fate. Those Vilisian DNA samples? One of them got into a human culture by accident. We never did know how it happened—probably just a tech not following proper lab procedures. But when it combined with the proteins we were growing in the culture—*she sat back and snapped her fingers. *There it was. The key to the self-replication problem.*

Mother glanced off-camera, and the image froze. The end of the vid.

I sat back in my chair. Vilisian DNA was the key to mother's breakthrough research? I never would have guessed that. And, I supposed, neither had anyone else, since the research had apparently never been duplicated.

Unless it had now, by Dr. Ndasa and Schulyer Corp. I wondered if the revelation would come as news to him.

I looked at the chipcase lying open on my desk. Two more chips, which might hold the keys to Mother's research. Or more evidence against PrimeCorp. Somehow I doubted they'd be protected by the same password as this chip.

I was about to watch the third vid on the *L/L* chip when Yuskeya commed me. "Captain, Baden and I have this data ready to send."

"Be right there." I put the chips away again. It was more important right now to get this data to Gusain Buig—if he would agree to help us.

I made my way to the bridge, and found everyone but Dr. Ndasa waiting for me there. I assumed the Vilisian was still in his former quarters, probably unsure of his status aboard the ship now. I'd have to go and speak with him later.

"How close is the *Trident* now?" I asked.

"Still a ways out," Yuskeya answered.

"I guess we'll chance it," I said.

"Did you get the message from Sedmamin?" Baden asked. "I didn't see it come through to me."

I shook my head. "No, it self-destructed. We'll have to forget about that for now and concentrate on what we do have. Go ahead and open a narrowband transmission to the Chairman for me."

When the Chairman came onscreen, he shook his head. He looked as haggard as I felt. "No word on your mother, Captain, I'm afraid. And the PrimeCorp ship isn't here yet, either."

"I'm sorry to bother you, Chairman, but I have a favour— another favour, I suppose I should say—to ask of you."

If he was annoyed at my temerity, he didn't show it, at least. "If I can help you, I will," he said graciously.

"Chairman, in the past few weeks, while we travelled here, there have been a number of illegal attacks on both my ship and my person. We've managed to retrieve some clues to the identities of the perpetrators—photos and DNA samples, but there are some planets where we suspect we wouldn't get far with any complaints."

The chairman raised his eyebrows. "Planetary Statute crimes?"

"And Primary Statute," I said, "piracy being one of them. And I suspect that they were committed by order of someone at PrimeCorp."

Now he frowned. "Those are serious accusations, Captain."

I nodded. "I agree. And I don't make them lightly. But the first thing I need to do is ascertain that the perpetrators did, in fact, have some link to PrimeCorp. And to do that, I need to know their identities."

"And that's where I come in," he said. "You need access to the Nearspace Worlds Database."

I held up a hand. "No, I'm not asking for access. I don't want to compromise you. But if you had the data, and could access the database yourself—well, any information you could pass along to me would be much appreciated."

He looked at me hard for the space of a few heartbeats, and I thought he might be wishing I were there in person so he could read me better. I didn't know what Mother had told him about me, but it must have been good because finally he said, "Captain Paixon, I would be happy to assist you. But the PrimeCorp cruiser is getting closer. Can you send me the data right away?"

"It's coming now," I said, and nodded to Baden. "We'll go back to radio silence until the *Trident* docks. If you know anything by then, you can send it along with that message. Thank you very much for your help, Chairman."

He smiled. "If it will help keep your mother out of PrimeCorp's clutches, that will be thanks enough," he said, and broke the connection.

I spent a few minutes watching Kiando whirl slowly below us, colours blurring and shifting beneath the clouds that wreathed the planet. Its hypnotic effect eventually made me realize just how long it was since I'd had any sleep. *Everyone else must be feeling the same way*, I thought guiltily, *but no-one's said a word*.

"I think everyone should get some rest," I said. "We have to stand a watch, but share it up, and get some sleep. That's what I'm going to do."

Rei, Viss, and Baden worked out a schedule to take the watch while we waited to hear from the Chairman, with promises to wake me if the PrimeCorp ship landed on Kiando or anything else of interest happened. Yuskeya demanded to take her fair share, but the others voted her down and she agreed, grudgingly, that she might have had a slightly more difficult night than the rest of them.

Hirin left the bridge with me and stopped outside my door. "Feel like some company?" he asked, and I was glad to curl up next to him.

"Luta?" he whispered, after we'd lain silent in the darkness for a few minutes.

"What?"

"Your mother—you found her once. You will again, I'm sure of it. And at least you got to see her."

He lay pressed against my back, but I could hear the smile in his voice. "You always said I would."

"I'm glad I was here for it." He reached up to stroke my cheek. His skin was warmer now, not as fragile-feeling. "Since . . . since the transfusion. I've been feeling so much better."

I rolled over to face him. His face was half in shadow, but I knew every line and plane. "I know. I think it worked. It's another reason I want to find Mother again—to ask her about the whole thing. But I think if Dr. Ndasa ran a scan on you now, the virus would be gone."

He nodded slightly. "I think so, too. I haven't felt this good in . . . well, in years. Thank you. If you hadn't thought of the transfusion . . ."

"I'm just glad it worked," I whispered. "It's been wonderful, having you here with me, especially now."

I sensed, more than saw, his grin in the darkness. "A useless old man like me? That's a pretty big compliment."

"Useless? Never," I said with a chuckle. "And honestly . . . you don't even seem as old anymore. The way you walk, the way you talk. You stand straighter. Your voice is stronger."

"Would you believe that my hair is starting to grow in a little *darker*?" he said wonderingly. "And my hearing is sharper. I'm sure of it."

My eyes filled with tears suddenly. It seemed as though whatever worked its age-defying magic in me was also toiling in Hirin, regaining at least some of what time and illness had taken away from him.

"I wish I'd thought of it years ago." I brushed away a tear with my fingertip. "You wouldn't have had to go through—"

"Stop." He put two fingers gently on my lips. "It never occurred to me, either. We just didn't understand what was happening . . . or at least we hadn't made as many educated guesses. It doesn't matter. What matters is now."

I nodded, his fingers still on my mouth. I kissed them.

"Luta," he whispered again. "I think I could . . . I wonder if we—"

I pushed his hand out of the way then and kissed him full on the mouth, stopping his question with my answer. Hirin's virus had virtually erased the sexual element of our relationship years ago, and although we made the best of it, we'd both missed the closeness. I'd noticed a tension building between us ever since the transfusion, noticed it without thinking about what it could mean. It was like slipping back into comfortable clothes that you haven't worn in a long time, the way we'd begun to banter again, to touch casually. I'd wondered if we might rekindle this aspect of our relationship, or if it was just wishful thinking.

It wasn't. Whatever was working on Hirin, I found out for sure that night, was doing a damn good and thorough job.

Chapter Eighteen

Hunters, Hunting, and Prey
Both Dead and Alive

Baden's voice woke me over the ship's comm a few hours later. His voice was low, as if he hated to wake me. "Captain?"

I touched my biochip implant and said, "I'm here, Baden. What's up?"

"Message request just came in from Chairman Buig. The *Trident* will be docking at the Ando City spaceport soon, and he wants to talk to you about the data we sent him."

"Be there in ten," I said, rubbing sleep out of my eyes. I couldn't say I felt truly rested, but I did feel better. Hirin was still asleep and I didn't wake him. Goodness knew he must be tired out. I quickly and quietly pulled on the one shipsuit I owned, dashed some water on my face, and scooted down to the bridge. Baden was alone there, and the ping from Chairman Buig was waiting on my screen.

"We'll be watching for the first opportunity to slip away from Kiando," I said to Baden. "You might want to wake Viss and make sure everything's set to go in Engineering. With luck, what Chairman Buig has to tell me will help us decide exactly where we want to go." I pinged him back and his image filled my screen.

"This will have to be brief," he said, sounding apologetic. "I'll have to put in an appearance and talk to someone from the PrimeCorp ship in person any minute."

I knew he would already have said something if it was warranted, but I had to ask. "No word from Demmar?"

He shook his head. "No, but I won't stop looking. I'll make a big show of searching for her for PrimeCorp, but the real hunt will be much more discreet. Don't want PrimeCorp to know if I actually do find her."

"Did you have any luck with the data we sent you?"

"I'd say so," he said. The data appeared on the screen, along with a full head shot of a face I recognized, although it had been dead by the time I'd seen it. It was definitely the intruder. I'd recognize the thin scar that curved along his jawline, if nothing else.

Chairman Buig summed up what the screen was showing me. "Oleg Borrano. He's been in PrimeCorp's employ for the past number of years. Security division, PrimeCorp Main. That is still listed as his current employment, and he has a top security clearance there."

The display switched to show three faces, each with its own personal data. I recognized my three captors from the warehouse on Rhea. "The three names you gave me, Sylvana Kirsch, Ben D'Epiro, and Anshum Chieng—they all also work for PrimeCorp Security, although not at the same clearance level as Borrano."

"Thanks, Chairman, that's all pretty much what I expected. Any luck with the DNA?"

He chuckled. "That took a little more work, but luckily, I have a few people around here who are good at that sort of thing. That DNA sample belongs to one Nikolai Cavan, who doesn't seem to have any employment record with PrimeCorp. In fact, he doesn't have much of an employment record at all, although he's worked from time to time as a general crewman on various traders and mining ships." He must have seen the disappointment on my face, because he went on. "However, the techrig he was carrying—well, I've also got a couple of folks here who are what I might call 'techdogs.'"

I smiled. "I know one or two of those myself. They're handy to have around."

He nodded. "They tell me this rig is a highly modified version—illegal modifications—of a piece of technology Ginteno Tech was making before PrimeCorp took them over. The mods look like mass-production, not things someone hacked together in their workshop. The opinion is that they would raise some eyebrows with the Protectorate and the Administrative Council."

"So there's a link to PrimeCorp there, as well," I said. "Chairman, if I wanted to pursue legal action on these matters, could I get leave to do it on Kiando?"

"You could certainly file a complaint here regarding the pirate attack," Buig said, "and bring the other matters in under that umbrella. Do you have further evidence besides what you've given me?'

"All of us who have been involved would give statements, and testify—whatever was necessary," I said. "We don't have much else in the way of hard evidence, I suppose."

He considered. "Well, it's enough to begin proceedings . . . but you only have your story regarding how you came by any of this information you sent me. To tell you the truth, a good advocate could probably poke holes in that pretty quickly—and PrimeCorp is going to have good advocates if you bring an action against them."

I nodded. "That's what I thought. I'll let you know what I decide, Chairman, and thanks for your help. We're going to take the first opportunity to leave without attracting attention. I want to speak to my brother; he's an admiral in the Protectorate. And I'd rather PrimeCorp didn't know I'm going looking for him."

"I'll get word to you if anything changes," he said. "I hope we'll speak again soon, Captain. And if you find Demmar before I do, tell her—tell her I look forward to her return, would you?"

"Will do."

I shut down the commscreen and turned to Baden. "Okay, it's time to scramble. Did you get Viss?"

"He's already down there."

"I want to be ready to burn for a wormhole as soon as the spaceport is facing away from it. I'll wake Rei—"

"Don't bother," she said, coming onto the bridge. In deference to Hirin, I suppose, she was wearing her souvenir crimson robe.

"Doesn't anybody sleep around here?" I asked.

"Who could sleep with so much excitement happening?"

"So where are we going, Captain?" Yuskeya asked, coming in, too. Apparently she wasn't going to pay much heed to any of us about getting some rest. Maybe I'd have to get Dr. Ndasa to have a little talk with her.

"That's what I'm trying to decide," I said. I drummed my fingers on the arm of the chair, thinking. "I want to try and reach Lanar. I want to tell him everything that's happened, and I have some videos he needs to see. My best chance of tracking him down is to get to a planet with a Protectorate outpost or find a Protectorate ship—either one will tell me where he's currently deployed."

Yuskeya nodded. "True."

I got up and paced around the chair. "Also, I'm thinking about Mother—if she's still on the planet, either hiding out or kidnapped, the Chairman has the best chance of finding her or getting a message from her. I can't do either if I'm trying to avoid PrimeCorp myself. However, if she's off-planet, then I'm the one she's likely to try and get a message to if she can, so that's another reason I should get away from here and out where we don't have to keep the communications locked down."

"Good thinking," Rei said.

I stopped walking. "And the other thing I want to do is skip into Keridre/Gerdrice and see if we can't find our missing cargo crate with the intruder's body inside."

"You think we need that for the case against PrimeCorp?" Yuskeya asked. "We do have his DNA, thanks to Rei."

"I know, but the Chairman is right—PrimeCorp will just say we could have gotten that anywhere. If we have the body, too, it's better proof that he was here, on the ship, and that our story is true. It's been frozen all this time, so they can do whatever forensic tests they like on it. And it's evidence that he was operating without an ID biochip. It's got to help our case."

Yuskeya nodded. "You could be right. And with the homing beacon and knowing where the pinhole exits, we should be able to find it."

I took my seat again. "So, knowing all that, where should we go?"

"Well, we don't know about your Mother—so other than getting out of this system, her whereabouts don't influence where we go," Rei said.

"The last place you knew your brother was heading was Beta Comae Berenices, right?" Yuskeya asked, calling up the wormhole map on the big screen.

"Right."

"So we can make one wormhole skip right into Beta Comae. There's a Protectorate outpost on Jertenda there, and then we're only one more short skip to K/G, to see if we can find the cargo crate," Yuskeya said. She smiled. "Sounds like a no-brainer to me."

"Okay," I said. "As soon as we're in an optimal position to burn for the wormhole to Beta Comae, we'll do it. Might as well wake Maja and Dr. Ndasa and let them know what's going on."

I left the bridge and headed back to my quarters. Hirin was awake when I opened the door and patted the bed beside him. "You still look tired," he said with a grin. "You should come back to bed."

"Ha ha," I said, leaning down to kiss him, but dancing away when he tried to pull me down next to him. "I don't know how much time we have before we break for the wormhole out of this system, and I want to watch the last video from Mother."

I explained my plan to catch up with Lanar and try to find the intruder's body while I got out the chip and inserted it.

"Well," he said, "for an old lady you aren't too senile. That's brilliant!"

I blew another kiss over my shoulder toward him. "Gosh, you'll turn my head with compliments like that. I don't know if it's brilliant, but it's a chance. All I can do is try."

"All *we* can do, Luta. You're not alone in this."

I reached over and squeezed his hand. "I know. The idea just takes some getting used to again. Now, do you want to watch this with me?"

He did, and I touched the screen to play the video.

Mother was back in a tiny, unassuming stateroom, likely on another of the big starliners that ferried people around Nearspace. This one had at least made a nod to décor, and a wall holo behind her displayed slowly morphing images of soothing Erian landscapes. She'd dyed her hair dark brown, covering up its signature bright auburn, and it made her look older.

I do want you both to understand why I've done the things I've done, Luta and Lanar, she began. *I had to test the bioscavengers on someone, and it seemed only fair that it be me. Once I knew they worked, and I had started to suspect that PrimeCorp wasn't going to play fair with them, I couldn't live with myself until I'd shared them with both of you. Few parents want to outlive their children, and I especially wouldn't have been able to stand it knowing I'd engineered my own longevity. I'd have treated your father, too, but he didn't want it. I've never quite understood why.*

And when your father died—you were probably angry that I didn't come to the funeral. I was there—in a way. I sent a good friend with a hidden recorder. But I also knew that PrimeCorp would be watching, expecting me to turn up. And it was so hard—knowing I could have saved him, if he'd let me . . .

Her eyes brimmed and she blinked quickly, denying the tears. I felt guilty. I *had* been angry, for a long time. Until I'd figured out what her reasons probably were. That's one thing about living on a far trader—lots of time to think.

She went on. *The generation of bioscavengers you both have should keep on self-replicating without errors for at least another ten years or so, but there is a new generation I've produced that's—well, they should last pretty much indefinitely. I did plan to contact you both sometime in the next couple of years and offer them to you. If something has happened to me, all the instructions for producing them are on the chip marked NB2897, which should be in the chipcase with this one. The password is the sum of your two birthdays, plus the ages you were when we first left Earth, written in standard format. You'll have to decide yourselves if or how to go about that.*

She leaned back in her chair, which squeaked in protest, and stared at the space above the camera as if gathering her thoughts.

My own mind was whirling at what she'd said. *Indefinitely.* That meant, barring accidents, I was, or could be . . . functionally *immortal.*

An idea like that takes some getting used to. I was quiet, too, while Mother composed her thoughts on the screen. I felt Hirin take my hand.

"Wow," was all he said, and then Mother was speaking again. *There are many things to consider if the choice has come to you. When I started this project I thought it was important, the best thing we could do for humankind. I sacrificed so much because I didn't want it to come at the price of putting us all at the mercy of PrimeCorp or one of the other corporations. All these years I've kept working at it, hoping the day would come when we could distribute it freely. But sometimes when I think about it, it seems like the worst idea in the world.*

On the one hand, we could accomplish so much more if we had more time, longer lives. So much misery could be avoided if there were no death. We would have limitless capacity for joy, for discovery, for loving.

Hirin squeezed my hand again, and I squeezed back.

Mother shifted forward in her chair. *Then I consider the other side. The necessity to keep expanding, to find room for all of us to live. The wars and disagreements that might never end because death doesn't hand the problem over to a new generation. The endless ways greedy power-seekers will invent to oppress others if they have all the time in the universe to think about it and implement their plans. How much longer it will take for views and attitudes to change if there's no dying-out of a generation. I don't know. Maybe it would be a disaster.*

She paused again and I considered that. What would Alin Sedmamin do with endless years in which to scheme and plan? Would he eventually get bored with money and power and turn to philanthropy? I doubted it. You don't know how a couple hundred years could change a person, but they'd probably only reinforce character traits, whether good or bad.

And what would my future hold if I got my bioscavengers refreshed from my mother's bag of nanotechnological tricks? I couldn't imagine running a far trader forever, however much I might enjoy it now. And even if I could share them with my family, would it be the same for them? I had quite a head start in the non-aging department. Maybe I'd still have to face losing Hirin someday and spending forever without him. Maybe Maja and Karro, too. I'd thought it might be a possibility before, but I hadn't let myself consider the ramifications because I hadn't *known.* I could have been programmed to drop dead on my ninetieth birthday, for all I knew before. It wasn't worth worrying about. Now it was different. Now I knew.

Or did I? With an infinite future lay infinite possibilities. It would be the same for all people. Perhaps that was how it should be.

Mother spoke again. *At any rate, there's one major reason why I haven't been forced to make a decision about whether to release the data—industrial espionage. No-one else has arrived at a workable prototype because PrimeCorp has agents in its major competitors—Schulyer, Genusana, AriAndas. They steal data, they subtly sabotage experiments, they do whatever it takes to make sure that PrimeCorp is going to be the corporation that wins this race.*

I glanced at Hirin and he raised his eyebrows, as incredulous as I was. I whispered, "How would they be able to manage an operation like that without someone figuring it out? Wouldn't someone get suspicious eventually, if none of their research ever worked out?"

Hirin nodded. "You'd think so, eventually. But isn't that exactly why Dr. Ndasa said he came out to find your mother? So maybe PrimeCorp's luck is running out."

You're probably thinking, Mother continued, *that with all of that stolen data at their disposal, along with their own legitimate work, PrimeCorp would have made more headway by now. It's true. But PrimeCorp has one little flaw.*

Hirin snorted. "Only one? I doubt it."

I shushed him.

Hubris, Mother said, one side of her mouth twisting up a wry smile. *They've never stopped to think that any game they can play, someone else can, too. I've managed to retain a little influence on what goes on at their facilities. Let me explain—and confess, I suppose.*

None of my colleagues were happy about what PrimeCorp planned to do, when we found out about it; and, well, most of us were friends. There was no question that the original research was mine. Most of them would have had moral scruples about using my ideas without my permission. Almost all of them left PrimeCorp just after I did. I stayed in touch with them—in roundabout ways—from time to time, to make sure we remained friendly. There was one who would eventually have gone along with PrimeCorp, but he had—gaps, let us say, in his ethical makeup. And with what he knew, he probably could have helped others duplicate the research.

But—one of those ethical gaps had allowed him to have an affair with one of the PrimeCorp executives' wives . . . an affair that involved some very embarrassing appetites. After I left, I contacted him and threatened to make it public if he ever used my research. I had holos to prove it. Very nasty and explicit holos that I had lifted from his datapad before I left, and I sent him one—just one—when I contacted him. He died a number of years ago, and he'd never worked in anti-aging research again.

You might call it blackmail, she said, *but I thought of it as firm persuasion. After all, I didn't want anything from him. I just wanted him to do the honourable thing.*

At any rate, almost my entire team left the corporation, but a few stayed on, claiming that their loyalty was to PrimeCorp, and that they'd keep working on the research, even though I'd taken the data. She paused. *I don't know if PrimeCorp really trusted them at first, but I guess in the end they were convinced. It wasn't entirely for show. My colleagues did some good work there on the Vigor-Us program. They were the ones who found out when PrimeCorp put moles in the other corporations and started stealing data, and they contacted me through a communication route we'd set up when I left. We decided the best thing to do was to quietly make sure that other research fell through. And as they aged, they carefully recruited people to take their places.*

I felt a little awed. PrimeCorp was the most powerful of the megacorporations, but she had managed to secretly manipulate them from the inside. And then a realization struck me.

It was like she read my mind, because she leaned toward the screen and said, *Yes. I set up a secret way to communicate with the colleagues I left behind—but not with my family.* Her face showed a sadness so deep I could almost feel it through the screen. *When I left PrimeCorp, I didn't think we'd be on the run forever. And I wanted a way to keep up on what they were doing, keep tabs on them, and on my colleagues, to make sure they stayed loyal. Years later, by the time I left you and your father, though . . .* she drew a deep breath and blew it out. *I knew how tenacious PrimeCorp was going to be. It seemed like the only way to keep you safe—to make sure you could have a normal life—was to cut our ties completely. All I could think of was keeping you out of it. If they somehow found out you could contact me, it might have made you a target.* She shook her head. *In hindsight, perhaps I should have done things differently. But I made what seemed the best decision at the time. I'm sorry.*

At any rate, my only leverage against PrimeCorp is the evidence from my contacts on the inside. To use that means pulling my people out of there, and once that happens, there's no going back. So I have to be sure that what I have is enough, and that the time is right to do it.

If necessary, you can trigger that. One prearranged, coded message, and they'll get out and take everything with them, and get it to me as quickly as possible. Or to one of you, if they can't contact me. That's what will take the time. It'll be a roundabout route, because I didn't want to put anyone in the position of actually knowing where I was. Safer all around. The message is on the chip marked PC35411, and the password is the sum of your father's and my birthdays plus the year I left you all on Nellera. Please use it if you need to, but not without due consideration.

She leaned back again. *Anyway, there it is. My explanations and my sins. As I said, I hope we'll have a chance to talk about it all together sometime. And if not—well, it's in your hands now. I love you both. Good luck.* She blew a kiss toward the screen and the image froze.

Chapter Nineteen

Gambles, Mysteries, and Playing the Odds

"Excuse me, Captain." Yuskeya's voice came over the comm. "We're ready to try and sneak out of the planet's sensor shadow now. Ando City's going into the shadow on that side and we have a clear run to the wormhole to Beta Comae Berenices."

I touched my implant. "Start to move whenever you're ready, then. I'll be there in a minute. Thanks." I didn't get up right away, though.

"That's a lot to process," Hirin said.

"You're telling me. And I feel guilty seeing these without Lanar."

Hirin stood, pulled me to my feet as well, and kissed me lightly. "Then let's go find him," he said.

By the time we reached the bridge everyone else was there, too. Rei had taken over the pilot's console from Yuskeya, who was back in her seat at nav. Maja and Dr. Ndasa stood near the archway into Sensors, talking quietly. The main drive ticked over like a clock, its pulse rumbling through the ship as Kiando fell further and further away behind us.

"Anyone noticing us yet?" I asked as I slid into the chair.

"Would everyone please sit down so I don't have to worry about knocking you over if I have to take evasive action?" Rei asked. Maja and Dr. Ndasa moved to take skimchairs.

"Not yet," Baden answered me from the comm station. "Only a few short traders have left the planet since we did; they all seem to be headed for Cengare. There's a starliner in orbit getting ready to ship out in a couple of hours, so there's a lot of shuttle

215

traffic between it and the spaceport, but that's it."

"Let's hope it stays that way. How long to the terminal point?"

"I guess we're a little faster than that bucket PrimeCorp sent," Viss said with evident satisfaction from the engineering station. "We'll get there almost an hour faster than it took them to come in."

"So we'll jump to Beta Comae, then take the wormhole there to Keridre/Gerdrice?" asked Maja.

I nodded. "Viss, I know you wanted to have a look at that tracking device we found in the cargo pod, but did you do anything to it yet?"

"Not yet. There hasn't exactly been an opportunity," he said dryly.

"I know, that's what I was hoping. I wondered if it might be a good idea to drop it somewhere—I don't know, like maybe near a wormhole we *don't* plan to take, just as a bit of misdirection in case someone comes looking for us?"

He grimaced. "What a waste of a perfectly nice little tracker! I thought we were going to have some fun with it."

"Well, you might have to sacrifice that in the interests of survival. If it looks like they're trying to follow us, I want to leave it as a red herring."

"Oh, all right. I'll load it into one of the jettison tubes so it'll be ready."

"Good thinking. And if we don't need it, I promise you can have it back."

We managed to burn toward the wormhole, apparently undetected, for almost an hour when Baden let out a yelp.

"Ship just took off from Kiando and it's moving this way at a hell of a pace!"

"What? What is it?" I punched up the sensor readings on my own screen.

"*Dio!* It's the *Trident*, but what's she burning? That's not the same power she came in on!"

"Unless she was hiding it," I said through clenched teeth. "Probably has one of those new burst drives."

"And at the rate they're going, they'll catch us before we get to the Beta Comae wormhole," Viss added.

"But we'll be far enough out that the Kiando Planetary Police won't have any jurisdiction," I said. "We can't call on the Chairman for help."

"If this was a trap, we played right into it," Baden said. "And there's a message incoming from the *Trident*."

"Put it through," I said. I composed my face. Whoever was on the bridge of the PrimeCorp ship, I wasn't going to give them the satisfaction of seeing me look worried.

"Captain Paixon? We meet again." Dores Amadoro's face appeared on my screen. Her blonde hair was secured in a somewhat severe knot behind her head, throwing her sharp features into even stronger relief. She'd traded her sleek PrimeCorp pantsuit for an equally well-fitted corporate shipsuit with a red-embroidered logo on the collar. It was obvious who was in command of the ship chasing us. Whatever attempts at softness she may have made for the environs of PrimeCorp headquarters, she had clearly abandoned them now.

"Good day, Ms. Amadoro," I said. "Small universe."

She smiled tightly. "Getting smaller all the time, in some ways. I believe you have something to which I'm legally entitled," she said.

I shook my head. "I'm sorry, but it will take more than a piece of paper—which you could very well have simply paid for—before I willingly surrender any samples to you."

Dores Amadoro shook her head and chuckled softly. "Nice try, Captain, but I'm not as interested in your DNA as I am in the origin of it. I'm talking about your mother. She's on your ship, but I intend to exercise my warrant and take her onto mine."

I leaned back in my chair, and it was my turn to smile. "That's quite a threat. You sound almost like a pirate. Sadly, you're mistaken. My mother isn't on board—as far as I know, she's still on Kiando. So you're wasting your time looking for her here."

She cocked her head at me. "Oh, yes, of course. And I'm likely to believe that and head back to the planet? You must take me for quite a fool, Captain."

"What I think of you personally hardly matters. My mother is not on board this ship."

"I suppose we'll do this the hard way, then, Captain," she said, and cut the connection.

"Well, they obviously didn't buy Chairman Buig's story," Hirin said.

"No. And I guess it makes sense to conclude that we'd be trying to get her off the planet."

"Yeah, if we were stupid," Viss said. "If we really were trying to get her away, we never would have done it this way."

"Talk about it later, folks!" Rei said. "What are we doing now? I'm giving it all I've got, but unless Viss has a secret burst drive wired up, they're definitely going to catch us before we make this wormhole."

"I know, I know. I'm thinking." I closed my eyes to concentrate. "Yuskeya, put the wormhole route map up on my screen, would you?"

The route map appeared in front of me, showing all the known wormholes and the systems they connected. I could have rhymed them all off without the map, but now I needed to visualize our options.

As soon as I looked at it, the answer was clear.

"We have to go through the Split again."

"What?"

"Are you crazy?"

"Not again!"

I didn't know who said what, but I knew that Rei had only drawn her breath sharply and that Hirin stayed silent. Maja's lips were pressed in a thin white line.

"I know it sounds crazy, but I'm looking at it right here in front of me. We're not going to make it to the Beta Comae wormhole, but if we change course now, we should make it to the one for Delta Pavonis. Then we have three options. We can take the wormhole out to K/G, but the *Trident* will catch us first, and even if they don't, we can't hide where we're headed—they'd come through and see us. We could head towards the wormhole from that system to Beta Comae Berenices—same situation. They'll just chase us from system to system until they catch us—which they will eventually. Even if they find out at that point that Mother's not on board, I'd rather not have them catch us at all."

"Obviously," said Viss.

"But, if we skip into Delta Pav and head for the Split into GI 892, we might make the terminal point out again before they're in the Delta Pavonis system, so they won't necessarily know that's where we went, especially if Viss can mask our drive signature or scramble it a little. We can jettison the tracking device in the direction of the wormhole to Beta Comae, which is where they thought we were headed anyway, so they might take that bait.

And even if they think we took the Split, they might not have a pilot who'll attempt it. They'll have to go the long way around even if they figure out where we're going. At any rate they won't know where we've headed out of GI 892."

"And from GI 892 there's another wormhole to K/G anyway," Yuskeya said. "But PrimeCorp won't necessarily be expecting us to take it. They're much more likely to think we'd head to Eri from there, trying a more roundabout route to Beta Comae to avoid them."

"Couldn't we do it in reverse?" Maja asked. "Leave the tracker near the Split as a red herring and actually take the other wormhole like we planned?"

"The Split's closer. We can't make it to the other one before they come through. They'd see us. And they're less likely to go through the Split anyway."

There was silence, then Hirin spoke.

"Luta's right. It's the best chance." There was no hesitation in his voice, and I loved him as much in that moment as I had in my entire life. He was the one with more to fear from the Split than any of the rest of us. If he were willing, I knew the others wouldn't balk.

"So, change course for the Delta Pavonis wormhole?" Yuskeya asked.

"Do it," I said.

"*Trident* is also changing course," Baden reported after a moment. He ran his fingers over his touchscreen, gathering data. "They've gained on us some, but we'll definitely make it to the Delta Pav wormhole well ahead of them."

"As long as we can get to the Split before they come through," I said.

"It'll be close, but if we can maintain speed, we could do it," Yuskeya said.

Viss left his console and sprinted down the corridor toward the engineering hatchway, shouting something over his shoulder about having an idea for re-routing more power to the main drive.

"Captain," Baden said, "Yuskeya told me you want to track down your brother. I could send a message through the K/G wormhole to the Protectorate base on Nellera, see if they can tell us where he is. We might get a response back before we leave this system."

Sherry D. Ramsey

"Good thinking, Baden, do it," I said. "With luck, he's still in Beta Comae; we can get there in two skips from GI892."

The overheads dimmed, the ship shuddered a bit and Rei gave a whoop. "Viss is as good as his word. That's a fifteen percent increase in power, so PrimeCorp should have a harder time catching us."

"Message coming from the *Trident*," Baden said.

"On my screen."

The cold eyes of Dores Amadoro stared out at me again. "Captain, I am prepared to disable your ship if necessary."

I stared back at her, considering. "You're bluffing," I said. "If you want my mother this badly—and you truly think she's on this ship—you won't risk harming her."

"That's why I'm sending this message," she said coolly. "I'm advising everyone on your ship to get into EVA suits, just in case your life support systems suffer . . . collateral damage. Or you could just stop, let us catch up to you, and allow your mother to come with us peacefully. I am anxious to meet her, you know, so that I can thank her."

"Thank her?"

Amadoro smiled, but it was not a nice smile. Too much wolf and not enough warmth. "When I recognized her and took that information to Chairman Sedmamin, it did wonders for my future at PrimeCorp. I can honestly say I wouldn't be where I am today without your mother." Her face hardened. "So I'm prepared to take whatever steps are necessary to secure that meeting."

I muted the feed. "Folks? Could they have any kind of weapon that might be capable of reaching us from that distance?"

Yuskeya shook her head decisively. "Not a chance. When they get closer, maybe. But not from that far away. They could fire torps, but we'd have so much time to get out of the way, it wouldn't be worth launching them."

"Nothing I know of, for sure," Rei agreed.

"Yuskeya's right," Viss chimed in from Engineering. "Tell her to blow it out her—"

I killed the feed from Engineering and switched back to Amadoro. She was still there, looking annoyed.

"Thanks for the warning, Ms. Amadoro," I said, and cut the connection before she could say anything else. "Everyone into EVA suits."

220

"They're too far away!" Rei protested.

"I think you were right in the first place," Hirin said. "She's bluffing."

I shrugged and left the chair, heading for the bank of EVA lockers near the bridge airlock. "Nevertheless, I am not taking any chances. Suit up."

They weren't happy, but they did it. I didn't like it, either, since the suits were bulky and got hot after a while, but I didn't trust Dores Amadoro not to have some new long-range weapon she was just itching to try out on us. PrimeCorp could easily have developed something that was still a corporate secret.

So it wasn't the most pleasant time I've spent on the bridge of the *Tane Ikai*, but it passed, and we watched the *Trident* slowly devour the distance between us as we neared the wormhole to Delta Pavonis. They still weren't what you'd call close—but I wanted as much distance as possible between us. They hadn't fired on us by the time Rei fired up the skip drive, and I smiled to myself. As bluffs go, Amadoro's hadn't even been a very good one.

"Torpedo away from the *Trident*!" Baden said suddenly. "Moving fast."

"Time?" I asked.

"We can dodge it or get into the wormhole, but we have to do one or the other. Immediately."

"Rei?"

"Initializing skip drive now," she said. The low whir of the drive thrummed through the ship and reverberated in the decking under our feet.

"Everyone take your seats," I said, and opened a channel to Dr. Ndasa's room. He'd excused himself from the bridge and gone back to his room, with a promise to keep his EVA suit on. "We're about to make a skip, Doctor."

"I'm ready, Captain," he answered.

"Going in," Rei said evenly as the mouth of the wormhole opened up and swallowed us. The mad swirl of colours spun us along its length, skipping and spinning as fast as the drive could propel us. Rei kept the ship rock steady, and I was sure we skipped that wormhole faster than it had ever been done before.

No-one spoke while we were inside. The instant we exited the terminal point, Rei cut the skip drive and Yuskeya's fingers flew over the touchscreen as she laid in the coordinates for the Split.

I told Baden to monitor the wormhole we'd just exited for any signs of the *Trident*.

"Aye, Captain." He touched the screen. "Message is away to Nellera regarding your brother. And I'm ready to launch that tracking device at your signal."

"Use your own judgment unless I say otherwise, Baden, because I might be distracted. Fire it off at the optimal vector for the Beta Comae wormhole. That's the best we can do."

"Will do."

I took off my EVA helmet and said, "Okay folks, shuck your helmets and gloves but keep them nearby." The air on the bridge felt deliciously cool against my skin.

I caught Hirin's eye and he smiled and winked at me as he unfastened his helmet. Then he crossed to Rei's chair and bent low beside her, telling her something in a low voice. My breath caught in my throat and I almost choked, but I managed to clamp it down. The last thing the crew needed now was a captain going to pieces on them, but this plan terrified me. What if the Split affected Hirin's heart again? He already had all the help I could give him.

All I could do was hope he wasn't going to get his wish to die in space just yet. Hope, in fact, that none of us were.

"Captain?" It was Yuskeya. "I was thinking—we should ask Dr. Ndasa to come back up to the bridge for this next skip."

I sensed a silent presence just behind me before I could answer. It was Maja, but she said nothing, simply put a warm hand on my shoulder.

"That's a good idea." I glanced over at Hirin, still talking to Rei, and Maja's hand twitched as she followed my gaze. She kept silent.

I lowered my voice. "I think he'll be fine, but it would be good to have the doctor up here just in case. The bioscavengers have been working in Hirin for a while now. They might have repaired all the damage that was done the last time *and* whatever caused it in the first place." I turned to look at Maja. "Are you okay with this?"

She pressed her lips together, then nodded. "Look at him. He's not worried. He wants to do this. I haven't seen him like this for a long time."

I nodded my agreement. "If I changed my mind now, and he thought it was because of him, he'd never forgive me."

I reached up wordlessly and squeezed Maja's hand. *Thank you.* She squeezed back.

"Maja, would you go and bring Dr. Ndasa up from up his quarters?" I asked.

"Right away," she said, with a final glance at her father, and hurried down the corridor.

Hirin straightened up from Rei. "We're going to go in cold this time, folks. You had last time to cut your teeth, this time, no babystepping. Rei's asked me to take the secondary helm, which I'll do if the Captain approves it." He looked to me and I nodded. "So we're going to be firing up the skip drive on the fly. I want everyone sitting down and buckled in when we do that."

He strode over to the secondary helm as if he owned the place—well, he did, half-ownership, anyway—and hailed Viss on the ship's comm. "Viss, about that power you've got re-routed to the main drive?"

"Oh yeah, can you feel it?"

Hirin grinned. "I can feel it. Do you think you could rig something to switch it directly over to the skip drive stabilizers when I give the word?"

"Give me half an hour," Viss said. "It won't be a smooth ride, but I think I can do it."

Yuskeya looked up from the nav screen. "Half an hour is on the outside edge of what you've got," she told him. "We have to be out of sight before that PrimeCorp ship makes the wormhole. It doesn't have to be pretty. It just has to work. Right, Hirin?"

"You've got it," he answered.

Diable, I could see the day coming when he'd be captain of the *Tane Ikai* and I'd be busted back to piloting again, if the crew got to choose. No, Rei was a better pilot than I was. Cook, maybe. Seemed like Hirin was becoming their favourite person, but it was okay with me. He was already mine.

Half an hour passes with a speed relative to what you're trying to do in it. If you were Viss, trying to set up the power crossover, I expect it would go amazingly quickly. If you were me, sitting and watching everybody else work while I waited for the *Trident* to burst out of the wormhole behind us, it was agonizingly slow.

Finally, we were there. I'd already picked out the dark mouth of the Split, and we were coming up on it fast. Maja and Dr. Ndasa had arrived and taken seats at two of the empty sensor stations near Hirin. The Vilisian caught my eye and nodded gravely. He knew why he was here.

"Data packet back from Nellera," Baden said.

"I'll look at it on the other side," I told him.

"Viss, you ready?" Hirin asked over the ship's comm.

"Well, I can't say for sure that it's going to work, but I'm ready to give it a try," he answered.

"Okay, Rei and Viss, listen up. On my mark, Rei's going to engage the skip drive. Viss, you count about three seconds and then do the switch. Yuskeya, just do exactly what you did the last time. It was perfect. Baden, you're going to jettison the tracking device as soon as you hear me give Rei the word. Everybody okay?"

I couldn't resist. "Anything I can do?"

Hirin didn't turn around, but I was sure he was smiling. "Cross your fingers, Captain."

I didn't. He knew I wasn't superstitious. Then Hirin barked, "Rei, skip drive now!" Baden said, "Jettison tube engaged," and Viss must have done whatever he was going to do down in Engineering because the ship bucked violently a couple of times and then we were swallowed up by the eerie half-presence of the Split.

I'd kept my eyes locked on the screen that showed the sensor readings for other ships in the area. Just as we entered the Split, they seemed to be picking up something—maybe the *Trident* coming out of the wormhole from Mu Cassiopeia, I don't know. I didn't think they could have gotten to the wormhole that fast, but I couldn't be certain, with that burst drive. I hoped, if it was them, they hadn't seen us go into the Split.

Maybe I should have crossed my fingers after all.

At any rate, there wasn't time to worry about that now. Rei and Hirin between them were piloting us through the Split, keeping the skips so short and close together that we barely moved from side to side down the length of the tunnel. Viss's extra power to the field generators must have held, because the ride was exponentially smoother than the last time we'd made this trip.

And Hirin—I could hardly keep my eyes off him, watching for anything untoward, but he seemed perfectly fine. He was deep in concentration, synchronizing his efforts with Rei's, but he didn't seem to be in the least distressed. I couldn't relax just yet, but I let out a breath I'd barely realized I was holding.

The passage was so much faster this time—or at least it seemed so—that before I knew it we were slipping out the other end, into the quiet darkness of GI 892's red dwarf system, and I gave them a chance to sigh and cheer and babble in delight.

"Okay, okay." I clapped my hands. "Great job, everyone, but it's not over yet. For all we know the *Trident* is still right behind us, so we want to high-tail it out of here. Viss, are you there?"

"Here, Captain. That was a hell of a ride."

"You got that right. Now listen, that magical power-boosting you were doing down there, how long can that work?"

"I know you'd like me to say indefinitely, but I can't. I'm stealing power from all kinds of places, but I can't keep it up or I might overload the system. We could burn it to the next wormhole if you think it's necessary, but I wouldn't advise switching it again or running it for longer than that. I should really put things back to normal then."

"Okay, keep the reroutes on the main drive until we get to the next wormhole. We won't need to switch it back to the stabilizers for that one, and you can put everything back in place then. But I'd appreciate any extra distance we can put between us and our friend Ms. Amadoro."

"No problem, Captain."

"Yuskeya, lay in a course for the Keridre/Gerdrice wormhole, and Rei, let's get there as fast as we can. Everybody else—take a break, I guess." I grinned. "I wonder what Dores Amadoro is doing right now?"

"As long as she's not running for the Split, she's not a worry," Baden said. "You want that message from the Protectorate on Nellera now?"

"Yes, please." It came up on my screen, brief, and not what I'd been hoping to see. My brother's ship, the *S. Cheswick*, was back in Sol system, too far away to help get PrimeCorp off my tail—or help me figure out where Mother was now.

Chapter Twenty

To Those Who Wait

"*Damne*," I whispered, but Baden heard me and turned in his skimchair.

"Not what you were hoping for," he said.

I shook my head. "I really want to talk to him," I said, "and I don't want PrimeCorp listening in. But Sol system is three skips from here no matter which way you go."

Baden cocked an eyebrow at me. "Remind me again what we're going to do while we're here in K/G?" he asked.

"Find the cargo crate, if we can," I said with a frown. "But I'm not going to spend too much time on it now. Talking to Lanar seems more—"

I broke off because Baden was looking at me expectantly.

"What?" I asked.

"And the cargo crate is going to be near . . .?"

"The pinhole," I said in exasperation, but by the time I got the words out I realized what he was getting at. "The pinhole! Which is a communications gateway to—"

"Sol system," he finished for me. "And if we get a message to him and bring him to that end of the pinhole, and we cozy up to this end, it'll be about as secure a communication as you could have face-to-face."

"As long as we get into K/G before the *Trident* catches up with us," I said. "Thanks, Baden." I stood up. "I think I'll go talk to Viss, see if he can't get us even a little more power to the main drives."

Trying to get somewhere in a hurry when you don't know if you're being followed is enough to make anyone want to scream, and this trip took almost twelve hours. It was a relief to arrive at the terminal point for the wormhole to Keridre/Gerdrice with still no sign of the PrimeCorp ship behind us. Viss had managed to get us a little more juice at the expense of the heating systems, but with extra sweaters we were all okay. I sat down next to Yuskeya while Rei and Viss did the last-minute preparations for the skip.

Baden's readings from his tracer scan had come from the planet Nellera, so the pinhole wasn't too far from there. The wormhole we would be entering the system through, on the other hand, came out somewhat closer to Stana, the middle inhabited planet. As long as the homing beacon on the cargo crate was still broadcasting, it shouldn't be too difficult to focus our efforts and find both the crate and the pinhole.

I wasn't surprised when everyone showed up on the bridge for the skip into K/G. It was something to do besides look over our shoulders for PrimeCorp.

The skip was nothing out of the ordinary, although the inside of a wormhole is always worth looking at—same as you can't really ever get tired of sunsets or starry nights no matter what planet you happen to be on. I held my breath as we neared the end of it, though, because no matter how cocky I'd tried to sound, I wasn't altogether sure there wouldn't be an armada of PrimeCorp ships lying in wait just beyond the terminal point.

I let it out in a long sigh when we cleared the end of the wormhole and the only thing waiting for us was the distant globe of Stana, shining in the reflected light of its double suns.

"Baden, can you get any kind of a reading on the pinhole yet?"

"*Hola*, Captain, we're still too far out. I'll start scanning, but don't expect any return for a while yet."

"I know, I know, but it doesn't hurt to ask. Okay, let's head toward Nellera with our sensors at maximum."

The fifth planet of the K/G system, Nellera, was just inside the double star's habitable zone. Much further out and it would have been too cold to be welcoming, but as it was, some nice little colonies gathered around the warm and watery equator. The hospitable spots on Nellera were mostly island chains looping around the planet's middle, and they did a booming tourist trade with the two other inhabited planets in the system, Stana and Tarcol.

The most likely scenario for the crate was that it had come

through the pinhole's terminal point and was still coasting along an unobstructed path that led in-system. While this wasn't necessarily a good thing, since it meant the path would take it further and further into more heavily travelled space, it was my preferred scenario because it made the crate the easiest to find. It also meant that it would be heading towards us as we pointed our nose towards Nellera, and that if we found it, the pinhole would also be easy to find.

We watched Nellera grow larger and larger in the viewscreen for a while. Baden said, "Well, I hate to say it, but if the crate had just come out and headed in this direction, I should be picking up the homing beacon by now. I think we'd better consider some other possibilities."

Damne. "Such as the chance that some piece of space junk or a small asteroid collided with it and changed its trajectory?"

Or smashed it to smithereens. No one said it, but I was sure everyone was thinking it.

"Possibly, yes. I can change the parameters of the sensor field, to extend further out to one side or the other from the ship," Baden said, "but there's not much else we can try. We at least need to get within reach of the beacon."

"I think we should concentrate on finding the pinhole," I said. "It would be great to find the body, too, but I think the priority has to be contacting Lanar. Turn the attention to that for now, but keep the sensors up. If we're looking for the pinhole and we come across the crate, too, so much the better."

But I didn't really feel that lucky. The initial anticipation I'd felt in the air on the bridge as we entered the last wormhole was fading fast, and we needed to focus. I wanted to have my discussion with Lanar before the possibility of PrimeCorp appearing at any moment made me any more anxious.

"Come on, folks, don't be so gloomy. You didn't expect it would be sitting outside the wormhole waiting for us, did you?"

"No, but a person can hope," Yuskeya muttered.

"Let's get to the pinhole first, and worry about the crate later."

Baden called up the data from his tracer scan and went about analyzing where it meant the pinhole should be. After a few minutes he said, "Rei, I'm shooting you some coordinates. Head for them, and if the pinhole's within sensor range of there, we should find it."

My nerves were running high, since two of the inhabited

planets in this system were PrimeCorp-controlled. The
Protectorate administered Nellera, and that was the only planet
we were planning to get close to. I didn't know how much notice
PrimeCorp took of the rest of the system. For all I knew they
might have their eye on Nellera, watching for data runners or
other corporations or who knew what.

And I wondered what Lanar was going to say about Mother's
revelations. As an admiral in the Protectorate, I didn't know what
he'd think of her confessions to things that had been outside the
strictly legal. Then again, he was good at turning a blind eye to
things I'd done when I didn't feel that "right" and "legal"
completely coincided. Maybe he would do the same for our
mother.

"Got it!" Baden yelled suddenly.

I jumped. "What?"

"The cargo crate, off to the dock side, almost outside the
sensor range." He entered coordinates on his screen. "Rei, you
want to take us over there?"

"Sure thing," she said with a grin. "That's easy compared to
some of the things I've been asked to do lately."

"So the pinhole should be . . ."

"Just got a fix on that, too," Baden said. "We can pick up the
crate, then head straight over there to try and contact Admiral
Mahane."

It wasn't long before we could actually see the crate onscreen,
hanging still and dead, looking like a discarded toy. I felt another
pang of conscience, much like the one I'd had the day we
jettisoned it. It didn't seem like a very dignified place for a body,
especially when I felt responsible for it being there.

"Why isn't it still moving?" I asked.

"Good question," Hirin said. "The only answer is, something—
or someone—stopped it."

"It might not be very . . . pleasant, when we open this," Viss
murmured. "Even if the body is frozen, and might not have
decomposed much—"

"Eww!" Maja said, wrinkling her nose.

"He might be starting to look sort of freeze-dried," he
continued.

"Do we have to talk about this?" Maja demanded.

Viss just grinned. "Are you going to lift it into one of the cargo
pods and keep it there until we get back to Kiando? They're all

empty now."

"That's what I'd planned. Put it in Pod Two, it's the smallest."
I hadn't realized until now how creepy it was going to be,
travelling all the way back there knowing what horrible cargo we
carried below.

When we got close enough, Viss and Baden went down to
Engineering, where the controls for the remote arms were. We
didn't use the remotes very often, but occasionally they came in
handy for transferring cargo between ships in space instead of at
a spacedock. With the remotes it wasn't necessary for anyone to
go on EVA—you just put your arms inside the big gloves and
mimed what you wanted the real things to do.

Viss was working the remotes and keeping up a running
commentary for those of us still up on the bridge. He'd latched
on to the cargo crate on the first try and then muttered, "Uh-oh."

"I don't like the sound of that."

"It could be a misreading," he said hesitantly.

"Just tell me."

"There's not enough mass."

"Not enough mass?"

"The remotes provide feedback on the mass of whatever
they're picking up, since it has to match up to the cargo manifest
especially on skip runs, where weight calculations are
important," Viss explained. "The reading I'm getting seems too
small for the crate and its contents. Unless I'm wrong about what
the crate weighs."

But this was Viss, the man who knew more specs about the
Tane Ikai and everything in it than I did, and I knew how likely
it was that he had it wrong—not likely at all.

"Where's the crate now?" I asked, getting up.

"Bringing it through the pod bay doors," Viss said. "I'll have
the doors closed and the air pressure equalized by the time you
get here."

He hadn't counted on how fast I was moving, though, and I
had to stand and tap my foot impatiently at the airlock hatchway
to Cargo Pod Two while the air was pumped back in. Everyone
else—including Rei, who really should have stayed at the helm—
gathered around it, too. When the indicator went green I opened
the hatch and climbed down into the cargo pod, the others
clattering one by one down the ladder behind me. The cargo crate
lay on the far side of the strapped-down groundcar, on its side

over near the bay doors, and we practically ran over to it.

I found out what I wanted to know soon enough, anyway. Not letting myself stop to think about what the inside of the crate might be like, I keyed in the simple unlocking code and lifted the lid.

Viss, as usual, had been right. The crate was empty, and the body of the identity-stripped operative, one of our keys to bringing PrimeCorp down, had vanished into the blackness of space.

I slammed the hatch closed. "*Damne, damne*! What do we do now?"

Hirin shook his head. "Doesn't make sense. How could the body be gone?"

"Are we sure it's our crate?"

"Yes, because of the homing beacon. And the unlock code worked."

"PrimeCorp," Maja said in a tight voice. "It has to be. Somehow they tracked him here—"

"I don't think so." I cut her off. I didn't want to believe it was possible. "They couldn't know he was in this system. He had no ID biochip for them to track him with, and there's no way they'd find that homing beacon by chance."

"Although they did have the tracking device on the *Tane Ikai*," Hirin mused. "They might have been tracking us but staying just at the edge of our sensor range from the moment we left Earth. Maybe they knew when we jettisoned the crate and knew it went into the pinhole, did the same thing Baden did to see where it went, then sent someone out to pick it up in case it could lead back to them."

"The tracking device couldn't have had that strong a signal," I argued. "Surely they couldn't have been close enough to pick up the signal but out of range of our sensors. And why leave the crate here?"

"They could have had a tiny tracker on the op's body," Viss suggested. "We didn't strip him down. Never thought of it."

"Or maybe someone just found the crate and opened it to see if there was anything valuable in it," Maja said reasonably.

"So when they discovered it was a body, why didn't they just put it back out in space?" Rei asked. "Anybody with any decency would. It's got no value."

"Anybody with any decency wouldn't have opened it in the first place," Maja said.

"It might be valuable to someone," Baden mused. "There are lots of traders out here, and not all of them are dealing in things we'd like to think about."

"Ick," said Yuskeya. "I know I don't."

I kicked the crate once, knowing it was childish. "Well, I'm freezing my butt off down here, so I'm going upstairs for a triple caff. I might even find something interesting to use as an additive. You're all welcome to join me. And then we'll see if I can get through to Lanar, or if this whole detour has been a waste of time."

We trooped back up the hatchway ladders again. I was starting to think I'd look into installing some kind of elevator when I put the *Tane Ikai* in for a refit. I'd never climbed the ladder as much as I had on this trip.

Rei and Baden went back to the bridge. I fetched a bottle of Vileyran whiskey from the secret compartment in my cabin and plunked it down on the galley table with a "Help yourself." When the rest of us had collected our beverages of choice from the galley we followed Rei and Baden to the bridge, taking drinks for them, too. The *Tane Ikai* was already moving toward the pinhole, and as I came onto the bridge, Baden said, "Message request queued up and ready to send on the WaVE, Captain. If Admiral Mahane is in Sol System we should know pretty quickly."

Baden was right. Lanar pinged back with a WaVE message within three minutes. I opened it up on my screen. Lanar was on the bridge of the *S. Cheswick*; I could see crewmen at consoles in the background. "*Saluton*, little sister! I didn't know you were back in Sol System."

It was good to see his smiling face, and I felt some hidden tension in my chest loosen. I hadn't realized just how badly I wanted to talk to him. "*Saluton*, Lanar, but I'm not actually in the system. If I send you some coordinates, can you tell me how quickly you can get to them?"

He raised one eyebrow. "Hmmm, all business today. Sure, send them along."

I nodded to Baden and he sent the data packet along the WaVE. I watched Lanar relay them to a crewman. "What's up, Luta? Are you all right?"

I let myself smile a little. "I'm not even sure how to answer that, Lanar. An awful lot is 'up.' Although I am all right, for the moment at least. And better now that I'm talking to you."

His eyes softened and he smiled. "No more pirate attacks, I hope."

I shook my head. "Fortunately, no. But then again, I'm not carrying any particularly interesting cargo, either."

He looked off-screen briefly and then said, "We can be at those coordinates in about six hours if we burn hard," he said. "And if it's important."

"I think you'll agree it's important," I said, "But I don't want to say anything else unless I know we're secure. Will you come?"

His grey eyes went very serious as he studied me on the screen. "We'll be there," he said, "although my navigator claims there's nothing of interest in that sector."

"Well, maybe your navigator will learn something new," I said with a wink. "*Gis la revido*, Lanar. I'll talk to you soon."

Six hours was a long time to wait and hope that PrimeCorp didn't show up. I retreated to my cabin and watched Mother's videos again, and tried to decide what she should do. Deep in my heart, I believed she'd been right to keep PrimeCorp from using the research unscrupulously. Whether she'd signed a contract or not, they were her ideas, and I felt she had a moral right to some control over them. And PrimeCorp had certainly proved itself an unworthy caretaker of humanity's future.

But now, with the Schulyer Group to consider, the situation might have changed. If their research turned out to be sound, the control that Mother had guarded so closely was about to be taken out of her hands anyway. And if Schulyer hadn't gotten there, someone else would before long. Mother would not be able to stop it from coming. All she could do would be to try and ensure that people had fair access. But some of the things she'd said in her videos were bothering me. I wanted to talk to Lanar about them, but that wasn't going to happen for a while. And for some reason I didn't want to go to Hirin or Maja with this.

I went down to Dr. Ndasa's cabin and lightly rapped my knuckles on the door.

"Come in," he called.

The doctor sat at the desk in his room, reading something on his datapad. He set it down when the door opened and got to his feet. As usual, his violet-coloured eyes were calm and his demeanour quiet. It struck me that this seemed to be his default state. "Captain Paixon. What can I do for you?"

I took a deep breath. "I want you to know that I don't really blame you for being . . . secretive . . . about your reasons for wanting to find my mother."

He lowered his head like a penitent. "Thank you. I did not enjoy deceiving you—although it was only a partial deception—but I felt that the importance of the cause perhaps superseded personal feelings."

I nodded. "I was angry, but I do get it. As long as Schulyer is not going to turn into another PrimeCorp—"

Dr. Ndasa shook his head vehemently at that.

"—then that's it," I finished. "But I do want to ask you something."

He gestured that I should take his vacated desk chair, and seated himself primly on the edge of the bunk, adjusting his shipsuit awkwardly. He'd left Kiando without any belongings other than his datapad and the clothes he'd worn to Chairman Buig's salon, so we'd lent him some shipsuits. He didn't seem entirely comfortable in them, although he didn't complain.

"You've spent a long time hunting for the secret to immortality, just like my mother," I began.

The Vilisian nodded, his long ebony braid swinging slightly.

"Did you have to struggle to decide if it would be a good thing, or a bad thing, in terms of the future of our races?" I asked. "Or has the answer to that always been clear to you?

He waggled his head. "Not always clear, no. When I first became interested in the field, it was all about figuring out *if* and *how* we could do it, not necessarily *should* we do it," he said. "There are arguments for both sides. How would we deal with near-immortality? Would it cause more problems than it would solve?"

I nodded. "I watched a video that my mother left for me. She seems to have struggled with the same questions, and never really been able to come to a decision. I think if she had, she would have released the data from her PrimeCorp research into the public or given it to other researchers long ago."

He chuckled. "It might have saved her a lot of trouble—or made more for her. She still might have had to run from

PrimeCorp, and from the law as well if they wanted to press their rights."

I couldn't sit still any longer, and got up from the chair to pace the small room. Since all of the Vilisian's belongings had been unloaded back on Kiando, it was back to the bare bones of bunk, desk, and dresser. I felt a little pang of guilt for hustling him along with us so unceremoniously. And yet he'd come along and stayed without protest.

"What I keep coming back to," I said, "is that I don't know if it's any one person's decision to make. I know my mother wanted the knowledge to be used responsibly, if it was used at all. She said she believed that no one should have sole control of human aging, when she was talking about PrimeCorp. But hasn't she put herself in exactly that position? She's the one hanging on to the control. So I think she may have been wrong in keeping the data secret."

"And that is difficult for you to accept," he said, the skin around his eyes crinkling as he studied me.

I nodded. "In the years since she left us, all that time spent looking for her, I've always assumed that when I found her—we'd agree on things. That whatever had made her leave us and stay away, was a noble cause. That I'd understand everything she did and why she did it, if she just had a chance to explain." I leaned against the wall next to the desk. "Well, I've heard her explanation—at least an abbreviated version—and I don't really agree with her."

"But you are still worried about her whereabouts," he said.

"Absolutely. I'm just worried that when I find her—we're not going to get along."

Dr. Ndasa regarded me, then seemed to come to a decision. "Captain, there is something about my race that is not well-known. We have the ability, if we choose, to change our memories. To adjust them to what we want to remember, rather than what actually happened."

I looked at him in confusion. "Humans don't have perfect memories, either, Doctor."

He shook his head gently. "No, this is different—a matter of control. The old memories remain, but we can keep them submerged, hidden beneath what we would rather remember. It makes life . . . easier, in many respects. We can literally change the past—or at least our experience of it. We can make it easier to bear."

"That's—that's really fascinating," I said. "I didn't know that. But I'm not sure I understand—"

"I mention this because I think I understand your Mother's choices. Without my people's memory-altering ability, she would be most concerned at making the wrong decision in this matter. She would feel responsible for whatever happened as a result of her actions—actions that could affect all of humanity and the other races as well. Because I would have the option to escape it, I can appreciate the enormity of that prospect."

I considered it. "And she'd be around to see those consequences. All the consequences. Potentially for . . . forever," I said slowly. "I guess that would be pretty daunting."

Dr. Ndasa smiled. "I think you also sell yourself short, Captain," he said. "I've watched how you 'get along' with everyone—even your daughter, with whom I gather you have had difficult times. I think you need not fear a relationship with your mother."

I fetched a deep breath. "Thanks, Doctor. I hope you're right."

And I hoped I'd get the chance to find out.

Chapter Twenty-One

Brotherly Love

The hours crept by as we waited for the *S. Cheswick* to arrive at the Sol end of the pinhole. It was far worse than hours spent travelling through space, when at least sometimes the scenery was interesting: nebulae, asteroids, wispy clouds of cosmic dust. At some point in the waiting process I went to the galley with Hirin and Maja and we had a meal together. Maja cooked up a delicious stir-fry and Hirin put fresh fruit over ice cream for dessert. We talked about our lives together and apart, and half of it I don't even remember, except that for a little while I let go of everything I was worrying about and it was kind of amazing.

So when the message ping came in from Lanar, I felt pretty good. I took the conversation in my cabin, because I wanted to talk to him about PrimeCorp and I knew we needed privacy.

"Aren't you the secretive one," he chided me when his face came on-screen. "How long have you known about this pinhole?"

The reception was incredibly clear, considering the almost unimaginable physical distance that separated us. Lanar was in his shipboard office, and the lettering on the wall plaque behind him was almost readable. I knew what it read anyway, though; *In Astra Pax*, the motto of the Protectorate. Peace Among the Stars. He had the lights low, his face thrown half into shadow.

I shrugged. "Not long, really; Baden discovered it when we were leaving Sol System the last time. He's convinced he'll get to name it," I added with a smile.

"And he should." Lanar studied me. "So, why this little rendezvous? Not that I don't like talking to you," he added.

I blew out a long breath. "Where to start? I'll give you the condensed version. I found Mother—and lost her again. I have

239

some messages from her that I want you to see. PrimeCorp is after me because they think Mother's on board my ship. We need to find her and make things safe for her, and I might have an idea how to do that. How's that for a start?"

Lanar grinned and shook his head, then took a deep breath of his own. "Little sister, I think it's time to pool our resources. But first I really want to see those messages from Mother. Can you narrowbeam them to me through the pinhole?"

I wondered what he meant by "pool our resources," but that was sort of what I was hoping for, anyway, so I didn't press him on it. I commed Baden and asked him to send the datapacket of the messages, which I'd already downloaded from the chip and prepared. A few moments later, Lanar and I were watching them together.

Even all together, they weren't terribly long. At the end, Lanar was solemn. "You sure look like her. Sound like her, too." He ran a hand over his face. "It's a lot to take in."

I nodded. "But Lanar, here's what you don't know. Dr. Ndasa, who skipped out to Kiando with us, works with Schulyer Group. They think they've come up with something just as good as Mother's nanobioscavs, and they want her to vet their research."

He pursed his lips. "So if that pans out, she won't have to worry any more about PrimeCorp having a monopoly? She could just give them back their data and step away from the whole thing."

"I don't think she'll see it as being that easy. She's held onto this data for a long time, and she feels responsible. Even if she gives it to PrimeCorp, she's going to worry about what they'll do with it—and how they might still come after her, legally, maybe. And after all the things they've done—not legal things, I might add—I don't want them to have the data, either. They can't be trusted. I think it's time for PrimeCorp to take a fall. A big one."

Lanar leaned back in his chair and laced his fingers behind his head. "What if I told you that we can't afford to have PrimeCorp take too big a fall? The timing isn't right."

"We? Who's we? Who wouldn't be better off with them out of the picture?"

"A lot of people, sadly. Think about it. PrimeCorp is Vigor-Us, it's techrigs, it's skip drive technology." He held up a hand. "I know, there are others in the same fields. But not nearly as influential or with the same kind of reach. It's also the government on five Nearspace planets. More than half of the people in Nearspace *depend* on PrimeCorp for one thing or another, and if we pulled the rug out from under them, it would hurt. Hurt industry, hurt medicine, hurt people all over Nearspace. To make matters worse, too much of the system is built on interdependent political connections, and who owes whom. A breakdown of that web might open the door for someone even worse to step into the gap while things were in confusion."

I stared at him. "So we just let PrimeCorp get away with whatever they want? Is that Protectorate policy? That's not right, either."

Lanar shook his head. "No, it's not. And it's not that we're doing nothing about it. In fact, I'm supposed to give you this." He touched the screen and a datapacket showed up on mine. "We've set up a hearing on Vele, before the Nearspace Worlds Administrative Council, to present evidence about PrimeCorp's illegal tech operation—the one Viss helped us with. Your datapacket is a summons to appear to give evidence—you and the crew. It's not going to bring down PrimeCorp, by any means, but it's not meant to, either. Just push back a little. Cut out one of the tumours."

I steepled my fingers and tapped them against my lips while I thought, realizing after a second that I'd picked up the habit from Hirin. "Okay. I had thought about bringing my own complaint against PrimeCorp. I've got a fair bit of evidence accumulated, which I was going to take to Chairman Buig on Kiando. Rei already suggested that I *could* bring the complaint—and then be 'persuaded' to drop the charges if they'd come to some agreement with Mother. This could work to our advantage. If they're already in trouble because of the illegal tech, they might not want any other complications right now." I chewed my lip. "It doesn't completely solve the PrimeCorp problem, but it would get them off our backs."

"Blackmail them into leaving Mother alone?" he said with a grin. "You sound just like her."

"Not blackmail." I grinned. "I'd prefer to think of it as firm persuasion. And if the Schulyer data turns out to be solid, PrimeCorp might be willing to forget any plans of action against Mother just to get their own data back."

He nodded. "It might be persuasive enough. And it wouldn't

interfere with the bigger picture of what the Protectorate's doing."

I sat back again and rubbed my hands over my face. "I just wish I knew where she was. She gave us the password—we could send the message to get her people out of PrimeCorp and take their evidence with them, and that would give us even more leverage against them. But I hate to do it without her permission. I don't know if the situation is really desperate enough to pull down what she has set up there, because once it's gone, it's gone." I sighed. "At first I was scared PrimeCorp had taken her on Kiando, but Dores Amadoro certainly didn't seem to think that. So in that case, I don't know where she is. Or even if she's acting as a free agent."

I stared at him earnestly. "Is there anything the Protectorate can do to help find her now? Could you start trying to track her from Kiando, or put out some kind of watch on her known aliases, or—"

Lanar sighed and gestured for me to stop. "I think before we go any further with that, it's time for me to come clean on something. Would you mind inviting your navigator to join us in this little chat?"

"Yuskeya?" I stared at him. "What's Yuskeya got to do with any of this?"

He smiled, the mischievous smile I knew so well from when we were kids. "Get her, and I'll tell you."

Shaking my head, I touched my comm button. "Yuskeya, would you come to my cabin, please?"

"Right away, Captain."

In moments she tapped on the door and I told her to come in. "For some reason, my brother the Admiral requests the favour of your presence."

She moved to stand just behind my chair, so Lanar could see her. "Hello, *Admiralo* Mahane."

Lanar nodded. "Good day, Commander. Luta, I'd like you to meet *Commander* Yuskeya Blue, of the Nearspace Protectorate. Under my command, and currently on covert assignment aboard the *Tane Ikai*."

I stared at Lanar for half a minute, trying to decide if he was playing some joke, then turned to look at Yuskeya. She'd stood to attention, and nodded when I met her eyes. Her cheeks flushed pink. "It's true, Luta. You can scan my implant if you'd like. The

Admiral will give you the Nearspace Authority codes you'd need to read the secure layer."

"Oh, no, I believe you both," I said. I waved her to the other chair. "You might as well sit. I have a feeling this might take a while."

Yuskeya? A Protectorate officer? And yet, maybe it made sense. She'd been shaken the night the intruder got aboard the *Tane Ikai.* She'd been extra cautious performing the transfusion—what had Lanar told her?—and running that scan on me when I'd been injured. She'd been the first one to Mother when she collapsed, the first one to think PrimeCorp might be following us. *The one who'd been with Mother when she disappeared again.*

Lanar had the grace to look a little sheepish when I turned to the screen again.

I leaned back and crossed my arms. "So, this is how you had my back, huh, little brother? You couldn't have *told* me?"

Lanar shrugged. "You wouldn't have let me put a Protectorate officer on your bridge if I'd asked you."

"No, I wouldn't! I don't like being spied on!"

"Come on, Luta, Yuskeya wasn't spying. She was just doing what I told her to do—keeping an eye on you to make sure you didn't get into too much trouble."

I shook my head. "Oh, sure, that's nothing like spying. But Yuskeya's been with me for over a year. PrimeCorp only started bothering me lately."

Lanar nodded. "Sure, they've only started bothering *you* again lately, but we've been keeping a close eye on them for longer than that. Ever since Sedmamin made his way to the top, we've been aware of changes in the way PrimeCorp does things—big changes, Luta. There are things underway that go beyond industrial espionage and stepping over the line of the law. I figured they'd be after you eventually, but in the meantime, there were other uses for an undercover officer on a far trader." He had the nerve to wink at me.

"So I've been unwittingly participating in covert Protectorate operations? First Viss, and now Yuskeya. Is there anyone on board besides me who *isn't* on the Protectorate payroll? Wait a minute—did Yuskeya know about the illegal tech, too?"

"No, I didn't," Yuskeya said, and there was a touch of ice in her voice.

Sherry D. Ramsey

Lanar shook his head. "No, our Commander Blue isn't one to look the other way when the Protectorate has to venture into grey areas, even when we feel the ends justify the means. I thought it best to keep her out of that loop."

I believed him. I remembered how shocked Yuskeya had seemed when Viss told us about our "secret" cargo. She hadn't been faking. "I hope she gives you hell for it, then."

"Don't worry, she already did, in a very strongly-worded coded message. So I've been suitably chastised, and we can just put that little issue behind us, *okej*?"

I wasn't about to let him off the hook that easily. "If the Protectorate knows how crooked Sedmamin is—and they certainly do now—why don't they go after him? PrimeCorp wouldn't necessarily fail if you took him out of the picture."

Lanar shook his head. "The Nearspace Council made a mistake in letting PrimeCorp get as powerful as it is," he said. "It's not just Sedmamin. The entire corporate infrastructure is rotten, and they're greedy for even more power. Yes, we could target Sedmamin and take him down, but the Board of Directors could replace him with someone even worse. We're building our case, gathering information, but if we move before we have enough, it's all going to come tumbling down. We can't have that. Nearspace can't afford it. So all we can do is quietly crack down on the worst of what they're doing and try to get some leverage at the top. A series of surgical excisions, rather than an all-out attack."

"Baden thinks PrimeCorp might have an informant in the Protectorate, so you might want to be careful who you trust."

He seemed to consider the possibility. "I'm doubtful, but I'll keep it in mind. One more thing—I think I can help you make your case against PrimeCorp look even better."

"Well, I want it to look as damning as possible," I said. "They're more likely to cut a deal if they're worried."

Lanar pursed his lips. "Yuskeya sent me a coded message not long after you left Sol system. About a certain . . . item that had gone missing."

At first I drew a blank, but then I realized what he meant. "The body from the cargo crate? You have it?"

He nodded. "Picked it up and put it into storage, just in case we might need it someday. And because we didn't want PrimeCorp getting its hands on it. I guess it was a good idea."

244

I turned to Yuskeya. "Why'd you bother letting us go hunting for it?"

She shrugged. "I was under orders not to reveal my identity—unless it was a life-or-death situation. And I wasn't sure if it had been picked up, anyway. So I had to just go along."

"Well, I'm glad *someone* has it, anyway," I admitted, and got up to pace. I'd been sitting too long, with too much new information coming at me. I turned to Yuskeya. "So, does this mean you know where my mother is? Was all that knocked-unconscious thing just a cover to help her get away?"

Yuskeya actually looked uncomfortable and touched the place on her head where the lump had been. She glanced an unspoken question at the screen, and Lanar nodded. "Yes, and no. The lump and the bruise—they were all too real," she said with a grimace. "I was under orders, if we ever found your mother and she seemed to be in danger, to get her to a Protectorate safe area as quickly as possible. That's why I volunteered to go with her. So I could contact one of our agents on Kiando and get her safe."

"She could have been safe with us!" I protested.

Yuskeya shook her head. "With the PrimeCorp ship on the way, I couldn't be certain of that. I thought it was best to get her into Protectorate hands as quickly as possible."

"So you do know where she is."

"No." Yuskeya bit her lip. "Your mother is a very—strong-willed person. She said she'd take my advice and not go back to the *Tane Ikai*, but she wouldn't let me get her to our agent. She had her own . . . contingency plan, she said."

I almost smiled at the image of my mother telling Yuskeya that she could take her protection and stuff it. But I didn't. I was hurt. "Why didn't you just tell me all this?"

She pulled a deep breath. "I'm sorry about that, Luta, I really am. But I knew that you'd be able to think clearer—and not have to lie—if you really didn't know where she was."

"So you let yourself get hit on the head to convince me that you didn't know what had happened to her. Were you really unconscious at all?"

She smiled a little and put hand to her forehead again. "Your mother apparently has a black belt in Warrior Chi. But she gave me a shot so that I wouldn't have to 'fake' being unconscious."

I shook my head. "Nice little conspiracy," I said with a certain amount of bitterness. "I wouldn't have thought I was that easy to fool. Or so untrustworthy."

"She did want me to make sure you got the bag, and the messages on the chip. Maybe it wasn't the right decision. But we had to act fast." She grinned. "And you have to admit, the *Tane Ikai* taking off like it did made a good distraction. We got the *Trident* away from Kiando, which might have made it easier for her to get off the planet."

"But," I said, "you don't know where she is?"

Yuskeya shook her head, her grin fading. "She wouldn't tell me her plan. Just that she had confidence in it." She looked up at me, and her eyes were dark and sincere. "And she told me to tell you, when I could, that she'd be in touch as soon as possible."

I wasn't sure what to say to that, but as it turned out, I didn't have to say anything. Because that's when PrimeCorp caught up with us.

Chapter Twenty-Two

The Company of Enemies

"Sorry to interrupt, Captain, but we've got company," Baden said over the ship's comm.

"Who is it?"

"Our new acquaintance the *Trident* just showed up on our sensors—and it looks like they brought some friends. I count four runners, all with PrimeCorp sigs."

"How far away?"

He hesitated. "That's the strange thing. Closer than they should be for our sensors to just be picking them up now. I can't explain it. Viss says maybe they have some new stealth technology or something. But they're here."

I swallowed. Even with three planets in the K/G system and Nellera in sight, we were far out of the local traffic lanes, and there were no known wormholes out here. This sector of K/G was pretty lonely, the equivalent of being ambushed in a dark alley. Even if I was, so to speak, on the phone with the Protectorate.

"I'll comm them, Luta," Lanar said.

I was happy to let him try, but I doubted it would do any good. Dores Amadoro was unlikely to care about a Protectorate ship in another system.

I opened the ship's comm so everyone could hear me; I wasn't sure where everyone else was. "Everyone take a seat somewhere and buckle down," I ordered. "I don't know what these oncoming ships have in mind, so we might have to get out of here fast, and when I say fast, I mean fast enough to take the pseudo-gravs offline."

"Aye, Captain," Viss said from Engineering.

"Dr. Ndasa and I are in the galley," Maja said over the comm. "What's going on?"

"With luck, not much, but I wouldn't count on it," I said. "It's PrimeCorp."

"They're not answering my pings," Lanar said.

"They don't know about the pinhole; they probably think it's some kind of trick I'm trying to pull," I said. "They can't see a Protectorate ship, so if they haven't noticed the pinhole, how could one be pinging them?"

"I'm going to see who else is in the vicinity. If there's another Protectorate ship anywhere close, I'll send them to you."

"Thanks, Lanar," I said. "Signing off now. With luck, I'll call you back in a few minutes. Don't go anywhere."

With Yuskeya at my heels I hurried to the bridge, and switched the bridge view to all the ship's screens. That way everybody could follow along with the rest of us.

When they hailed us a few moments later, the angular face of Dores Amadoro did nothing to improve my mood. I'd thought, with the summons to Vele, at least I wouldn't have to see her again until I got there.

"Captain Paixon," Amadoro said in her coldest voice. "Here we are again. I'm still looking to execute this warrant for the arrest of Emmage Mahane. I'll have to ask that you prepare for boarding so that my agents can carry out their duties."

"I'm afraid that won't be possible." I did my best to look perfectly relaxed. "This ship is en route to a hearing before the NWAC on Vele, where, frankly, I expected you would be headed as well. I hear the Council is pretty testy when it comes to Primary Statute crimes. I don't think they'll be happy at this delay."

"Primary Statute crimes? Which ones?" she asked nastily. "The one in which your mother violated the terms of her employment contract and stole PrimeCorp property, or the one in which you helped her escape apprehension knowing full well we had a warrant for her?"

I crossed my arms casually. "Neither. My mother is still not on board my ship, and those are only *Planetary* Statute crimes in any case. I'm concerned with more serious matters here. For instance, the development and manufacture of illegal tech as defined under Nearspace Authority law."

Tiny wrinkles appeared at the corners of Amadoro's eyes as she took that in, but she was still belligerent. "PrimeCorp is not involved in the production of any technology classed as illegal," she said flatly.

"No? But strangely, it seems that one of its subcorps is. I'm sure you personally have no knowledge of such a thing," I said sweetly. "If you don't like that one, how about the one where someone—whose identity I think you already know—sent a stripped op onto my ship to steal DNA samples directly from my person?"

Amadoro allowed a slight frown to crease the skin of her forehead. "I don't understand what any purported invasion of your ship has to do with me, Captain."

"Oh, spare me the crap, Ms. Amadoro. I don't like dancing with you out here, any better than I do with your boss Earthside. It may not have to do with you directly, but it certainly involves PrimeCorp. Now, the Council is expecting us to arrive with this evidence very soon, and they know where to look for answers if we don't."

"What sort of evidence?"

Her voice was smooth, but her body language was telegraphing all sorts of things. She was trying to rattle me, catch me in a lie, but she really was interested in what I had. "That's confidential."

"Because there is no evidence," she rejoined, "and PrimeCorp has committed no crimes. To get back to my warrant—"

"Well, what if I told you I know that PrimeCorp has been engaged for years in a comprehensive campaign of industrial espionage, focused particularly on anti-aging research, at several other corporations' research facilities? And that PrimeCorp has systematically stolen, compromised, and otherwise interfered with research, data, and experiments owned by those other corporations."

She stared at me, and then threw back her head and laughed with ostentatious merriment. "Oh, Captain Paixon, you are amusing. This whole thing is intriguing, but it's fabrication from beginning to end. Now," she said, her smile disappearing as if someone had wiped it off, "if you're quite finished, we're coming aboard."

I shook my head firmly. "No, you are not. You're completely welcome to accompany us to Vele, but you are not boarding my ship. There's a Protectorate officer on board with me, by the way. No doubt she'll be happy to give evidence of what's happening here." I saw the puzzled look that passed between Baden and Rei and remembered that no-one else knew about Yuskeya yet. Well, this wasn't the time. "Tell your people to stand down and let us pass, because if you don't I'm going to start blasting a pathway through you."

"Oh, really? I'd heard that you didn't believe in carrying weapons on a far trader," Amadoro said with a smirk.

"Well, times change. Would you like me to prove it? I'm formally giving you notice that my ship is going to begin moving away and you are not to interfere. I'm certain I can justify my decision if I'm forced to take defensive measures."

Of course *that* was the bluff; despite my mental vow to start carrying torpedoes again after our run-in with the pirates, there simply hadn't been an opportunity to get it done. I hoped Amadoro wouldn't take the chance. I'd always done my best to set myself up as a don't-care, kickass mercenary to PrimeCorp, so the bluff *could* work.

Amadoro pursed her lips, considering. I hoped I'd made her nervous, but not nervous enough to start taking the *Tane Ikai* apart.

Viss, from the engineering station, said over the ship's comm, so Amadoro could hear it, "Forward torpedo bays on standby, Captain. Ready to fire on your command."

It was a brilliant bit of backup that I hadn't even asked for, but Dores Amadoro wasn't buying it.

"I don't think so, Captain Paixon. I have the law on my side. Stand by to be boarded. Resistance will be met with force."

One of the PrimeCorp runners began to move forward, presumably making ready to hook up to one of our airlocks.

Damne, damne! I couldn't think of a single thing to do. I'd tried my best bluff and it hadn't worked. *Lanar, this would be a good time to have one of your Protectorate buddies show up.*

"Captain?" Viss interrupted her. "Shall I fire a warning shot across their bow?"

What was he doing? The bluff was over. Maybe he'd rigged up something that might look like a torp?

"Go ahead," I said with more conviction than I felt.

A single torpedo burst out of one of the forward bays and toward the PrimeCorp runner that had moved toward us. It hurtled silently through the space between us trailing blue-tinged exhaust, and *damne* me if it wasn't real. I watched the sensors track it all the way until it skimmed the runner's nose and kept going harmlessly past.

It wasn't easy to keep my voice steady, shocked as I was, but somehow it came out okay. "Well, Ms. Amadoro, are you going to move aside? The next one will not be merely a warning. I'm certain if you follow us to Vele, the Council will look at everything and make a fair decision."

She hesitated only a fraction longer. "I don't get paid to take that kind of chance," she said, and the connection went dead. I suddenly realized that maybe taunting her about all the evidence I had on board hadn't been the smartest move. Now we were more of a threat than ever.

"Viss, where the hell did you get a torpedo?"

"Yeah," said Baden, "and do we have any more?"

"*Trident* and runners are readying weapons systems," Yuskeya said in a voice that seemed preternaturally calm.

"Evasives, Rei," I ordered. "Hang on, everyone."

It was fortunate that I'd told everyone to sit down earlier, because Rei hit the thrusters almost as the words were coming out of my mouth. The *Tane Ikai* bucked and jumped up and away from the PrimeCorp ships. An auto-alarm blared, triggered by the sudden acceleration. I hoped the others had heeded me and been prepared.

Damne, I thought. *I should have had everyone in EVA suits before we made the skip.* If the PrimeCorp ships fired on us and made enough of a hole in the outer plating to compromise life support, we wouldn't survive long.

"Ready to fire on your word, Captain," Viss said over the comm.

"Not unless they fire first, Viss," I said. "We still might get out of this without anybody getting hurt. But I want a full weapons report immediately."

Hirin surprised me by answering. "I bought the torpedoes, Captain, and I had Viss bring them aboard when we were at Ando City. Thought they might be needed. I just got him to load them into the bays in case they were needed. We have a full complement, everything the *Tane Ikai* was built to carry."

"Torpedo away from the *Trident*," Yuskeya said. "Heading straight for us. No warning shots here. Runners seem to be equipped with wasp missiles and—"

A flare of orange light burst from the front of a runner that had managed to get close on our tail.

"—particle beams," she finished, as the flash from the superheated dust and gas particles the beam had encountered in its path faded. "Very narrow, reasonably weak, and fortunately for us, badly targeted that time. A lucky hit will poke a hole in us, though."

"Fire rear bay torpedoes, Viss," I ordered. I hadn't wanted this fight, but they were obviously willing to kill us. I had no trouble defending my ship and crew. "Hirin, take the front guns. Both of you, fire at will. Rei, try your best to get us the hell out of here."

The *Tane Ikai* shuddered as Viss released two torpedoes toward the runner, and groaned as Rei veered sharply downward. Something hit the floor and smashed in First Aid, and I wondered how many other things weren't secured for this kind of flying. Another alarm klaxon blared, echoing down the corridor behind the bridge. The *Tane Ikai* wasn't an agile fighter or an armoured battle cruiser. I wasn't sure how much fighting action she could take.

A rhythmic, metallic clanging echoed from the main corridor behind me and I turned in my chair thinking something had shaken loose. Instead I saw two EVA-suited figures, their arms heaped with more suits, making their way toward the bridge with heavy steps, the magnetized boots allowing them to stay swayingly upright.

"We thought these would be a good idea," Maja said, her voice emerging hollowly over the ship's comm from inside her helmet. She handed me a suit and crossed to set one down beside Rei, who was obviously unable to stop and put it on. The third was for Baden. Dr. Ndasa took one each to Hirin and Yuskeya.

The ship jolted again and Rei whooped as the rear screen lit up in a flare of white light.

"Torpedo hit on that *bastardo* behind us," Yuskeya said.

"Shock wave do any damage?"

"We're okay so far," Baden said. Now that communications had broken down, he was monitoring the ship's systems.

"*Trident* is using their burst drive to try and get close," Yuskeya said.

"Can we get in position for me to get a shot with the forward torps?" Hirin asked Rei. "I don't need more than a few seconds to get a target lock."

"See what I can do," Rei said, and the ship rolled sharply to starwise and shot forward.

I was trying to struggle into my EVA suit from a sitting position, not an easy task especially at these speeds and erratic flying. Once I had my feet and legs in, though, I could trigger the magnetics and stand to finish the job. My helmet tried to roll off my lap and I grabbed it, ramming it over my head even though I couldn't connect it to my suit yet. At least it would stay put.

I stamped my foot and the mags triggered, the electromagnetic force gripping the metal decking. I stood up then, just as the ship juddered and the lights flickered. I would have fallen over without the mags.

"Report!"

"Looks like a wasp went through Cargo Pod Two," Baden said. "Losing pressure in there."

"Is the access hatchway sealed?"

"Showing green, Captain," he reported.

"Viss," I said over the comm, "can you get to an EVA suit?"

"Little busy, Captain," he said. "But the bulkhead between Engineering and the access hatches is sealed. I'm fine down here."

Unless the next missile goes through Engineering. "Maja, can you try and get down to Engineering, get a suit to Viss?" It wouldn't be easy to climb down the ladder in a suit, but he was completely vulnerable without one.

"Aye, Captain," she said, sounding just like one of the crew. I heard her clomping off down the corridor as fast as the mags would let her.

"Torps away from the *Trident* and two runners," Yuskeya reported.

"Hang on, folks," Rei said, and the ship veered up and rolled to dock. I hoped Maja had stayed on her feet. Struts creaked over my head and the floor beneath my mag boots trembled against the metal decking.

Hirin had his own EVA suit on and I clomped over to him as quickly as I could. "Can you pilot while Rei gets into her suit? I'll take weapons."

"I think I can manage," he said with a flash of a grin. Hirin had piloted the *Tane Ikai* for decades. I just hoped his recent de-aging experience had restored his reflexes.

I sat down at the console just as the targeting locked onto another of the runners. Without hesitation, I touched the button to fire the torp and watched it launch from the bay soundlessly, arcing toward the runner bearing down on us. The pilot rolled to avoid it, but it contacted the edge of a wing and an orange bloom scattered sparks and debris in all directions. The impact sent him spinning away out of sight below us. With luck, it might be enough to take him out of the equation.

"Message from the *Trident*," Baden said.

"Audio only," I said.

"That's all she's sending."

"Captain Paixon, this is your last warning," Dores Amadoro's voice was as cold and icy as the space around us. No battle heat there. "We will try to disable you only, but at this point I'm sure you understand that I can't make any promises."

"Thank you, Ms. Amadoro," I said. "I'm sure you can understand that I can't, either." I broke the connection, tired of the woman's threats and games.

Hirin sat at the secondary pilot's console and Rei bent over, pushing her feet into the EVA suit. I hadn't noticed even a stutter in the handling of the ship when they swapped control. "Any chance we can just outrun them?" I asked, although I already knew the answer.

"Not with that burst drive," Hirin said. "The runners, maybe."

"All right, then. Concentrate on taking out the main ship," I ordered. "Disable them if possible, but don't hesitate to take any opportunities, either."

A chorus of *ayes* met the order.

"Try to get a lock on the *Trident*, Luta," Hirin said. "I'm going to try a chicken run."

I swallowed even as my hands danced over the controls. Hirin certainly hadn't lost any of his nerve, anyway. A "chicken run" was old jargon from our early spacefaring days together. It would take us in a swerving line toward the enemy ship, hoping to get a shot away at them before they could get one off at us. Part of me wanted to order him not to, but I'd always trusted him in the past. How could I refuse to trust him now?

We'd been trying to put distance between ourselves and the *Trident*; now Hirin pushed the ship into a sharp climb relative to the far cruiser and brought us around in a tight turn to make a run toward it.

"Searching for lock," I said, and Hirin started the ship veering left and right, sharper than should have been possible, it seemed to me. I heard Dr. Ndasa gasp, but kept my eyes on the targeting screen. The *Tane Ikai* trembled under the stresses and a low whine sang along the walls.

"Torpedo away from the *Trident*," Yuskeya said. Even now her voice was steady and strong. I guess my brother had trained her well.

I should have ordered Hirin to break off, but I didn't. He swerved harder, more erratically, and I waited, finger poised over the screen, for the lock to turn green. Or the ship to fly apart at the seams.

Then Maja's scream came over the comm, and cut off as abruptly as it had begun.

Chapter Twenty-Three

The Company of Friends

"Maja, what happened?" I demanded. I could not move from my seat or take my eyes off the targeting console, or risk all of our lives.

For a long, long moment there was no answer. "Maja!"

"I'm okay," she said, her voice small and strained. "I fell off the hatchway ladder. But I'm okay." She ended with a sharp intake of breath that did not sound okay at all.

The lock went green and I fired the torpedo. "Away!" I said to Hirin, in the same breath as Yuskeya said, "*Trident* has fired again."

Now it was just a question of who could dodge faster. The *Tane Ikai* immediately veered starwise in a sharp twist, and the metal all around us screamed in protest at the forces pulling at it. On one of the viewscreens I saw the bulk of the *Trident* dart to one side as well, then I couldn't keep following it. I was too busy trying not to black out as Hirin pushed the ship through maneuvers that were near-certain to tear us apart.

"Torp has a trace lock on us," Yuskeya said.

"Jettison the trash," I ordered. "We might confuse it."

"Done," said Baden, as the flotsam and jetsam that would usually be dropped at at spacedock for recycling trailed out behind us.

Light flashed in a brilliant rush on the viewscreen, painting the dimly-lit bridge like moonlight. "That's a hit," Rei said with satisfaction. She'd finished suiting up, but wasn't about to take the piloting controls back at this point. "Looks like we might have taken out that burst drive, she's coasting now."

I started to grin but it didn't last long. Hirin sent the ship into a rolling dive that threatened to bring up the contents of my stomach, and I remembered the PrimeCorp torpedo still chasing us. The *Tane Ikai* jolted suddenly sideways and an even brighter light roiled over every viewscreen. Metal shrieked and a horrible rushing sound filled the comm.

"We're hit," Yuskeya said with the tiniest catch in her voice. "Cargo Pod Four and Engineering."

"Main drive is losing power," Hirin said.

"Switching to secondary," Rei answered without missing a beat.

I was up and on my feet before I realized what I was doing. Luckily my mags were still engaged or I would have gone flying across the bridge. I yelled into my helmet comm. "Maja? Viss?"

I started clomping toward the rear of the bridge, planning to take the ladder down to the lower deck.

"Captain?" Hirin's voice sounded behind me. Just the one word, and he didn't shout. But it halted me in my tracks, and I shook my head to clear it. No. Despite what my heart was telling me, I couldn't go running to see what had happened on the deck below us. I was in command. I started walking again, but I stopped when I got to the command chair and sat down shakily.

"Reports," I said. My throat was so tight, the word seemed to scratch it, heart thumping so hard and painfully it must be audible over the comm.

"Emergency bulkhead between Decks One and Two has sealed," Baden said. His voice was shaky, with no trace of his usual cockiness. "Engineering deck is depressurized."

Maja, I thought in agonized silence. I knew he was thinking the same thing.

"*Trident* appears to be disabled," Yuskeya said. "One runner left, and it's coming this way."

"We still have secondary drive and manoeuvring thrusters," Hirin said. "Coming about to face the runner."

"Fire everything we have at it," I heard myself say calmly. My voice sounded like it came from someone else.

The ship shook as a volley of torpedoes vaulted out toward the oncoming runner. It got just close enough to launch one of its wasps before one of our torps took it squarely in the body and it blossomed into a silent red ball. I felt nothing, not even relief. My mind had gone to some place where it simply did whatever came next.

Another tremor ran through the ship as the last wasp missile hit, but our luck held one more time. Hirin had managed to keep the manoeuvring thrusters turning us sideways once our torps were away, and the wasp struck the door to Cargo Pod One. The reinforced doors were possibly the strongest parts of the ship, and although the wasp detonated and the *Tane Ikai* juddered harshly again, I didn't think the missile had penetrated.

"We're okay." Maja's voice came weakly over the comm. She was panting. "At least, I'm okay, and I think Viss is . . . I hurt my leg when I fell . . . might be broken . . . so I couldn't get the suit to Viss as fast as I should have." Her voice rose in pitch and her words tumbled over each other, hysteria vibrating beneath them. "He didn't have the helmet all the way on when we were hit. But . . . it's on him now, and he's still breathing. It doesn't sound right. Someone . . . should get down here, soon."

I let out a breath that was almost a sob. "Good—" I had to clear my throat and try again. "Good work, Maja. Glad to hear you're okay."

"All threats seem to have been eliminated or disabled, Captain," Yuskeya said, and for the first time her voice had a tremble in it. "Weapons systems on the *Trident* appear to be offline. Permission to render medical aid in Engineering?"

"Go ahead, Yuskeya," I said. "Folks, we're going to have to seal all the bulkheads and depressurize the corridor to open the hatch to Engineering. I don't know how good our overall integrity is, so everyone check your suits and say when you're ready." We'd have to go and inspect the damage soon, see if we could patch ourselves up to get to Vele, but first I wanted everyone safely on the bridge deck.

"Captain?" Dr. Ndasa's voice came over the comm from his helmet mic, shaky but resolute. "I will go with Yuskeya and help her see to the others."

"Thank you, Doctor."

There was silence from Dores Amadoro or anyone aboard the PrimeCorp ship. The *Trident* itself seemed to be coasting, slow and blind, and I wondered with a pang if they had wounded or dead to care for. I set my jaw. If they did, it wasn't my fault. She'd risked the fight, and it definitely hadn't gone the way she'd expected. But I did have one other thing on my mind.

"Hirin," I said, and he turned in the pilot's chair. "You didn't see fit to consult with me before loading up the ship with torpedoes?"

He had the decency to squirm in his seat. "You were busy . . . you had a lot on your mind. I didn't think it was a detail you needed to be bothered with."

"A load of torpedoes is something I don't need to be bothered with? Let me state for the record, here and now with everyone paying attention, that any munitions brought aboard this ship constitute a detail that I need to be bothered with. Anything else will be considered mutiny. Is that clear?"

It was greeted with a quiet chorus of "Aye, Captain."

Rei said, "I bought a new plasma rifle when we were on Eri . . ."

And at the same time Baden was saying, "I picked up a—"

I waved my hands to stop them. "Personal ordnance excepted. All right?"

Nods and smiles all around. Much later, I thanked Hirin properly for saving us with the torpedoes, but those details aren't important here.

"Captain, your brother is pinging us like mad," Baden said.

"Put him through."

Lanar was on his feet, leaning on his desk with white knuckles as he stared at the screen. "Luta! Are you all right?"

I nodded, realized he might not be able to see my face very will inside the EVA helmet, and said, "I think so. Viss is injured and Maja might have a broken leg. Yuskeya and Dr. Ndasa are seeing to them. The ship has a few more perforations than it did the last time we talked, but we're holding together."

"I've got a far cruiser on the way but she won't be there for an hour or so. Are you secure?"

I laughed. I couldn't help myself. My ship sported numerous holes, was partly depressurized, and the "enemy" was still within sight. As far as I knew, PrimeCorp still wanted samples of my DNA, Mother continued to be missing, and I'd had a Protectorate "spy" on my ship for over a year without suspecting it. *Secure?*

"I guess we're as secure as possible under the circumstances, little brother," I said. "But I'll certainly be happy to see the spacedock on Vele."

Not one, but three Protectorate far cruisers showed up to

escort us to Vele, along with the disabled *Trident*. By the time they arrived, Viss and Maja had been brought back up to the bridge deck, and Hirin and Baden made a cursory inventory of the damage we'd suffered. The *Trident* turned out to be in worse shape than we were; the torpedo that had taken out their burst drive had also caused a chain-reaction failure in their main and secondary drives, so they were pretty much dead in the dark. Generators strove to keep life support at least minimally functional, and that was it. One of the Protectorate cruisers had to call for a tug to get them moving again.

I did hear that no-one on the *Trident* had been killed, but beyond that, nothing. I wondered briefly what Dores Amadoro had told the Protectorate officers about what had happened here, but decided that I didn't really care. I'd had my own Protectorate officer aboard the *Tane Ikai*, who had witnessed the whole altercation, and I was pretty sure that Amadoro's hot-headedness would prove to be a game-changer in our dealings with PrimeCorp. After her stunt, Lanar and the Protectorate might not get their wish to take the corporation apart little by little. I couldn't say the thought made me sad, despite Lanar's conviction that a PrimeCorp collapse would be bad for Nearspace.

We had fared much better than the *Trident*; we needed some emergency patch materials from the Protectorate ship that had taken us into their care—the *Winchester*—and some electronics, but our secondary drive would get us to Vele all right. The main drive would have to be replaced. Maja's leg was in an ultraplas cast, a weird echo of the ultraplas cuffs from our kidnapping episode on Rhea. But she was limping around just fine.

Viss was confined to his quarters, where Dr. Ndasa and Yuskeya had moved a load of equipment from First Aid to monitor him. He'd been exposed to vacuum for a mercifully short time, but one lung had collapsed, and some small blood vessels in his eyes and face had burst. Once Maja had secured his helmet and the suit had repressurized he'd seemed stable, and Dr. Ndasa had been able to treat him quickly, but they were keeping a close eye on him. Viss was helping his own recovery mostly by complaining a lot and trying to get someone to let him onto the Engineering deck.

It would be three skips to get to the Beta Hydri system, where Vele and its sister planet Vileyra circled the yellow-orange star.

That meant I had lots of time to think, when I wasn't overseeing repairs and visiting the patients. And what I mainly thought about was my mother. My mother and all her worries and fears and sacrifices, and how she'd looked on Kiando when she said *it wasn't because I didn't care about my family.* I thought about her, and the bioscavs, and Hirin and Maja and Karro. And me. And how this mess with PrimeCorp was all going to sort itself out.

The conclusions I came to were these: she was tired of running. And I was finally tired of chasing.

So one day I sat down and loaded the chip marked *PC35411* into my datapad. I added up the numbers for my parents' birthdays and the year she left us on Nellera, punched it in as the password, and it opened up the message like a charm. But I didn't send it, not that message. That decision was my mother's to make, unless and until she wasn't able to make it herself and I had proof of that. Instead I took the address it was to be sent to, and wrote my own message.

STATIC ELECTRONIC MESSAGE: 25.7

Encryption: securetext/novis/noaud
Receipt notification: disabled
From: "Captain Luta Paixon"
<lutapaixon.taneikaireg.nearspace*web>
To: "Anonymous" <ID 32597564512>
Date: Sat, 14 Dec 2284 11:16:55 -0500

To whom it may concern: Please forward this and the attached message along the route established. There is no danger to you or recipient.

Many thanks,
Luta Paixon,
Captain, Tane Ikai

Encoded inside that message was the one I wanted Mother to read. I used the same password she'd placed on the *L/L* chip; she'd figure it out.

Mother,
You said: No one should have sole control of human aging.

Think about it?
Come home,
Luta

Four days later I was lying on my bunk, trying to get some rest. That goal was being thwarted by my brain insisting on trying to figure out how I was going to pay for a new main drive, when Baden commed me. We'd made the skip through to Beta Comae Berenices the day before, with the *Winchester* hovering behind us like an anxious mother, and tomorrow we should make the wormhole to MI 2 Eridani. One more skip from there would take us to Beta Hydri and the proceedings on Vele.

"Captain, message for you."

I sat up and touched my implant. "From Lanar?"

"No." Baden's voice sounded strange. "It purports to be—from you."

"On my datapad," I said, bounding for the desk to snatch it up. It wasn't vid, only a text message, and it was brief.

Received: from [205152.59.68] Eri Main Datastation
STATIC ELECTRONIC MESSAGE: 25.7

Encryption: securetext/novis/noaud
Receipt notification: enabled
From: "Captain L. Paixon"
*<lpaixon5064.public.nearspace*web>*
To: "Luta Paixon" <ID 59836254471>
Date: Wed, 18 Dec 2284 6:25:22 -0500

Dear Luta,
You may be right. I'll see you on Vele.
M.

I thumbed my implant comm. "Baden, where did this message come from?"

"Through the comm relay from MI 2 Eridani," he said.

It did have the relay stamp from the Eri datastation at the top, but that didn't mean it had originated there. It could have bounced around Nearspace for a while before it got to me.

It seemed like, at least when this message had been sent, she'd been safe. And somehow, she knew about what was happening on Vele. I wondered if Lanar had found a way to get a message to her, too, or if her network of contacts was just that good.

Either way, it seemed like everything was going to come together on Vele. I rolled over, closed my eyes, and this time my brain let me sleep.

Chapter Twenty-four

One's Aspect to the Sun

Vele was a smallish planet, about the size of Mars, circling its star at a distance similar to Earth's from Sol. It was Earthlike and yet somehow alien; it had little axial tilt and so seemed to have one long temperate season that rarely varied, and something in their biochemical makeup made a lot of the plants look *wrong*. It was a nice enough planet, though, and I would have liked it more had it not been the place where Hirin originally took sick.

Mother was as good as her word. We said goodbye to the *Winchester* and set down on Vele late one mild, starry night, and the next morning I was barely dressed when I got a message ping. It was voice-only, but it was Mother. "Are you accepting visitors?" she asked.

"Dock One-Eleven," I said. "I'll be at the bridge deck airlock."

"Wait inside. I'll knock," she said.

I supposed it was to avoid drawing attention; me standing alone outside the door, obviously waiting for someone. She was the expert at all this cloak-and-dagger stuff, so I did as she asked.

When the knock came, I opened the airlock immediately and there she was, standing at the top of the metal staircase. Her hair was a rich, dark brown with pale highlights now, and she wore the midnight blue uniform of a dockworker. She carried a canvas carryall slung over her shoulder and vidshades hid her eyes, but it was her. She was smiling.

I waited until we were inside before I said anything. "So, you're here to see if PrimeCorp can wiggle out of this one?"

She pulled me into a quick hug. "Actually," she said, "I'm

mostly here for you."

"For me?"

She slid the vidshades off and tucked them into her carryall. "Do you have any caff?"

I shook my head. "Sorry, not being much of a hostess, am I? Let's go to the galley."

Strangely, it was deserted. I pulled us both steaming mugs from the machine, and we sat down at the long table. "That was some message you sent me," she said, looking around the room. "Nice ship you have here."

"Thanks," I said. "There wasn't much to it. The message, I mean."

"No, but you certainly got straight to the point, and it made me think." She blew across the top of her caff, making the liquid ripple and steam writhe in the air. "I hadn't really stopped to think about things for quite a while. I was on automatic pilot, you might say. It was . . . a wake-up call. Anyway," she went on, pulling a datapad from her carryall and setting it on the table between us, "I've sent this data to Lanar. Dates, names, and details on the research data PrimeCorp appropriated and sabotaged, what companies were involved—everything."

I looked up from the pad, meeting her eyes. "You sent the message."

She nodded. "I sent the message."

"And your people? Are they out of PrimeCorp's reach?"

"No-one on that end realizes what's happened yet. By the time PrimeCorp gets notice of this, they'll be well away."

"PrimeCorp's going to have a lot of things to worry about, all of a sudden."

She shrugged and turned the datapad around with a finger. "Let's hope so. At any rate, I've decided that I have to let it go," she said simply. "I'm going to go and talk with Schulyer, release my research data publicly, and let PrimeCorp take me to court if they want. They'll stop bothering you, at any rate." She put a hand on one of mine. "It was probably the hardest thing I've ever done to leave you on Kiando. Leave you *again*. Seeing you, and Hirin, and Maja—it sort of cracked something inside me."

"I would have helped you, you know." I couldn't stop myself from saying it. "You didn't have to disappear."

She sighed. "I know. You know what happened?"

"Yuskeya told me, what she knew, anyway."

Mother sat back in the chair, cupping her mug in both hands and staring into its depths. "I just did what I've been doing for so many years. Put the plan into action. Keep moving. I had a dummy ticket booked on that starliner that was orbiting Kiando—that's standard practice for me. So I took a shuttle up to the starliner under one of my other identities, changed my appearance in a stateroom, caught a shuttle back down to the planet, and hopped on a short trader to Cengare. From there I shipped out for MI 2 Eridani. And the whole time, I was thinking what a fool I was, and how I should have just gone with you."

I smiled wryly. "Turns out, that would have been a bad idea. PrimeCorp caught up with me almost right away and ended up nearly destroying my ship."

She met my eyes then. "But I still would have *been* there. I would have been part of your life for once, instead of just watching from the outside."

We sat in silence for a few minutes. Finally I said, "I watched the videos. Showed them to Lanar, too."

"So you know the best and the worst of it."

"You didn't do anything I wouldn't have done."

She smiled at that.

I sipped from my own mug. "You know what I got out of it all? That at some point, people should start benefiting from your research. Isn't that what all your work has been about?"

She didn't answer, so I went on.

"I know it's a worry—what will happen. But you can't take all the responsibility on yourself. We've been hunting immortality, wishing for it, working towards it, for centuries. You're only the locus that all that work has led to. You're the last function in the equation. Most people will probably embrace the technology, but some won't. Society will change, of course, evolve just as it always has when conditions change. You can't take it on yourself to be responsible for what immortality will mean to humanity. You have to give people the chance, and the choice. What happens then—well, it can't be your worry."

"Your message made me come to a similar conclusion," she said. "But the letting go—I want to. It won't be easy."

"You don't have to stop your own research," I said. "It's what you love doing. You just have to focus on the people you'll be helping. Take Hirin, for example. I gave Hirin a blood transfusion a few weeks ago, and the changes in him have been—

well, unbelievable."

Mother stared at me. "What?"

I realized that Mother didn't know about Hirin's virus, and told the story as succinctly as I could. "He had a bad reaction when we went through the Split. The virus surged, and it affected his heart. We decided to gamble that a transfusion from me might help."

"Transferable bioscavs? I wouldn't have thought—especially that generation, and after so long . . ." She stared into the distance, likely envisioning complex formulae and nanostructures I couldn't even begin to imagine. "They didn't have any adverse effects?"

I chuckled. "Well, they seemed about to kill him for a few days, but then he got better. Since then they—the bioscavengers, I guess—have been reversing a lot of the damage age has done to him. It's noticeable already."

She still seemed stunned. "After so long in your system . . . I wouldn't have thought—" her voice caught and tears sprang to her eyes.

"What is it?"

"If I'd realized sooner . . . but it never worked in tests—"

My heart lurched. Perhaps the transfusion had been an even bigger gamble than I'd thought. I caught her hand briefly and squeezed. "It's okay. I know you would have told us if you'd known. Maybe it had something to do with the particular virus Hirin had."

"Is Hirin here? I'd like to run some tests, if he'd let me."

I smiled. Whatever else I might convince my mother to do, she'd never stop being a scientist. "I'm sure he will." I touched my implant and messaged Hirin, asking him to meet us in the galley. "What about the new generation of bioscavs—the ones you mentioned in the video? Will they work for Hirin?"

"Ye-es," she said hesitantly. "They'd be more limited. I wouldn't say they could prolong his life indefinitely. But they'd extend it for a good many years yet."

Hirin came into the galley, stopped dead and did a double-take. "*Hola*, that is weird. Even with the different hair colour, you two look amazingly alike. You're going to have to wear name tags if you're both going to be on this ship. I don't want to start making passes at my mother-in-law by mistake."

I took a swipe at him as he passed me, which he ducked with

newly-reacquired speed. "If a man can't tell his wife from her mother—" I started, but he cut me off.

"Hey, I get to plead extremely unusual circumstances," he protested as he filled a mug with chai for himself.

"Mother wants to take a look at your virus, and your bioscavs," I said. "Do you mind?"

He shook his head and held out his arm, implant facing Mother. "But will there be anything of the virus left to find?"

"Oh, I think so," Mother said. She placed her datapad gently over Hirin's implant, waiting for the connection. "The bioscavengers would deal with the virus in one of several ways— by neutralizing parts of it or by altering the body's reaction to it— but they wouldn't necessarily erase it. And I want to see how they've adapted themselves to your body, too."

"I still have all the data Dr. Ndasa collected," Hirin volunteered. "He gave me a copy to keep for my own records."

The datapad chittered and Mother removed it, pressing her fingers swiftly over the screen. "I'd love to see it, Hirin. The comparison would be valuable. This will just take a few minutes to analyze."

He found it on his datapad and sent it to her, and while the datapad performed its operations, Mother questioned Hirin closely about his condition at all stages of the virus's progress. I sat back and sipped my double caff, savouring not only the hot, sweet bite of the drink but also the fact that we could talk about Hirin's illness in the past tense.

The datapad alert announced that the analysis was finished, and Mother looked it over, frowning.

"What?"

She shook her head. "Let me check something." She pulled a chipcase from her bag and loaded another chip into the datapad.

"Is something wrong?"

"The virus," she said distractedly, scrolling through pages on the datapad. "There's something—it's familiar."

Hirin and I shared a look, but said nothing. Mother studied the screen, occasionally pursing her lips and squinting at the data. The suspense was almost intolerable and I was about to speak when she abruptly got up from the table, still staring at the datapad screen. "I don't want to believe this."

I just looked at her until she continued.

"The virus contains a gene sequence that belongs to

PrimeCorp. They own the patent on it. I know because I helped create it."

"Dr. Ndasa told me it was synthetic—engineered. That it must have been spread by accident."

"It should have been completely destroyed when we were finished with it. It shouldn't still be in existence." She sat down again. "And it definitely shouldn't be in Hirin."

"So . . . you think PrimeCorp wasn't careful enough with it? Or sold it?"

She didn't answer, drumming her long fingers on the table and staring at a spot on the far wall. Finally she said, "No. It's too much of a coincidence. My guess would be that PrimeCorp deliberately exposed you to it in an attempt to find out what your bioscavengers could do."

"But it happened here, on Vele! They would have had to follow us out here, and then find a way to infect us! And how could they do that without risking exposure for other people?"

"Maybe they didn't care. This is PrimeCorp, remember?" Hirin said. He rubbed his stubbled chin contemplatively. "It would explain some things. Like why the doctors never could pinpoint what kind of virus it was."

"There'd be nothing obvious to link it to PrimeCorp, not for anyone who hadn't worked on the project." She stood again and paced the length of the galley. "What did you do when Hirin first got sick?"

"We headed straight back to Earth." I looked out the viewport, remembering those terrible days. "There were reasonably good medical facilities close by on Vileyra, but the colonies were still young. We thought the newest and best treatment would be Earthside."

"And it kept getting worse on Earth, then regressed once you left?"

Hirin shook his head. "For a long time it was up and down. We kept trading, tried to ignore it. I'd have flare-ups, then it would calm down, just simmer for a while. Didn't seem to make a difference if I was Earthside or anywhere else in Nearspace."

"But when you . . . reached the point where you couldn't manage the trade runs anymore?"

"It got steadily worse once I went into care," Hirin said. "Slowly, but steadily. It didn't improve until I left Earth the last time."

"Almost like someone was trying to make sure Luta stayed to look after you?'

I broke in. "What are you saying? That PrimeCorp—"

"Do you think it would be difficult for them to find someone in a care facility who could make sure a patient got sicker instead of better—if the price was right?"

I stared at her. When I could speak, my voice was only a whisper. "You think PrimeCorp was making sure Hirin got worse, and he started to recover when he came with me because they couldn't . . . get at him any longer? That's monstrous!"

Hirin narrowed his eyes. "But it makes sense. And it explains why they were so reluctant to let me leave. They couldn't forbid it, but they did everything short of that. Including trying to say I was crazy."

I still didn't want to believe it. A sick churning roiled in my stomach. All this time I'd thought I was doing what was best for Hirin, and in fact I'd only been leaving him in jeopardy alone. I didn't want to accept that it might be true. "What about the Split? When the virus surged again? PrimeCorp couldn't have engineered that!"

"I can't answer that part of it, Luta," Mother said. "It could have been something caused directly by the Split, or the virus could have been engineered to surge after a certain amount of exposure to wormhole radiation—that would be an effective way of limiting travel."

"I'm going to have to kill him." My voice seemed alarmingly calm, even to my ears. "Sedmamin. For doing this to you."

Hirin took me by the shoulders and turned me to face him. His blue-grey eyes were intense as they fastened on mine and his hands were strong and firm, not the weak, fragile hands of such a short time ago. "You're going to do no such thing, Luta. Listen, PrimeCorp is going to get what's coming to it. The Protectorate is going to see to that. We're going to let them take care of it, and we're not wasting any more time or worry on Sedmamin or the rest of them. This is not the beginning of a vendetta. I've been given the gift of more time, and I have better things to do with it." He gave me a gentle shake. "Got it?"

That's when I burst into tears. I guess I got it.

Hirin told me later that Maja cried, too, when he told her about it.

I can say unequivocally that giving evidence in a proceeding before the Nearspace Worlds Administrative Council is the most boring thing I've ever done. Lanar arrived on Vele just a day before the actual hearing was due to start, and we had a nice reunion, he and I and Mother. It made for a welcome break in the monotony, because by then we'd all been interviewed, signed affidavits, turned over evidence, been interviewed about the evidence, and then been cross-interviewed about everything again by PrimeCorp's lawyers. A lot of paperwork and bland meeting rooms and hurry-up-and-wait. There were no courtroom dramas, no damning accusations from a witness stand. This was the Protectorate's show, and Lanar had done his part remotely from his ship. I would have given almost anything to simply slip away some night and burn for the nearest wormhole, but that would have solved only the boredom problem. I wanted to stay around and see how it all fell out.

And how it all fell out wasn't the most I could have hoped for, but it was pretty satisfying. The Protectorate had quite a bundle of charges, thanks to our evidence, to take to the Council. In addition to its own evidence of manufacturing and transporting illegal tech, there were the instances of piracy, kidnapping, industrial espionage, use of illegal viruses and stripped ops, and unprovoked firing upon a civilian ship.

It certainly would have been interesting to observe the proceedings, because I'm sure that delicately balanced web of interplanetary relationships throughout Nearspace that Lanar had talked about came into play—who sided with PrimeCorp and who with the Protectorate, and what political leverage was brought to bear. The media certainly gave it full play on the vids and the web (although they weren't privy to the deliberations, either, so a lot of it was speculation) and PrimeCorp's net worth valuation took a pretty deep hit. Not enough to ruin the corporation, because as Lanar had said, ruination wasn't feasible—at least not yet. They couldn't make all the charges stick, or possibly some were negotiated away. But the PrimeCorp foundations shook, no doubt about it.

Predictably, Alin Sedmamin came out smelling—if not like a rose, at least mostly free of the odour of corruption. Dores Amadoro didn't fare so well, and was facing time in prison. Sedmamin managed to sidestep most of the responsibility for the criminal activity, allowing it to land squarely on her shoulders. Somehow it came to light that all those criminal happenings had been instigated or carried out by her, acting on her own initiative. The Board of Directors was shocked—simply shocked, that such a viper had been sheltering within its walls.

I didn't believe it one bit, obviously, but I still didn't feel sorry for her. Dealing with someone like Sedmamin, she should have known he'd be the last person to take responsibility for failure.

It was Lanar who stopped by Dock One-Eleven to give me all that news. "It'll be pinging all over Nearspace tomorrow," he said, "but I wanted you to hear it first."

We were in the galley, in the two big armchairs facing each other, mugs of double caff in hand. It was quiet, except for a dull thumping that signalled Viss was labouring away on the repairs to Engineering.

"I'd rather hear that Sedmamin was going down," I said, "but I'll take Amadoro as a consolation prize. Do you think they'll go after Mother when she leaks the research data?"

He shook his head. He was off-duty, and had traded his Protectorate uniform for jeans and a transform t-shirt. "If I know Mother, she'll do it in a way that won't be directly traceable to her. If anyone knows how to do that, I'm sure she does." He grinned. "And don't be too certain about Sedmamin. His day is coming. I expect his Board of Directors is going to be very unhappy with him after this, if only because it happened on his watch."

"Thankful for small victories," I said, and raised my mug.

He leaned forward to touch his mug to mine. "Speaking of victories, your evidence really helped us out, Luta. No-one could argue that it was just Protectorate harassment or trumped-up charges. The Protectorate is going to be grateful. Quiet, but grateful."

"Huh. If they'll turn that gratitude into a new, upgraded main drive, that might compensate me for my trouble." I was still not entirely over the way Lanar had gone behind my back with Yuskeya, but I never could stay very angry with him. I changed the subject. "So I suppose you'll be wanting my navigator back now. Where am I supposed to find another one as good as Yuskeya?"

Lanar glanced away, not meeting my eyes, then back. "Actually, I want to talk to you about that. I hear you're taking

Mother back to Kiando. Could I leave Yuskeya with you for that trip? I want her to meet with our agents there to—discuss a few things."

I narrowed my eyes at him. "I'm suspicious already, but sure, I'll take her back. She can spend the time bringing me double caff and cinnamon *pano* to make up for lying to me."

"I don't think that's in her job description," he said, grinning again. "Any of them. But you can try."

Maja knocked on the door of my cabin one evening as I was looking over cargo manifests for likely jobs. The repairs to the *Tane Ikai* were almost complete, and we'd be shipping out for Kiando soon. Might as well travel with full cargo pods, even if the Protectorate had paid for the new drive. I put the datapad aside when she came in.

She wasn't the same Maja who'd come aboard on Eri. Her blonde hair spilled down from a girlish ponytail and her blue eyes were lively. She smiled at me as she settled herself in my big armchair and tucked her feet up comfortably.

"Are you making plans for taking Grandmother back to Kiando?" she asked.

I nodded. "Looking for some likely cargo to haul on the way there, anyway. She's anxious to see Gusain Buig again, so I don't think she'll want me to make too many stops along the way."

She licked her lips. "I've been thinking . . . I'd like to stay on for a few runs, if it's all right with you. I'm starting to think that I didn't give space travel enough of a chance when I was younger."

"Does my communications officer have anything to do with that idea?"

She flushed slightly. "You know about that?"

I raised my eyebrows. "Maja, I'm your *mother*. And we both know why, despite my age, I'm not senile just yet."

She laughed then, a sound I couldn't hear often enough. "Do you mind?"

"Why should I mind? Baden is a good man. He wouldn't be on my crew if I didn't think so. He does have a bit of a reputation—"

"As a womanizer. I know all about it."

"—and I thought he and Rei had something going—"

"Baden told me about that, so I talked to Rei, too. She laughed, very nicely, and said he was 'amusing' on long runs, but that she has a fiancé back on Eri whom she'll be marrying 'when he's old enough.'" Maja raised her eyebrows. "What's that about?"

Sankta merdo! I'd known the crew had secrets, but the ones I'd learned lately were not what I'd expected. "I have no idea, and nothing you or anyone else does is any of my business. I can't keep track of it, anyway. So yes, I'd be very happy if you stayed with us for awhile, and so would your father. There's a lot in Nearspace I'd like you to see."

She leaned her head back against the chair. "I had a nice talk with Grandmother, too, today. I thought at first I'd feel angry with her, since she was really the beginning of all this. But I don't." She took a deep breath and looked around my cabin thoughtfully. "Everything I worried about for so long seems to be awfully far away now. And everything important is right here."

I smiled. "That's a good thing."

She nodded. "That," she said, "is a very good thing."

Weeks later, back on Kiando, Mother and I took a long walk together, a real outdoors walk through some of the vineyards where the fruit for *jarlees* wine grew. They were reminiscent of vineyards on earth, although the *jarlee* vines grew over tall, arching trellises and sported pale, burgundy-veined leaves. Anyone seeing us would think we were sisters, not mother and daughter, and I was thinking about how alike we were, and how alike Maja and I were also turning out to be.

"So you're staying on here for a while." It wasn't really a question; the relationship I'd suspected she had with Gusain Buig had turned out to be very obvious, and she'd already been talking about getting back to her ongoing research. The trip to Schulyer Group's labs was in the works, and Dr. Ndasa was keen to show her what they'd done.

She nodded and sighed. "And you're not, I suppose."

I smiled. "Part of me would like to. We still have years' worth of things to catch up on. But you're going to be pretty busy for a while."

"That's for certain. But I'd squeeze you in."

"I know. I think it will be even more fun if I come back later, and bring Karro and Aliande, and their children, if they'll come. I'll mention it to Lanar next time I talk to him. We'll have a real family reunion."

"That would be wonderful." Her voice was warm, and there was a catch in it.

I pulled a dark violet *jarlee* fruit from one of the vines and rolled it in my fingers, enjoying the plump promise of sweetness.

"Hirin came to see me about the new breed of bioscavengers," she said. "I explained what they could and couldn't do for him. But he seemed happy for whatever they'll accomplish."

"He's already had the treatment?" I was surprised he hadn't told me.

"Yesterday. Maybe he wanted to surprise you."

"Hmmm. Maybe." I thought it might be something else, but I'd have to ask him later. "Mother, it's kind of strange, but—now that the die is cast, I think I understand your hesitation to unleash immortality on humans."

Mother laughed. "Oh, really? You told me rather bluntly that it wasn't my business to decide for the entire race."

"Well, something like that, I guess. But when I think about people like Alin Sedmamin and Dores Amadoro, I wonder if you weren't right after all. We could do a lot of harm if mortality isn't an issue anymore. There seems to be an almost limitless capacity for greed and mean-spiritedness in us as a race."

"We could." She picked a *jarlee* fruit and popped it into her mouth. "On the other hand, we might get over the short-sightedness that's plagued us for centuries. Might be more mindful of the hundred-year consequences of our actions if we have every expectation of being around to experience them. We have great capacity for kindness and compassion, too."

"True." I grinned. "I guess we'll just have to wait and see, won't we?"

"I guess so. There's a quotation from an old Earth writer that's always intrigued me. It goes, 'I don't believe in ageing. I believe in forever altering one's aspect to the sun.' I don't know what she actually meant by that, since she killed herself years later, but I've always taken it to mean that instead of worrying about getting older, we should instead be able to use time to change our perspective on things. Change how we see the universe and the face we present to it." She laughed a little. "I guess that's what I hope this research will ultimately enable people to do. Alter their perspective from time to time, because they'll be around long enough to do it."

"Sounds good to me," I said. "I guess that's what I've been

doing for years, I just didn't realize it."

We walked a long way in silence after that, and it was perfectly *okej*.

That night when we were getting ready for bed, I told Hirin about my visit with Mother.

He smiled. "I'm so glad you finally found her. All that time—it wasn't wasted."

"I wouldn't have said it was wasted, anyway." I sat beside him on the bed. "We had a lot of good years out there on the *Tane Ikai*."

"And a lot of close calls," he said with a chuckle. Then his face grew serious. "Luta, this has turned out so differently than what we talked about when I left Earth. You've gotten into something you didn't expect . . . or maybe even want."

I'd suspected as much. I turned to meet his eyes, eyes I'd looked into for decades, loving them with every glance. They were no longer clouded with age, no longer sunken—the bioscavengers had taken a good fifteen years off his appearance and probably fixed him up inside even better than that.

None of that mattered to me at all. I'd never felt that he'd aged beyond me, only that he'd been subject to forces that had bypassed me, like an illness to which I'd been blessed with immunity. Our souls were the same age, and that was what had brought us together and kept us together all that time, anyway.

"Mother said you went to see her yesterday. Looks like you don't have to worry about dying in space—or anywhere—just yet."

He nodded. "But you weren't counting on that, and I'll understand if you'd rather—"

I kissed him, which shut him up briefly, but then he pulled away and said, "No, I'm serious about this—"

"And so am I." I kissed him again, harder this time. "You silly old man. You're not getting rid of me that easily. Unless you're thinking you want a younger woman now—"

At which point he made it very clear that, in fact, he did not.

THE END

Acknowledgements

Every novel bears the name of at least one author on the cover, but in truth, no book comes into being through the efforts of just one individual. This one is no exception. I've had readers, consultants and editors galore in the process of creating this novel, and I thank you all.

In particular, I'd like to mention the folks at National Novel Writing Month, under whose crazy auspices the first draft of this novel came into being, and the (anonymous) Atlantic Writing Competition judges who provided valuable commentary on an early incarnation of the novel. For feedback, advice, and proofing on many and various stages of the book (until I'm sure they were sick of looking at and hearing about it), huge thanks to Nancy Waldman, Julie Serroul and my sister Krista Miller, and special thanks to my husband Terry Ramsey for helping me untangle the intricate web of Nearspace wormholes. For advice, cheerleading, and general encouragement, I must thank my incomparable writing group colleagues in The Story Forge and The Quillians.

I owe special thanks for many thoughtful editorial insights to my editor, Margaret Curelas, who in particular helped me find my way to the best ending for the book.

And of course, none of the rest would really matter at all without the ongoing and unfaltering support of my family and friends.

Finally, thanks to anyone who ever told me (sincerely or not) that I did not look my age, since that's what sparked the whole idea.

Even with all that help, there will still be imperfections . . . they are entirely my fault, and I can only hope that perhaps in some alternate universe, even those have been fixed.

About the Author

    Sherry D. Ramsey is a writer, web & indie publisher, jewlery-maker and self-confessed internet geek. She lives in Nova Scotia with her husband, two children, and two dogs, where the rest of the family is also creative in various ways, even the dogs (who consistently develop new ways of begging).

    She interacts with fellow members of the species *Homo scriptor* through the Writer's Federation of Nova Scotia, SF Canada, and other workshops and writing groups both online and off.

    Visit Sherry's blog and website by surfing to www.sherrydramsey.com, or keep up with her more pithy musings on Twitter @sdramsey.

CPSIA information can be obtained at www.ICGtesting.com
Printed in the USA
LVOW11s0741270315

432275LV00001B/5/P